Dead
But
Dreaming 2

Dead
But
Dreaming 2

edited by
Kevin Ross

Associate Editors:
Tom Lynch and Scott David Aniolowski

Miskatonic
River
Press

New York • Florida
2011

Table of Contents

Foreword
Messrs. Cthulhu And Lovecraft Have Arrived

Every year it seems the cult of H.P. Lovecraft and his be-tentacled creation grows in some fashion or another. From the Arkham House volumes of the 1940s and beyond, to the paperback explosion of the '60s and '70s, to the film adaptations and roleplaying gamebooks of the '80s and '90s, to biographies and documentaries and countless anthologies and computer games and half-witted movie adaptations (special thanks to the SyFy Channel, for its sub-moronic brain-rape version of *The Dunwich Horror* -- surely we'll never see a more inept Lovecraft adaptation) and comic books and plush animals and so on and so forth, ad infinitum (and often ad nauseam), HPL and his famous creations continue to infiltrate virtually every form of media.

But events of the past couple of years have, I think, insinuated Lovecraft's name even deeper into the mainstream -- for better or worse.

First off, Cthulhu has invaded our cartoons, for R'lyeh's sake! 2010 saw explicitly Lovecraftian/Cthulhoid episodes of *Scooby-Doo! Mystery Incorporated* and *South Park*. Between the two of them, almost every single follower of animated cartoons on the planet has now been exposed to Lovecraftian lore, whether via the juvenile nyuk-nyuks of the Scooby-gang or the outrageous antics of the South Park kids (AKA Coon and Friends). *Scooby-Doo* boasted a character voiced by monolithic fantasist (and occasional *enfant terrible*) Harlan Ellison, whose participation undoubtedly lured in a few of his fans curious to witness his latest non-writing venture. *South Park*'s "Coon and Friends" trilogy of episodes threw out a non-stop barrage of Mythos references, from the Necronomicon and the sacred couplet ("That is not dead...") to appearances by shoggoths and elder things and even the *Arkham Horror* boardgame (South Park, Colorado's Cthulhu cultists are apparently avid boardgamers) -- and of course Cthulhu himself. Summoned to Earth via the latest cock-up by British Petroleum, the big tentacled guy laid waste to the Gulf of Mexico before teaming with Cartman/ The Coon to destroy the rabid right-wing child's "hippie" enemies. Cartman's relationship with Cthulhu is a perversion of *The Neverending Story* and various anime tales where a child befriends a giant monster and the pair share wondrous adventures: Cartman even sings Cthulhu a song. In Cartman's case, however, those adventures involve the destruction of San Francisco and the slaughter of Justin Bieber and the hippies at the Burning Man Festival. You never saw that in The Neverending Story.

Leaving behind the corruption of youth through animated cartoons, after five seasons of chasing down all manner of ghosts, monsters, demons, and angels, the latest season of the monster-hunting television series *Supernatural* finally got around to referencing Lovecraft. HPL is depicted onscreen on the day of his death, swilling whiskey as he pounds out the final page of "The Haunter of the Dark", just before a dreadful, bloodsplattered, and lethal visit from some unseen force he and his friends had summoned up earlier. As you might have guessed, the Lovecraft references are mostly inaccurate and entirely gratuitous, though several story titles are named and eagle-eyed viewers might catch glimpses of the covers of a few Lovecraft books and Cthulhu comics, artwork by *Call of Cthulhu* game artists, and posters for the HPL Historical Society's film adaptation of *The Call of Cthulhu* and the HPL Film Festival. Unfortunately, the plot ignored the rich possibilities of Lovecraftian horror while sticking to the series' continuing storyline about a new war in Heaven between different factions of angels. So close, but no cigar...

As if this weren't enough, in the past few months the world just missed getting smacked in the face with an even bigger dose of Lovecraft. For several years, fantasy filmmaker Guillermo Del Toro (*Cronos, The Devil's Backbone, Hellboy, Pan's Labyrinth*) has been talking about adapting Lovecraft's novel *At the Mountains of Madness* for the cinema. Scripts have been leaked to the internet, and there were even a couple of brief elder thing cameos in Del Toro's *Hellboy II: The Golden Army*. Del Toro had always been eager to do Mountains, but the studios were understandably reluctant to back a big-budget film whose relatively minor cult following and intellectually stimulating premises might not appeal to the movie-going masses. Then the King of the World -- AKA James Cameron -- attached his name to the project as producer, and for a couple of weeks it actually looked like the project might get off the ground this time. Unfortunately, as things often go in fickle, nanosecond-attention-span Hollywood, Del Toro dropped *Mountains* in favor of another project. So I guess we'll just have to settle for whatever the SyFy Channel decides to defecate out in our direction instead.

But the Del Toro situation led to what I think was another apocalyptic sign that Lovecraft might have finally "arrived". While making the talk show circuit last summer, Del Toro appeared on Craig Ferguson's late night chat show and the pair started talking about Del Toro's upcoming projects, including *At the Mountains of Madness*. Del Toro and Ferguson briefly discussed Lovecraft and his works, which even Ferguson was familiar with. This might not seem like much, but I think it's important. Here is one of the top handful of fantasy filmmakers of our time speaking on a nationally televised talk show about the work of a rather obscure pulp-fiction writer who died over 70 years ago. This isn't Bob Kane, or L. Ron Hubbard, or Robert E. Howard, or even Lester Dent, whose creations have been staples of comics and films (and offbeat religions) and thus recognizable in pop-culture for decades. This is H.P. Lovecraft. Think of the last time you saw a writer or filmmaker on one of these talk shows. Did he or she mention the names of their inspirations? Let alone somebody other than the latest bestselling novelist or the King of Horror himself? It seems unlikely -- I certainly can't recall such a thing outside of Charlie Rose or the old Tom Snyder show from way back when.

So depending on how you look at it, it's either a pity or a blessing in disguise that Del Toro's film didn't actually make it to the screen, as we would've seen a freaking *supernova* of interest in Lovecraft if it had happened. The XBox game. The novelization of the film (remember *Bram Stoker's Dracula* -- by Fred Saberhagen!?). The comics adaptation. Action figures. Cell-phone apps. Any number of newly-packaged Lovecraft books and themed Cthulhu Mythos anthologies. (I imagined mash-ups of Cthulhu with Jane Austen, zombies, and the Twilight sparkle-vamps -- hopefully all not in the same book, but you never know.)

I'm tellin' ya, if Del Toro's *Mountains of Madness* would've happened we wouldn't have been able to get away from this Lovecraft guy and his tentacled horde.

Hopefully we'll be able to ride the crest of this new wave of Lovecraftian interest with *Dead But Dreaming 2*. The first *Dead But Dreaming* anthology was originally published in 2002 by DarkTales Publications. DarkTales shut down about a month after *DBD* came out, and apparently only about 75-90 copies were produced in that original printing. Most of those copies ended up in the hands of the contributors, but those that did circulate quickly developed a reputation for *DBD* as one of the best Lovecraftian fiction anthologies ever produced (he said, sort of humbly). Three stories from *Dead But Dreaming* earned Honorable Mentions in Ellen Datlow's annual *Year's Best Fantasy & Horror* collection, though frankly I thought at least twice that many more deserved it as well. The book's extreme rarity and good word of mouth quickly drove up prices on the collectors' market: a handful of shrewd folks (including *DBD*'s co-editor and my best friend) eventually put copies up on Ebay and were rewarded with winning bids in the $200-$300+ range.

My wily *Dead But Dreaming* co-editor, the late Keith Herber, always intended to get the book reprinted somehow, and when he was granted a license in 2008 to produce *Call of Cthulhu* roleplaying products, the *DBD* reprint was the first release by Keith's Miskatonic River Press. The reprint allowed folks who had heard so much about this unspeakably rare volume to see if there was any fire to go with all the smoke that had been blowing around. Once again, the reviews were generally more than kind, and often just as glowing as with the book's first appearance. *Dead But Dreaming* was again a minor cult hit, and Keith thought we ought to do another one. (If you've read his Foreword to the first book, you know that by "we" he meant "me", but I doubt he had in mind the exact circumstances through which *DBD2* would have a single editor.)

In assembling the first *Dead But Dreaming* I had wanted to concentrate on stories with larger, more cosmic themes than one usually finds in a Mythos anthology. Most Lovecraftian pastiches don't have any depth: they're rooted in the "here and now" of the individual tale, with little sense that there's a history, a mythology, or any kind of a world or universe outside of them. I sought stories with more depth and heft to them. The absence of name-brand Mythos elements in *DBD* was daunting to some, and my contentious introduction caused further dismay: one reader admitted to enjoying the anthology even though he had been tempted to throw the book across the room upon reading the anti-pastiche manifesto in my intro.

This time around I loosened up quite a bit in selecting stories. There are lots of name-brand Mythos elements in these stories, and a lot of more subtle Lovecraftian stuff too. There are deep ones, cults, Cthulhoid horrors, weird books, hidden races, and family curses. But there's something more here, I think. Many of the stories in the first *DBD* dealt with the psychological impact of human beings discovering alien forces representing a godless universe in which humanity had no significance whatsoever. *Dead But Dreaming 2*, on the other hand, digs right into the emotional lives of the stories' protagonists. *DBD2* is less cold and cosmic, more emotional and human, than the first *DBD*.

This book also offers a broader range of settings and themes, and, as I said, a lot of explicit Cthulhu Mythos references. We have tales dealing with cryptozoology, pop culture, psychedelia, decadent subcultures, some surprisingly human aspects of Mythos races, age-old conspiracies, historical settings, Lovecraft Country, urban horror, academic horror, near-apocalypse science fiction, and -- as with the first volume -- a final terrible revelation involving Cthulhu himself (save that one for last, please). Like its predecessor, *Dead But Dreaming 2* offers a mix of newcomers and established authors, but with perhaps a few more names familiar to readers of Lovecraftian fiction. There's a little bit of something for everyone here, I think, a veritable cornucopia of flavors and textures.

But hopefully nothing that'll make you want to chuck the book across the room.

Kevin Ross
desolation angel
Boone, Iowa
January/May 2011

Acknowledgments

Extra special thanks to my Associate Editors, Tom Lynch and Scott Aniolowski, who steered countless stories and authors toward me, and helped out with rights and contracts issues. Thanks also to all those writers who submitted their stories and were patient with me through extended deadlines. Thanks also to John Stavropoulos and Terry Romero, who helped Tom limp his way through layout to make this book a reality. And thank you Jason Williams for your work on copyediting this beast. Finally, thanks and salutations to the authors included in this volume, for their enthusiasm, patience, and understanding -- it was a pleasure working with all of you.

Dedication

My biggest thanks of all goes to my late friend, mentor, and co-editor on the first *Dead But Dreaming*, Keith Herber. Doing a Mythos anthology was Keith's idea, way back when. Keith died just a few months after the Miskatonic River Press reprint version appeared, but he already had plans for a second volume. This time he really did leave me to edit this one on my own. I hope he'd approve of the results. *Salud*, amigo.

Dead
But
Dreaming 2

WALTER JARVIS grew up in Central Texas and attended college in Tennessee. He was a photographer in the Vietnam war. and worked for newspapers and trade magazines in Virgina, Texas and California. Presently he lives in Los Angeles, a city where tagging has been raised in some circles to an art form. He discovered Lovecraft as a teen-ager and has been hooked ever since.

Taggers

by Walter Jarvis

The boy was lying face down at the bottom of the concrete embankment, almost at the water's edge, dressed in a tagger's standard-issue uniform: baggy black shorts that came down below his knees, a blindingly white t-shirt, a black Raiders cap that hid his face.

There was something about the death of a kid that still affected Morell, despite all the years he had spent on the force. In his career as a police officer, he had seen perhaps half a dozen deaths involving children, victims of violence or traffic accidents, with an occasional drowning or electrocution to round things out, but had never become inured to it. Each new death was like a kick in the gut. It was one of those things that you never hardened yourself into accepting, no matter how much you might want to. Perhaps that was good, he told himself as he stared down at the body of the dead boy. It meant you were still human.

Scuttling sidewise, almost on all fours, Morell descended the steep concrete embankment. He could hear his partner Jiminez, who was overweight and even more out of shape, swearing softly under his breath as he made the same awkward descent behind him.

Morrell approached the motionless shape. The riverbank was silent except for the steady rumble of traffic on the Mission Road bridge as workers headed into town during the early morning commute.

A can of spray paint had landed in the soft muck just above the dead boy's outstretched hand, and his splayed fingers looked as if they were reaching out for it even in death. Two other cans lay near him in the grass. He had finished the first letter of "Vaqueros," the name of his crew, in Day-glo crimson bordered by white, before he had died. It was so stylized that it was hard to recognize it as a "v", but Morell had had long experience identifying graffiti and its perpetrators. The Vaqueros had been active in this area for decades; membership was passed down from brother to brother, uncle to nephew, father to son. It was a stepping stone to real gangs that were involved in everything from auto theft to drug dealing. Jimenez was the one who bent down and turned the body over. He drew in his breath with a hiss and instinctively crossed himself when the boy's face came into view. Morell looked over his shoulder. He didn't cross himself because he was not a religious man, but at that moment he almost wished he

3

were. Never had he seen such absolute terror on anyone's face, dead or alive.

"I know this kid," Jimenez said. "Name's Jesse Alvarado. I arrested him about six months ago for doing exactly the same thing. Been tagging since middle school. Jesus Christ, what the hell happened to him?"

"He must have fallen off the edge of the embankment, then landed on the concrete the wrong way."

"Maybe. But look at his face. Something scared the shit out of him."

Morell saw what he meant. The wide-open eyes. The lips frozen in an "o" of shock. The boy certainly looked as if he could have died of fright. But people didn't die that way in Alvarado's world. Gunshot wounds, knife punctures, overdoses—yes. But not frightened to death. These kids were hardened by years on the street, and it took a lot to frighten them to begin with. More likely Jesse had died by falling and hitting his head against the unforgiving concrete.

Then why that look of terror?

"Those other letters aren't the Vaquero's tagging," Jimenez said, pointing toward the embankment. "I don't recognize them at all."

Morell didn't either. They began about 20 feet from the "V", stopped at a cavernous concrete storm drain, and picked up on the other side. They were so highly stylized that they didn't even look like letters of the Roman alphabet. It was some kind of writing, but Morell didn't recognize it. Almost like Arabic characters, he thought.

"Get a picture," he said to Jiminez. "If it's a new crew, we need to know about it."

Jiminez was staring transfixed as if he hadn't heard him.

"Jesus, have you ever seen spray paint do that before?" he asked.

As the rays of the morning sun struck the letters, they began to rapidly steam and then evaporate until there were only the faintest ashy outlines left on the concrete walls. With a start, Jiminez pulled out his camera and began snapping pictures; but by that time the letters had mostly disappeared, leaving the dead boy's "V" standing alone in crimson clarity.

The boy in the baggy pants caught the principal pointing him out and turned toward his locker, pretending to examine the textbooks inside. That'd be a first, Morell thought. Bet you've got books in there you haven't opened since the beginning of school.

"Aldo, could you come here for a moment, please?" the assistant principal called out in a firm but not unfriendly voice. "These gentlemen want to have a word with you."

Reluctantly, his head bowed, the boy shuffled over to the two men, refusing to meet their eyes.

4

"In my office, Aldo," the a.p. ordered. "It'll only take a few minutes. I'll write you a pass when we're through."

The boy was thin, dark, with enormous brown eyes that gave an almost feminine cast to his face. His hair was cropped close to his head and he wore a t-shirt that was bleached white. His black work pants sagged well below his waist, and the chain that dangled from his belt loop looked heavy enough to drag them down further. The school had a policy prohibiting gang-related attire, so this outfit was this was the closest that Aldo could get to let the world know he was a gang banger, or at least a wannabe.

"Aldo, this is Lieutenant Morell and Sergeant Jiminez from the LAPD," the principal said once they were seated. A broad-shouldered man in a sports coat and tie, he looked a little like an ex-Marine gone slightly to seed. Morell imagined you had to be something of a drill sergeant to deal with these kids on a daily basis.

"They need to ask you a couple of questions about Jesse Alvarado," he went on. "I know you're still upset about your friend's death—we all are—but it's important to make sure that there aren't any open questions about how he died. You agree with that, don't you?"

The boy hesitated, and then silently nodded his head.

"Aldo, were you with Jesse the night he died?" Jimenez asked softly.

"I didn't do no tagging," the boy said defensively. "I quit doin' that stuff after I got out of juvey."

"We didn't say you did," Morell interjected. "We just hope you can help us get to the bottom of Jesse's death."

"I was with him early, then he left us. We tol' him not to tag around Mission--some weird shit's been goin' on down there--but he wouldn't listen to us."

"What kind of 'weird shit', Aldo?" Jimenez asked.

Aldo shook his head. "I don't know 'xactly how to say it. That used to be the Kutter's turf. You tagged in their hood, you was in big trouble. Then 'bout three weeks ago they pulled out. At least that's what we heard, we don't talk to them directly. We also heard a new gang had come into the 'hood and run them out. This crew's got no name, nobody knows nothing about them. Some said it made the river up for grabs. That's when Jessie thought he could sneak down there and tag for the Vaqueros. Mission Road, that's prime territory, man. Everybody can see your sign drivin' across the bridge. Anyway, we told him not to do it, to wait awhile, but he went anyway."

"You think maybe he was ambushed by this new gang?" Morell asked.

"I don't' know…Maybe. Thing is, nobody knows nothing about 'em. They haven't shown their colors. Even if they's tagging, nobody's seen it. We don't even know where they from."

Morell pulled out one of his cards. "If you hear anything, call me at this number. You don't have to leave your name, and nothing you say will be held against you. Don't do it for me, Aldo. Do it for your friend Jesse."

The boy stood up to go back to class. "Oh, one more thing," Morell added. "Have you ever heard of a paint that disappears when the sun hits it? A spray paint that taggers use?"

Aldo gave him a perplexed look. "A disappearing paint? You tag so people can see you was there—that it was your crew that did it. People got to see it during the day for it to mean anything. To have the tagging disappear when the sun comes up—What would be the point?"

Morell was just about to leave for the day—he had shoved his half-filled coffee cup over to the side of his desk, next to the stack of the paperwork he had not had time to get to during his shift, and had just logged off his computer--when Latasha, the desk clerk, stuck her head in his office.

"Lieutenant Morell, there's somebody who wants to talk to you. Says his name is Professor Kensington. You want me to tell him you already left?"

Morell sighed and glanced at the clock on the wall. Ten till six. He was definitely ready to call it quit.

"Did he say what it was about?" he asked.

"Something to do with that tagger's death at the Mission Road bridge."

"Send him in," Morell said. Suddenly the time wasn't that critical anymore.

Kensington turned out to be a short, rather plump man in his late fifties. In his tweed jacket and chocolate-colored vest, he certainly looked the part of a professor, but there was an almost childlike excitement in his eyes and a certain breathlessness in his voice that made it hard for Morell to take him too seriously.

"Thank you for taking time to see me so late in the day," he said, shaking hands. "I read in the Times about the tagger you found on the bank of the L.A. river bed. The story quoted you as saying you also found some graffiti that you couldn't identify but which you said might be associated with the boy's death."

"That's correct."

"Would it be possible to see an sample? I'm assuming you took photos. I'm something of an expert in the field. Perhaps I could help you identify the crew that was responsible."

Morell doubted whether Kensington was more of an expert than he, but he nonetheless pulled the blowups of the unknown graffiti that Jiminez had managed to photograph before it all steamed away in the light of day.

Kensington stared at them intently and then looked up at Morell. "Just these fragments, right? This is all you have?"

"It wasn't exactly a Kodak moment," Morell answered. "The letters were disappearing faster than we could shoot them."

"What do you mean, 'disappearing'"?

"I really can't explain it. When the sunlight hit the side of the embankment, the letters sort of faded away. Evaporated."

Kensington was suddenly very excited. "Did you do any kind of analysis afterwards, take any scrapings off the embankment itself, perhaps?"

Morell had thought about that, but after the fact. When he finally got around to doing it, it was the day after an unexpected rain shower, and the embankment had been washed clean. To cover his own feeling of incompetence, he answered a little gruffly: "Professor, we had a dead boy on our hands. That was our first priority."

"Of course, of course. I didn't mean to imply otherwise."

"And what's your interest in this case?"

"Before I answer, detective, let me show you something." He pulled a well-worn notebook out of his briefcase and opened it to a page onto which a Photostat had been pasted.

The picture was dark and grainy, and filled with an unknown writing that looked nonetheless familiar. The more Morell stared at the letters, the more he realized they were the same as the graffiti that had vanished off the side of the embankment.

"It looks like what we saw near the boy's body."

"Good. I was hoping you would say that. Now let's make a comparison between this Photostat and what you photographed."

Morell studied the two intently. The resemblance was remarkable. There were some slight differences, but they were obviously the same overall.

"You've identified the crew that did this?" the detective asked, pointing to the photograph.

"No, but I would like to," Kensington said with a strange smile. "The Photostat is from the tracing of a tablet in the National Museum in Baghdad. They are the symbols of a cuneiform language that dates back at least 4000 years."

They were crouched behind a rusting pile of oil drums on the other side of the river from where Jesse Alvarado had fallen to his death. He and Kensington had been there for some time, and the stench from the river, no more than a few inches deep here, fulsome with the wastes deposited along the bottom, was beginning to stick in the back of his throat. They had bought infrared binoculars, but the moon was bright enough so that Morell did not think he would need them. Kensington, though, had them pinned to his eyes.

What the hell am I doing here? Morell asked himself again. waiting for taggers who might or might not come back to the scene of the crime, simply on the faith of one crackpot professor?

If the crew were smart, and had anything to do with the kid's death, they won't come back, unfinished tagging or not, he told himself. They'd have to figure that this place might be under surveillance. But again, maybe they weren't that smart after all. In his experience, kids did dumb things all the time. Which was one of the reasons that so many of them wound up in jail--or worse.

"What makes you think they'll come back?" he had asked Kensington when the latter had first broached the idea of waiting for the taggers by the river's edge.

"Because they didn't finish what they started. They were interrupted by your young man. He scared them off."

"Judging by the expression on his face, it was the other way around."

Kensington glanced away. "Yes, I can see how you could say that. Whether that led directly to his fall we may never know."

Did the man know more than he was saying? Morell still wasn't very clear about the relationship between the professor's area of expertise—ancient languages—and the tagging. Kensington was infuriatingly vague in answering the detective's questions, mumbling something about writing a book comparing modern-day tagging with graffiti in ancient times. "It existed, you know," he said. "The walls leading to the Forum were covered with Latin inscriptions, and the tomb robbers carved their initials in ancient Arabic in the tunnels of the pyramids." Morell wasn't impressed. To him, tagging was tagging, a way for young punks to mark their turf, no different from a dog pissing on a hydrant. It was ugly, destructive, and, in a larger sense, indicative of the gang violence that was metastasizing in the inner city like a cancer.

The professor, on the other hand, seemed to look it at it as something that had intrinsic value, almost as if it were art form. Oh, Morell knew the academic was not alone in this. The newspaper had written articles about graffiti artists, for chrissakes. Kensington must have thought the graffiti at the site of Alvarado's death was important, or why else would he have spent so much time laboriously try to retrace the letters on the side of the river bed earlier that afternoon, never once complaining about the heat or mosquitoes? It was all for naught: there was nothing left after the rain.

"They'll be back," Kensington had insisted. "In fact, I expect to see them again tonight."

"What makes you so sure?"

"Full moon," the other man had replied.

Morell didn't know what a full moon had to do with it—usually taggers liked it dark; the darker the better. Again, Kensington seemed so confident that

Morell was willing to return to the river bed with him—at least this once. He had also managed to talk his partner Jiminez into accompanying them, although the man had complained bitterly that he would have been better off drinking beer at a local taverna.

So far tonight there had been no signs of any activity. It was after one a.m., and the area was completely deserted. If there had been any movement along the banks of the river bed, it would have been easy to detect. It was a dismal foreboding place even at high noon, and now, empty, full of lightless brick buildings and stockpiles of industrial supplies, it was sinister enough to intimidate the most aggressive tagger.

"Someone just came out of that storm drain," Kensington said, his voice electric with excitement. "No, more than one. At least three of them."

"I don't see anyone," Morell answered, squinting into the darkness.

"Take the goggles."

Then Morell saw them clearly. Three diminutive figures, dressed in black, making their way down the side of the concrete river bank. He was struck first of all by the smallness of their stature—they must have been nine or ten years old, judging by their size. They moved with a surety of purpose that did not seem typical of young taggers, who were more afraid of being caught than their older brethren. And something else: their proportions were all wrong. The bodies were short, squat, but the heads, hidden beneath the black hoods of what he supposed were sweatshirts, seemed disproportionately large to a man. And even in the moonlight, it was hard to discern their features.

Maybe they're all brothers, Morell thought, a faint creeping sense of unease working its way up his spine. Or even triplets. If that were the case, someone had dipped into a very curious gene pool indeed.

Kids or dwarfs or whatever, they were still taggers, and Morrell intended to pick them up and bring them in for questioning.

"My God!" Kensington hissed. "Their eyes. Look at their eyes!"

Hurriedly he passed Morell the binoculars but the trio, turned to face the sloping concrete flank of the river bed, now had their backs to him.

"What about their eyes?" Morell whispered.

"They're red, red like a feral animal's."

Morell watched for a moment and then said in a voice that that had a thrilling note to it that normally wasn't there: "That's not spray paint they're using. What the hell? Do they have some kind of paint on their fingers?"

From a distance that was what it looked like. Almost in unison, as if the motion had been choreographed, they were moving their hands across the concrete, and with the night binoculars Morell could see they were leaving wet, gleaming marks on the embankment.

It almost looks like they were marking the concrete with their naked fingers, but that wasn't possible, was it?

"Jiminez, get over to that storm drain and block them using from that as an exit while I go down the embankment," he ordered. "Between the two of us, we'll get at least one of them."

Kensington grabbed his arm. "Wait!" he said fiercely. "Let them finish what they're doing. I need photographs of their work. It has a greater value than you might think."

"Sorry, Professor," Morell said. "I know these kids. As soon as they're through, they're going to split. We've got to act now."

Ignoring Kensington's further whispered pleas, Morell let Jiminez get a head start and then began to lope down the side of the embankment and across the river bed. It must have been the sound of his feet splashing through the water that alerted the trio, for he saw them jerk to a rigid stance. Almost as if they were one entity, they turn around to look in his direction. Thick hoods hid their faces, but Morell saw their eyes glow redly beneath their cowls. It was not a glow that came from any reflected light, but from within.

"Hey, stop where you are!" he yelled. "Police."

Ignoring his command, they moved with incredible speed toward the entrance to the storm drain. Desperately he lunged at one of them to bring him down, and his hand made contact with flesh beneath the black outer garment. With a cry he let go: it had been like touching something soft and almost gelatinous. He nearly lost his balance, and, catching himself before he fell, he saw Jiminez grab one of the taggers at the entrance to the culvert. Sergeant Jiminez was a big man, close to 200 pounds, so what happened next did not seem possible. The tagger lifted the policeman as if he were a child and then threw him down. With a hoarse cry, Jiminez rolled down the side of the embankment and landed in the shallow water at the bottom.

Morell forgot about the taggers and went to his partner's rescue. He had looked over his shoulder to see the trio disappear silently into the culvert.

"Man, you OK?" he asked Jiminez trying to help him up.

"The little fucker knocked the wind out of me," Jiminez groaned, unsteadily rising to his feet. "I may have broken a rib."

"I'm going to take a look in the culvert," Morell said. "Those bastards may be right inside, waiting for us to leave. Are you gonna be OK?"

"Yeah. Sure," Jiminez nodded, although he was in visible pain. "You go ahead. But be careful. They not your run of-the-mill crew."

As Morell made his way up to the entrance of the viaduct, out of the corner of his eye he saw Professor Kensington furiously photographing the graffiti which seemed to gleam liquidly in the moonlight.

10

Morrell stopped at the entrance and shone his service light around. The tunnel stretched back several hundred feet until it curved to the right, probably to join a sewer line. Of the three taggers he saw no sign. Of course, they could be lurking just beyond the bend in the tunnel. Waiting for him.

He knew he should go deeper into the tunnel to investigate, but something, some primal instinct, held him back. Perhaps, he rationalized, they weren't there after all. Maybe they had kept going and entered the sewer system which ran throughout the city. If that were the case, they could be anywhere. The thought of the using the sewers as an escape route was disturbing in itself. He decided to go no further but instead to go back to help Jiminez. Pursuing the taggers would have to wait another time.

He had trouble finding Kensington's office at the university. It was tucked away in the back of an annex to the School of Archaeology building, just past a freight elevator. It was painfully obvious by the location that Kensington's academic standing among his peers at the university was not particularly high, and somehow that came as no surprise to Morell.

When the professor opened the door, he seemed a little surprised to see Morell standing there, even though they had made a three o'clock appointment.

"Come in, lieutenant, come in," Kensington said, ushering him inside the cramped, narrow little room. "Excuse the clutter. One of my New Year's resolutions was to get organized, but it hasn't happened yet."

Curiously Morell looked around. There were books stacked haphazardly everywhere, and he made out what looked like a photograph of Egyptian hieroglyphics spread out across the professor's desk. On one wall hung a faded color picture of a much younger Kensington knee-deep in desert sands somewhere, holding a cracked piece of pottery up for the camera, a triumphant smile on his face.

"How's your partner doing?" the professor asked, pulling a stack of student tests off of a beat-up chair so Morell could sit down.

"Broke a rib, but he'll be OK."

"Sorry to hear that. It could have been much worse, though. That was quite a tumble he took."

Morell didn't tell the professor that Jiminez had been picked up and hurled to the ground by someone the size of a child but with superhuman strength. "I got a look at one of their faces," Jiminez had confided to Morell afterwards. "It wasn't no teenager. It was old, old and wrinkled with burning red eyes. And there was something wrong with his mouth—It—it---." He had shuddered, unable to say anymore.

"Don't worry Omar, we'll find 'em. They won't get away with what they did to you."

Jiminez had turned his head. "I dunno. man. It may take me awhile to get back on my feet. Now my back's starting to hurt. Maybe you better get someone else to go out with you to round 'em up."

Morell had realized with a shock that his partner was afraid. Jiminez, Mr. Machismo, the man who had never said no to a fight, had been spooked by a trio of kids.

But what kind of child could lift a 200-pound man and then throw him down as if he weighed nothing? And had that been the same fate suffered by Jesse Alvarado?

Kensington shook his head. "The gangs today are so much more ferocious than they were even a couple of years ago. Absolutely merciless. They—"

"It wasn't a gang," Morrell interrupted.

"What do you mean?"

"Knocking down a police office—a gang would claim bragging rights to that right away. They wouldn't be able to keep it to themselves. It'd be all over the 'hood. So far, not a peep. So in my opinion, it's not a gang. Or at least not the kind of gang that I'm familiar with. But you already knew that, didn't you, professor?"

"I don't understand what you mean."

"How did you know that that crew was going to show up again? How did you know the time? Have you been in communication with them, Professor Kensington?"

"I'm an academician, Lieutenant Morell, not a gang banger."

"I'm afraid I'm going to have to take the photos you took of the tagging as evidence."

"Those photos are for my research into the nature of graffiti—"

"They were taken at the place where Alvarado was killed. They may be useful in identifying the members of the gang who came back to the same site to finish their tagging."

"I can give you copies."

"Sorry, professor, but I'm going to need the originals. If I have to, I'll get a warrant for them."

Kensington took a deep breath as if to calm himself and then said: "Look, lieutenant, it's very important that my work remain a secret until I have finished it. If those pictures become public, and it gets out why I consider them important, it's going to raise all sorts of questions, questions that could upset a lot of people, even cause a panic. We wouldn't want that, would we?"

"I'm not following you, professor."

"Let me show you something." Kensington dug around on his desk and pulled out a photograph so old that was beginning to yellow around the edges. Passing it to Morell, he asked: "What does this look like?"

12

"It's some sort of graffiti," Morell said, squinting at the picture. "It looks like that stuff on the side of the river bed."

"It was a picture taken in 1923 during the excavation of Pompeii. A wall on the Via Roma. Graffiti was quite common in the Roman Empire, as I've mentioned before. Citizens expressed themselves anonymously, usually after dark, writing on walls because there were so few outlets for self-expression in what was an authoritarian regime. There were a lot of disaffected people in the Roman urban centers. Sounds like Los Angeles today, doesn't it? But this graffiti is not Latin. It bears a remarkable resemblance to what was written on the sides of the L.A. River, don't you think?'

Morell nodded. "Same strokes, joined together in the same way."

"One big difference is you can see the letters in the light of day. They didn't evaporate like the letters we saw. Something to do with the composition of the ash from the eruption of Mount Vesuvius that covered them. Now look at this."

He handed Morell another picture. This one also was yellow with age, curled and worn around the edges. It was a street scene in some city in Japan, shot during the 1940s, Morell judged, by the style of the few visible cars and the garments people were wearing.

"Now take this magnifying glass," Morell said, "and tell me what you see in the lower right hand corner."

Morell gave a low whistle. He could barely make out the graffiti on a wall that was in shadow from an overhanging porch, but it was still discernable. It was the same graffiti that had been on the banks of the river and on the wall at Pompeii.

"Apparently the letters disappeared as soon as the sun hit it, but this picture was taken early enough so the wall was still in shadow. The city was Hiroshima, Lieutenant Morell. The picture was taken a few hours before the Enola Gay dropped the bomb. The photographer was shooting something else, and just happened to catch the graffiti in the background."

Morell handed the picture back to Kensington. "What the hell does this have to do with the death of Jesse Alvarado?"

Kensington hesitated, as if weighing whether he should say more. "Just before every great tragedy in human history, these words written in an unknown language have appeared, scrawled on a wall or, in our case, on the concrete bank of a river bed. They —or something like them—were reported just before the Great Fire of London of 1666. They were witnessed by a night watchman just hours before the San Francisco earthquake. Dr. Joseph Goebbels, Hitler's propaganda minister, mentions seeing them on the shadowy courtyard wall in front of the bunker, before the fall of Berlin, in one of his last diary entries."

"Are you saying that these letters predicted those events?"

"They didn't predict them. Somehow the graffiti brought them about."

Morell shook his head, thinking that now he had heard everything. The lowly tagger had been elevated to some kind of supernatural force, responsible for the destruction of entire cities. He had invested time in listening to this crackpot when he should have been out looking for new leads in Alvarado's death.

"What does this have to do with Jesse?"

"He must have started his tagging earlier in the evening, left the river bed and then came back to finish it. He made the mistake of interrupting our friends while they were in the midst of their tagging. Apparently they're working on a deadline."

"Are you saying your taggers have plans for L.A.? What's it going to be, professor? A volcanic eruption? Earthquake? Hell, it's not even earthquake weather."

"I don't know," Kensington said, "and even if I did, nobody would believe me. All I know is that, based on my research, the taggers are working on establishing a grid of graffiti across the city. They are the minions of a greater power, a malevolent force that has had it in for mankind since our creation. I believe that when the grid is completed, then something momentous will happen. Once I narrow down to where they will strike next, perhaps I'll have a better idea of what they plan. Then I want you to go with me and try to stop them. The future of Los Angeles may depend on it."

Morell shook his head. "Sorry, Kensington, I've got better things to do. I'm investigating the death of a 15-year-old boy, remember, and I don't think anything you've said is going to help me solve it."

Kensington's shoulders slumped. "I thought…because of what you saw at the culvert…you might be more open to helping me."

"Maybe later, after the Alvarado case is put to bed. In the meantime, I am going to need those photos."

"I need a little time to get them all together and make copies for myself. Why don't you come back around five? I'll have them ready by then."

"Fair enough. See you at five sharp."

When Morell returned to the university, he found Kensington's office locked, the lights off. A pool secretary who was in the department office—much more spacious than Kensington's—reported that the professor had gone home for the day.

"Are you Lieutenant Morell? He left this for you." She handed him a sealed envelope. Morell opened it and read the contents:

Dear Lieutenant Morell,

I'm sorry I'm not where I said I would be, but I think you'll understand me better after you read this. After you left, I got a call from a friend who said new graffiti had been reported this morning on the river near the Sixth Street bridge. I'm going there tonight to investigate. If I can interrupt the grid, perhaps the disaster set to strike the city will be mitigated somewhat. I will bring the photographs with me. If you want them, meet me at midnight at the top of the incline leading down to the river. I will be there with a video camera to record what I see, and hopefully you will, too.

I have been working all afternoon plotting coordinates based on reports on the graffiti that I have collected, and apparently the grid is almost complete. There should be some activity there tonight.

Once you join me, and see the same thing that I expect to see, I believe your request for the photos will be superfluous.

Sincerely,

Professor Edwin Kensington

Morell arrived about a 12:30 a.m. at the place where he was supposed to rendezvous with Kensington. He had been delayed by being called out on several different incidents beginning with a store burglary, followed by a cocaine bust. He parked the patrol car about a block from the bridge and hurried by the empty buildings. He could hear the sounds of distant traffic, but the surrounding area was deserted and silent—the perfect work place for a crew. Up ahead, parked under in the jaundiced glow of a street lamp, was an old Volvo that he knew belonged to Kensington. So the professor had gotten here ahead of him. He half expected to find the man seated inside the car, waiting for him, but Kensington apparently had already gone down to the river bank. Perhaps he had seen something or heard something that had made him act before Morell had arrived.

Not very smart to go down there by yourself, Morell thought, thinking of how easily Jiiminez had been assaulted by one of the taggers. It's not a group of pimply-faced kids we're dealing with now.

The graffiti, new and glowing in the moonlight, stretched as far as the eye could see. The taggers had been particularly busy tonight; perhaps they were in a hurry to finish so they could meet some unknown deadline, as Kensington had suggested. Of the professor he saw no sign.

"Professor Kensington," he called out. "It's me, Detective Morell. Where are you?"

No answer.

At the gaping black entrance to a massive storm drain that fed into the river he found Kensington's camcorder, lying in the grass, where he had dropped it or…where it had been hurled by one of the taggers. The red power light was still flashing monotonously. Morell picked it up and looked around with a frown. Surely the professor wouldn't have gone off and left it, no matter how much of a hurry he was in. Which led to the next question: Where *was* Kensington?

He could have gone into the culvert itself, perhaps in pursuit of the taggers. Morrell didn't know if the man would do anything that foolhardy, but it was possible. The opening was almost big enough for a man to stand up in, and, crouching over, Morell edged inside, shining his flashlight ahead of him. His shoes sank in the soft detritus left from the winter rains, and his nostrils were assaulted by the rancid smell of decaying trash. The tunnel was preternaturally silent; Morell heard no sounds of running footsteps, no distant cries for help.

Every nerve tingling, he descended until the tunnel split into a "v." Morell shone the flashlight down both ends, but again saw no sign of Kensington. Still, he had the strangest sensation that he was being observed, that somewhere in the darkness beyond the reach of his flashlight hostile, alien eyes were watching him. He would have to go back to his car and call for backup. The tunnel had to come out somewhere; with enough men they could flush the taggers out and perhaps find Kensington as well.

He took the camcorder back to his car and examined it under the glow of a street lamp. Something had been recorded. He hit the "rewind" button and watched. He saw the ghostly sides of the river bed through Kensington's eyes, and then a jiggly, sea-sick motion as the professor descended the side of the river at a fast clip after catching a glimpse of something that he wanted to document. Now Kensington was fairly running across the grass, making the image bounce up and down so it was almost impossible to make out anything.

Then he must have jerked to a stop, driven either by caution or the need to steady the camera to better film what he saw. The camcorder zoomed in on three figures with their backs to Kensington. They were marking graffiti on the wall. Morell couldn't tell what they were using for paint brushes. Again it seemed that the markings were almost flowing out of their finger tips.

Morell felt a thrill of horror as he saw how they moved almost in unison, scuttling insect-like up and down the concrete, leaving a gleaming black trail of letters in their wake.

They're not human, Morell thought. I don't know what they are, but I know that much.

It was at that moment that the taggers must have become aware of Kensington's presence, because almost in unison they turned around. The professor had zoomed in one the nearest one, its face filling the tiny screen in the harsh white light, and the close up made Morell cry out in fear. He let go of the camcorder and it tumbled over the concrete lip of the embankment. He heard it shatter into a thousand plastic pieces as it hit the bottom.

With a cry he rushed down to find it, but saw the remains were already disappearing beneath the surface. Even if he could have retrieved it, the water would have ruined the chip inside.

What had he seen? He was still trembling from the remembrance of it. Just a glimpse before the tape went black, but it would be enough to haunt his nightmares forever: the pasty-white, almost leathery looking skin, the vertical mouth crisscrossed with needle-like fangs, the burning, soulless eyes. He had lost the one piece of proof of what he had just seen, but he doubted whether anyone would believe it even if he had been able to save the camcorder. Kensington might have been able to convince people, but the professor was gone, perhaps forever.

Kensington disappeared without a trace. The police, led by Morrell, made a thorough search of the area without finding any clues. Nor did they find anything that might have led to the taggers. It was as if they, too, had dissolved into thin air, much the way the graffiti itself did when the first wan, slanted rays of the morning touched it.

Finally, a little after ten a.m., having given up the hope of finding Kensington, Morell went home and tried to rest. As exhausted as he was, he could not sleep. He kept seeing that grotesque face in the tiny screen of the video recorder every time he closed his eyes. But had he actually seen it, or only imagined he had? It could have been the way the camera's light had caught the features, the shadows harshly distorting them somehow. Since he had inadvertently destroyed the camcorder, he would never know. About what had happened he had told no one. The water had carried away the pieces of the camcorder, and with them, the flimsiest evidence, but evidence nonetheless, that the taggers were not human.

Finally he got up and went back to work. He checked to see if there had been any developments on Kensington. Nothing. Desultorily he shuffled through some old reports on the Alvarado case, hoping that there might be overlooked clues buried there. He kept thinking about what Kensington had said about the grid connecting the bands of graffiti being almost complete, and what it might possibly portend once it was finished. He had heard from the grapevine that there had been other reported sightings of hooded taggers, working in threes and fours, not affiliated with any known gang, all over the city, but no one had gotten as close to them as he had.

He was dozing off at his desk when someone touched him lightly on the shoulder. Morell started, still spooked by what he had seen the night before. It was only Jiminez, smiling down at him, standing stiffly because of the tape around his ribs.

"Hey, man, you're falling asleep at your desk. Go home and get some shut eye."

"I'll be OK," Morell said. "I got a couple more things to do before I call it quits." He and his old partner had barely spoken since the other had refused to go out with him to rendezvous with Kensington. Morell was sure that Jiminez felt guilty now about not being there to back him up.

"It'll still be there tomorrow. At least get away from this place for awhile. You'll think better when you come back."

"Maybe you're right," Morell said, standing up. "I got to swing by the San Pedro station. Maybe I'll go from there to the beach."

"That salt air'll clear your head out. You'll be doing yourself a favor, man."

He wound up going to Manhattan Beach. It was a little more upscale than the places Morell normally frequented, but he could walk along the Strand, in the shadow of the multi-million dollar homes that faced the Pacific, and pretend that the rest of the world as a right as things were in this beach community.

Before he got there, he had to follow the Los Angeles River one last time on the way to San Pedro. This was one of the most depressing vistas in the whole city, with the railroad yards to his left and warehouses and manufacturing to his right. It made him think of another place on the river, where a boy had been killed and a man had disappeared. There were storm drains all along the river, interconnected and tunneled into the earth; it would be easy for an army of taggers to hide inside of them.

The artificial river bed was the key to the mystery, he thought. The tagging had followed it and had, from what he had been able to ascertain, branched off it in certain places to form Kensington's so-called grid. It had been designed to protect the low, flat plain from flooding, and over the years had done its job well; Morell was sure that its designers had never dreamed that its storm drains would be put to a more nefarious purpose.

It was late afternoon by the time he finished making his stop at San Pedro and shot the breeze with the desk officer. He had the all-news channel on during the remainder of the drive up the 405; the newscaster was talking about a major quake that had occurred off the coast of Baja California a few minutes before. Someday, he thought, we'll get ours, and turned the radio off.

He parked about two blocks up from the beach, and, after putting on tennis shoes, descended to the pier. It was late in the afternoon, with the sun beginning its descent below the horizon, and the beach was largely deserted. A few families had camped out at the water's edge, and two surfers were paddling out in unison to meet the waves.

Morell was about to turn up the Strand, past the beach front houses of millionaires, when his attention was caught by something underneath the pier. Something had been marked on the massive concrete legs, and with a chill of recognition Morell thought he knew what it was. Forgetting about his walk, forgetting about everything else, he scrambled down the concrete steps to the beach.

The graffiti had not faded—at least not yet—because it was well-protected by the overhang of the pier. It extended from the top leg all the way down to the water's edge; most of it would be washed away when the tide rose.

How had the demon taggers been able to come down here and do their work even at night, when Manhattan Beach had a popular after-hours scene, and the streets as well as the bars were full of people late into the night? He looked up the beach and thought he had his answer: a huge concrete storm drain loomed dark and mysterious at the Strand's edge.

So the grid began just above downtown and ran all the way down to the sea. Morell imagined he could find traces of the graffiti on other piers or on the sea walls themselves if the sun had not burned it away. But why end here? he wondered, as dark green water licked at the graffiti on the last leg of the pier.

Then, as he watched, the water began to receded with a hissing sound, rolling backwards with ever increasing speed. He heard terrified shouts and saw the two surfers were struggling not to be sucked out with it. The disappearing water revealed a flat endless expanse of beach where the bay had been such a few moments before. A large fish flopped helplessly on the grayish sand.

Morell could not have said at exactly what point the emergency sirens went off. He looked over and saw the surfers were standing on dry ground where the water had been over their heads a few moments before. Far out at sea he heard a distant rumbling like an approaching storm, but the sky was clear.

Only then did he realize what was happening. The graffiti on the beams of the pier, and wherever else it terminated at the water's edge, was an end point... and an invitation.

"Run!" he yelled to the surfers, to the family who were gawking at the endless expanse of sand. "Get out of here!"

He took his own advice and clambered up the concrete steps to the street, and sprinted past the bars, past the huge homes that would soon be reduced to rubble.

Manhattan Beach was built on higher ground; it might survive—part of it, anyway. But through his mind flashed the names of the other cities hugging the coast—San Pedro, Carson, Long Beach, a good part of Los Angeles—that were barely above sea level. The home to hundreds of thousands, perhaps millions of people. He glanced over his shoulder and redoubled his speed at the sight of the tsunami's seventy foot wall of water rushing inexorably toward the shore, knowing at last what fate for them the alien graffiti had spelled out.

WILLIAM MEIKLE is a Scottish writer with ten novels published in the genre press and over 200 short story credits in thirteen countries. He is the author of the ongoing *Midnight Eye* series among others, and his work appears in a number of professional anthologies. His ebook *The Invasion* has been as high as #2 in the Kindle SF charts. He lives in a remote corner of Newfoundland with icebergs, whales and bald eagles for company. In the winters he gets warm vicariously through the lives of others in cyberspace, so please check him out at http://www.williammeikle.com

The Unfinished Basement

by William Meikle

Dave Collins stood at the kerb and gave the house the once-over. From the outside it didn't look like much, but that was sometimes a good thing in this business. A quick flip, both interior and exterior, could polish the unlikeliest derelict. It wouldn't be the first time that Dave managed to turn a hundred grand profit on something that no one else had seen money in.

I've got a nose for it.

He'd heard about this one on the grapevine - a Fifties mock-Tudor on a corner lot that had gone to seed. It wasn't even on the market yet - Dave had a day's head start on the competition, and he intended to make the most of it.

First he made a quick survey of the outside. To his trained eye the structure looked sound. There would be some work needed on the guttering, and one of the rear windows needed replacing, but there was nothing to frighten him off. As he stood on the back lawn he felt a vibration run through him, like the *thrum* of a giant guitar string, but it passed as quickly as it had come. He made a mental note to check on any possible sewer work in the area, then went inside.

The ground floor looked like it hadn't been decorated since the house was built. Flock wallpaper had peeled in places, exposing patches of damp beneath, but again it was nothing that had him worried.

She's an aging beauty. All she needs is some fresh make-up and new clothes.

The main living area surprised him. Where the rest of the house felt empty and neglected, he had the feeling that someone had left this room just seconds before. The second surprise was the large piano sitting dead centre on the polished hardwood floor. It looked to be a full sized grand in good repair, and Dave was at a loss to understand why the previous occupants had left it. But he knew from experience that pianos were a notoriously difficult sell in the trade.

Maybe it was just too big to be worth the trouble? Or warped and out of tune?

He ran a hand over the keyboard. The instrument rang and chimed. Somewhere below him the ground vibrated again.

There's definitely something going on down there that needs looking at.

Dave didn't have a musical bone in his body so there was no way he was going to be able to tell if the piano was salvageable. But he knew a man who might. And maybe the instrument would help squeeze even more profit out of the deal. As he left his footsteps on the hardwood floor set up a sympathetic vibration and the piano *droned*. He felt it rise through the soles of his feet.

It's as if the house is singing for me.

It wasn't an unpleasant sensation.

*   *   *

He signed the papers that same morning, and early the next day was back at the property with his contractors, knocking on walls and assessing the scale of the work that needed doing.

They were just about to move down to the cellar when Dave's piano man arrived.

He'd used John Thorpe's experience before, and knew him as a quiet, steady man not prone to emotion, so Dave was surprised at the man's reaction to the instrument.

Thorpe whistled in appreciation as soon as he set eyes on the piano.

"This is a real find Mr Collins," he said, running a hand along the instrument's flanks as if it was a lover. "There's no maker's mark, but a craftsman put many weeks of love into this, no mistake."

"Just tell me it won't cost more to take away than it's worth," Collins replied.

Thorpe smiled.

"Mr Collins... it might just be worth more than you'll make on the house. Leave me with it for a bit and I'll let you know."

Collins joined Thorpe in smiling, and he still had the grin on his face as he led the contractors down to the cellar. But his good humor was to be short lived. Where the upstairs of the house held an air of faded grandeur, down here it was as dark and dank as a cave. The single lightbulb flickered, sending a spluttering strobe effect through the cellar. There was no plasterboard on the walls, or flooring on the ground. Instead it looked like the area had been hewn straight out of the bedrock; the appliances and old furnace looking strangely out of place in a space that could easily have been made to contain something *older*.

The three contractors he had brought with him stood at the foot of the wooden stairs, looking to Dave for guidance. He saw the look in their eyes, and felt the same concern himself. What had been an opportunity to make quick easy cash had suddenly turned into a potential money pit, for no-one in their right minds would buy a house with a cellar in this state.

"Let's just get on and assess the damage," Dave said. "Maybe it's not as bad as it looks."

It was worse.

A dark, almost black, pool lay still and stagnant across the whole far end of the basement, an acrid odour rising from it that made all four men step back, hands to mouths. Over to their left, where the cellar stretched beyond the limits of the house above, white pallid plant roots hung from the ceiling, wafting in the air almost as if alive.

Collins stepped over and kicked at what passed for a furnace. His feet hit the casing... and kept going, knocking a large hole in the rusted metal.

One of the contractors poked with the tip of a knife at a timber column supporting the floor above. It went into the wood as if cutting into soft butter.

This is a disaster.

Thorpe chose that moment to start playing the piano in the room above.

Dave felt it first in the pit of his stomach, but soon his whole frame shook, vibrating in time with the rhythm. His head swam, and it seemed as if the walls of the cellar melted and ran. The lightbulb receded into a great distance until it was little more than a pinpoint in a blanket of darkness, and Dave was alone, in a vast cathedral of emptiness where nothing existed save the dark and the pounding beat.

Shapes moved in the dark, wispy shadows with no substance, shadows that capered and whirled as their dance grew ever more frenetic. He tasted salt water in his mouth, and was buffeted, as if by a strong, surging tide. He gave himself to it, lost in the dance, lost in the dark. He had no conception how long he wandered, there in the space between. He forgot himself, forgot where he was, in a blackness where only rhythm mattered.

He only came to his senses when Thorpe stopped at the end of the piece. Something roiled in the pit of his stomach. Collins headed for the stairs at a run, and made it as far as the kitchen sink before he lost his breakfast in a steaming bundle. He slowly became aware that the contractors were in a similar state, and when he went back to the main room he found Thorpe slumped over the piano in a stupor.

He had to shake the man twice before he stirred, coming up as if out of a deep sleep.

He looks worse than I feel, Dave thought.

The contractors had already fled by the time Dave dragged Thorpe to the front door and sucked in welcome fresh air.

"What did you do?" Dave whispered. "What the hell did you do?"

Thorpe didn't answer. Dave noticed the man staring intently at a sheaf of papers in his hand. At first he thought it was a musical score, but a quick glance showed that it was what looked like random scrawls, strange groups of lines and dots.

Thorpe shuffled the papers, folded them, and put them in an inside pocket.

"I found them inside the piano," was all he would say. "I'll do some research on the instrument and get back to you. Just don't move it anywhere. It's precious."

Dave had no intention of going *near* the piano. He turned to tell Thorpe that, but the man was already scurrying away down the driveway.

Dave closed the door behind him and turned his back on the house. As he went down the path he thought he felt a vibration under his feet, and his stomach rolled over. He went home and fell into a fitful sleep. He dreamed of dark pools and ringing chords.

When he woke the next morning it was amid a tangled mess of sweat-damp sheets and he was more tired than ever. He dragged himself to the office only to be told that his contractors had, to a man, resigned rather than return to the old house.

I know just how they feel.

He spent the day finding any excuse he could to stay away from the building, but the sound of the piano continued to reverberate in his head whenever he found a moment of quiet. He had just about determined to head for a bar and attempt to drink it away when he got a phone call from one of his competitors.

"Dave? Phil Johnson. I thought I'd check out the Fifties Tudor, but it seems you got there first. Did you know there's someone still living there? I took a look at a new one on the market across the road, and they said there was someone in the Tudor last night, and the piano playing kept them awake for hours."

The bar seemed like a good idea again, but the call of money was stronger. Dave couldn't afford to take a big hit on the Tudor house. Piano or no piano, the renovations were going to have to start.

He drove straight over.

He wasn't surprised to find Thorpe sitting on the stool by the keyboard. The piano-man looked like he hadn't slept since the day before. He looked up from the keyboard and waved the sheaf of papers towards Dave.

"I know what you've got here," Thorpe said. "You have to demolish this place. Raze it to the ground and concrete over the ashes."

Dave didn't get time to ask why. Thorpe tried to stand but his legs gave way and he tumbled, insensate, to the floor. The thud as his head hit the boards caused the piano to ring and thrum in sympathy.

*   *   *

Dave spent the whole evening in the E.R. while doctors fussed and fiddled over a still-unconscious Thorpe. As the night passed an air of deepening worry grew, and by the time Dave came back from a fruitless search for coffee at eleven-thirty the worry had turned to sad resignation.

"There's nothing we can do for him," a tired doctor said. "He's lapsed into a coma, and the cancer might take him at any time."

"Cancer?"

The doctor nodded.

"End stage... very near the end. I'm surprised he was mobile long enough to get here. How long has he been bedridden?" It came from so far out of left field that Dave didn't understand the question, let along be able to answer it.

The rest of the night was reduced to a jumble of snatches of sleep stolen in waiting rooms and bad food in the hospital canteen. Thorpe was *stable* acording to the doctors, but they gave little hope of him waking. Dave was near ready to head for home and his own bed when he was called into Thorpe's room.

"He's asking for you," the doctor said. "He says it's important. But he may not live long enough to tell you."

Dave could not stop the shock showing as he walked into the room and looked at the shell of a man on the bed. If he hadn't known better he'd have thought he was in the wrong room... the *thing* on the bed looked soft and pulpy and somehow *decayed*. But it was Thorpe's striking blue eyes that looked out of the sweat-drenched face, and the piano man's voice that spoke.

He had the sheaf of papers clutched to his chest.

"I know what you have there," he whispered. Flecks of blood showed at his lips. "It's all in these papers."

"Shush man," Dave said, moving to stand at the side of the bed. "Save your strength."

"It's too late for me," Thorpe said. "But not for you. I told you. Raze it to the ground Mr Collins. Burn it, then make sure nothing else is ever built on the spot."

Dave didn't get time to respond. Thorpe's eyes rolled up in their sockets and he fell back, unconscious once again. The doctors ushered Dave back out into the corridor, but on his way he lifted the sheaf of papers and stuffed them into his jacket pocket.

"I'd go home sir," the attending nurse said. "It's doubtful that your friend will wake up again. We have your number. We'll ring if there's any change."

Dave took his weary body home and fell, fully clothed into bed.

Sleep wouldn't come. His mind filled with images, of dark pools and pale roots, of Thorpe's greasy skin and the blood, too red, bubbling at his lips. He rose, unrested, in the early hours and made a pot of coffee.

It was then he remembered the papers. He took them from his jacket and smoothed them out on the table. The top page had been ripped from a diary and was dated March 29th, 1959.

I had visited several Neolithic tombs, in Carnac, in Orkney and on Salisbury Plain. This gave the same sense of age, of a time long past. What I hadn't expected, what was completely different, was the overwhelming feeling that this place was in use. The walls ran damp and there was a stale taste in the air but there was no sign of moss or lichen on the walls - only softly wafting roots, milk-white and smooth like mouse-tails.

Roger moved over to one wall and held the flashlight closer.

"Here," he said. "Here's why I called for you."

The wall was covered in small, tightly packed carvings. At first I thought it might be a language, but it was none that I recognised from my studies, indeed, it bore no resemblance to anything I had ever seen before.

"'I can't make head or tail of them,'" Roger said. "But I believe they hold the secret.'"

The remainder of the papers seemed to be a transcription of the aforementioned symbols, page after page of dots and lines that looked like gibberish to Collins. But whoever had written the diary entry had done better. Tagged on at the end after the notation were two more lined pages, dated March 30th 1959.

Roger drummed his fingers on his piano, a martial beat, only a few seconds long. The piano rang in sympathy... and the answer came to me, all at once.

"It's not a language... it's a musical notation."

Roger merely looked at me in astonishment as I jumped out of my chair and headed for the piano. I spread the transcribed papers over the top.

"Look. These lines, separated into groups corresponding to quavers, minims and crotchets... but it's not music as such... there is no sense of a scale."

Roger drummed his fingers once more, and again the piano resonated in sympathy.

I moved him off the stool and sat down at the instrument.

"So if it's not music... it must be rhythm," I said. "Rhythm and vibration."

I shuffled the papers and placed them on the music stand in front of me.

"How do you know where to start?" Roger said.

"I don't. Let us just see if I am right first."

I picked a solid minor chord, and began striking the keyboard in time with the rhythm transposed on the pages. Almost immediately I felt the sympathetic resonance rise from the chamber beneath.

"It's working," Roger shouted. But I was already lost in a world of pounding chords.

Something was far wrong. I knew it at an intellectual level. But the music controlled me deeper than that, in the hindbrain where the evolutionary equivalent of a gibbering monkey hit a log with a stick and enjoyed the noise. My hands pounded the keyboard, hands clenched into fists. The beat sped up a notch and the walls shook, loose mortar falling from the ceiling. Just as I felt I could go no further, the beat slowed, mellowed.

My head swam, and the walls melted and ran. The fireplace receded into a great distance until it was little more than a pinpoint of light in a blanket of darkness, and I was alone, in a vast cathedral of emptiness. A tide took me, a swell that lifted and transported me, faster than thought, to the green twilight of ocean depths far distant.

I realised I was not alone. We floated, mere shadows now, scores... no, tens of scores of us, in that cold silent sea. I was aware that Roger was near, but I had no thought for aught but the rhythm, the dance. Far below us, cyclopean ruins shone dimly in a luminescent haze. Columns and rock faces tumbled in a non-Euclidean geometry that confused the eye and brooked no close inspection. And something deep in those ruins knew we were there.

We dreamed, of vast empty spaces, of giant clouds of gas that engulfed the stars, of blackness where there was nothing but endless dark, endless quiet. And while our slumbering god dreamed, we danced for him, there in the twilight, danced to the rhythm.

We were at peace.

I came to lying on the floor beside the piano. The first thing I was aware of was the pain in my hands; my knuckles bloodied and torn. At some point I had vomited, and the sweet sickly odor drove me away and up to my feet. The door to the cellar creaked and I heard stumbling footsteps headed downstairs. I called after Roger, but there was no reply.

I followed as quickly as I was able, stumbling down into the dark room.

But there was no sign of my friend, just a white sticky trail leading straight to that dark pool in the corner.

I fled back upstairs.

That was an hour ago. I have fortified myself with whisky, and on completion of this memoir I shall once more venture downstairs. It knows I am here... I have felt its vibrations. But if my friend is still there somewhere, I must go to his aid.

Collins turned the last page over, but it was blank. His gaze kept turning back to the scrawls and scratches on the papers.

Rhythm and vibration?

It made no sense at all to him, and he was too tired to think. He drained his coffee just as his phone rang, causing him to jump and spill the dregs over the papers on the table.

It was the hospital.

"He's gone?" Dave asked.

There was no answer at the other end for some time.

"Not exactly sir." He recognized the voice of the nurse he had spoken to earlier. "He's gone all right... his bed is empty, and we can't find him anywhere."

A sudden chill hit the back of Dave's neck, bringing with it a whiff of damp and mold that he recognised all too well. He turned, just in time to see a pale bloated arm raised above him. It smacked into the side of his head and Dave fell sideways. His temple hit the table and darkness took him down and away. He went thankfully.

*   *   *

When he woke it was to thin morning sunshine washing across the kitchen floor. He stumbled to his feet, having to climb up the table-leg to keep balance. He had to stand still and quiet for long seconds before the dizziness abated.

The transcribed papers were gone from the table, only a rectangular clear patch in a drying coffee stain showing where they had been. And there was something else -- a white viscous fluid, disturbingly seminal, that was tacky to the touch. A trail of it led to and from his apartment door.

Thorpe. And he's heading for the house. Raze it to the ground? Over my dead body.

He was hampered by nausea and dizziness, but the thought of the house burning, and his investment money along with it, got him on the move. He drove through the early morning, hoping he wasn't too late, his mind full of the thought of burning.

It was a momentary relief to find the house still standing, but as soon as he turned off the car engine he heard the thumping martial rhythm of the piano. Even out here on the lawn he felt his head spin and threaten to send him back to the rushing tide of oblivion.

He stuck fingers in his ears and made for the door. Even then he felt the beat through his feet. He pushed through the open door.

At the same instant the music stopped and the house fell deathly quiet. He ran into the piano room just in time to see the cellar door swing shut. There was a moist *slumping* sound from the stairs on the other side. He walked across the floor, kicking aside coffee stained papers, and listened.

What if he's taken gasoline down there? He could burn the place down around me.

Despite his better judgement he opened the door and moved to the top of the stairs. The smell hit him immediately... the same dank odour he'd been smelling since he first went down into the basement.

"Thorpe. Come back up here. Let's talk about this."

There was no answer. He went down three steps. The single light-bulb sputtered and flickered, revealing only a trail of white mucus stretching down the stairs and off out of sight across the cellar floor.

"Thorpe?"

There was still no answer, but *someone* was down there... he could sense it. He stepped down to the cellar floor. The only noise was a soft *hiss* from the lightbulb overhead.

"Thorpe?" he called.

In answer there was a *splash* from the pool at the far end of the cellar.

There's no way I'm going over there.

But his legs thought otherwise. He stepped slowly forward, taking care not to step in any of the pale slime that showed him Thorpe's path. It led straight to the dark pool of water.

There was another splash, and something white moved in the darkness.

"Thorpe? Is that you?"

Two more steps took him to the edge of the pool.

He looked down into the water.

What he saw there sent him screaming for the stairs, out into the world in search of as much gasoline as he could get his hands on.

Later, as he watched the house burn, he knew he would never forget the sight of the white bloated mass that sank slowly into the pool, receding into some far depths where shadows surged in the tide... and all the way down as it descended, Thorpe's startling blue eyes staring back up.

DON WEBB has stories in Norwegian anarchist magazines, Bengali experimental literature magazines, a Norton anthology, *Truckers USA* and a few hundred other places. His fifteenth book *The War With the Beletren* is coming out from Wildside Press. He has written nonfiction on the Greek Magical Papyri and Aleister Crowley. He teaches Creative Writing for UCLA Extension. He is a Texan, so he has a secret chili recipe. He lives in Austin with his lovely wife Guiniviere.

Plush Cthulhu

by Don Webb

As soon as the excuse left his lips Larry Ellison felt slightly lower than the belly of a rattlesnake in a wagon rut. Larry had tried for years to reach his students at James Bowie Junior High with Western metaphors, reasoning (incorrectly) that kids in central Texas had something of the Old West about them. His principal Miss Rebecca Gonzalez looked appropriately shocked. His assistant principal, Mr. José Wong Jr, who had not smiled at him in his five years of employment, actually put his hand around Larry's shoulders. Larry had no idea where the excuse had come from, and was amazed at some deep level that God hadn't smitten him on the spot.

Larry had just told the administration that he had missed Monday because his mom had died on Sunday. He had missed because he was high on ecstasy and balling some woman, whose name (he thought) was Chandra Azathoth Nibiru, or maybe it was Sandra? Although now he realized that was probably a stage name; she was probably named Rebecca Fielding or some such. His mother was (to the best of his knowledge) alive, if not well, at the Machen Assisted Living Center about twenty miles north in Austin, Texas.

"If you need to take more time off Larry, the District gives a five day leave for death of a parent or spouse in addition to the normal state and local days." Said Mr. Wong. Wong had never used his first name before. But the big lie had apparently made his heart grow three sizes larger,

"I'll need Thursday and Friday off for the funeral." It was snowballing now. "But otherwise I want to stay at work, keep my mind focused on things."

"I was the same way when my mother died." Said Miss Gonzalez. "She had been in a rest home like your mom. Is the funeral going to be here, I mean in Austin?"

"No, Ma'am. It will be in her hometown of Amarillo."

"Let us know where we can send flowers." Said Wong.

Oh god. "I, well my brothers and I, are asking that donations be made to Book Aid International." Mom had probably never heard of Book Aid International, it was one of Larry's favorites. Oh god I am going to Hell for this, for sure. Larry made an exaggerated stare at the Brother brand clock in Miss G.'s office, "I need to get to first period."

He left her office and made an effort to stare at the brown terrazzo floors. Larry was not a frequent liar. All of his lies had been small ones, Yes he was sure the copy machine was turned off, yes he had all of his grades in, of course he knew his autistic student's IEP by heart. He made his way to the second floor, not enjoying running his hand over the age-smoothed banister or the Latin motto in the wall Non scholae, sed vitae discimus Not for school, but for life we learn. Seneca. Bowie Junior High was one of the landmarks of Doublesign, Texas – and he had enjoyed its solidity as he had his own until today. He had about ten minutes to get his days objectives for English 8 on the board. It was almost the last day of the poetry unit, and most of the students had still not written the poem and paper required.

When noon came, all the teachers made their way over to him: Mrs. Spradlin, Mr. Henley, Mr. Gutierrez, Miss Leach, Miss Mertin, Mr. Ousley, Mrs. Olrun, Mr. Watson. All Larry could do was think what was going to happen when Momma really died? She was almost 90 for Christ sake.

He wanted to call the nursing home during his conference period to make sure she was still alive, or he fantasized grimly maybe she has died. He was reaching for his cell phone when it started to vibrate. He hoped it was Chandra, but to his horror he saw it was the nursing home.

His mother may have had a stroke. They had rushed her to Seaton Hospital, but the hospital had returned her asking that she be closely observed for the next 24 hours. Could he come and see her? He said that he would be out immediately after work, and they must not call the school because, because, because they were doing standardized testing.

The next two periods might have been dipped in lead. Cotton filled his ears; his corneas were surely tinted with weak tea. The eighth graders muttered little rhymes like miniature witches and warlocks. Just before the last bell, he could've sworn he heard some girl saying, "Step on a crack, . . ."

He felt too drained to run, and too anxious to collapse. So he made his way to his car. Teachers weren't supposed to leave until half an hour after the last bell, but given his recent bereavement: he knew no one would stop him. Some of the para-professionals were putting up cardboard snowmen, others symbols of a New England Thanksgiving. It was a warm afternoon; he wondered how long the decorations made for school would take to catch up with global warming. None of his students had ever seen more than a half-inch of snow – they had no reference to a world covered in pristine white.

He had taught middle school too long, he decided as he drove north into Austin. He had given a middle school excuse. Probably the ecstasy has fucked his mind. He was having some mid-life crisis. It was probably the girl's fault. Oh great another middle school response. He hadn't planned to go to Austin for Halloween, at least not be in the city after nightfall. Austin had a huge drunk party on Sixth Street fueled by revealing costumes, live music and cheap drinks. There were over forty thousand students in attendance at the University of Texas. He had stopped at a used music store. This amazingly tall bronze woman in a deep purple miniskirt disrupted his thumbing through jazz CDs by bending over to look at psychedelic vinyl. With her white go-go boots and long raven hair, she looked as though she belonged to the psychedelic era. She stamped her boots and sighed loudly, inviting comment. Despite the twenty-year difference in their ages, Larry played along.

"Can't find something?" he asked.

"My girlfriend told me that she had seen an Electric Commode album here today. I've been hunting it for years."

"I take it that it hasn't made itunes yet."

She smiled and he was lost in her liquid brown eyes.

"It was an obscure band even then. Part of the Arkham sound. They did some work with a theremin like device I am trying to rebuild."

"Like in that documentary, who was she? Clara Rockmore?" asked Larry.

The woman's face lit up. "Oh cool. Yes Clara was a lover and student of Leon Theremin. Are you interested in alternative electronica?"

Larry had never heard the phrase, "alternative electronica" in his life, but he hadn't been laid in three years. So his agreement sounded genuine and enthusiastic.

Larry pulled up at the Machen Assisted Living Center. A bright yellow-green ambulance was parked in front of the light gray one story building. But that was nothing new. He swallowed as much guilt as he could, and then headed inside. It didn't smell as strongly as the place his grandfather had died in twenty years ago. Maybe there had been breakthroughs in anti-death smell chemistry. The administrator at reception looked professionally sad.

"Mr. Ellison, when your mother began living here, we talked about the stages of our process. Your mom won't have her own room anymore. We're going to have to watch her a little more closely. Would you like to see her?"

Mom's hair was white as snow, her skin translucent. She had shrunk so over the last three years. She wore a faded Sears's housedress, no doubt older than any of his students. Her eyes had faded from a rich brown to the color of weak tea, and they looked angry. She sat in the "sun room" in a gerry chair, the restraining wheelchair that kept mindless patients from roaming the halls on their own. She smelled of piss. Some one had given her a plush Cthulhu doll. She clutched the little green monstrosity fiercely. It was an odd gift. Mom had never been much of a reader, and preferred Danielle Steele to Stephen King or certainly to Lovecraft. It was a silly, stupid toy dark green plush with a lighter green underbelly as though Cthulhu were a relation of Kermit. Its soft blunted tentacles and soft wings removed any sense of cosmic evil, and its brown eyes were almost shy. It tore at Larry's heart; the toy's eyes were more alive than his momma's.

She looked at Larry.

She didn't know him.

He actually heard his heart break. Well not his heart, but the emotional break had a sound accompanying it – it sounded like a hollow reed had been snapped behind his neck.

Larry walked over to where she was and sank on his knees. He looked at her and nothing really looked back. He said, :Momma" six or seven times. No change in her face. He tried to take Cthulhu away from her. She resisted, but it was easy to deprive her of the toy. She made a sad sound and tried to get the doll back. The other seniors looked at him with the same horror one would give to the thief of an infant's candy. He gave her the doll back. He had a hard time standing. His face was wet. He hadn't cried in a very long time.

"Did you step on a crack?"

He wheeled on the administrator. "What did you say?" he asked.

"I said it's so hard the first time they don't know us. I remember how it was with my own mother." She began.

The room seemed very unstable. Larry opened his mouth and couldn't make a sound. He tried again and managed, "I know you are trying to share a helpful story, but I can't really hear anything right now. I've got to go, I'll talk to her doctor tomorrow,:

He made it to the parking lot. This was Mamma. Mamma who had helped through a bad marriage, Mamma who had worked two jobs so that he could get his English degree at UT. Mamma who had rocked him when he had those terrible earaches as a kid. He was going to have tell his boss the truth. Surely she was about to die. It was all wrong. All fucked up.

He had heard that sound before. At Chandra's apartment.

Her apartment was over a Mexican import shop on South Congress. It was jam-packed with books, CDs, old vinyl and strange looking electronic instruments. She told him some of the names: the Persephone, the Electronode, the Tepaphone, the Haken Continuum, the Trautonium, the Sonorous Cross, the Shaggaipolyphonic.

She had painted a slogan on the ceiling in purple, "Music is divided for Love's sake."

She had slipped into the bathroom, slipping into something more comfortable. Larry spotted a framed page from a children's book:

There was once a poor woodcutter, who lived in front of a great forest.

He fared so miserably, that he could scarcely feed his wife and his two children. Once he had no bread any longer, and suffered great anxiety, then his wife said to him in the evening in bed: take the two children tomorrow morning and take them into the great forest, give them the bread we have left, and make a large fire for them and after that go away and leave them alone. The husband did not want to for a long time, but the wife left him no peace, until he finally agreed

"'Hansel and Gretel'?" he asked as she returned in a short purple nightgown that matched the color of the quote. "Why?"

She smiled, "It's about splitting. Freud studied fairy tales for this. The young child has to split the image of the Good Mother and the Bad Mother. The kid's tiny brain can't deal with the Good Mother that gives him the tit and the Bad Mother that is angry when he poops himself. So he makes up two mothers. The witch in the gingerbread house is actually the regular mom. That is where humans get good and evil."

"OK, but why frame it?" Larry was split between curiosity and horniness at that moment.

"Music is all about splitting. Rhythm is about breaks, notes are about breaks, and noise and sound are about breaks. All of my lifework is about splitting things and putting them back together. You ever done X? It can help you see beyond splits. That can take you beyond Love and Fear. That's my work, besides it makes sex better."

Larry attempting to be cool just smiled.

The sex was great. Super-nova great. Hallucinogenic mother-fucking awesome great. Mythic volcano erupting beyond Good and evil great. She played weird music, and the drugs kicked in and he had a million weird flashes like screwing atop a pyramid altar, or having sex with hundreds of women and men and fauns, or making love to his ex-wife, or having an erotic frolic with mermaids, or seeing stars explode. At some point they left the flat and walked to Sixth Street and milled among the costumed and the drunk and the horny – or maybe they had gone to a Black Mass in Hell or some mixture of both and the one clear memory was a snapping sound behind his neck and Chandra saying, "Well Cinderella your ball is over now."

The next thing he knew was that he was laying in her narrow bed and was staring at the quote on her ceiling. It was not the Sunday morning he had been expecting. It turned out to be Monday morning. Chandra had split, and he was famished. He went to his car, and he dove back to Doublesign. He got there about noon, and he was sure that he didn't want to face his classes. Every now and again he seemed to see green or yellow lights shimmer at the corners of his vision. Doublesign had two stoplights and one actual apartment building, but Larry lived in a garage apartment belonging to Mrs. Irma Johnson, who also ran the FedEx store. He crawled up the stairs to his apartment, ate three bologna sandwiches and crashed. Somehow he would make it right

It was getting dark. He needed to drive home from the home. He would have to call his sister in Florida and tell her, but he couldn't think of the words. He knew the guilt that filled him was irrational. Momma didn't have a stroke because he had lied to his boss. He tried calling Chandra. When she answered he hung up, and turned his cell phone off. No words for that either.

He didn't remember the first nightmares. Suddenly it was 6:30 and his alarm was going off and he was scared. His bed was dank with sweat and his stomach too upset and it was Wednesday morning. Frost silvered everything; a front had come in during the night. He couldn't remember what his lesson plans were. He remembered telling his principal that he was taking for the funeral. Was it Thursday and Friday? Or just Friday? Were his actions too shitty to tell his friends? It was going to be a great day, he could tell.

Someone had told the kids. They kept their heads down. No joking around. Many of the girls made him little cards out of folded notebook paper and colored pencils. The para-professionals told him that they would remember his Mamacita in their prayers this Sunday. What was her name? The football coach bought his lunch. Someone left a white rose in a vase on his desk. Students whispered outside of his room.

His cell phone vibrated with messages of consolation. Email came from HR, Dr. Simms -- the Superintendent, the English department of the High School.

He remembered his nightmare that night.

He was sleeping in his childhood home in Amarillo, Texas. He was wearing pajamas, his blue fuzzy pajamas so it would be when he was in Junior High, and Momma had been so ill from her hysterectomy. She was calling from her bedroom. "Larry darling, I need you! I need you!"

He ran down the hall. She stood by her bed. Well something stood there in the dark. A column of some thick liquid that kept reforming itself. It seemed to have tiny feelers. Its mouth was vagina shaped, near the center of its body. Some of the feelers, near where a human's hip should be held onto something, possibly the Cthulhu doll. "Larry you can't shut me out. You have to love me."

He must have been thrashing about on the bed. The dank sheets held him. He was so confused by their wet restraint that he couldn't tell when he passed from nightmare into the waking world. His room stank. He thought for a moment that he might have shit himself. The alarm clock read 4:32. It was Thursday morning. In theory he was flying to the funeral.

He would have to leave town. Doublesign was small, if he were out and about this weekend, everyone would know. He got up, got dressed and drove into Austin. He would stay at the Hotel Six near his mother's nursing home. Maybe if he spent sometime with her – serious focused, loving time it might help her. And he didn't care how she felt about the damn stuffed toy – it was headed for the trash. He didn't even turn the sheets back in his hotel room; just lay his dressed sweaty self on top.

His phone woke him at noon.

His mother had passed away. He was horrified at the relief he felt.

She had a prepaid funeral policy a Blackwell Brothers in Amarillo; the home was going to make the call. Did he want to view her body before they arranged for transportation?

With the sick thought that everything would work out now he drove off to the home.

"She's at the end of the hall."

She's not at the end of the hall. A body is in a room at the end of the hall.

Music, sort of spacey Muzak, came from the end of the hall. Larry heard one of the old men reading poetry. They probably have to have these little impromptu services all the time. It wouldn't be like a hospital where the scandal of death had to be hidden.

The poem was ending as he entered:

"The darkness drops again; but now I know
That twenty centuries of stony sleep
Were vexed to nightmare by a rocking cradle,
And what rough beast, its hour come round at last,
Slouches towards Bethlehem to be born?"

Yeats' "The Second Coming" seemed the most inappropriate poem that could possibly be uttered at a mother's funeral, but Larry's revulsion was held in check by the sight of Chandra playing some sort of electric lyre strumming something complicated some twelve tone melody with angular tonalities.

"What the hell are you doing here?"

His mom lay on the bed, dressed in the pants suit she wore when he moved to Austin three years ago. She held the Cthulhu toy like a baby. The old people were shocked by the profanity and began to shuffle out, he was unsure which of the men had been reciting the poem.

"I do volunteer work here on Thursdays." Said Chandra

"What are you doing?" Larry asked.

"Hey a little respect this is your mom."

"That was my mom and where do you go on Monday morning?"

"I work for a living. I tried to wake you up."

"Why are you here? Why were you with me?"

Chandra said, "I am doing my art. You can take it or leave it." She had stopped her weird music and was clearly going about to leave. Larry thought about stopping her physically and then stopped himself, surprised at how far he had changed in less then a week.

She looked at him and responded as though she read his mind. Probably easy enough to read his face. "You haven't changed. You're just noticing how you really are because you heard my music. You are seeing some of the monstrous you that you have learned not to see. But the real world is split further away from your views than you know. If you want the Real, go with what you are beginning to see."

"What's your real name?'

"Same as your mom's, dummy. Hannah. I was born Hannah Maria Nibiru."

She walked out and suddenly the real shock of his momma's death hit him. He crumpled into a chair and cried and forgot his excuse or strange drug trips with mystic musicians.

Somehow in the next hour, he called his sister and the funeral home and booked a flight for tomorrow. He didn't give a damn about gossip and drove home to his Doublesign apartment.

That night he had the last nightmare.

He was sleeping in his little bed at home. It was cold, he could hear the gas heater turn on, and the Santa Fe train in the distance, and so it must have been about ten o'clock when the train rattled through town. Beyond the curtains he could see the Christmas lights at the Casey house, and his room smelled of gingerbread. He could hear momma crying and he could hear his sister in her tiny bedroom snoring lightly. Sissy had had breathing problems in the old house, and it was always so cold. Mamma called out to him, "Where is my little man? Where is Larry? Come help me Larry. Come help me.!'

He sat up (and with the ease that such changes happen in dreams) he was his adult self, "Mamma you don't need me! You need Sissy!"

"Sissy can't help me no more. She can't see me!"

"Mamma she can't she you because you're dead! This is a nightmare and I am sorry that I said you're dead."

"Baby, baby. That's one of those fake splits you make. There is no line between Dead Momma and Live Momma and Good Momma and Bad Momma. Now come to me baby. Don't you love me anymore? After all I have done?"

So Larry got of his bed and walked down the hall. In Sissy's room, she was sleeping in her childbed, but it was adult sister and somehow he knew that they slept in this house every night. And Momma would always be in this house, where she had been sick and the family had been poor. Not the nice house, not the nursing home.

Momma was saying, "There is no line between Dead Momma and Live Momma and Good Momma and Bad Momma" and he heard Sissy mutter in her sleep, "Iä! Shub-Niggurath!" Which also made sense. Fear and Love. Guilt and Innocence. Curves and Angles.

At the end of the hall, Larry opened the door to his mother's bedroom. It stood there in the darkness with a voice coming from the middle of a column and the stench of vomit and decay and this time it was holding soemthing squirming not a Cthulhu plush toy, and Larry knew it was him as a baby. Little Lawrence Derby Ellison , and he could tell by some reflected points of crazy Christmas lights from next door that momma had too many eyes in the wrong places. "Please look at me baby, please know." He could hear Chandra's melody off in the distance.

Despite his best intentions he reached back and flipped on the light. They say you can't turn a light on in dreams, but they are wrong. And Lawrence Derby Ellison saw what his mother really looked like and what he looked like and what the world really was. Before he merged with his mother and was born again, he heard the last notes of Chandra's music, which he realized sounded flute-like.

The next morning, his landlady, who had heard of his mother's death from her cousin, who was the janitor at James Bowie Junior High, knocked on the door of his apartment. When there was no answer, she opened the door and went in. The coroner latter said heart failure, but Irma said she will think of the poor boy's expression the rest of her days. Some things aren't meant to be seen.

For James Wade

41

DARRELL SCHWEITZER won the World Fantasy Award in 1992 for co-editing *Weird Tales* (which he did between 1988 and 2007). His fiction has also been nominated for the World Fantasy Award and the Shirley Jackson Award. His novels include *The White Isle, The Shattered Goddess,* and *The Mask of the Sorcerer.* His short fiction has appeared in *Twilight Zone, Amazing Stories, Night Cry, Cemetery Dance, The Horror Show, Whispers, Interzone,* and in numerous anthologies. His story collections include *Sekenre: The Book of the Sorcerer, Tom O'Bedlam's Night Out, Transients, Necromancies and Netherworlds* (with Jason Van Hollander), *The Great World and the Small,* and *We Are All Legends.* Also look for his story-cycle/novella *Living with the Dead.* He is also an essayist, reviewer, poet, interviewer, the author of books about H.P. Lovecraft and Lord Dunsany, and editor of *Discovering H.P. Lovecraft, The Thomas Ligotti Reader, The Robert E. Howard Reader,* etc. He is also famous for rhyming Cthulhu in a limerick.

Class Reunion

by Darrell Schweitzer

"In the old days, Jeffrey," Victoria said as the two of us wound our way up the cramped, stone staircase, "my real purpose for sneaking off with you like this would have been to get inside your pants."

"As good enough reason as any," I said.

Of course back then, when we had been in school together, she had been Vickie, not Victoria, and I knew perfectly well that behind my back she called me Dopey, a play on Opie, the wide-eyed, naïve kid played by Ron Howard on *The Andy Griffith Show*, and if she'd been any more forward with such lofty ambitions, I probably would have gaped at her and said, "Jeepers ..."

Not that I normally used such an expression as "Jeepers" when I was a kid. I was very self-conscious of my alleged dignity in my dim, ill-remembered, and decidedly insecure youth.

Now, out of breath already, I eased myself down onto a bench on the first available landing and sighed, "Jeepers ..."

I leaned on my cane. I'd already started to use a cane at fifty-seven, because of my weight, after one of my knees went bad. I looked up into the semi-gloom. This room was unlighted, but moonlight streamed in through the diamond-shaped windows, sparkling, as the windows themselves were made up of dozens of smaller, diamond-shaped pieces of glass in the oldest New England style. Well, anything good enough for the House of Seven Gables in Salem was good enough for Orne Academy, which, so it was rumored, was even older than English settlements in North America, if you cared to believe the stories. The very first school building must have been some kind of Indian longhouse, or even a cave. This fancy woodwork and the diamond windows were all added later.

I'd been on this landing before, although not in forty years. We kids had called it the Edge of the World, because it was the limit of where we were allowed to go. Often we would meet here, with a teacher, or even with the Headmaster, Elder Sathaniel, on some private matter of instruction, or more often discipline. Not a happy place, but one I remembered, and saw now completely unchanged after all this time, with that tall, curiously ticking, absurd clock in against the wall – a clock which had several extra hands, not all of which went in the same

43

direction, and which kept no system of time anyone could figure out – flanked on either side by ancient portraits of the Academy's two founders. I knew now from my subsequent education that they were 18th century work, and very second rate, the kind an itinerant painter of the day would knock off for a few shillings, inserting the subject's face onto a pre-painted body with a conventional setting. There was old Joseph Curwen, tall, pale, dignified, with his finger in a book, probably supposed to be a Bible; next to him Jedidiah Orne himself, who despite the painter's best efforts looked inescapably like a toad.

Beyond this landing, the clock, and the two portraits, was what students had always called "The Forbidden Zone." We were strictly *not* allowed through the door at the far end, or up the stairs beyond it.

After a moment, Victoria's eyes met mine, and then she glanced at the door, which was slightly ajar.

"Shall we?" she said.

"Better late than never."

*   *   *

It was already late, late enough to admit that none of this made a whole lot of sense, that there wasn't, as my therapist had insisted, any pressing reason after forty years to attend a class reunion at the so, so exclusive prep school which had beclouded a brief interval in my youth. After so long, faces you once knew look like distended wax masks, half-melted, with teeth and hair falling out. *Sic transist Gloria something or other –*

Yet I came, driven by some urge like that of a salmon swimming upstream to its birthplace to spawn and die. There were gaps in my memory. I couldn't quite remember leaving home, or what my therapist or other doctors had finally said or ordered, if anything. I was drifting on some current I didn't understand, but it was so much easier just to *go*, not to resist, and I couldn't even remember boarding the plane to fly coast-to-coast, first to New York, then a second flight to Albany, then renting a car for the drive up into the mountains of Vermont.

I stayed one night in a little motel outside of Brattleboro and dreamed of flying, as if something with huge, bat-like wings had lifted me up and was carrying me toward the frigid, impossibly distant stars.

But that was merely a dream, and in the morning I continued and completed my journey, as if coming to the end of some ancient ritual, and I saw the vast, eccentric pile of the Academy before me, nestled among thick and gnarled trees.

There were already cars in the driveway, and fat and aging strangers shuffling about, who must have been my classmates. Here and there, a glimpse, maybe just because of the angle, of a familiar face, but more often a completely

44

unfamiliar face and a voice completely mismatched to the speaker, as in the case of the tall, thin, white-haired fellow who grabbed hold of me suddenly, pointed at the imposing edifice, and said, laughing without much conviction that he was actually being funny, "Well, it isn't exactly Hogwarts, is it?"

"No," I said, hurrying on. "I think not."

That voice. Jimmy Kleiber? But hadn't I heard, years ago, that Jimmy Kleiber had shot himself?

*   *   *

"I always knew it would be like this," Victoria said.

"Like what?"

"I'm not sure, actually."

We'd entered what must have been a private area, a library or common-room off limits to students, lit by a chandelier that didn't use electricity or even candles, but some sort of faintly glowing, blue stone. I tried to keep my distance from it, wondering if it was radioactive.

In the center of the room was a long, wooden table – not factory work, or even high-grade Colonial, but rough-hewn, as if it had been carved with a hatchet – on which were placed several candlesticks, an empty glass bowl lined with dust, and a massive, handwritten book in Greek which, having been away from my lessons for so long, I could not even begin to read, though some of the text on the open page did look familiar.

I closed the book gently.

"What exactly did we study here?"

"You know . . . the usual . . ."

"No, I don't know."

That was the truly strange thing. Either I was coming down with premature Alzheimer's at fifty-seven, or I was like one of those UFO-abductees you read about, whose mind has been messed with, the genuine memories suppressed or erased, and "screen memories" left in their place.

Only sometimes there can be holes in the screen. Flashes, glimpses leak through.

*   *   *

"Hey, what about that time the wooden *gargoyle thing* at the top of the dorm stairs *came alive?*" That was Jimmy Kleiber again, the one who was supposed to be dead.

"No, I don't remember that," someone else said over dinner that night.

"Yeah, it flapped around all night. Jeffo here –" he pointed at me – "claimed it was catching mice. *But I don't think so.*"

"I don't think so either," I said.

". . . and Master Eberhard tried to swat the thing down off a shelf with a broom and the fucker bit the his *nose off*. . . him yowling, so much blood . . . it was really gross." Jimmy Kleiber, if that really was Jimmy Kleiber, had a small circle of an audience. "Now I ask you, *who* was reading books he shouldn't outside of class?" He leered toward me, as if this *were* somehow intensely humorous, but I just gave him a blank look.

Nobody laughed, because that was when Headmaster Sathaniel appeared on the podium at the head of the great hall.

"My *God* . . ." someone muttered, and I could only concur under my breath, not because the Headmaster was anything resembling divine, but because when we'd been kids, in this oddly repressive and oddly progressive institution (Hey, it was co-ed, back in the mid-'60s), Headmaster Sathaniel had looked *exactly* as we saw him now, imposingly tall, white-haired, bearded like a Biblical prophet, though with some indefinably disquieting look in his eye or some oddity of his otherwise expressionless, almost mask-like face permanently excluding him from any Charlton-Heston-as-Moses look-alike contest; thin and gaunt, almost frail, for all we knew from experience how strong was the grip of his hand and how swift and filled with purpose were his movements when the occasion called for it.

That much I *could* remember.

If Headmaster Sathaniel had been like that in 1965, if it had not been merely the distortion of memory and an older man seen through the eyes of adolescents; if he had, in fact, not aged at all, *how* old did that make him in now?

He spoke, in a voice like thunder, as he always had.

*　　*　　*

Up. Up. The stairs seemed to go on forever. Victoria and I both had to pause again for breath, in the middle of the stairs. She put her hand on my shoulder, gently, not, I think, because she was about to get into my pants then and there, or even because she was afraid. I think she did it just to reassure herself that I was real, actually there, someone under all this blubber and graying hair whom she had actually once known.

We weren't sure anymore about anything else.

We passed dozens – could it have been hundreds? – of small, empty rooms, like monastic cells, I thought, some just smelling of dust and old wood, others with a foul, subtly repellent odor I could not place. Vaguely reptilian, like a badly cleaned crocodile house at the zoo. One room had chains and manacles fixed to the walls, but they were rusty, and didn't seem to have been used in a long time.

I was completely disoriented now. The Academy was large, but not *that* large, and I could not imagine where we had come to in the overall architectural plan of the place. There were turns of the stair, strange doorways, angles that the eye could not quite follow.

Once, groping in the dark, we flung open a wide set of shutters and looked out, not on the wooded Vermont landscape by moonlight, but on an infinity of stars, as if we were already deep into space, and the Earth were not even a visible speck among billions. I clung to Victoria and she to me, for solidity, because somehow up and down were not right, and we were falling, into that infinity. Then I saw one star blink, and then another, as if something dark had momentarily eclipsed them, and I had a sense, beyond sight or reason, that something out there had *seen* us and was coming toward us.

It took a great effort of will to turn away and grope – it felt like *climbing* – back into the corridor outside.

Wind howled in through the open window.

*   *   *

The Thunder spoke, I tried to tell myself, like something out of a T.S. Eliot poem, but, no, it was not like that, so peace surpassing all understanding, no *Datta, Dayadhvam,* not even a *Hieronymo's mad againe,* or anything as human as that, nothing *of the Earth* at all; a voice like something out of deepest dream, relentlessly, inexorably, describing how each of us had been selected by a destiny written in the stars, etched down the centuries, our bloodlines observed and subtly *adjusted* or *directed* by those who, like Elder Sathaniel, were *priests* of Those Who Dwelt in the Spaces Beyond; each of us carefully and subtly collected, examined, recruited, and brought here in our youth to something that was far more than a *school.* Yet the dark secrets of our lives *could* be learned here by those whose minds were open. For there was great wisdom in the darkness, the Thunder said, an inner truth only dimly glimpsed by those seekers who had gone before us, the Templars, the Gnostics, the sages of Babylon, those who met the Black Man in lonely places.

We who knew the Dwellers Beyond, could take the dark shards of mystery left behind by our predecessors and assemble them into their true shape and meaning, here, now, at the end of history, the Thunder said.

*   *   *

That was when Victoria took me by the arm and led me away from the table and out of the hall, and I went with her willingly, half convinced I'd thought of the idea myself; and this was the bond between us, that for all the Elder taught that our empty, unfulfilled, and shipwrecked lives had amounted to nothing, *could* amount to nothing – maybe that was why of the fifty-four graduating students in our class, only twenty three were still alive in good enough condition or otherwise available (as in not institutionalized) to attend this reunion – for all we had been directed and controlled and shaped and run like pinballs down a pre-ordained chute because our parents and our parents' parents unto the umpteenth generation had belonged to a secret, absurd, and utterly depraved cult devoted to the return of the Others or Ancient Dwellers or whatever you wanted to call them from the spaces between the spaces, into the physical world we knew – for all that, because of that, *despite* that; yes I am ranting now; now, now, *now* was the last chance we had to rebel, to do something we're *not* supposed to be doing, as if this could somehow cancel out everything that had happened since the age of 17 and give us a chance to start over.

With that kind of desperation, then, all joking aside now, Victoria and I made our way up, up, through the forbidden turns and dimensions of Orne Academy, uncovering its many secrets, violating its sacred places, until we emerged onto a kind of roof garden where the trees and plants and pale, strange flowers *sang* or merely gibbered in some hideous language no human mind could fathom, and *two pale suns* hung in a still starry, but alien sky. Around us loomed vast, indescribable statuary created by no human hand, conceived by no human imagination; hulking, lurking things, bat-winged and tentacled some of them, or in shapes beyond the ability of words to grasp; the very images of the Others whom we were all supposed to serve, even if this service, unwitting as it must be, was buried deeply beneath a lifetime of screen memories.

*　　*　　*

Now the Thunder called into my mind the memory that I had *been here before*, that on the last day of my final term, as part of a ritual or *graduation exercise* no student could ever describe to another, because the contents of his mind had been *revised* to make this quite impossible, whatever psychoses might spring forth like gibbering midnight flowers as a result; a ritual in which, as the hooded Elders stood around me chanting their prayers, I lay cold and naked -- very skinny but very *soft* in those days -- bound and outstretched on an altar here, beneath those pale, heatless suns and alien stars, while something foul and many-faceted and many-shaped descended from those same stars, eclipsing them with its dark mass like spilled ink

48

spreading across the sky, reaching down to *touch* me and make its flesh and my flesh as one.

*   *   *

For it is learned by those whose minds will inquire, from all the secrets in the forbidden books gathered here by Joseph Curwen and Jedidiah Orne and by *their* predecessors before them, in keeping with the immemorial ritual and the immemorial truths, that contrary to the popular, clichéd misconceptions on the subject, virgin sacrifices are not necessarily girls, for the differences in the human flesh are of no importance whatsoever to the will and the utility of the Others.

Nor do such victims necessarily die in the sacrifice, however much they might yearn to do so.

For there are things beyond death, and far worse.

*   *   *

And the Thunder invoked the terrible name of Shub-Niggurath, the Black Goat of the Forest (by which we may understand, symbolically, the Forest of Lightless Stars) with a Thousand Young, whose selfsame Young, in order to enter into this terrestrial, three-dimensional world and wreak havoc upon it, must be born *into human flesh* and *make that flesh their own*, then be *delivered out of it* into the fullness of the foulness of their ultimately incomprehensible Shapes.

And the Thunder said that on this night, at this time, after many years of preparation, because the stars were right, holy Shub-Niggurath would welcome the birth of her Spawn.

*   *   *

Victoria screamed. I think the memories were flooding into her mind too. I could see it in her eyes, the terror, the *recognition*.

She screamed, even as Elder Sathaniel said in his thunderous voice, "Ah, Jeffrey, Victoria, how good of you to join us," and the other Elders of the faculty stood in their hooded robes, chanting their prayers (which I had once learned out of the huge, handwritten Greek book), as the rest of the Class of '65 trembled and slouched, naked and fat and sagging, looking slightly ridiculous as they were herded toward the altar and slit open one by one.

Victoria screamed, and clung to me, and we two fell back among the singing, babbling shrubbery -- some of those voices I thought I recognized, or remembered – clasping one another in an obscene parody of our original mischievous intent, which a *human* might have phrased as, *Hey let's sneak up on the roof and screw while Old Windbag here delivers his boring sermon; it's never too late.* But it was too late. It was entirely too late. It has *always* been too late, as our lives had been written out in advance to the last detail in the vast, forbidden Greek book.

"We could have loved each other," she said, sobbing.

Could have. Might have. Perhaps. Not that any part of our human lives mattered; not that it mattered that in my more lucid moments I had been a minor academic and even more minor poet with a famously erratic, tragic career, in and out of mental hospitals, wretched, unfulfilled, occasionally given to strange visions in between the suicide attempts.

What had she been? How had her life played out?

Too late to ask about that.

I screamed too, as something like a molten, iron serpent stirred to life in my gut.

And the stars and the twin, pale suns were blotted out by That which descended upon us.

And the voice of the Thunder spoke.

Iä! Shub-Niggurath!

*   *   *

The Thunder whispers, in the depths of a disquieting dream: What is left when the flesh, when humanity itself sloughed off like a discarded afterbirth?

Only a wraith. A phantasm. A thing of nightmare which enters your mind and makes you copy out this account or makes you read it from the hand of another, that you might know that *you too* are part of that ancient destiny and design which is ultimately called Azathoth, the chaos and pain that surpasses all understanding.

This the Thunder says.

SCOTT DAVID ANIOLOWSKI is a self-styled hermit and amateur agoraphobe. He lives in a large old Colonial home in western New York dubbed The House of Secrets, complete with library. Scott loves nothing more than a scone and cup of tea in front of the fireplace with a good book and a cat in his lap. He has written dozens of scenarios and books for *The Call of Cthulhu* RPG since 1986. He is an active member of the Horror Writers Association, and his fiction has appeared in several anthologies from Chaosium and in Barnes & Noble's omnibus *365 Scary Stories*. Scott has edited four fiction anthologies -- *Made in Goatswood*, *Singers of Strange Songs*, *Return to Lovecraft Country*, and the forthcoming *Horror for the Holidays* – and the Donald Burleson collection *Beyond the Lamplight* for his own Jack O'Lantern Press. Scott's weird poetry has been published *in Deathrealm Magazine*. His literary influences include Lovecraft, Robert Bloch, Thomas Ligotti, William Hope Hodgson, the poetry of Richard Tierney, and many more.

First Nation

by Scott David Aniolowski

The late October sun hung low and cold over the lake as the small boat slid toward the dock. On the rocky shore, a two-storey cabin crouched mutely, its rough-timbered form black with weathering. Except for an artificial bare spot between the lakefront and the building, towering thin pines crowded around the cabin and as far off in every direction as the eye could see. Some stunted trees spilled to the edge of the lake, huddling there precariously, their roots partially exposed by the erosive powers of the water. The odd oak and maple peeked out through the gently swaying sea of evergreens, their few last leaves flushed of their autumnal golds and reds into weary browns.

Rob waved at a figure on shore as he jockeyed the fourteen-foot aluminum boat into place along the rough dock. A clump of yellowed water lily pads bobbed in the boat's gentle wake. "Hello," he shouted.

"Hello," returned the figure from shore. It was a small man with pure white hair gathered in a long ponytail down the back of his neck. He stood before a crackling bonfire, sparks dancing into the air like fireflies as he poked at it with a long stick.

The small outboard motor sputtered and coughed and then fell silent. Rob and his passenger stood cautiously, tethering their craft to the dock. Jase leapt out first, steadying the boat and extending a hand to Rob. The grey weathered wood bowed and creaked beneath their weight as though the whole of the dock might tumble into the lake at any moment. The young men quickly gathered their gear and made for solid ground.

"Hello, Uncle Billy," smiled Jase as he embraced the white haired man. "Its great to see you."

The old man smiled and regarded the pair for a moment. The long autumnal shadows and the flickering bonfire light distorted his smokey features. His face looked like coppery leather, weathered and full of deep creases accumulated over a long lifetime. Despite his outward antiquity and small stature, however, the old man projected an air of strength and greatness.

Jase towered a full foot over Uncle Billy and was crowned with a thick tangle of jet-black hair. He shared deep-set smokey features with the old man, yet had the sleekness of youth. He wore an earring in each ear and a short scruffy beard on the end of his chin. "This is Rob, Uncle Billy," Jase gestured to his companion.

"Nice to meet you, sir," Rob addressed him. Although he could look Jase square in the eyes, Rob was a sharp contrast to his friend with blond hair buzzed short and clean-shaven fair features. An innocence danced in his grey-blue eyes and peered through his thin, crooked smile.

"Uncle Billy. Call me Uncle Billy, my boy. I'm pleased to meet you. How was your journey?"

"It was good. Took us almost two hours," he answered. "I didn't realize you were so far out here."

"That's the way I like it. Nearest town miles away. No neighbors. No roads. Can't get here only by boat or float plane. No one to bother me. A few fisherman rent rooms in the spring and summer. Sometimes duck hunters in the fall. Otherwise, no one." He poked at the bonfire and gazed into the sky. The quickly setting sun made everything glow an October orange. "Almost dark," he said, tossing a pine cone into the fire. The pine cone popped and sent sparks leaping into the air. It was followed by another. As the old Indian continued adding pine cones to the fire he produced an almost hypnotic sing-song sort of sound from deep within his throat.

The boys stood silently around the fire watching the sun slip beneath the tree-lined horizon far across the lake. Shadows grew longer and danced around the bonfire until they finally disappeared into the deepening twilight. Rob shivered once. The temperature had noticeably dropped with the setting of the sun. A cold wind rustled through the trees and kicked up dry leaves, sending them spinning in tiny vortices around their feet.

"There, that's good. We should get inside," Uncle Billy finally said, his words coming out in thin wisps of fog. He poked the fire one last time and tossed in another pine cone.

"What's that all about?" Rob asked, nodding at the pile of pine cones, red in the crackling fire.

"Keeps away unwanted visitors," Uncle Billy said matter-of-factly.

The young men looked at each other and shrugged before turning to follow Uncle Billy up to the cabin. A warm, guttering glow waved from the cabin's black windows, and a curl of smoke wafted out of a crumbling stone chimney. Behind them, the lake faintly licked the rocky shore and their aluminum boat bumped randomly against the dock, making a hollow thumping sound. With several steep strides they reached the cabin's log steps and climbed a few feet up to the porch. Fishing rods hung on hooks behind a pair of Adirondack chairs, and several piles of firewood leaned against the wall.

Rob and Jase took in the view from the elevated porch. The rising moon played across the rippling lake and made the encroaching forest look black. Infernal black-red embers pulsed in the waning bonfire, the occasional tongue of flame licking the chilly night air. Somewhere close by an owl sang out. Then echoing from far off in the deepening darkness came the sound of wood against wood. Knocking. Slow, steady and rhythmic. Deliberate and incongruous in the whispering of trees and soft lapping of water against rocks.

"Did you hear that? What was that?" Rob asked to anyone who might answer. It came again. Wood on wood. Knocking. Unmistakable. A hollow yet somehow firm sound. "There! There it is again!"

"I don't know. Woodpecker?" Jase shrugged.

"That would have to be one hell of a big woodpecker!" Rob blurted.

"Its just the sounds of the forest. Come in. Its stopped now, anyway," Uncle Billy reassured them.

Rob strained to listen, but the knocking had stopped just as suddenly and inexplicably as it had begun.

"Sounds of the forest," Uncle Billy repeated absently. "Now come in. Its getting cold out here." The boys followed him into the cabin, Rob scanning the blurry darkness one last time as the old man pushed against the battered screen door causing it creak and the rusty spring to pop.

The squeaky door opened into a large room whose focal point was an enormous stone fireplace. A comforting fire blazed in the hearth and warmed the cabin. To the left of the fireplace a wide staircase led up into darkness; on the right an archway led into back rooms. High above the fireplace mantle hung a gigantic moose head, its majestic antlers stretching more than six feet across. With cold glass eyes, the behemoth cast a watchful gaze over the room. Several other taxidermied trophies – mostly fish – adorned the walls alongside pieces of Indian art. Built-in shelves crammed with yellowed and dog-eared books rose on either side of the fireplace, and a large table with a dozen mismatched chairs sat to the right of the front door. Several similarly random and outdated chairs and couches were scattered around the great room and in front of the fireplace.

Rob thought to himself how the place smelled like a museum: wood and dust and old musty things. Combined with the earthy, sooty scent of the blazing fireplace, he found it all soothing and welcoming.

Uncle Billy retrieved a pair of oil lamps from the large wooden table and lit them. "No electricity, so this is what you have for light," he handed a lamp to each of the boys. "There are four bedrooms upstairs. You can take any you want," he said, gesturing to the staircase. "No one renting rooms now, so its just us. Mind you don't kick over a pail. Roof leaks some. Heck of a storm last night. Wind shook the old place. Thunder. Lightning. One struck close by. The sky lit up and everything shook. Anyway, the pails probably got a lot of water in them."

"We'll watch that," Jase nodded.

"And back there is my bedroom and the kitchen," the old man continued, nodding to the dark archway.

"Bathroom?" Rob wondered.

Jase and Uncle Billy looked at each other and chuckled.

"Got the lake for washing. Or you can heat up a big pot of well water on the wood stove in the kitchen," the old man explained. "And when you gotta go, there's an outhouse just out behind the cabin. Be sure to take a lamp: it gets mighty dark out there."

Rob sighed. "Great."

"Ain't got no internet or phone service way up here, neither," the old man said, disappearing through the dark archway with a third oil lamp. The faint light guttered and vaguely illuminating the antique kitchen in sallow light.

"So you're Jase's uncle?" Rob hung his coat on a rack near the front door. It was made of four deer hooves attached to a board.

"No," came a voice from the murky kitchen. He returned momentarily with three mugs of steaming coffee. "No. I'm an old friend of the family. Everyone calls me Uncle Billy."

"Uncle Billy's from the Me-Wuk in California," Jase explained as he hung up his jacket and took a sip of the thick, oil-black coffee.

"California? What the hell are you doing way up here in the Middle-Of-Nowhere Ontario?" Rob asked. "Don't you miss your home?" He made to sip at his cup of coffee but found the brew far too strong and bitter for his taste.

"The mountain is my home. The forest is my home," Uncle Billy smiled.

"Okay. But you're Iroquois, right?" Rob turned to Jase.

"Right. My family is from around here," Jase nodded. He took another drink from his cup and made a face.

Uncle Billy laughed. "That'll put hair on your chest," he said, taking a deep gulp from his cup. "That's real campfire coffee, not that stuff you get at those overpriced fancy coffee shops in the city."

The young men chuckled politely and casually lowered their cups to the table.

"So I'm glad you boys could come out and help me close up the cabin for the winter. Normally I'd stay, but it gets harder for me every year," the white haired man explained.

"Yeah, Uncle Billy's agreed to stay with my mom and aunt over winter," Jase told Rob.

"And it was very kind of them to offer, too," Uncle Billy raised his coffee cup in a sort of toast. "This will be the first year I didn't stay."

"How long have you been here?" Rob asked.

"Let's see," the old man looked to the ceiling as if searching for the answer. "I bought this place almost thirty years ago."

"Oh, I figured you built it," Rob said.

"No. A couple doctors from Toronto built it. They used it for summer holidays for fishing and family trips. Back then everyone with money had to have a place in Cottage Country. But then one of them had a heart attack and died out here in the woods. After that the other decided to get rid of the place. I got it pretty cheap. He just wanted to unload it," he surveyed the great room. Light sparkled in the moose's glass eyes and the fire in the hearth popped and crackled. "Anyway, you two go settle in and I'll get some food on the table."

The young men gathered their belongings and their oil lamps and climbed the stairs to the second floor, stepping over a bucket of water sitting just at the top of the stairs. The upstairs was divided evenly between the four bedrooms, two overlooking the lake and two the thick forest behind the cabin. The rooms were musty and rough but adequately furnished with beds and a dresser. Each room had a narrow closet and two large windows. A dusty piece of fabric hung over each closet, although none of the windows were curtained. Both Jase and Rob occupied the rooms overlooking the lake.

Rob opened one of his windows. Instantly a cool gust of fresh air blew in. He breathed it in deeply, taking in the faint scent of the waning bonfire below. The moon was climbing higher in the night sky, casting cold white light over everything. It was a monochromatic landscape of blue-black punctuated by white. The sea of treetops swayed in unison and thin white ripples shone on the lake. As he stood in front of the windows he realized that he was fully exposed to everything beyond. There were no curtains or drapes to shut out the wilderness, and the sputtering flame of his lamp against the solid darkness illuminated him up here like a lighthouse beacon. Suddenly, Rob became very uncomfortable. He felt as though he were being watched: that somewhere in the forest something was gazing at him standing in the window. He took a step back and tried to settle his nerves: he knew they were the only people around for miles. If there was anything looking at him it was an owl or racoon. He told himself he was being silly.

Resigning himself to settle in, Rob unpacked his nap sack. Then he emptied two coffee cans half full of water out the window and replaced them, in case it rained again. The old bed seemed spared from the leaky roof – he sprawled out and found it dry. The mattress was soft and lumpy, yet strangely comfortable. He lay there for several moments, taking in the sounds of the wind in the trees outside. The lake was too calm to make a discernable noise, but he heard the occasional hollow bump of their aluminum boat against the dock. Rob stretched and watched the long shadows cast by his oil lamp playing across the ceiling. He wondered about the many fishermen and hunters who had stayed here over the years – what they thought about the place. Rob was more a towny than a wilderness buff, although he enjoyed fishing and hunting. But he also appreciated the convenience of modern technology, like indoor plumbing and electricity: this was too primitive for his taste.

"Great place, eh?" Jase wandered into Rob's room.

"Its okay. A little rough for me."

"The lack of electricity?"

"And plumbing."

"Don't be such a city boy. Its only for a couple days. We just have to help close the place up, then we head back to town."

"Yeah, I know."

"And we'll do some fishing while we're here. And enjoy this wilderness."

"Its pretty cool, I guess. Just can't help feeling like we're being watched, though. Its creepy."

"Probably are. You know how many critters are out there?"

"Yeah. Whatever."

Just then the old man called from below, telling them food was on the table. They descended the log staircase back into the great room where Uncle Billy was waiting for them at the huge table. There were three place setting of mismatched dishes, cutlery and glasses. In the center of the table their host had placed several plates and pots of food along with a six pack of beer.

"Come and get it," called the old man. "It ain't much, but it'll fill you up."

"It looks good," the boys said in unison.

"Corn soup, pan fish, acorn mush, and ghost bread," presented Uncle Billy.

"And cold beer!" Jase smiled as he opened a bottle.

"How do you have cold beer without a refrigerator?" Rob wondered.

"The lake. Great way to keep bottles cold."

"Clever," Rob said as he poured himself a cold one.

"You make do," said Uncle Billy. "I'm mostly self-sufficient out here. Got a fellow who brings me canned goods and a few supplies every couple months. Otherwise, I get everything I need from the lake and the forest."

After dinner they cleared their dishes into the old cast iron sink in the kitchen. The older man scraped food scraps into a large pot and then disappeared through the back door into the darkness. Rob and Jase retrieved the last two bottles of beer from the dining table and settled into a pair of well-worn chairs in front of the fireplace. Rob lit a cigarette, inhaling deeply and blowing out a great puff of smoke.

"Still feeling creeped out?" Jase asked.

"No."

"Okay."

"You think he'll mind?"

"Mind what?"

"This," Rob waved his cigarette in front of Jase's face.

"Uncle Billy? No."

"Okay, so what's his deal?"

Jase shot Rob a questioning look.

"I mean, all this living in the middle of nowhere, wilderness stuff."

"I don't know. Just the way he likes to live, I guess. You heard him."

"Yeah. But way out here all alone?"

"He's got fishermen in season."

"I guess. Not for me, I'll tell you."

"What's not for you?" came the old man's voice as he returned through the creaky front door.

"Oh, just living way out here all alone. Roughing it. That kind of thing," Rob said.

"Rob's scared. Says the place creeps him out," Jase tattled.

Rob kicked at his friend and shook his head in embarrassed denial.

"I suppose it isn't for everyone," the old man winked at his guests.

"Where'd you go?" Jase inquired.

"Whatever I can't finish I leave out back for the animals. I take so I also give back."

After several minutes of conversation and the last of his beer, Rob stood and headed toward the kitchen. "Well, if you'll excuse me," he said.

"Don't forget your lamp," the old man reminded him. "It gets mighty dark out there."

"So you said," Rob grabbed a lamp and headed through the kitchen toward the back door.

"Your friend is a city boy, eh?"

"Well, not really. He likes hunting and fishing. This is all just a little too rough for him."

"You boys have it too easy these days. Too easy."

As he stepped outside, Rob was instantly engulfed by the night. The wind had picked up and blew louder through the trees. He could just make out the shape of the outhouse in the dark distance – from here it appeared to be a mile away. A shiver ran down his spine. Bare branches scraped along the side of the cabin, making shrill scratching noises; fallen leaves crackled under his feet. Strangely, there were no animal sounds. No birds. Nothing. Just the wind and the sound of his own footsteps. Rob told himself that this late in the year there were no insects and few animals or birds left to make sounds.

The cold air made his bladder feel like it was about to burst. Finally gathering his nerve, Rob marched defiantly toward the out building. It felt as though he had walked hundreds of yards before finally reaching his destination. All the while he scanned the forest for eyes, still feeling as though he were being watched.

The outhouse was a narrow tall building with a crooked door. The only window was a rough crescent moon cut into the door. If the whole idea didn't disgust him, he would have thought it all ridiculously cliched. Even before opening the door, he could smell the contents. Immediately he began to breathe through his mouth so as not to take in the odor. Rob grasped the rope handle dangling from the door and yanked it open. He scrambled inside, slamming the door behind him and flipping a small metal hook to lock it. Suddenly he felt foolish: he was acting like a child hiding from the boogey man in the dark. He shook his head and laughed at himself before settling in to do what he had to do.

Suddenly, something slammed into the outhouse. Rob jumped, his heart skipping a beat. The rickety old structure shuddered. He cursed loudly, assuming Jase was trying to scare him. Then he heard the deep breathing. Branches snapped and broke. Something big was moving around just outside. He gulped in breath, heart beginning to race. Now he feared it was a bear, attracted by the food scraps left out by the old man. In a panic, Rob pounded on the wall of the building and shouted, hoping to scare the animal away. Something moved away: the thunderous breathing and branch breaking got fainter until Rob could no longer hear it. He gathered himself and went to the door, peeking through the crescent. All he could see was the darkness. His heart racing, he slowly unhooked the latch and opened the door with a shaking hand. Glancing in both directions, Rob cautiously stepped out. He saw nothing but trees and the cabin in the distance. That's when the stench hit him. The stench of rotten eggs and a wet animal, but infinitely worse. He gagged.

Fearing some savage encounter, Rob took off running for the cabin, all the while anticipating an attack by a ravenous bear. He thought he heard labored breathing just behind him, yet was too scared to turn and look. He pushed himself, heart pounding in his ears, breath coming in deep quavering gulps. Rob struggled forward, feeling as thought his legs were in cement. He pushed on, wheezing hoarsely. It was a herculean effort to lift each foot as he raced for sanctuary.

Rob finally slammed into the back door of the cabin. He threw it open and leapt in wheezing and gagging for breath. Threads of sweat trickled off his nose as he lay crumpled on the cold floor.

"What is it? What happened?" Jase shouted as he and the old man raced into the kitchen.

Through gasps Rob managed to get out, "Bear. There was a bear."

"A bear?" the old man said.

"Where?" Jase asked.

Rob just pointed toward the back of the cabin, still trying to catch his breath. The back door hung open, the night's cold breath billowing in.

"It couldn't be. Bears hibernate this time of year," Uncle Billy tried to reassure him. He poked his head out the door to survey the back of the cottage. "There's nothing out here, son," he pulled the door closed.

Rob sat in a heap on the bare floor for several minutes, wheezing and trying to gather his thoughts. His face was flushed and his eyes wild. Finally he rose shakily and went to the sink, washing his hands and splashing water on his face from a large jug. "Something's out there," he stood panting. "Something big."

"Did you see it?" Jase asked.

"No. But I heard it. Something big shook the outhouse. I heard it walking through the brush. And breathing."

"What was it?" Jase asked again.

"A bear! I don't know!" Rob yelled. "It was big. And it stunk."

"Stunk?" Uncle Billy put a hand on the young man's arm to try to calm him.

"Like a wet dog, only worse. Like rotten eggs. Something dead. I don't know. It was the most awful thing I've ever smelled."

They all stood in a long silence until Uncle Billy finally laughed.

Rob just looked at him. He was incredulous. "What?" he said.

"Skunk," the old man explained. "It was a skunk."

"No," Rob argued.

"Had to be," Uncle Billy insisted.

"Yeah. He's right, Rob. He put the food scraps out back and a skunk came for them. You scared it and it sprayed. That was the stink. That's all," Jase said. "Good thing it didn't get you."

"I know what I heard and it wasn't any damn skunk. There's something big out there. A skunk wouldn't make the building shake like that."

"The wind probably. A gust of wind made it shake. That old outhouse ain't as sturdy as it used to be. Been meaning to replace it for years," the old man reassured him. "Your imagination just got the best of you. That's all. It happens. The woods is scary at night."

Rob gave up further argument, suddenly feeling foolish again. "I don't know. But it stunk."

Uncle Billy brewed another pot of his extra-strong coffee and they retired to warm spots in front of the fire. They chatted cordially into the small hours without any more mention of bears or skunks. Finally, they agreed that it was time for bed. The old man poked the fire, toppling charred logs into a black-red heap. It popped and crackled, little fingers of flame playing over the burnt wood.

"Okay. See you two in the morning," Uncle Billy said, swallowing the last gulp of his now ice-cold coffee. He strode toward the archway.

"Do you want us to lock up?" Rob offered.

"Ain't got no locks. Doors don't lock. No need," Uncle Billy's voice trailed off as he passed through the kitchen and into his bedroom. A lamp was left burning in the kitchen, in case either of the boys needed anything in the night.

"Whatever," Rob mumbled.

Jase chuckled. "You coming?" he said as he climbed the staircase.

"In a few minutes. Going to have another cigarette. I'll be up in a few."

"See you in the morning," Jase called from the darkness at the top of the stairs. Rob heard Jase's bedroom door close.

Then Rob was alone in the great room, the fire little more than red embers, and the glassy-eyed moose still staring down at him in diligent silence. He retrieved a new pack of cigarettes from his coat pocket, lit one and settled into a well-worn coach under the front windows. Facing the fireplace, his back to the lake, cold moonlight streamed in around him. A few spatters of thick rain began to hit the windows: any colder and the rain would have been snow.

Rob finished his smoke, flicking the butt across the room and into the fireplace. He yawned and stretched, feeling the weight of the day on his shoulders. He slumped over, half reclining on the couch, his feet still on the floor. The moonlight disappeared as the rain increased; he could hear the sound of drops falling into the bucket at the top of the stairs in a slow, steady rhythm. The dying fire let the cold in and Rob shivered once. He swung his feet up onto the couch and pulled an old quilt over himself, staring absently at the winking embers in the belly of the fireplace. The rhythmic patter of the rain sang softly to him.

A dark, hulking shape stalked Rob. Something that moved unseen through the primal forest watched him. A stench filled his nose and he gagged. He ran, the monster at his heels crashing through the forest, its breath deep and growling. Terror swept over him as the unseen primal horror bore down on him, reaching for him. He could hear the sounds of its heavy foot-falls getting nearer and nearer.

Rob's eyes popped open. He lay there motionless. It took him several seconds to realize where he was. He exhaled deeply: he had been dreaming. The rain had stopped and the moonlight was back at the window. A heap of cold ash lay in the bottom of the hearth. He closed his eyes, listening to the cabin creaking in the wind. His mind began to cloud again, a steady familiar thudding coming closer. He was just slipping back into sleep when he realized that he was listening to heavy footsteps. Outside, the wood porch snapped and groaned, and then the sound stopped. A tingle shot through the young man's body. Without moving, Rob slowly opened his eyes. The moonlight on the cabin floor cast an elongated pale halo. He gazed at it and the inner circle of the halo moved: he wasn't looking at a halo but at a silhouette. Something very large was standing at the window. Just behind him. It could have been a huge man with long arms, but its shadow was shaggy. He felt icy, as though all the blood had been drained from his body. He was frozen with terror, unable and unwilling to move to see what was peering at him through the window. Rob squeezed his eyes shut, listening to his heartbeat explode in his head. His body trembled uncontrollably and his breath came in random quavering spasms.

*   *   *

"Morning," Jase yawned as he trudged down the stairs, wearing only boxer shorts and a blanket draped over his shoulders. The morning sun streamed in through the windows, and beyond he could see the rippling blue of the lake. Jase could smell the aroma of Uncle Billy's black tar coffee boiling away.

Rob sat in a chair next to the fireplace, facing the front windows. A nearly-burned up cigarette dangled form the corner of his mouth. Dark circles ringed his eyes and sandpaper stubble covered his jaw. He said nothing as Jase descended into the great room.

"You look like shit," Jase said. "Rough night?"

"Your friend did not sleep well," Uncle Billy came into the room with three cups of steaming black coffee clutched in his arthritic hands.

Rob glared up at Jase, his eyes an unreadable chaos of emotions. He looked down and took a final drag from his cigarette before flicking it into the cold fireplace. "Something came to the cabin last night."

"What? What do you mean?" Jase asked.

Rob sighed deeply, "Whatever was outside the outhouse came up on the porch last night. A bear. An animal. Something big. I don't know."

"You saw it?" Jase squatted down so he could look eye to eye with his friend.

"No. But it was on the porch. Watching me through the window. I heard its footsteps. I saw its shadow through the window. It was big."

Jase caught Uncle Billy's gaze but the old man just looked away.

"Are you sure it wasn't just a dream?" Jase asked.

"Its wasn't a damn dream. Something was on the porch. Looking at me through the window."

Jase stood. He shook his head and teased his chin hair with one hand. "I don't know," he said. "I mean... I don't know. A bear? Could it have been a bear?" Uncle Billy avoided his gaze; pulling open the squeaky front door, he went outside.

"Whatever this bear – this bear-thing – this whatever – is, its bold enough to come up on the porch. And to bother someone in the outhouse," Rob said.

"But it didn't actually do anything?"

"Well, no."

"If a bear or some other big animal wanted to come through those windows it could. Probably just curious. Or hungry. We just need to be careful. Let's not...." Jase's voice trailed off. He was staring out the window, watching the old man do something.

Rob stood. Jase pointed toward the old man stooping just feet from the bottom of the porch steps.

Curious, they stepped out onto the porch. Immediately the chilly morning air hit them. Jase inhaled deeply, pulling the blanket tight around his chest. "What you find?" he called to the old man.

Uncle Billy did not respond. He gazed at something on the ground and then at the forest and then back again. The old Indian stood. He stared toward the forest and then mumbled to himself: "Where are you, grandchild? Where are you, grandchild? Where are you? Where are you? Yes. Yes. I am lost. Where are you? This way. Where are you, grandchild? Someone comes. Look out. Get ready. Prepare yourself, for Yayali comes."

Rob looked at Jase. "Its an old story," Jase explained. "An old tribal story."

That's when they both noticed what Uncle Billy had been looking at so intently on the ground. Incredibly, it appeared to be a human footprint of enormous proportions. The imprint looked to be about a foot and a half long and probably six to eight inches wide. They looked at each other, startled, and then both squatted to better look at the print.

"What is this?" Rob finally said. "This can't be what I think it is."

Jase stood, planting his bare foot next to the print in the mud: it dwarfed his foot. He looked at his friend but said nothing.

"It can't be. Impossible," Rob said.

"Yayali," Uncle Billy said, still looking across to the vast expanse of forest. "Yayali?" Rob said.

"Yayali. Big Brother. Hairy Man. Heavy Foot," Uncle Billy recited the names breathlessly.

Rob looked at Jase, puzzled.

"Sasquatch," Jase said.

"Yeah. You're talking about Bigfoot," Rob nearly shouted. "Bigfoot?"

"My people call them Ot-ne-yar-hed. The Stonish Giants," Jase explained.

"All Native people know them, but by different names."

"But they're just stories. They aren't real," Rob insisted.

"They are," Uncle Billy put his hands on Rob's shoulders, looking him squarely in the eyes.

"We need to leave, Jase. We have to get the hell out of here," Rob stared into his friend's bewildered face.

"Yeah, dude, we will. Later today. Maybe tomorrow. At the latest. This is nothing. We just have to help Uncle Billy close up the cottage and we're out of here."

"Yayali cannot harm you," Uncle Billy reassured Rob.

"Yeah, they're peaceful forest people. We know of them but we're told to leave them alone. They won't hurt you," Jase said.

"No. Uncle Billy said 'they cannot harm us'. That's not the same thing as 'will not harm us'," Rob looked into the old man's eyes.

Uncle Billy looked away. He exhaled deeply and went back inside the cottage, the boys close behind. The old man settled at the large wood dining table. An uncomfortable silence hung over the room for several moments until Uncle Billy finally gestured for the boys to join him at the table.

"My grandmother told me a story long ago. I was younger than you. She made me promise to memorize the story and pass it on one day," the old man said.

Jase and Rob just looked at the man, not knowing whether they were to speak or just listen.

"Jase, the stories you have been told are lies," Uncle Billy said. "Yayali is not a peaceful creature of the forest. The truth has been hidden. Only a few know."

"I don't understand," Jase said.

Uncle Billy took several noisy sips of his coffee. He sighed deeply and then took another sip of coffee. Finally, he took a deep breath. "Before People there were the animals and the Yayali, who were the first Men. The Yayali were Giants who had been made by the animals and given the gifts of language and fire and tools so they could help the animals and protect the Earth. The animals and the Yayali lived together in peace, sharing the mountain and the forest and the river. But the Yayali became proud and selfish. They turned their backs on the animals and on the Earth. They discovered dark Spirits and made offerings to them. These Spirits were older than the animals and the Earth and had no names Man could say. The Giants took up the worship of these Spirits from outside who told the Yayali that they would be given eternal life if they ate the meat of Men. So the Yayali began to build altars of stone and sticks in the shadowy places and began to eat the meat of their own.

"So all the animals gathered at Hocheu to make People, who would be the new Men and the friends of the animals and the Earth. But soon the Giants discovered that they could eat the meat of People instead of their own kind, and this angered the animals. 'The Yayali have turned their backs on the animals and the Earth,' Eagle said. 'They eat the meat of Men and shall never die and never go to the Happy Hunting Ground.'

"So the animals decided to punish the Yayali and take away the gifts they had given them.

"Owl said, 'I take away the Yayali's tools, and make them forage for food.'

"Coyote said, 'I take away the Yayali's language, and make them grunt and howl.'

"Vulture said, 'I take away the Yayali's clothes, and make them grow hair.'

"Lizard said, 'I take away the Yayali's fire, and make them eat meat raw.'

"Bear said, 'I take away the Yayali's homes, and make them live in the forests and mountains.'

"Turtle said, 'I take away the Yayali's names, and make them less than Men.'

"Wolf said, 'I take away the Yayali's family, and make them live alone.'

"And Eagle said, 'And I take away the Yayali's spirit, and make all animals fear and shun them.'

"As the Chief of the animals, Eagle was chosen to bring the punishment on the Yayali. He waited until nightfall, when all the Yayali giants had gathered in their village and were asleep in their homes. Eagle flew over the Yayali village saying 'Yayali, you have turned from the animals and the Earth to dark Spirits. You eat the meat of People and shun the Happy Hunting Ground.' Then Eagle fell to the Earth like a great winged fire, burning the village to ashes. Eagle said 'Giants, the animals have taken away their gifts to you. We take your language, your fire and your tools. You are banished to the lonely places and shall forever be alone, shunned by animals and People.'

"Then at every lonely place were a Yayali went, Eagle marked the Old Symbol on a stone as a sign of warning. The Giants feared the Old Symbol and could not go near it. They also could not make offerings to their dark Spirits nor wield any power over People so long as the Old Symbols remained.

"And so to this day the Yayali live alone in the dark and lonely places, feared by animals and Man. They are occasionally seen, but can never be captured or killed," Uncle Billy finally finished and sighed.

"So you're saying Bigfoot is real and that its out there? You knew it was out there?" Rob was incredulous.

"He cannot harm us," the old man insisted.

"Has this thing done this before? Come up on the porch? Bothered someone in the outhouse?" Rob asked.

Uncle Billy looked past the boys and out the front windows. After a long moment he replied, "No. Yayali has never come this close to the cabin."

"Something's not right. None of this is right. We have to get out of here," Rob stood, grabbing Jase's arm.

"Dude, relax," Jase tried to calm his friend. Rob shoved him aside, pushed open the door and hurried down the porch steps.

"It is too much for some people," Uncle Billy sighed.

"He'll be okay once he calms down. But I can't believe all this. Is this true, this story?"

"Yes," the old man nodded. "Yayali has great power. He sometimes comes to us in dreams and vision quests. He is more terrible there. A horrible giant monster. Some never recover from meeting the giants in their dreams. Those who see them in dreams call their name 'Gug'."

"I just don't believe all this. I thought Ot-ne-yar-hed were just from stories. Not Real. I mean, not really."

Uncle Billy just sighed and shrugged.

"I'm going to get dressed and go see what Rob's doing." As he was halfway up the stairs, the front door burst open and a flustered Rob rushed in.

Panting, his face a mask of panic, Rob blurted out, "the boat's gone!"

*   *   *

The three men stirred up a thick mustiness as they trudged through the forest's carpet of leaves and pine needles, up to their knees in some spots. A few green things peeked out from beneath the blanket of leaves, but most of the vegetation was bare branches and dead-brown. Leaves scattered in crackling waves as they pushed through them, sounds echoing in the cool, damp forest air.

Rob guessed they had walked a mile from the cabin, all the time in uneasy silence. The tall thin trees all looked the same; turning in any direction, everything looked exactly like any other direction. He understood how easily someone could become disoriented and lost in the primal wilderness. The morning's sun had become obscured by heavy autumn clouds, casting a cold greyness over the landscape. The vague illumination made the woods glow weirdly under a shadowless shroud.

Uncle Billy suddenly stopped and noiselessly put up a hand. Rob and Jase stopped and looked at each other. The old man was intently staring at something several yards away. Slowly, he walked toward it. As they neared, the boys could see something large and metallic protruding up out of the leaves. It was their boat – or a what was left of it – turned up on its side. The aluminum craft was dented and smashed, and partially buried beneath leaves and mud. Creased and buckled in the center, it looked as though something had effortlessly folded the boat in half before discarding it. There was no sign of the outboard motor or any of their gear.

"Jesus! That thing carried our boat all the way out here? And then bent it in half like it was tin?" Rob flustered.

"Well, maybe..." Jase started. Rob cut him off with a look.

"What the hell? That thing doesn't want us to leave?" Rob's voice wavered between fury and fear.

"Very bad," Uncle Billy mumbled. He gazed curiously upward, and then scanned the thickness of trees.

"What?" Rob said.

"Come. We have to check," the old Indian replied cryptically.

"Check what?" Rob's query went unanswered.

They continued for another mile in screaming silence, the forest unnervingly quiet and still; their footsteps through the leaves sounded thunderous. Rob was sure the others could hear his every breath, his heart pounding in his chest. He felt eyes on him. Something was watching them: following them behind the trees. He stopped for a moment, letting the others get ahead of him. Slowly he turned, scanning the crowds of trees. Was there movement? Something dark? The wind changed direction and he caught scent of something pungent. Like rotten eggs but worse – musty and animal-like. In the distance leaves crunched under some unseen weight, and a dark indiscriminate shape moved between trees. A cold, wet shiver slid down Rob's spine, and he turned and ran after his friends. He stopped several times to survey the shadows and listen for any sounds, but he saw and heard nothing.

By the time Rob caught up with them, the others had stopped in a small clearing. In the middle of the clearing lay a large bare-branched tree broken and splintered across a boulder: the big mossy stone appeared to have been cleaved in two by the fallen tree. Around the boulder was a wide ring of large toadstools, black and slippery with age. A few yards from the cracked boulder sat a large pile of stones deliberately stacked into a flat-topped mound about five feet high and eight feet long.

Uncle Billy stood inside the fairy ring of toadstools, intently pulling broken branches from the broken boulder. Quickly, he uncovered an odd pictograph in the side of the rock and Rob saw that the split ran right through it. Rob couldn't make out the design, but it appeared to be the symbol of a branch or an eye or some combination of the two: it didn't appear to be of Native origin, although it looked ancient.

The old man ran his hands over the sharp fissure in the boulder, tracing the broken pictograph with his fingers. "The Old Symbol is broken," he said as much to himself as to the boys.

"What? What does it mean?" Rob studied the ancient carving, trying to make sense of the shape.

"The Old Symbol. Put here by Eagle to keep Yayali under control," Uncle Billy explained.

"Yayali can't make offerings to their evil Spirits as long as the Old Symbol remains," Jase said, remembering the story the old man had told earlier.

"And cannot eat the meat of men," Uncle Billy added.

"Wait. You knew this was here? That all this was really true?" Rob blustered.

"I did not know the Old Symbol had been broken," the old man said.

"But you said Bigfoot couldn't touch this Old Symbol or go near it," Rob countered.

"He can't. This tree just happened to fall here. The lightning must have struck it in the storm," Uncle Billy shook his head.

"Then you have to make a new carving. Fix the broken one," Rob demanded.

"I cannot make the Old Symbol. Only Eagle can do it."

"Then we need to get out of here. Back to the cabin. We'll be safe there," Jase grabbed the old man by the arm.

"Yeah. Can you shoot it? You have a gun, right?" Rob hoped.

"Man cannot kill Yayali," Uncle Billy said. "It is too late. See," he pointed at the mound of stones, "Yayali has already built his altar to his dark Spirits."

Another cold wet shiver slid down Rob's spine when he suddenly caught scent of something rotten. "Its here!" he blurted out. He turned to scan the surrounding forest as something came crashing out of the trees to one side of him. There was the ponderous thudding of heavy feet, and deep growling breaths. With a bone-chilling howl, some hulking shaggy darkness swept past him, knocking him to the damp ground.

There was a blood curdling scream followed immediately by another unearthly, bestial howl. Rob felt something warm spatter his face, watching as if in slow motion as a hairy creature towering over eight feet tall twisted Uncle Billy's head to some unnatural angle. The old man slumped to the ground in a twitching and contorted pile. Jase sprinted away but was quickly snatched up by a long hairy arm. Without effort, the giant hoisted the young man up and snapped him in two like a stick, instantly silencing a scream. The creature tossed Jase's limp body aside, and turned its gaze to Rob.

The sound of his own heart pounding exploded in Rob's ears. His panting breath fogged out of his quaking mouth, and he felt something warm streaming down his leg. He struggled to move, but something inside him seized up his muscles and bones. He was frozen to the spot, unable to do anything but stare at the towering hairy creature standing over the broken bodies of his friends. The creature stood staring at the quivering young man, its large brown eyes studying him. For the first time Rob saw it clearly. The thing was over eight feet tall, broad and muscular, covered in coarse shaggy hair. It stood slightly stooped on two powerful legs, its hands and feet human-like but exaggerated in size. The head was long and conical, but the features were wide and flat and crossed between man and ape. The thing's most disturbing features were its eyes: large, dark, and human. Rob's trembling gaze met the creature's and he realized that he wasn't staring into the eyes of some wild animal, but of an intelligent being: a giant, hairy man.

Keeping him always in sight, the creature scooped up the limp bodies of Rob's friends and lay them atop its stone altar. Every fiber of his being was screaming for Rob to run – to flee this nightmare place – yet he couldn't move, couldn't look away. Something unseen held him in place. The creature tore great chunks of meat from Jase's body and hungrily ate them, blood and gore frothing around its mouth. The sharp, wet sounds of bone and tissue being torn and chewed sickened the young man. The giant gorged itself on the bodies, consuming great portions of both.

The day's lingering greyness was deepening by the time the shaggy giant finished its cannibal feast. It began to pound on the top of the bloodied stone pile with a log, producing a steady, rhythmic knocking. The creature howled and made a series of deep guttural chattering sounds. As he listened, Rob began to notice the same sounds repeated. It was like a language or a chant – some sort of communication to something unseen. Strangely, the wind began to howl, blowing great clots of leaves and dirt around and swaying the towering trees. The air was alive and electric. Ground fog swirled and thickened. The creature let out a final bestial scream that caused goose bumps to cover Rob's flesh, and with that his limbs went limp and he fell to the ground.

Before he could lift himself, the hairy creature pulled him up and off his feet. He was carried to the giant's cairn and roughly deposited amidst what was left of Jase and Uncle Billy. Rob struggled and squirmed atop the bloody remains of his partially-eaten friends, but the creature held him down with a powerful wide hand. It began to chatter again, pressing like a vice against Rob's chest until bones began to crack. The young man screamed but the sound was swallowed up by the shrieking wind. He looked into the creature's deliberate and calculating eyes; instinctively he knew what was happening. Glancing past his monstrous captor and into the roiling sky, Rob saw vague, primal forms taking shape. The clouds parted and stars peered down like cold eyes as things began to coalesce in the night sky.

As Yayali smashed its fist into Rob's chest and pulled out his beating heart he knew, as the life faded from his body, that the dark Spirits were coming back.

For Justin Smoke

First Nation

W. H. Pugmire has been a devoted Lovecraftian since 1973, and has worked at establishing himself as an author of Lovecraftian fiction these many decades. He has now had stories in many professional anthologies, the most exciting being his tale, "Inhabitants of Wraithwood," published in S. T. Joshi's *Black Wings*. The year 2010 saw him writing like a thing possessed, and the among his many books to be released these next two years are *The Tangled Muse* (Centipede Press), *Some Unknown Gulf of Night* (Arcane Wisdom), *The Dark One -- Strange Tales of Nyarlathotep* (Mythos Books), *Uncommon Places* (Hippocampus Press) and *Gathered Dust and Others* (Miskatonic River Press). He dreams in Seattle, WA.

Your Ivory Hollow

by W. H. Pugmire

Yes, I know I seem a bit nervous. Here, let me pour us a drink. This is from South Africa, and although they are noted for their white wines, I think this red is especially good. That's better. My nerves have been on edge since our friend's death. I miss him more than I can say. He led me into a world such as I have never encountered, an intoxicating realm; and now that he is gone that world haunts my ivory shell with dim and dreamy reveries. I have a feeling that you too know of these things, because of your secret heritage. No, don't look surprised; you must realize by now that Johan and I shared everything, that we had no secrets from each other. We were brother poets as well as lovers, and our passion was for Decadent Literature, as you know. It was his aim to write something that would astound the prosaic world, similar to the way that Baudelaire so astonished his age. Well, Johan has certainly shocked the world! I think, over the decades, his last book will take on new significance and power. It has already led to one suicide, which is such a compliment.

Ah, your eyes keep shifting to that ornamental box. I have no idea where he found it, but I know what he used it for. It's made of resin, and the inlaid motif on the lid is gold. It's rather heavy, although it no longer holds its former occupant. But I keep the other thing inside it, that small unearthly gem. Go ahead, open it.

The lid is heavier than one expects, almost as if it protests the touch of your silver hand, your attempt to explore its mystery. Yes, take it out, the small black gem looks so lovely against the mesh of your antique gloves. You can see, of course, the hollow indentation left by the thing for which the box had been composed, the smooth small skull. When Johan first showed it to me, I mistook it for the delicate cranium of some woman, and thus I was astounded when he revealed to me that the skull belonged in fact to the Marquis de Sade. Do you smile? I smiled too, I confess. Johan's imagination was what one would have called extravagant. His means were modest, and I told myself that such a gem as the skull of the Scarlet Marquis would be a costly treasure. And yet – the first time he actually showed me the thing, I confess that it had its weird effect; indeed, I took it for some artifact cleverly composed but obviously fake. It was small and looked frangible; its osseous surface was yellow with age yet well preserved, except for the small hollow that had formed upon the brow bone. It took me some time to realize what made this skull so utterly different from any others I had encountered. It was as I studied the rows of teeth and finely structured jaw that I suddenly noticed – *it did not grin.*

I am prone to bad nerves, as you know, and for a moment I was stiff with horror, my flesh prickled and I grew slightly dizzy. An overwhelming sense of emanate danger engulfed my being. As I studied the skull I felt a weird sensation that I was part of some mesmerized crowd who ogled it adoringly – I could feel their sensuous eyes behind and above me. As I studied the grim thing, Johan spoke of it in his remarkable voice, that voice that so captivated audiences when he read his work publicly.

"You'll probably think it's a fake, Frank, but I can assure you I know otherwise. I've been sleeping with it beside me, which has resulted in uncanny dreams. Dreaming is a form of magick, if you do it right; it can transform space and time. I lived de Sade's secret life, the one for which we have rumors only, his life as a sorcerer. He trafficked with daemons of the pit, with devils in the deep abysses above. He tried to whisper their names to me, but his voice was like the wind and I couldn't understand it. He revealed, darkly, the thing that squatted in its subterranean cavern for centuries, hungering for homages of carnage. He revealed the shapes that fell to earth, the beings who brought their images with them. I remember them especially, keenly, and so you can imagine my reaction when I encountered a woman with one of these images carved in obsidian and fastened to a necklace that she wore!"

I noticed a wildness of expression in his eyes that had never been there before, an intoxication and a madness. It was almost like some primitive force, the lunacy that burned in his eyes. Ah, your glass is empty. Here – more wine. It's a beverage that he introduced me to, and it has a subtle potency. I thought, at first, that the drink added to his dementia, for he spoke of it as "that loathsome, bestial thing from Africa." Well, I *thought* he was referring to the drink and its effect on him; you know as well as I do his flare for the melodramatic, how he loved to act the victim to the things that gave him intense pleasure. Johan had always been a performer, but I never considered him unbalanced until I learned of his actual participation in what I think is called Solitary Magick, a form of witchcraft. He had begun to talk to me of Baudelaire's Satanism, of de Sade's supposed sorcery which demanded the spillage of blood as a procurer of boon.

You remember when Johan took that mysterious trip to Chicago? I think that's when he obtained his magick skull. Yes, we laugh, but it's a serious matter, for it touches on Johan's art. Because at the same time he introduced me to the skull, he showed me something else – his new poem, which he recited from memory as I perused the lines. I was riveted! The combination of those

magnificent lines and the sound of his sonorous voice ringing inside my head
– god! The sound of it sent waves into the air, seemed to taint that air and fill
it with half-seen forms, undulating shadows. You know that his publisher is
now preparing an audio edition of his last book, having found a cassette that
Johan recorded reading a large portion of the poems. The sound quality is poor,
so perhaps it won't do the harm that I imagine it could, the delirium it might
otherwise cause.

I'll never forget what happened next. He reached for the necklace that
he had begun to wear and pulled it out from under his shirt so as to reveal the
little trinket. I must have smirked when I first laid eyes on it, he had spoken
of its potency in such a way that I was expected something astounding and
monstrous. Morbid art doesn't shock me, especially when it reveals genius. The
gemstone was inside a kind of prismatic locket that was attached to the silver
chain. I remember the queer way the room's light played upon that locket, and
then how that light subdued as Johan opened the locket and took out his little
gem. He placed it in my palm and I shuddered, for it was as cold as some dead
moon. It seemed, as I first studied it, to be a smooth yet shapeless mass of pure
obsidian, but the more I peered at it the more – suggestive – the thing became,
the more I could see that which it represented. You can see it yourself as you
hold it, but perhaps your strange gloves robs you of the experience of touching
it. But you *can* see it, can't you, the way it seems to entrance your eyes and thus
reveal its unspeakable form, bewitchingly? And once the thing reveals itself, it
never leaves your mind; some aspect of it is within you, always, haunting the
darkness within the hollow of your skull.

You'll remember I mentioned the indentation on the brow bone of de
Sade's skull. I never learned if Johan chiseled it there himself or if it was formed
by some – other means; but when he took that black gem from me and placed it
into the cavity of bone it fitted perfectly. There was something utterly macabre
about the sight of that dark emblem within its bed of bone, and I wanted to turn
my eyes away – but of course I was captivated, and could not help but observe
the look of mad ecstasy in Johan as he bent to the skull in its box. I watched as
he placed his face against it, touching the gem with his forehead as he pressed
his mouth to the malformed teeth of the death's-head. The queerest sound of
humming filled the air, and I could not understand how his human mouth could
produced so unearthly a sound – and then I realized that the noise was coming
from different places, from some distant place outside the house, and from the
space between my ears. I covered my ears with my hands momentarily, but that
merely resulted in increasing the eldritch noise, which rose in crescendo until
Johan began to speak, at which point all other sounds extinguished.

You've experienced the sound of his voice, the way it transformed when he uttered his poetry. It was, in every way, a tool of *evocation*. It is merciful that he took his life when he did, because had he continued to give readings... There was only one suicide that we know of, that young man who, after having attended a poetry reading, stabbed himself in the neck after screaming snatches of Johan's verse in some public place. It was a ghastly business. Yes, I think I know why Johan took his life. Johan Sebastian Goodrich, the greatest poet since Baudelaire! But let me continue my tale. It's almost told. He lifted his head from that beautiful box and its ghastly occupant and reached for a pen and pad on a nearby stand. He spoke lines of verse that shook me to the core, and as he spoke he wore a double countenance. Beneath his normal features I could see a visage of someone else, a face that wore a semblance of that blasted death's-head. Johan spoke the lines in English, but then he would falter and mumble to himself in French. It was entirely bizarre. I noticed a place where his mouth bled, from some minute slit in the fabric of his lower lip, and I assumed that he had bit himself. I had to shut my eyes as he scribbled into his pad, for the combination of his twin countenances filled me with profound vertigo, as if I were about to tumble into some abyss. I found a chair and fell into it and kept rubbing the moisture from my face with my hands. I became aware of silence, moved my hands from my face and looked at him. He was studying the lines that he had etched onto the page of his notepad, and then he looked at me, smiled, and read his new poem in a quiet voice.

"Rather good, I think," he told me, to which I could not reply, and something in my inability to speak amused him. I heard in his laughter something I had never experienced from him – cruelty.

It was then that I deserted him. I will say quite frankly that I shunned him. But I could not kill my interest in him and thought of him always. Our romance had been a mild affair, it hadn't affected me profoundly; but his poetry continued to seduce me utterly, and when at last he published his new book, I rushed to obtain it, and I devoured it, and I knew such ecstasy as I have never undergone, mental sensations that seemed to turn my bones to jelly so that I could not stand for hours afterward. I was surprised when he telephoned me and told me that he wanted to give me a special limited edition of the book that contained some poems he felt were too powerful for public consumption. Would I come to him and accept his gift? I could in no way resist, although I wanted to. Yes, I was very shocked when he answered my tapping at his door; but of course I had not seen him for half a year, and I had no idea that there would be such alteration. It was most evident in his sickly palsied face; why, one could almost detect the shape of the bone beneath the thin covering of flesh, and his *smiling* was absolutely cadaverous!

"I've penned some new lines," said he as we entered his abode, "and I thought, if you would give me audience, that I would perform them for you, hmm? Sit there." I did as he commanded, and watched as he picked up some sheets of paper and lowered the lights. There was a fire burning in the hearth, which caused shadows to dance upon his diabolic face as he uttered his damnable posey. His words seemed to slice through my eyes and prick my brain with uncanny horror. I could almost see the things of which he sang and feel their cosmic hunger, their appetite for human blood and dementia. I felt like I was standing on some rim of an unknown dimension, above an abyss of nightmare that was ravenous for my puny soul. He read three new poems, and then he stopped and looked at me in such a way that I feared him as I have never feared anyone or any thing. His eyes were like smouldering black coals, and in the weird firelight his pale skin looked more like bone than living tissue. And his smile – great heaven! How could any human have a smile like that, with a mouth that stretched too widely?

I rose to leave, not caring for the promised special edition of his book. He placed a gentle hand on my shoulder and whispered, "I can teach you the trick. I know you've ached to write poetry of power, wondrous words of verse that would make society adore you. I can show you the way." Linking his arm with mine, he walked me to where the beautiful box sat on a velvet cushion. He opened its lid and I could not help but gaze at the skull. The black gem was in its place in the chiseled hollow. "All you have to do is kiss him, Frank, let him drink your longing." At this he moved directly before me and pressed his lips to mine, and I trembled with a passion that I had not felt in a long time. Savagely, we kissed, and then he took hold of my head and guided it downward, until my mouth touched the morbid thing in its box. My forehead pressed against the chilly black gem, and as he kept my head there, his hand pushing as it wound its fingers in my hair, I imagined that I could feel something burning into my brain. I saw visions – the things of his new poetry, the mad vortex and its inhabitants. I beheld a small figure that I knew to be the living de Sade, saw him kiss a dagger that was coated with dripping gore. Blood spilled into my mouth, filling me with delicious ecstasy. I grew dizzy and momentarily lost my footing, upsetting the stand on which the box and its occupant rested. The box and I fell onto the floor, where I knelt and watched the death's-head that rolled near my hand. I saw the blood upon its teeth – the teeth that now, impossibly, formed a lurid grin!

Something snapped within me. Screaming, I jumped to a standing position and stomped with one sure foot onto the skull, crushing it, not stopping until it was a heap of yellow dust. I expected Johan to attack me, to yowl with protest. Instead, he merely looked at the mess on the floor, sighed, and went to where he kept his decanter of wine. "Will you join me?" I did not take the proffered glass, and so he drank from both, then sat in a chair and shook with agony as the poison took his life.

Will you have another glass.? Ah, but you cannot, for you have also expired. Here, let me clean the vomit from your pretty mouth, from which your fragrant breath no longer issues through those petals of soft flesh that have so often been kissed. After I abandoned Johan, you see, I did some research into his life, his movements, his friends and so on. I wanted to know the source from which he obtained that black gem. He had, before his final madness, named me the executor of his estate, and thus I inherited this house and its contents – and finally I found his secret journal, in which he writes of you as "that loathsome, bestial thing of Africa." I can see it now, as I study your dead face, the deceitfully slight proportion of racial heritage that names you. You gave him that black gem, didn't you, as you seduced him with your animal lusts and primitive sorcery? You whispered to him of the secrets of the void, of how to conjure forth the cosmic daemons with rituals of blood and necromancy. I have tasted that unholy fare, and I need to relish it anew. I ache to write with the power that Johan Goodrich possessed – the power that so possessed him. And that is why I am going to debauch your corpse with my lust, and as I spill my seed into your clammy vortex I will work the saw that frees your head from its place above your shoulders. I will claw away your face and bring forth your beauteous bone. I shall place this black signal of your alchemical tribe onto your skull and watch it embed itself therein, and then I will kiss you with all the passion I possess and learn your secrets of the tomb.

MICHAEL TICE has long been a devotee of Lovecraft, due primarily to their shared aversion to seafood, partiality for cats, and Weltanschauung of an indifferent and/or inimical cosmos. Some of the details in The Spell of the Eastern Sea are drawn from Mike's experiences sailing the waters off his native California. The extent of his nautical understanding is such that he can reliably tell port from sherry. When his waking life as a Los Angeles businessman does not intrude, his dream-self composes poetry, fiction, nonfiction, and role-playing game material. His vanity imprint, the Elegantly Amused Press, has only published one slim volume of poetry, as Mike continues to struggle in his efforts to enlarge his vanity.

The Spell of the Eastern Sea

by Michael Tice

The melodious slap of halyards against hollow metal masts gave the only indication that numerous sailboats were moored in the fog-blanketed harbor of Kingsport. My restless feet had once again led me on an evening sojourn to the wharves, where I could discern the diffuse forms of securely tied fishing boats. To the chimes of the unseen pleasurecraft were added the creaks and groans of the lines securing the fishing smacks, an audible complaint that mirrored the sad state of the Kingsport fisheries. The sea does not provide an infinite bounty, and the eighties and nineties had witnessed a precipitous decline in the local catch. I knew from my recent walks that many of the boats hadn't moved from their berths all summer.

The evening gloom grew darker and more palpable, indicating that the unseen sun had set behind the western hills. Moisture settled on my skin as I regarded the lifeless fishing smacks and listened to the song of the invisible sails. The luxurious yachts and unsightly motorboats of the vacationers were quartered elsewhere in the harbor, but they held no fascination for me.

My parents had moved from Boston to Kingsport when I was a child. Ever since the first time I beheld the gay sails pirouetting about the harbor, dancing with the coy winds, I was enamored of sailing. Now, twenty years later, as I walked the wooden boards of the dockyard, fancies and memories of the sea still drifted pleasantly through my mind, like so many airy skiffs on the seas of imagination.

Early on, my parents had indulged my desire for a small sailboat of my own. Much of the free time of my youth and adolescence had been spent in that craft, learning the many moods of the local waters. I discovered the complex regularities in the mysterious mist as it crawls inland from the sea. I recognized the effect of rain on the confluence of waters at the mouth of the Miskatonic. I slowly internalized the subtle and seemingly patternless interplay of sun, storm, sky and sea.

And yet my parents always expressed a hint of disapproval in my avocation. There was no future, they seemed to be saying, in the sea, only a glorious past. My parents, before their early retirement, were both successful Boston lawyers, and their aspirations for me were consequently very ambitious. The present summer was drawing to a close, and I knew I would soon be returning to Harvard. Many would consider me privileged, but I felt little enthusiasm; two years of studies had succeeded only in dulling my appetite for what the university had to offer. But the expectations of my parents provided sufficient cause to return, if no motivation.

My life had been planned for me in broad detail: an undergraduate degree in political science, Harvard Law, a career and family, perhaps even a bid for public office. And the reward? Early retirement and relocation to some pleasant New England town like Kingsport, just as my parents had done. Originally part of the vacationing summer crowd, my parents had been captivated by the town, and bought land in the foothills on the western edge, where other wealthy immigrants to Kingsport had constructed an ever-widening crescent of palatial homes overshadowing the cramped and archaic buildings of Kingsport proper. Only the great headland that provides Kingsport with its most distinctive landward feature remains devoid of houses. Its steep sides preclude their construction, apart from the enigmatic structure that presides over the town from the pinnacle of the headland.

Although I had lived most of my life in Kingsport, there was still no question that my family and I were interlopers in the eyes of the established residents. Some great divide parted those who lived in the well-organized modern communities on the outskirts, and those who lived in the archaic maze of narrow streets in the ancient heart of Kingsport. My parents were content with the situation, recognizing the reserve of the New England temperament. The Boston community in which they both had been raised was just as exclusive and chilly to outsiders. For me, however, the aloofness of the natives had troubled my youthful psyche.

I was repulsed by what I felt to be actual resentment on the part of the Kingsporters toward the newer residents, and yet I was paradoxically drawn to the town itself. I wanted desperately to belong, but there was no way for an outsider to become a full member of Kingsport society. Efforts to become more than superficially friendly with the natives were politely rebuffed, so I sought other means to learn the ways of Kingsport, though little genuine success attended my efforts. When not mastering the secrets of Kingsport's wind and waters, I frequented its libraries and tiny historical and nautical museums; on many nights, like tonight, I walked the sloping streets of Kingsport and inhaled the soft, salt air, hoping thereby to become an integrated part of the town.

I suddenly found that I had reached the end of a pier, and had been standing there for some time, wrestling with my continuing conflict. My return to Harvard was imminent, and I was loath to turn my course toward home; nevertheless, I was on the point of doing so when I noticed a faint luminescence out on the waters.

The heavy fog still lay thick upon the water, but a hazy group of lighter patches signified the existence of a ship. She was a two-masted sailing ship by the pattern of lights. Something about the placement and quality of the light suggested to me that the vessel was of antique design; however, the all-enveloping mist precluded a better view.

The spectral lights drifted soundlessly closer, and I marvelled that the fog was sufficient to muffle the noise of the motor. Certainly, the chill, opaque vapors of Kingsport are legendary, but I still felt a rising excitement at the ghostly nature of the apparition.

I strained my ears, and could just make out the unintelligible sound of shouted commands on board. At the same time, the ship's glide slowed to a crawl, as a result of her few scraps of sail being taken down. To the music of the harbor's halyards, the crew made the ship fast and moored her with anchors fore and aft.

I watched this performance in a dumbfounded silence, for, despite the cloak of fog, I could tell now that the ship was indeed of an antique cast. The schooner's masts bore quaint topsails, currently furled to their gaffs, of a kind unseen on any modern sailing ship. Only in the fleets of centuries past did mariners strive so industriously to catch elusive winds beyond the reach of their masts: winds that might prove the difference between life and death in the days before the auxiliary engine.

Although surprised, I was by no means overwhelmed by the appearance of a sailing ship in the harbor. There had been a time, a hundred and fifty or two hundred years ago, when such ships had been a common sight in Kingsport. In that bygone age, as I knew from my visits to the local museums, the commerce between the old world and the new was carried out in such vessels, as was the bustling trade up and down the reaches of the American coast.

By the beginning of the twentieth century, though, wind and sail had been entirely replaced by steam and oil. The larger ports of the East Coast soon dominated merchant shipping, and the fortunes of Kingsport had suffered a concomitant diminution, leaving fishing as the only remaining business. Lately, even that trade had failed, despite the favorable catches achieved by the residents of another coastal town not far away.

Nevertheless, as a reminder of the former days of splendor, sailing ships were no strangers to the city. The Fourth of July celebrations brought historic tall ships to the shelter of Kingsports well-situated and capacious harbor. The local boats were festooned with garlands and flags, and the visiting ships had no need for additional decoration. Their very existence heralded the triumphs of an earlier age, when even something as utilitarian as a cargo ship was a work of breathtaking art. Perhaps tonights mysterious visitor was a restored vessel of this kind.

Still, despite my tentative explanation of the newly moored ship, I was filled with some disquiet. For Independence Day lay many long summer days in the past, and few such ships were seen in Kingsport at other times of the year. Furthermore, I thought to myself, what sane captain would hazard his priceless ship by bringing her in under the dual cover of night and fog?

While I pondered these matters, growing colder as the damp exhalation of the sea continued to condense upon my face, the crew had set about lowering a small rowboat. That act completed, a lone man embarked. With a long-practiced rhythm, the boat's passenger impelled it to shore.

His back was turned to me as he rowed, and a lantern set on a thwart before him projected strange rays into the swirling fog. I noticed that the men remaining on the ship had doused, one by one, all the other lights on board, until the ghostly outline had been completely enveloped by the welcoming fog of Kingsport. I tried to hail the rower, but the night had constricted my throat; only a croak emerged.

I cleared my throat with difficulty, feeling and tasting the heavy salt. By that time, the rower had neared enough for me to see him better by the light of the lantern. My hypothesis that he and his ship were part of a travelling display of antique maritime history grew to a certainty in my mind. For he was outfitted in naval clothing of a style consonant with that of the ship.

He was nearly at the docks, making for a point some distance from me. Quietly, I walked over to the pier for which he was headed, intending to welcome him heartily to Kingsport, however late he might be for the Independence Day observances. Anyone who had braved the mist in a sailing ship deserved a heros welcome.

I coughed softly, so as not to startle him, and called out to him, "Welcome to Kingsport." My voice was still somewhat frogged, and the salutation was not as I had hoped. He turned suddenly, and his face, limned from behind by the glow of the kerosene lamp, was disfigured by fright. For an instant, I was afraid he might dive into the water, but he recovered his poise and tossed me the painter.

I made the line fast to a cold, iron cleat and helped him to the planking. His boots sounded reassuringly solid as they struck the wood.

"Thank 'ee", he murmured, acting his historical part for an audience of one. I fumbled for something suitable to say, and spent the time looking him over thoroughly.

His boots bore marks of both age and wear, as did his thick woolen jersey. The cap upon his head was distinctly nautical and looked warm. In his left hand, he held a leather satchel; in his right, the lantern. His age I set at forty: his youth had certainly gone, and his face was weatherbeaten with the indelible stamp of years spent at sea, but there was as yet little grey in his hair. The whole ensemble, coupled with his emergence from the cold, solid fog, lent him an air of weary competence.

He had been regarding me with similar curiosity, while the ring of the halyards measured time. At last I asked, "How old is your ship? I can't see her well in the fog, but she looks to me to be a good two hundred years old."

His face clouded for an instant, and slowly he answered, "Well, she was built in 1815, so I hear."

"So not quite two hundred, then."

He seemed to mentally check this calculation before giving his cautious approval: "Not quite."

After a pause, I asked him the name of his ship.

"Reckless Kite."

Another pause ensued, and I felt pressured to say something.

"I'm afraid you've missed the Fourth of July festivities by a few weeks. But at least I'm around to appreciate your arrival. Of course, the night and the fog are hiding the ship at the moment, but I'm sure the townsfolk will admire the schooner in the morning."

As I spoke, I tried to appear encouraging, for the man seemed to grow more and more nervous. As he made to move away from me, he said, "We'll not be here in the morning. Excuse me, young sir, I've business in town that awaits me."

Incredulous, I couldn't help blurting out, "Business in town? At this time of night?"

And then, as the costumed salt made his way down the pier, the solution to the mystery became apparent to me. There were certain traditions in Kingsport, I knew, ceremonies known only to the locals and carried out according to a secret schedule. Just as Poe's tomb is visited on the anniversary of his death, there are equivalent rituals in Kingsport, alluded to but never described in the histories I had read. What could be more natural than for the town to commemorate the ancient ships of its last flourishing age?

With this explanation in mind, I chased after the man before the fog completely engulfed the glow of his lantern. I soon caught him up, for his stride, though purposeful, was slow as he made his way into town. I felt some trepidation about disturbing him in his historical reenactment, but there seemed to be no audience to observe it, and when he turned at my approach, he appeared comforted by my company.

I asked, "Is this a performance? One of the old traditions of Kingsport?"

He laughed bitterly, "That it is. That it is. For near two hundred years, in a manner of speaking, one of our number has done this duty."

"Surely you're not a Kingsporter, though. I've lived here nearly my entire life, and I don't recognize you."

"Oh, we're from Kingsport, all right. Not but that we don't make port here only every few years. Nowadays."

He certainly had the accent of the Kingsport native. Kingsport's relative isolation has kept its dialect relatively unchanged, though now that outsiders like my parents have moved in, the children of Kingsport are starting to lose their linguistic eccentricities.

We left the harbor area behind, and the sounds of the sea diminished, but the narrow channels of the streets in old Kingsport were still thickly filled with sea-fog. The streetlights illuminated hazy spheres at regular intervals, and by their stronger light, I noticed more clearly how grimy and shabby were the clothes the sailor wore. I wondered at this, for even if they formed an authentic period costume, surely they shouldn't be as dirty as this.

Anxious to be congenial, I offered my name. He murmured his own, Abel Taylor. I recognized the Taylor name as that of one of the most eminent families of Kingsport, the source of their present wealth lost in an obscure past.

My companion sighed and slowed his gait somewhat. Thinking that it was to converse more easily, I asked him how many men made up his crew. He slackened his pace further and absently said, "Only eight left now."

"Are you the Captain? Is that why you have to attend to this matter yourself?"

Abruptly, he stopped. Fear seemed to seize him again, and he whispered, "There's no captain aboard the Reckless Kite. We cast lots for this task."

He had halted in the middle of a steeply sloping block, inspecting the darkened storefront of a large chain clothing store on the northern side. Taylor stared at the silent building before him as if it were a mirage that would soon pass away.

He turned to me, anxiety making his voice tremble. "Cooper's Alley," he quavered, "Where's Cooper's Alley gone?"

I searched my mind for the answer, A couple years ago, there was a fire, and the city tore down the buildings on either side of the alley. When it came time to rebuild, the lots were consolidated to build this store. "Cooper's Alley still continues on the other side of the block. We'll have to backtrack and go around."

Although he said no word, I think then that he truly appreciated having me at his side. Up until that moment, I had merely been an interloper in this strange business, but by providing these directions, I had become his companion. I felt satisfied at having some small beneficial effect on an ancient Kingsport tradition.

Taylor relaxed as we circumnavigated the obstruction and pressed on toward the heart of Kingsport. Strangely, now that he had accepted me, I felt little pressure to continue making conversation, and so we passed through the misted streets with no sounds but our own footsteps for company.

By degrees, the inclination of the street grew steeper beneath our feet as we climbed the slope toward the center of town, the streetlights continuing to periodically illuminate our way. The incline was so precipitous that the globes of light seemed to soar eerily into the sky. By the turnings he took, I soon knew his destination. We were drawing ever closer to the Congregational Hospital and the surrounding cemetery that predates it by more than two hundred years. The hospital is prominently situated on Kingsports Central Hill, which overlooks the twisted lanes of the town and the mercurial sea.

Where once a church stood, now the imposing edifice of a modern hospital presides over the graves of three centuries. The electric lights that blazed about the building formed an impressive beacon in the fog, dominating the indistinct expanse of the darkened cemetery crouched at its feet.

My companion broke the long silence with a laconic comment. "That the hospital? Larger than what it was."

As commonplace as the statement was, its effect on me was profound, for I knew that the expansion of the hospital had taken place not long after the second world war. Perhaps, in the Kingsport fog, I had mistaken my comrade's age, but could I have been so greatly in error?

I murmured something inconsequential; in response, the old man startled me even further by saying that he remembered a previous visit to Kingsport. He had been the first of his crewmates to see the hospital in place of the Congregational Church. If that were true, then the crew must be eighty years old at the very least, a conclusion clearly belied by his untroubled climb of the steepening grade as we neared the hospital gate.

My mind struggled to fit all the facts of the evening into a consistent pattern, and failed. The hypotheses that swarmed through my head were that the man was either mad, peculiarly preserved, or acting out his historical persona in earnest. But none of these satisfied, and I became more and more convinced that I had stumbled across one of the hidden ceremonies of Kingsport, never discussed in books at all. I had always known, on some level, that they existed, and each of them has left its indelible imprint on the mystic atmosphere of Kingsport.

As soon as we passed within the hospital gates, he turned unhesitatingly to the side, leading straight into the vast darkness of the burial ground. The darkness enclosed us, consigning everything but the hospital, haloed in a watery illumination, to oblivion. The graveyard's dolorous atmosphere appeared to diminish the power of the sailor's oil lamp until it shed only enough light to reveal the ground immediately before our feet.

But Taylor seemed to know his way well enough, despite his momentary confusion in town, and I shuddered momentarily as I reflected that the stone landmarks about us were the most durable and permanent in the city. Two hundred years ago, this section of the graveyard would have looked much the same on such a night as this.

Hoping both to extract a sensible explanation and to dispel the gloomy silence, I asked him, "How frequently does your ship come to Kingsport?"

He trudged on for some yards before answering, "Hard to reckon. Twice a year or once a decade ... can't tell the difference anymore."

Although I could see little more than his silhouette in the light of the lantern, I sensed his anxiety increasing again and I forbore to ask him to elucidate his cryptic response. I hoped, as we threaded a course through the obelisks and headstones, that the terminus of our passage would provide a clearer explanation.

That terminus proved to be a large stone crypt, shielded by an encroaching oak, nebulous in the feeble light. As the sailor searched through his leather bag, the swaying lamp revealed the incised name upon the stonework: WARING. I didn't recognize the name, but the imposing architecture of the tomb indicated that at some point in Kingsport's early history, the Warings had been a wealthy family. But, so far as I knew, their line had come to an end -- in Kingsport, at least.

He produced an iron key, antiquely fashioned yet brightly gleaming in the lamplight. He moved to unlock the door, but paused when a dry rustling disturbed the still air. I felt no wind, only the damp kiss of the blanketing fog, but the oak must have been responding to some such current.

Shadows danced in response to the lantern, which shook in the sailor's suddenly trembling hand. "I can't do it," he murmured, "Not yet."

The terror in his voice sent a chill down my spine, and I utterly discarded my prosaic explanations for the ship's appearance this night. Though I felt a keen pleasure at finally being admitted to one of Kingsport's true mysteries, and one revealed to me alone this night, my companion's reaction made it clear that the experience was not without an accompanying danger.

The key went back into the bag, and the mariner faced the ancient crypt, steeling himself against some potent dread. He continued to shiver in the night, and I felt the chill begin to penetrate my own flesh as we stood in the midst of the dark and seemingly boundless ocean of the cemetery.

At last I could no longer endure to remain silent. "Tell me the story," I implored, "Why have you come here? What task is so dire that your crew have cast lots to decide who shall perform it?"

I'm sure he would never have told me, had not two aspects of his condition made that option attractive. First, his continued silence before that troubling *memento mori* was not having the calming effect for which he had hoped. Dispelling the quiet with voice was at least one way to make the night seem at least a little more agreeable. And secondly, every sentence he spoke delayed for some few moments the performance of his terrible duty.

"Back when the British were trying to discourage the slave trade, a fast ship could make a lot of money running a few slaves from Africa to the Indies, or the South. Although we men didn't want no truck with ferrying blacks in the hold, Captain Waring wasn't satisfied with the gold dust, ivory and dyes that we could get lawfully. So he struck bargains with the Ashanti slave traders of the coast, in the hopes of satisfying his endless greed. We brought them guns and rum, and they parted with a few hand-picked slaves guaranteed to fetch a premium price."

Taylor paused for a moment, gathering the courage to continue, giving me time to calculate that the story he told must date from near the beginning of the nineteenth century. Also, the somber fact that we stood at the site of the Captain's family crypt had not escaped my notice. A low-pitched creaking emerged from that edifice, but before I could react, the sailor resumed his story, speaking more loudly in order to eclipse the other sound.

"And then they sold us the slave that altered our fate forever. A medicine man he was, of the Oyo, ill-favored in appearance and shunned by the Ashanti people for his evil ways. Even the slave-owners of the coast, not a timid lot, were afraid of that Oyo sorcerer. Despite his fine physique, none would buy him at any price.

"But Captain Waring wasn't subject to their superstitions, and was curious about the witchdoctor's infamous reputation. Soon after the Oyo boarded our ship, the captain had him pulled from the hold and delivered to his cabin. The witchdoctor whispered outlandish blasphemies to the captain, convincing him that there was a magical method to satisfy his lust for gold. One of the spirits worshipped by the Oyo ancestors could provide good fortune for the Reckless Kite and her crew.

"It took some doing to convince the captain. After all, a captured slave will say anything to save himself from his doom, and can hardly claim to be under the protection of a spirit of good luck. Nonetheless, during the passage, the two were often closeted together in the captains cabin, and strange lights filtered out through the cracks in the wooden panelling. That black sorcerer must have appealed to the Captain's covetous nature. Leastways, he wasn't sold, but came back with us to Africa. Once there, he promised, he would give us the god of his ancestors.

"When we arrived, the captain insisted that none of us accompany him as he and the repulsive witchdoctor made their journey to the Oyo shrine. We tried to warn him of treachery, but he wouldn't hear us. And so he left, issuing one final order: no matter what happened, he would still be the captain of the ship when he returned. On no account were we to choose a new captain. That was the last thing he said before going off.

"And when he reappeared, three days later, the captain was being dragged to the shore behind a brace of the sorcerers kin. That damned medicine man had a smile wide as Africa as he led them to the Reckless Kite. Angry, a company of us went to meet them, to demand an explanation. Spanish Joe was the only one of us, apart from the captain, that could speak the language. Of course, Joe can't much speak ours, even now. But this is how Joe rendered the black witchdoctor's speech, near as I can remember.

"'Your captain is now with the god. This is what he wished. You must keep the body of the spirit safe. When he calls you, you will come at different times. You must feed him these things: three dry cakes of meal and a cheese of mother's milk and blood. If you do this, you have luck. If you fail, then he will eat your body. But your spirit will never sleep. Never. It will haunt the earth forever.'"

"We didn't think much of his answer, and our blades and bullets ensured that the medicine man would never play any such tricks again. The captain's body we brought back to Kingsport, and laid to rest in yon crypt, the last of his line to lay there. We elected Martin Flagg to be our new captain, and continued our trading.

The sailor paused again, and stared blankly into the distance as threads of fog were softly combed by the headstones of the cemetery. The cold continued to sink into my flesh, freezing me where I stood as I waited numbly for the end of the story.

"But the captain would not rest quietly in his grave, and he remembered his last orders to us. We were summoned to his presence. The Reckless Kite was becalmed near Hispaniola, and night brought a dense fog with it, a fog such as never is seen among the Caribbean islands. And with the fog came a soft breeze that carried us off like a feather. And the darkest hour of that night found us entering the misty harbor of Kingsport.

"The breeze carried us just to the docks and then departed. Bewildered, we dropped anchor and argued among ourselves. Jack said it was the captain calling us. None of the men would gainsay him, but Captain Flagg struck him and called him a fool and said he'd go himself to cut up the old devil in his tomb.

"Flagg never came back, and when the sun burned the mists away, we were back in the West Indies. And two things followed this. First, favorable luck shone on us all the time, and our trading efforts became profitable beyond our wildest dreams. Since we knew from whence that luck stemmed, we arranged, on our next trip to Africa, to obtain the rare foodstuffs the Captain demanded.

"And so when the next call came, a year later, we were prepared. Lots were cast to determine who should go, and Peters was sent to care for the Captain. To tell him of the success of the ship, and to offer him the cakes and that damnable cheese."

The sailor's nervous fear suddenly increased, and he trembled for a moment before he could go on with his tale.

"And as our fortune grew, it brought us no joy. Of what comfort is gold when you have no home, when you have to sail the seas in search of the horrible means to appease the divine monster that rules your life? We kept the ship in good repair, and for a time we revelled in rich clothes and food and women. But by and by, the only use we had for gold was to offer it to our families in Kingsport. They were sundered from us by the Captain's Call, but on our occasional returns to Kingsport, we could offer them money, if but little familial cheer.

"As year followed year, we noticed another thing about the Captain's Call. Not only is it no respecter of distances, but the call doesn't respect the seemly flow of time. For we travel farther and farther into the future with each passing. On our regular trading trips, Kingsport is as it should be, but when the Call comes, everything is changed.

"By ship's time, we are Called once a year, always at the end of summer, but the Kingsport we find on our midnight arrivals has always aged and advanced a few more years. Reckless Kite finds herself surrounded by newer and fancier ships, and fewer and fewer landmarks stay the same for the one who has to perform his needful duties. But each morning, we're back in our own time.

"But that's not the worst, for even at the natural rate of time's passage, it becomes harder and harder, even among the savages of Africa, to find the captain his savage provender. Blood and grain we can obtain in all the abundance we need, but not so mother's milk. Now that the missionaries are doing their work along the coast, we sometimes can't find it.

"Mother's milk is not the kind of thing that can be stolen, either. Glad we would be to do so if we could. But instead, we have to do without sometimes. And those men don't come back. And now I..." He gestured helplessly with the leather sack in his hand. "It's mare's milk. We already know that cow and goat wont work, but maybe this time."

He fell quiet and lowered the lamp so that I might not see his weeping.

Awkwardly, sensitive to his pain, I asked him, "Couldn't you run away? Quit this life and live a new and better one?"

He shook silently with stifled sobs, and I heard again that queer rustling noise, caused by no wind I could detect. The sound seemed to inflame his rage, and he shouted, "Run away? Can't you hear the Captain calling me?"

Producing the lustrous key, he said, "This is the fourth one the Kingsport locksmith has fashioned for us. God help me, it wont be the last!"

He lurched into motion, setting the key quickly to the ancient lock before he lost his resolve. In a moment, he had wrenched the heavy doors open, and thrust his lantern in.

From where I stood behind him, I could perceive the cavity only indistinctly, the black of oblivion clinging to its corners. The wooden caskets within had rotted away with the damp, leaving mouldering piles of disintegrated wood, iron and bones on low, stone platforms.

But though most of the coffins had eroded away to practically nothing, there was one larger mass within the tomb, enthroned in a corner. The lamplight provided it with a halo of impossible shadows. Nausea swelled within me as I struggled to comprehend that horrible shape. It seemed to be composed of a mushy, bloated corpse permeated by a horrifying tangle of thin articulated twigs.

Unconscious of danger, I stepped closer to see it better until I stood just behind the sailor's shoulder. I was at first surprised by the lack of odor emanating from the thing, but then I realized that such a stench attends only the dissolution of something dead. This, whatever it was, was horribly alive.

The flabby lips smacked, the fingers curled bonelessly and one drooping eyelid quivered over its paste-filled socket. However, most of the animation of the thing was reserved for the bundled mass of thin sticks that sprouted in a flourishing bouquet from the abdomen of Captain Waring. The thin spines shuddered to some unearthly tempo, clicking against each other, scratching tenderly at the stone confines of the tomb and whistling rapidly through the moist Kingsport air.

I hadn't had time to truly examine the scene in detail before the sailor set down his lantern and knelt before that blasphemous thing and opened his sack. He drew out some pale white cakes and cast them toward the corrupt divinity. The crowd of angular limbs grew more vigorous as it whipped the cakes into crumbs, the volume of the unearthly noise increasing with the activity. But once the particles of cake had been distributed about the thing, it pulsed with a horrid air of expectancy.

I can only guess what went through Taylors mind as he produced a quantity of runny cheese with a disquietingly rosy hue. His back faced me, and the lamplight gave away no clues. For the most part, my attention was still fastened on the writhing mass in the crypt, and the semi-liquid, incorruptible corpse from which it sprang.

As soon as this second offering was made, the thing swelled up alarmingly. The volume of madly whirling feelers shrieked through the air, engulfing and penetrating the sailor.

Immediately and instinctively, I fled. But not before I gained one last glimpse of the altercation in the crypt, dimly illuminated by the guttering flame of the lantern which had fallen on its side. Taylor's body, clothes and all, was rapidly fragmented into smaller and smaller pieces, until there was nothing left but an atomized mist, embraced and absorbed in some queer manner by the crypt-bound demon. The vision was suddenly cut off by the ponderous doors as, with a titanic crash, they slammed shut.

Bereft of any source of light, my flight through the graveyard was a mad career of bone-jarring collisions with the immobile memorials and horrifying scrapes against the foliage, inspiring anew my terror of the inhabitant of the tomb.

Following the path of least resistance, my feet led me ever downward from that cursed hill in the center of Kingsport, down the slanting streets of the archaic town center, down to the very wharf where my adventures had started.

Was it insanity that impelled me to board that ancient rowboat, and force it through the sluggish waters of the harbor? Or was it rather a rational choice inspired by a sudden clarity induced by the shock I had experienced in the graveyard? An escape from the clutch of the dull realities of my life, and entrance to the exhilaration of life before the mast on the Reckless Kite?

They took me aboard and asked few questions, preferring to hear my tale in the light of day, since they already guessed the story's end. And so, under the balmier skies of a nineteenth century morning off the coast of Cuba, I met them all for the first time: Spanish Joe, Long Tom, Mate Ellis and the others. They soon grew closer to me than any of the friends of my insipid modern life. They needed me, for the ship's complement had been depleted by three over the past fifteen years.

I spent eight years sailing the waters of the Atlantic and Indian Oceans with them, finally fulfilling my dreams of the sea. Eight times I helped obtain the rare ingredients needed for the annual ceremony in Kingsport. In that time, I promised them to do what I could for the ease of their souls, to protect them against the rapacity of the Captain. I learned forbidden arts in the port towns of the African coast and the Indies both East and West. Nowhere did I discover how to release them, but I did learn how to communicate with and protect the lost souls of the dead crew of the Reckless Kite.

I also imposed upon the crew to hire on some younger men, to aid the aging mariners in their endless questing. The plentiful gold they continued to bring from distant shores seemed an adequate inducement, but no Kingsporter would join their ill-regarded vessel. However, in other ports, less knowledgeable seamen were eager to join the crew.

Nevertheless, after those eight weary years, I had had my fill of the wide sea, and since I am not bound by the same curse that keeps the Reckless Kite upon the waves, I have settled in the Kingsport of that long-ago age that has now become my present. Having been seen in port with the crew at irregular intervals, I have been accepted by the Kingsporters as one of their own, though the reputation of the Reckless Kite seems to have clung to me.

I have my memories of the sea, as well as the gold and treasures that are the tangible reminders of the Reckless Kite's dreadful and unsatisfying good fortune. But none of that is as important as the realization of my long-unfulfilled desire: at last I truly belong to Kingsport, even if the townsfolk regard me as a constant reminder of one of Kingsport's more lamentable legends.

Despite the fact that I have largely forsaken the sea for a settled life in town, my kinship with the cursed and pitiable crew still remains. On the nights that mark that hideous anniversary, when they find themselves in the occluded waters of Kingsport, I am there, transported to that future time by some unknowable power. It is strange to think that I have walked the streets of Kingsport in four centuries.

To that accursed graveyard, I accompany him to whom the burden has fallen. I help him navigate the fog-shrouded streets as best I can, for I too have become an anachronism. Should he perform the ritual correctly, I wish him well and see him safely to the ship. Should he fail, I look to the care and comfort of his forsaken soul, cast loose by a demonic god to drift among the eternal mists of Kingsport.

KEVIN ROSS has written for the *Call of Cthulhu* roleplaying game for over 25 years, contributing to more than 40 books in that time. The Yellow Sign symbol he designed for the game has spread across the globe, adorning everything from book covers to clothing to album covers and tattoos. Outside of *Call of Cthulhu*, Ross has contributed stories and articles to *Made in Goatswood*, *The Anthology With No Name Volume One: A Fist Full o' Dead Guys*, *The Asylum Volume One: The Psycho Ward*, *The Dragon*, *The Unspeakable Oath*, *Crypt of Cthulhu*, and *Cinescape Online*. With the publication of this volume he has now edited two anthologies of Cthulhu Mythos fiction in the *Dead But Dreaming* series. If nothing else, his achievements in the fields of applied reclusiveness and advanced misanthropy are the stuff of legend.

Dark Heart

by Kevin Ross

Daniel Curry tried not to run. His father and Mr. Matthews had taught him to take his time when tracking, to study the depth of the tracks and the distance between them, the debris atop and within them, and so forth. All of these signs would tell the hunter much about the prey he sought. Daniel didn't need to be very careful in following the tracks of these creatures: there were four or five of them at least, and the only thing he needed to know about them was where they had taken his little brother.

Abel was a few months shy of eight years old, five years younger than Daniel. Daniel had all but raised Abel himself, since their mother had died bringing Abel into the world and their father had to devote his time to taking care of the cabin, the crops, hunting game, and in all other ways providing for the Currys' needs. Marcus Curry was a good man, but his wife's death left him with a grief that could only be quashed by hard labor on the farm.

So Daniel and Abel were virtually inseparable. Daniel cooked and cleaned for them, played with Abel, and even tutored him his ABCs and what little arithmetic he himself had learned. They hunted and fished along the small stream that fed into the Miskatonic, but always took care not to wander too far into the dark woodlands west of Arkham. Their neighbor, Mr. Matthews, had sometimes accompanied the boys on their expeditions, teaching them woodcraft and telling them stories of the Massachusett Indians that used to live in the region. Mr. Matthews was older than Daniel and Abel's father, and he had sons of his own to take care of his land, allowing him to fish and hunt for game for their larder. Some of the people of Arkham thought Mr. Matthews might have been part Indian himself, since he dressed in deerskin shirts and breeches like them, and was such a fine woodsman.

Daniel now wondered what Mr. Matthews would have done in his situation. He had awakened late, sometime after dawn. His father had already risen and gone into Arkham for some flour and tallow candles, and Daniel should have already been up himself, but he had overslept. Rubbing the sleep from his eyes, he saw that Abel's bed was empty, the quilt spilled onto the floor. Stepping onto the cold wooden floorboards, Daniel neither saw nor heard his brother in the little three-room cabin. He cracked open the door onto a bright but chilly fall morning, but Abel was nowhere to be seen in the farmyard. Daniel was not yet afraid, for Abel might have gone out to the barn or behind the cabin for some reason. He called out, received no reply, and called out again. No answer.

With Mr. Matthews' tales of savage red Indians racing through his brain, Daniel dressed quickly, then went to the cabinet where the family's guns were kept. He took down his own short-barrelled musket and snatched up a little powder horn and a pouch containing musket balls. He slung the horn around his neck and stuffed the pouch into a coat pocket, then cinched his hat around his chin and went out into the yard.

It took him a few minutes to find the strange footprints in the hard bare ground several yards from the cabin. Daniel was confused, however, for rather than the moccasined feet he expected to discover, these tracks were barefoot -- and small. If there hadn't been so many of them, he would have thought that Abel had been running around without his shoes on in the October chill. No, this was strange, nothing like the stories Mr. Matthews had told them while puffing on his clay pipe. Could the tracks be Indian children who had somehow taken his brother while the Curry boys slept? Perhaps some evil rite of passage they undertook to prove themselves to their bloodthirsty tribe?

Daniel shuddered and plunged on into the woods. The trail had led from the cabin around the hill into the nearest stand of trees, and within minutes Daniel found himself alone, surrounded by dense forest. It was eerily silent within the wood, with the trees standing tall around him, so thick that even though they had lost most of their leaves they still blocked out the morning sun. Daniel was alone in the dim twilight, the only sounds those of his own footsteps as he followed the barefoot tracks where they joined an old game trail leading deep into the woods.

The musket was heavy in his hands, but he was reassured by its weight. Daniel doubted the Indian boys would be so armed, and he hoped a single shot would scare them off. He didn't want to actually shoot any of them, but to save his brother he would do so. Once the musket was fired, he would have to use his hatchet if any of the Indians remained, since it would take time to reload the rifle. Still, it would be better to die this way than whatever the Indians had planned for Abel and his would-be rescuer. Daniel hoped his father and Mr. Matthews would be proud of his efforts, assuming they ever found out.

Several times Daniel was forced to slow his pace and kneel down to examine the game trail closely to make sure the Indians still followed it. Yes, there, along with the round pellets of rabbit droppings, the walnut husks left by squirrels, the long-fingered prints of raccoons, and the hooved prints of several deer of varying sizes, were the barefoot tracks he pursued into the ever-darkening forest.

Daniel's attentions were on the ground when his attackers sprang upon him. In the last instant he saw one of them dart from behind a tree ahead of him, not more than three yards distant. Even as he fired the musket from the hip, he knew another was leaping toward him from the side. The musket ball slammed into the first little man's belly, spinning him around and hurling him to the carpet of leaves on the forest floor. Then a thin, rough-fleshed arm circled Daniel's throat and two bony knees ground into his back, as the second of the lean little men pounced on him from the side. Daniel dropped the musket and twisted in the creature's grasp, suddenly finding himself face to pinched bestial face with yet another of the creatures as it rushed to grab him by the legs. Daniel jerked his hatchet from under his belt as soon as he dropped the musket, and he swung it back and forth in a clumsy arc to hold off the third attacker. The one gripping his neck, however, tightened its grasp, choking him and digging its ragged fingernails into his scalp.

Daniel couldn't shake the clinging creature loose with one hand, and the other thing, leering, danced away from the desperate swings of his hatchet. Daniel swayed on his feet, and the thing on his back, sensing his weakness, now sank its teeth into his shoulder. Daniel screamed, more from the horror of the act than the pain of it. He staggered, and now the other creature rushed forward and tried to grab Daniel's hatchet arm. Instead, Daniel drew the weapon away and slashed down at the thing's arm, connecting on the back of its wrist. It yelped and before it could back out of reach, Daniel quickly swung again. The steel blade caught the surprised creature where its left eye met the bridge of its nose, biting deeply into its face and wrenching the weapon from Daniel's grasp. The thing spun away, screaming as blood gushed from its ruined face, stumbling blindly into the brush.

Now Daniel grabbed the bony arm of the remaining creature and hurled it from around his neck. The snarling, hissing thing was on its feet in an instant, rushing back at him. Daniel kicked the little man in the knee, and as it staggered backward he grabbed up his empty musket. The creature froze, hurt and confused, uncertain what to do, and as it hesitated Daniel reversed the musket and crashed the stock into its face. Its feeble arms had raised to stop the blow to no avail, and it went down with broken fingers and a shattered cheekbone. Stunned, the thing tried to rise to its feet. Daniel raised the rifle butt and brought it down on the thing's face, again and again.

When he stopped beating on the creature, he stood panting, leaning on the musket. A few yards away, the one he had struck with the hatchet still feebly tried to crawl away. Having caught his breath, Daniel strode after it, bringing the butt down on its back with a sickening crack, then caving in the back of the now-motionless creature's skull.

Daniel again paused to catch his breath. Once again the forest was silent. Daniel quickly reloaded the musket, turning in a slow circle as he did so, looking out across the leaf-strewn forest floor in case more of the little men heard the fighting and came running. But no further threat showed, and once his gun was loaded and his hatchet retrieved, Daniel finally went to examine his strange attackers.

They were scarcely three feet tall -- shorter than Daniel. They were naked but for crude animal skins wrapped around their trunks and tied with leather or gut straps. Their hair was long, dark, and unkempt, clotted with twigs, leaves, and dirt. Their bodies were dirty, as if they never washed. But it was their now-ruined faces that alarmed him most of all. For while their size had suggested that they were children, their faces were lined and scarred, their teeth old and crooked, and their general countenances bespoke age and malice. These were not children, but miniature adults.

Daniel shuddered, looking at the little people, the shock wearing off that he had killed these things and a new dread creeping upon him when he realized just how alien and *other* they were. These were not Indians, nor anything else he had ever heard of, not in the stories his father told nor those of Mr. Matthews.

These were the creatures that had taken his brother.

The thought spurred Daniel on. He left the dead little men where they lay and set off down the trail. Now, at least, he knew what he faced. But how many? There didn't seem to be more than two or three of them left from the party that had taken Abel. And what did they want with his brother? Could they be some lost Indian tribe, with similar motives? Would they torture Abel? Enslave him? Sacrifice him? *Eat him?*

The afternoon grew old, and still Daniel Curry followed the trail. How many miles he had traveled into the dark woods west of Arkham he could not begin to guess. By now, he hoped, his father would have returned from the village to find the boys gone. Maybe even now his father was following the trail somewhere behind him. Or maybe Marcus Curry had gathered others to help search for Daniel and Abel. Maybe a search party was even now gaining on Daniel and his brother.

These hopes buoyed his spirits, but still he pressed on. Now the sun was in the west, and the forest darkened further. He hoped he would find Abel soon, since he had brought no lantern. If his search continued after dark, he would have to make a torch, or -- God forbid -- stop to make camp. He had brought no food, and the only water he had drank was from a small stream not far from the game path he followed.

The darkness had grown even deeper when the little people's tracks left the game trail and veered toward an even more thickly forested glen that descended before him. Daniel's glances darted all around him as he followed the tracks of the remaining abductors into the gloom. Cold sweat dribbled down his lower back, and his palms were slick on the musket.

Here in the glen, the trees were shorter, thicker, and stained with patches of grey moss and lichen, their bare black arms reaching toward the unseen sky as if in prayer. Still there was no sound in the silent woods. No bird songs, no squirrels foraging among the leaves. Just silent stillness.

The path leveled off among the trees, and ahead Daniel glimpsed a clearing. A great fallen oak was visible at the far end of the clearing, its barkless trunk shockingly white in the encroaching night. Daniel crept forward, and as the forest opened into the glade his heart soared. There, sitting on one end of the fallen oak, was Abel. The boy was barefoot, clad in his nightshirt in the evening chill, and seemed to be simply sitting, absently kicking his feet, as if waiting for something. Daniel paused before entering the glade, scanning the surrounding trees for signs of Abel's abductors, the strange, fierce little men, but he saw nothing. The musket clutched tightly in his hands, Daniel crept into the clearing.

"Abel!" he hissed.

The boy turned toward him and smiled. "Dan!"

"Abel, let's go, before they come back!" Daniel trotted toward his brother, the musket still held ready to fire.

"They're already back, Dan," Abel said casually. "We've been waiting."

Daniel stopped, still some yards from Abel. Now he noticed the squat dark tree stump off to one side of the clearing. It was old, perhaps the source of the fallen oak. But where the fallen trunk was bleached white as bone, the stump was black and stained, as if from some dark sap. The stains were crusted, black, brown, and red, and Daniel knew they were not made by any kind of tree sap. He started to edge away from the stump, and now from the surrounding trees he heard furtive movements. He tensed as he saw their shadowy silhouettes as they darted between the trees, the glint of their eyes in the dying light, their grimy hands as they clutched at tree trunks and crept into the clearing. He could see at least a dozen of them, and knew there were many more still in the forest. They moved slowly, cautiously, their slanted, squinting eyes fixed on him, their lips pulled back in silent menace. Abel hopped to his feet and stood among them.

"Abel--? What--?" stammered Daniel.

"We've been waiting for you to come," said the boy. "My friends needed my help, and I told them about you." Abel stepped forward, toward the bloodstained tree-stump. The little folk began to fan out, slowly edging into a circle around Daniel, who swung the barrel of the musket this way and that, vainly trying to cover them all.

"You see, this is their forest, Dan. And it's *old*. It's old and it's *alive*. It even has a heart. It beats even. You can't hear it though, no matter how hard you try. But the heart is old and sometimes it needs fresh blood to keep it beating."

"Abel, what are you talking about?" But Daniel already knew. He could see there was something wrong with his brother, something in his eyes, and the way he regarded the twisted little men. Daniel's hands gripped the musket tightly, and his eyes darted back and forth at the leering, misshapen creatures that surrounded him in the dark glade. His heart beat faster, the blood drumming in his ears.

Daniel Curry fired the musket without aiming, then quickly dropped it as his hand flew to the hatchet in his belt...

*   *   *

It was Mr. Matthews who found Daniel stumbling through the forest the next morning. Marcus Curry had searched for his sons most of the previous day without result, and he had desperately sought the help of his neighbors. There had been no sign of the boys that first day, but early the next day Mr. Matthews had set out before dawn, traveling several miles west of Arkham. He had followed Daniel's trail diligently, and eventually he came upon the boy himself.

Daniel was apparently unhurt, but dazed and unable to speak. His clothes were torn and stained with dirt and what appeared to be blood. Egon Matthews shook the boy repeatedly, but he could not bring him to his senses. Matthews took the unresponsive Daniel back to the Currys' cabin, calling out as he returned through the forest.

At the cabin, Daniel was cleaned up, and other than a few scratches and a bite mark on his shoulder, he wasn't injured. His father shook him, slapped him, and dashed water in his face, but Daniel merely blinked and stared, still mute. Where was Abel? Where have you been? What happened to you? If you were going out, why didn't you take a musket with you? Mr. Curry's flood of questions was answered only by Daniel's blank stare. Curry and his neighbors shook their heads sadly.

Mr. Matthews, meanwhile, returned to the forest. He followed the tracks left by Daniel and Abel as they wandered into the woods. He traveled quickly over familiar paths and game trails. He had traveled nearly ten miles into the wilderness when he found the boys' trail descended into a shadowy copse of trees at the bottom of three hills.

There he found Abel Curry's body.

Matthews carried the small lifeless form back through the silent woods. When he reached the Currys' cabin, he laid Abel on his small bed, watching grimly as the boy's father sank to his knees and wept over his dead son. Sitting on his own bed, Daniel still stared and said nothing.

Egon Matthews ushered Benson, one of Curry's neighbors, outside the cabin. He had followed the boys' trail into a secluded little glen, he said. The only tracks he had found were the two boys', and from the looks of it they had scuffled in a clearing in the glen. Then -- God help them -- as far as Matthews could tell, Daniel had brutally slain his brother with a hatchet, which Matthews had found there, still clotted with blood.

Benson shut his eyes. Yes, he said. Daniel was never right after Mrs. Curry's death giving birth to little Abel. The two men agreed that Daniel must have hated his brother for causing their mother's death. Daniel had always been imaginative, always eager to have Matthews regale him with tales of dangerous hunts and red Indians and heroic settlers. Always wandering off in the woods to who knows where. The men shook their heads, lit their pipes, and muttered to themselves. If Daniel recovered, they would have to take him to Arkham for trial, and he would surely hang. If he remained in his stupor, perhaps he would never hurt anyone again.

* * *

This time of year, deep in the forest west of the village of Arkham, the only sounds you are likely to hear are the rustling of fallen leaves and the wind rattling the branches of barren trees. But if you stand very still, if you close your eyes and concentrate, blocking out the leaves and the wind, you might hear a slow reverberation, a low pulse. Like the beating of an old heart, alive with new blood.

After spending over a decade working as a screenwriter in Hollywood, T.E. GRAU recently embarked on his long overdue sojourn into speculative and weird fiction, dark fantasy, and cosmic horror. He currently resides under the shadow of a leering palm tree in Los Angeles, with his wife, daughter, and bunny named Cthulhu. He counts skepticism, imbibing fermented grapes, and misanthropy as hobbies. *Dead But Dreaming 2* marks his first anthology publication. T.E. Grau's random scribblings can often be found at *The Cosmicomicon* (cosmicomicon. blogspot.com).

Transmission

by T.E. Grau

Even this far out, away from the light and the bilge and the clamor and the droning nouveau bullshit lounge music rasping from a purposely old LP, things were still sort of a blur. The same blurry party with the same blurry people with annoying hipster headgear and piercings and tattoos and ironic t-shirts and uniformly blurry faces. The off-brand bottle of cut-rate blurry liquor in his hand. The blurry, slurry skank pressing in too close that he had seen before but never recognized. The shouting. The broken furniture. The fight. The blood. The various faux ghetto insults hurled his way as he ran out of the blurry room in the blurry house on a blurry street in a forgotten Midwestern city. A blur. All of it.

Max scratched at the crusted-over gash on the side of his face and concentrated on the shrouded pavement ahead of him, trying to clear the blur from his mind as he drove west, ever west, in an effort to outrace the smudge of his past. This was it, he felt. A wagon train of one, fueled by a last hope for blessed clarity waiting amongst the swaying palms of the Pacific coast. Failing that, he'd drive off the goddamn end of the continent and drown in the uncaring murk of the darkened deep.

Max blinked his eyes and lit up a cigarette, focusing on the cheap plastic compass he picked up at a dingy truck stop in Salt Creek, Nebraska, stuck lopsided to the cracked dash of his shitty late model Dodge. West, the tottering arrow assured him. West. He was still heading in the right direction. At last that much was certain.

Max knew that he stayed too long at his last stop, but he had gotten lazy, figuring roots would sprout from the bottoms of his shoes if he just loitered in the same place long enough. But the roots never came. Only rot. And that's when he knew he had to get out. That night. That second. By whatever means necessary.

And so he did.

It made no difference that he had a belly full of poison and eighty-seven dollars to his name. He just knew it was time. And so it was.

And so he went.

Max would keep moving this time, for as far as his shitty late model Dodge would take him. He was pretty sure he had hurt some people pretty badly, maybe even fatally, during his abrupt, violent exit from the blur two nights ago, so going back from whence he came wasn't an option at this point. He just had to keep his head down and keep grinding forward, in the vain hope of finding his unrevealed destiny out in the mythic west, as so many intrepid souls had done before him. A bit of true reality discovered amongst the fairy tales. He'd change his name, maybe stop shaving and take up surfing. But most importantly, at least in the short term, he would lose himself in the crowded anonymity of the city of fallen angels, where everyone is too busy looking at themselves to spot the disheveled fugitive sitting across the bar.

Max's erratic wanderlust was almost congenital, born out of an unsettled soul and dissatisfaction with nearly everything around him. Because of this, he became a human tumbleweed from the first time he learned how to thumb a ride, spinning from city to hamlet to dusty campsite, in search of something bigger than himself to tie him down and make him WANT to stay, to become something outside of himself. Some people looked for God. Some looked for love. Max just looked for MEANING, for him and all of us and all of IT. All of everything that was and would someday be. There had to be a point – a greater purpose - to all of this terribly self-important nonsense, and the answer had to be out there somewhere, around the next bend, over the next rise in the road...

But he never found it. He just found more of the same. He just found more blur.

So here he was, knifing down Highway 50 west of McGill, Nevada, as the last two days and nights – hell, the last 32 years – melted into just another portion of an unbroken line of bleary days and blurry nights spent doing nothing with a thousand nameless nobodies, all bored to panicked tears hidden behind stiff masks of sardonic smiles.

Somehow Max had gotten off I-80, that great tentacle of government-issue cement that stretched the length of this vast, savage land. But it didn't matter. His cheap plastic compass assured him that he was heading west, and that was good enough for Max. At least that much was certain.

Exhaling a small nimbus cloud of smoke into the windshield, Max sat back, and for the first time in what felt like forever, he relaxed, and opened the window, allowing the cool dry air to clean out the car. The blur finally began to recede, which finally allowed him a smile. He was moving again, and the road behind him was growing. He was carving a proud wound into the hide of the central Nevada desert, and no one could tell him to do otherwise. Max had finally found his footing again, and felt his rhythm return as the highway danced beneath the floorboards.

Settling back into his nearly forgotten routine of forward motion, Max turned on the radio, switching immediately from the damning FM presets of his last stop to the strange, innocent anonymity of AM.

A veteran of the road, Max loved to scan the AM dial when moving through the most remote, desolate areas of the country. AM radio in major cities is the home of blustery right wing shitsuckers and Madison Avenue country pop. But out in the forgotten hinterlands, especially in the desert southwest, it was a mesmerizing mixed bag of yammering Spanish, mournful cowboy crooning, thunderous Evangelical sermons, and that rare treat – the UFO nuts who always seemed to concentrate in the dried out, forgotten places, using the AM airwaves to rant and warn the deafened masses about the dangerous, reptilian "others" who were already moving amongst us. The desert seemed strangely suited to the curious lot of castoffs, eccentrics, weirdos, and criminals that were drawn to the dusty fringes. Meth cooks, anti-government militias, New Agey art nuts, murder cultists… All headed to the sandy heat like Jesus himself, looking to face down their demons, or possibly create them, away from the prying eyes of the better irrigated. Owing to the circumstances surrounding his exit from his last stopover, maybe Max should join these sun blasted freaks, but something else was out there for him, that extended far beyond the arid wasteland. At least that much was certain.

Max pressed "scan," and skimmed over an offering of MexiCali accordion music and a low rent advert for industrial shedding, finally arriving on what he loved the most – the Born Againer martyrdom rant against the encroaching forces of the nebulous but ever present AntiChrist. No matter what latitude or longitude traveled, Max could find cold comfort in the certainty of religious zealotry flooding the AM airwaves in the forgotten places of North America.

"And so the days of the tribulation are nigh, my brothers and sisters!" roared the firebrand, buzzing Max's tiny speakers. "And ye shall hear of wars and rumors of wars: see that ye be not troubled: for all these things must come to pass, but the end is not yet. For nation shall rise against nation, and kingdom against kingdom: and there shall be famines, and pestilences, and earthquakes, in diverse places. All these are the beginning of sorrows!"

The signal faded a bit, but came back in strong after a few seconds, allowing Max to continue his front row seat to the bloody, self-righteous theatre. "The signs are everywhere, if one knows how to look with the eyes of Jesus and the mind of God! The return of the Chosen Ones to their ancient land, the gathering of crows, the massing of armies… It's all in the Word, and the Word shall come to pass!" Hoots and hollers from the unseen audience gave credibility to these ravings that would be deemed insanity in the western world if spewed under a different banner.

The WORD. Max chuckled and lit up another cigarette, shaking his head at the dead set certainty of the Evangelical blowhard. How can one be so certain of ANYTHING? If we were a country settled by Bronze Age Norsemen and founded on the teachings of Odin and his hammer-wielding sprat, we'd have a totally different outlook on the afterlife, and pine for blood-soaked laurels while ascending to the Halls of Valhalla after a good death on the field of battle. But no, we get the longhaired peacenik from Galilee, who Max surmised was more dope smoking flower child than patriotic capitalist.

Unfortunately, after a few minutes, the signal from the Born Againer station faded, as expected. Max sighed, and pressed scan again, starting the lottery anew.

Outside his bug-dotted windshield, the sign for "Fallon, NV – 30 miles" whizzed past. Max paid it glancing heed, only concerned with how far he was from the Pacific, where his future would be made or broken on the chewed coastline of California. He just needed to get through the desert, and he'd be fine. The answers would be waiting for him at the water's edge. They had to be.

As the radio scan continued to cycle through dead air, Max looked out into the night around him. The range of his headlights hinted at untold stretches of dried out nothingness, populated by scrub brush, creosote, and most likely a fair share of bleached bones of varying size and species. This was broken by the occasional odd, squatty house, set far back from the highway, as if the structure itself was trying to run from civilization and - reaching the end of its tether - collapsed glumly onto the dusty ground in defeat. Max could never figure out why anyone or anything with viable options would choose to live in such a forsaken environment. No appreciable water, daytime heat that could kill a man, and a misanthropic landscape entirely populated by flora and fauna that is either poisonous or covered in menacing thorns, or both – a brutal ecosystem crafted with an eye on repelling or killing any non-native species that was stupid enough to wander into the neighborhood. And yet, people came in droves to dry places such as these, pumped in borrowed water, set up artificial air conditioning, and hunkered down inside their suburban pillboxes, waiting out each day as if they lost a bet.

The radio finally found faint electronic life and stopped on a fuzzy station espousing the tourist attractions of the area. "--orthern Nevada, some of the most accessible examples of these mysterious petroglyphs can be found at Grimes Point, about 12 miles east of Fallon on Highway--" And just like that, the signal was gone again. Scan...

Max was pondering the important issue of how petroglyphs differed from hieroglyphs when the radio stopped again at the very far end of the electronic dial. After a brief silence, the weak signal transmitted sounds indistinct and indecipherable, like whispers, intermingled with an odd, guttural chanting that moved in and out like a spectral dirge. Intrigued, and hoping for a broadcast of lonely Indian Pow Wow, Max turned up the volume, but the higher it went, the softer the voice and chanting became, finally going silent. There was no apparent signal, but the radio scan was still stopped, locked in on something.

Perplexed, Max noticed that the compass on his dash began to twist and oscillate, even though the road ahead was straight as an arrow.

Just then, booming, otherworldly intonations blasted from the speakers, startling Max, who looked down to adjust the volume, barely noticing the large, brownish, misshapen… *thing* that lurched onto the highway ahead of him just out of the range of his headlights, gripping something in its massive paws. Max unconsciously mashed the brakes while cranking the wheel away from the creature, which dragged a half eaten mule deer up the rocky embankment, as the Dodge swerved wildly by, skidding onto the shoulder and burying the front grill into the opposite hillside as the radio went silent again.

In the heavy quiet, the car engine skuddered and pitched under the slightly crumpled hood, then wheezed to a jerky stop. Max, breathing hard, glanced wide-eyed at the compass. It was spinning like a top inside the plastic housing. Was this from the crash? But, the car wasn't moving, and probably wouldn't be anytime soon. The radio too was cycling through dead air. And what was that huge fucking thing that ran across the road?

Max sat frozen and blinked his eyes that were obviously playing tricks on him after too many hours on the road. Was that a desert inbred? Some sort of mutated bear who wandered too close to Nevada nuclear test sites? Max was unnerved, and felt as if the car was closing in around him, like a tin can prison. Clearing his head, he locked the doors, not sure if what was out there was worse than what he heard inside, as what most terrified him was that the radio would once again find that horrible, baritone chanting, like an arcane incantation that seemed to echo from somewhere vast, foul and impossibly deep. He reached out hesitantly to turn off the radio, when it again stopped on the far end of the dial, but this time, he heard… weeping… The strange, uncomfortable sound of a man crying, as if deeply grieved by the already occurred. Or the knowledge of that which is unfortunately inevitable. This stayed Max's hand, before the sobbing turned to sudden, spastic, tittering laughter. What was this? Max was incredulous, then just pissed. What sort of psychotic local pirate station owner or ham radio operator was pranking over the air, scaring the shit out of those who scanned the far end of the dial? This fucker owed Max a new, shitty, late model Dodge. Or at least a ride to the coast.

The laughter suddenly stopped, and in the silence, the radio mic picked up sounds of papers being shuffled, and tapes being stacked… Then, a hollow, flat voice that sounded oddly far away began to speak, occasionally quivering, at which time the speaker would stop and collect himself before continuing: "You can hear everything in the desert," the voice began, then went silent. "You got that right," Max chimed in with irritation to no one but the unhearing voice at the other end of the radio transmission, which came to life again: "The buzzing of insects, the hooting of owls, the mad yap of the coyotes... But sometimes, those sounds fall away, and one can hear, can SENSE, the softer, more terrible noises that lurk underneath the normal nighttime din..." The voice paused, and then continued: "The desert whispers to me, telling me things I never knew existed, never dared dream, giving up primordial secrets from within and beyond... I record these secrets, as I have been tasked, and broadcast them when I can. But the recording is the key, and I have been diligent, as were those who came before me."

Outside, dry lightening carved the sky, highlighting clouds that looked like seething shapes forming in the sky above. "If you could rewrite the Bible, directly from the source, would you sacrifice your life to do it?"

Another loony toon religious whack job, Max thought, trying to chuckle to himself in spite of a nagging fear that began to tug at him. He quickly turned the key and tried to give life to a halting ignition, glancing furtively out into the darkness. He was still shaken by the crash, and nervous that he might be stranded out on this forgotten ribbon of highway with this obviously insane misanthrope with excellent hearing and whatever loped up into the hills.

After much protesting and cajoling from Max, the battered engine sputtered to life. He backed out from the embankment and out onto the highway, jammed the car into drive, and drove wobbly on in the same direction he was going, the voice droning on, with Max trying not to listen. The compass still spun like a mindless dervish, so it was no good to him. But Max knew where he was going. West. Ever west. He had to leave this weird fucking place behind.

As he drove on, the radio signal got stronger, and Max found himself listening more intently in spite of himself, increasingly fascinated by this obviously deranged individual who somehow attained access to the radio airwaves. It was like an auditory train wreck, the ultimate metaphysical reality show, and Max couldn't turn his ears away, or move himself to turn off the radio. "It's late in my mission, and nearly time for me to move on. I'm waiting for my replacement so the work and the message can continue. They tell me that the time of the awakening is at hand, and as such, the preparations have become more urgent than ever before."

The signal started to fade, and so Max slowed. He was now fully fascinated by this mournful monologue, and felt somehow compelled to keep listening, as if guided by a gentle outside force. Nearly losing the signal all together, Max stopped the car in the middle of the empty highway, dropped into reverse, and trundled backwards in the darkness cut open by his white reverse lamps, until the signal increased in strength again. He stopped and idled, leaning forward, as if to better connect with this lone voice in the darkness.

"The desert tells me to do this, and I do as I'm told, because you never, ever argue with the desert." The voice giggled again, this time with more mirth, but it ended with a terrified edge, as before. "So, now I whisper to you, speaking for the desert, speaking for those behind the desert, and speaking for myself, as my time here has lately become short."

The car engine shuttered, seized, and expired. Max didn't even notice.

"There is beauty and horror here, wisdom and madness, and I have drank deeply of it all. Will you do the same?" The voice went silent. Lightening licked the sky. Max, again feeling the car close in around him, began to wonder if this was just a one-way conversation. "Will you?" the voice asked again. "Me?" Max answered. "You," the voice continued, as if in confirmation. "Will you do the same?" The signal wavered and buzzed, then faded into fuzz again.

Max flung open his door and got out of the car. Rushing to the smashed hood, he pushed against the cracked grill with all of his might, and pushed the car backwards, gaining momentum as he labored. As it picked up speed, Max ran to the open car door and jumped inside, breathing hard as he turned up the volume. Finally, the signal came back in, and Max quickly veered the car off the road into the gravelly shoulder, then sat behind the wheel and listened.

"--slicing open the forbidden fruit forever, as knowledge is not evil, it is the natural progression of humanity, and a realization of what we were placed here to do by the creators. I and others in the service of the truth are just another signpost, another step forward in the awakened dream... The work is the most important thing that humanity is doing right now on this planet, battling the old war against those who call madness those things they dare not understand..." The radio strength dipped, and Max was about to hop out and reposition his car yet again, when it resumed.

"My time with the work is almost complete, as my vessel has been filled to the cracking point... I now wait for another... One who has been promised, who will come to pick up the transcription while I move on...." More fuzzy static, until: "The work isn't about good or evil, as good and evil do not exist. Only order and chaos. Only light and dark. Only knowledge and ignorance... Out of these primal forces spring everything we know. And I now know MUCH of what is out there, and sometimes wish I didn't, as in its transcendent power, it has ended me for this sphere... My brain has heard too many whispers, dreamed too many times beyond the First Gate, has seen too much revealed... and now aches for an eternal rest, to exhale after a decade-long upload. I seek the silence of the teeming abyss; to rest, and to dream, as has been promised... The veil has been lifted and the bliss of ignorance has been shattered forever, and so now I sit in a state of unsettled wisdom, blinking my watery eyes as if I have looked too long at the sun... The unimagined beauty... The indescribable horror... The unimagined beauty of the indescribable horror..." The voice trailed off in clenched awe, then took a deep, shaky breath. "Who out there will take my place? Who dares peek behind the veil, to see the truth in all its many splendors and terribly endless vistas? Who will listen to the whispers when I am gone?"

Max sat in his car, mesmerized by this voice, hanging on every quaver and sigh. This man was obviously bat shit crazy, but in his insanity, there was a powerful knowing certainty about topics and realities that Max could scarcely imagine.

"The work MUST go on, as the truth MUST be told," the voice continued, finding strength once more. "We weren't created to live as ignorant insects our entire existence, putting around with our heads down in the terrarium of our own making. The lost knowledge handed down from Beyond must be brought back, maintained, and again disseminated across our land, if we are ever to rise to the dancing dimensional heights we once knew as a young Arcadian civilization, buoyed by the magic of sacred geometry, cosmology, and outer technology, that was brought down and hidden in the mud by not just natural disaster, but more so by rank superstition of the falsely chosen elect, steeped in the bureaucratic fear of an enlightened human race. We are now taught to fear the forbidden fruit, and are lesser for it..." The voice trailed off with a zig-zagging reverberation, as if impacted by an outside power source, before returning again. "... For I speak of Gods and Monsters, creation and destruction, the birth of stars and those things living inside them... I speak of the Truth of Truths, of the way and wherefores of all realities discovered by those cosmic entities who whisper secrets to those who refuse to live their lives deaf, dumb, and blind. I speak of transcendence, liberation, and terrible paradise... And now, I await my replacement so the work and the message can continue. The Book was stolen from us, the Knowledge ripped from our minds, so it is up to us to rebuild The Book, and relearn the Knowledge... They tell me that the time of the awakening is at hand, and as such, the preparations have become more urgent than ever before--"

F₂₂₂Pop! And with that, the battery, the last life force of Max's shitty late model Dodge, blinked and died.

Max sat behind the wheel, scarcely able to breath, scarcely able to believe what he was hearing, as his eyes rimmed with tears. It was as if a balloon popped inside his brain, leaving behind nothing but an uncluttered view of his destiny of meaning. He felt reborn, and he felt a hunger he never knew existed... No longer was he worried about reaching the coast. All he knew now was that he HAD to keep listening to this transmission, at whatever cost... The weak, oscillating signal meant that the tower - and most likely the speaker - was close. Max scrambled out of his car, intent on finding this voice and learning more. This broken, impossibly enlightened man knew something, BELIEVED in something with every fiber of his tortured being, and Max had to figure out why.

Max ran up the road, and soon discovered a weed-choked access road that lead off from the highway and up into the semi-tamed wilds of the Nevada desert. Max's gaze followed what he surmised was the direction of the road up into the hill country, where he noticed a small red light floating in the higher elevations, like a disembodied eye keeping watch over the weird sand below.

Max looked back at his car, threw his keys into the darkness, and set out for the guiding red light that lurked somewhere out there, waiting for him.

As boney fingers of lightening crackled above him, strobe-lighting the ominously shaped clouds, Max walked quickly below, his path between lightning flashes barely illuminated by a gibbous moon, hanging low and sallow over the ring of mountains gnawing the sky like the craggy molars of a monstrous exposed jawbone. His shoes crunched over the volcanic gravel, pushing out the noises of the desert that the quivering, hollow voice described. The hovering red light was getting closer, and so Max moved onward, continuing his tumbleweed journey by rootless foot.

After nearly an hour, Max spied a stand of trees that seemed to coalesce out of the darkness on a ridge slightly above. As he neared, he could finally make out a dilapidated shack squatting amid the timber, blasted ghostly white by decades, or maybe centuries, of enduring the spite of the brutal Nevada sun, which seemed extra angry with this part of the world. Every hundred yards or so, a rough hewn stone monolith of greenish gray stone - which didn't seem to originate from the surrounding hills, or anywhere, really - stood sentry, forming a wide, easy-to-miss circle around the circumference of the ridge.

Unknowingly passing through the loose knit ring of stone, Max quickened his pace and approached the old shanty, which was built on a frame of crumbling adobe, like those found in the ruins of the cliff-face domiciles constructed by the brutal, mysteriously vanished Anasazi that Max had explored several years back while tumbling through New Mexico. On top of this ancient clay foundation, random building materials were haphazardly pasted and lashed, to keep out the wind and sun and sporadic bouts of angry downpours that sought to wash away those godless things that made their home in the desert.

Max walked to the front door, and listened. The faint, hollow voice that was now so familiar could be heard inside. Emboldened, Max tried the door, and found it unlocked. He opened it and pushed inward. As the door creaked on protesting hinges, Max steeled his resolve at his unannounced intrusion, and walked inside.

The small outer room was lit by several hanging, naked light bulbs, buzzing with flies and beetles, which cast harsh shadows on stacks of moldering newsprint, boxes of moth-eaten clothes, and various detritus that one would normally associate with a bunker existence. The voice was coming from a back room, sectioned off by a ratty curtain. Max walked through the maze of refuse and pushed back the curtain, terrified and thrilled in equal measure to finally meet the owner of the voice that had brought him from the known road into the weird wilderness.

But Max found no one beyond the curtain. Instead, he discovered a cramped yet deserted room hemmed in by high racks of notebooks and journals, facing a corner stacked with a precariously arranged amalgam of new and surprisingly old radio equipment surrounding a makeshift broadcast booth. Analog modulators, reel-to-reel players, a turntable, magnetic cassette docks, CD ports, and a laptop, all wired together in the same haphazard fashion as the shack itself. A DIY broadcast station carved out of overstuffed shelving and countless stacks of yellowing paper.

The chair behind the microphone was empty. A digital recording was playing, continuing a pre-recorded monologue transmitted out into the desert night, into Max's car, into countless other cars, and homes, and minds. "And so," the recorded voice continued. "The work must go on, even here, at this broadcast station at Grimes Point, built here because here has always been, and shall ever remain, a doorway to what the Early Ones called Star Nation before moving on, what we call The Outer Places, and the Realm of the Elders, where all is nothing and nothing is all in this dance of divine illusion..."

As the voice continued, Max explored the room, picking through the reams and reams of notebooks and folders, blowing off the red dust that was thickly settled everywhere, and reading a few lines of arcane and wildly advanced learning, mind-bending formulas, non-Euclidean calculus, quantum physics, interlaced with blurbs of history and a shocking understanding of the universe and inter-dimensional travel. Max moved to the broadcast table where lay an open journal. Paging through it, he discovered bizarrely grouped information assembled into monologues, written out in a sort of movie script format, similar to the ones heard on the radio, similar to the one the voice was relaying at the moment, with which Max followed along: "Upon receiving my assignment and arriving here, I spent some time alone among the rocks and discovered the promised doorway that I shall soon revisit for the final time..."

Max shuffled through the notebooks and tapes around him, noticing dates that went back, far back, several hundred years. This was not just a broadcast booth, Max realized, but a library - a repository of arcane and antiquated knowledge off the scale of normal human imagination.

Stunned by the implications of what loomed around him, Max then noticed a line of several dozen framed photographs on the wall, of different people manning the microphone, moving back through the ages, from color pictures, to black and white, to muddy sepia tone. Two dozen men and women of varying ages, races, and obvious social standing, all sitting in the same pose in front of the same microphone with the same grim expression and slightly unbalanced gleam in their eyes.

The most recent speaker went on, as he moved in closer and squinted at the last photo to the right, showing a man not much older than him, staring haughtily into the camera of an unknown photographer, the instruments of transmission glowing behind him. "I felt as though I had passed into a pin hole in realty, outside linear time and into the seething void... Grimes Point is a wrinkle in the fabric of this brittle plane, a carefully plotted and placed dimensional distortion allowing access to and from the Place of the Beginning, and the measureless vistas of the Continuing Chaos; a place forgotten or shunned through the course of human history. But a place that was also sought, by those Seekers who heed not The Fear... This is just one outpost, numbered six, and is one of many, where others like me continue the work to rebuild that which was stolen from us, a primal birthright ripped from understanding and our molecular memory. They took from us our Book, our Knowledge, but we will rebuild it, and again teach the Truth, through the written word, through the electronic ether, through the radio waves... We seek to swing the wrong back to right, through darkness and light, and ready the awaiting flock..."

The fly-spattered light bulbs flickered, and Max looked up, noticing mind bending lines and curves etched into the ceiling, surrounding what appeared to be several intricate, overlapping star maps. But, the maps didn't feature any of the known constellations, or none with which Max was familiar.

"I speak of what was whispered to me, through the sounds of the desert, of elder mathematics which is the language of all creation, the root and the key of what we know as eldritch magic. That which sank R'yleh, raised Atlantis, and built the sacred pyramids and other abandoned monuments to the Outer Gods across our crowded sphere..."

Max sank slowly into the rickety broadcast chair and gazed wide eyed around the room, as if a sudden realization clicked in his head, giving confirmation to something he had always surmised, but didn't dare believe, and rarely dared dream... Max's eyes bulged as he listened with every fiber of his being, taking in the words as the voice went on to tell of the Outer Gods, who will come and take away those who know how to ask. About how he and others throughout history and prehistory and the dawn of sentient life were mere chroniclers of these impossibly old entities and their exploits, from drawings in the primordial clay, to paintings in caves, to those driven mad finally compiling the Dread Book, to now - transmitting the stories and knowledge throughout the atmosphere, into the charged particles of our finite space. All the same. All working in the same service. Those who chronicle and spread these revealed truths are members of the enlightened few, and are assured a place of exaltation beyond the stars, spared the coming reclamation of this tiny blue rock by the errant overseers who have seeded all of the living worlds in the infinite dimensions of their influence. The workers at Outpost Six at Grimes Point are the newest members of these few, collecting information imparted in purposely small, disassociated segments to keep the recorder sane for as long as humanly possible. These are the Further Writers of the Book of Knowledge, continuing The Work of Alhazred, von Junzt, The Scribe of Eibon... Mason, Curwen, Carter, and Ward... These and we are the chroniclers of the Higher Wisdoms to prepare the earth for the promised Coming and the Transformation, when the Old Masters return home to check on their children. An enlightened assemblage needs to host and hail the Old Masters, when They come back to check on their forgotten petri dish in a far flung corner of nowhere... "This is what the desert told me," the voice continued, "And what I and others have recorded for decades, centuries, eons, before our poorly made vessels became too full and started to crack..."

Sitting in the chair with his eyes staring straight ahead while his mind began to venture several dimensions away, Max didn't see the bathroom just off the broadcast room, where hastily shaved body hair and a bloody razor clogged the sink. Max didn't see the trail of blood that led out the splintered back door, over the dusty yard, past the unnatural mounds and monoliths surrounding the property, and into the sand of the endless desert. Max didn't see the speaker of the voice, just hours before his arrival, standing on the brink of Grimes Point, and flinging himself down onto the curiously arranged rocks below. Max also didn't see the body of the man disappear into the void before it hit the craggy bottom, warping away to a swirling, unnamable infinitum of places unknowable, where he would join the roiling mass of omnipotent chaos that probed for a way back into our tiny plane of existence, settling in the meantime for psychic missives sent from the Beyond, transmitted to our time, place, and space in hopes of teaching one of us the correct formula to open up the dimensional gaps dotting our universe just wide enough for something substantial to come through, to return to a place unvisited in a billion years, but never, ever forgotten.

Max didn't see these things, for he was sitting at the microphone - his station at Outpost Six - taking in The Words in preparation for continuing The Work. The voice in the darkness had sliced open the forbidden fruit and offered a taste to Max. He took a reluctant bite, and was now changed forever - a doomed man enslaved by this terrible growing wisdom, joining all those curious souls who had been drawn to this place before him.

"So," the speaker in the picture, the speaker who dove into Grimes Point and into the boundless, structured abyss just hours earlier, concluded in his strange, hollow voice: "I leave this sacred burden to you who have found your way to this humble temple of the Outer Gods, the true gods of this universe and many others, who have revealed themselves to those who were forced to forget... They are There, and They are waiting, watching, and whispering... Tend to your task with seriousness, and be mindful in your work, for the birth and destruction of all we know demands rigorous attention and strict vigilance..." The speaker's voice began to give, but he mustered enough strength to continue, if only to breathlessly croak: "Fare thee well... and worry not... for understanding beyond measure is nigh!... A replacement draws forth, even now!... Signing off... and bid this forgotten place goodbye... knowing that you are already here... and the cycle... continues..."

The voice gave out and the transmission ended.

In the dead silence of the tiny shack, the noises of the desert began to creep in, as well as those softer, more terrible noises that lurk underneath the normal nighttime din.

And Max was listening.

An insidious menace to sanity and decency, JOHN GOODRICH lives in the haunted Green Mountains of Vermont, the last refuge of true Lovecraft country. He has published several Cthulhu Mythos stories, all of which reflect some aspect of his unsavory life-style. When not reading or writing, he is in school looking to enter the medical profession. Think about that next time your doctor orders a test.

N Is For Neville

by John Goodrich

"Thank *Christ* Simon kept the goth crowd out. Whenever they show up, everything's just a *disaster*." Lise Endicott dangled a champagne flute from her hand. "They're all so irredeemably dull; not one of them knows any language but English, most of them wouldn't know the *Malleus Maleficarum*, let alone a truly esoteric work. And the sex..." Her gesture toward the heavens was plaintive. "No time for romance or seduction. Just a mopey hello, their Myspace page, and then they're naked and needy."

Neville pursed his lips, gazing at her tantalizing low-cut bodice. The rich red brocade perfectly complemented her chocolate coloring. But madness lay that way. In bed, Lise gave more directions than his car's GPS. And in about the same flat tone. With clothing to separate them, he liked her company. She knew books, even if she didn't share his passion for them.

Simon Townsend's occult parties cut across all social strata. Not six feet from Neville, a wealthy dealer in illegal antiquities, dressed in flowing silver and grey silk, was deep in conversation with a greasy-haired street-corner prophet who smelled like a dumpster. Beyond them, laughter erupted from a conversational knot as a local scribbler of horror tales, well-known for his home-made Bishop's mitre adorned with a picture of Barbara Streisand, held court. The same crowd which had been attending for years, and the same tired conversations.

Neville did not believe in any god or divine power, but he longed to find something beyond mere humanity, some evidence of existence after death. He did not think he would find it in these nouveau religions with their sixties-holdover hallucinogens and shabby rockstar showmanship. Answers would come from authentic ritual, with roots that went back centuries or millennia. Simon felt the same way; old and forbidden ceremonies from the dark corners of the earth were the centerpieces of these parties.

Neville scanned the room with dispirited gloom. Aside from Lise, no one interesting was here. Then he brightened.

"Who did you come with?" he breathed.

"I haven't seen any new or interesting faces. Who are you talking about?" Lise asked.

"He's dark. Dark and gorgeous, wearing a white silk shirt, black jeans, and demi-boots with silver buckles."

"Sounds delicious. Point him out." Lise looked in the direction of Neville's gaze.

"Standing near Jane."

"Jane Waite, the slut overflowing her corset?"

Jane displayed her expensively-sculpted breasts like a jeweller's best diamonds. She would use them to attract the lowest life-forms she could, preferring ex-cons, morgue assistants, and child molesters. After a rushed, sticky assignation in a dark corner, she would go home and tell her husband all about her evening.

"His head is shaved. He's wearing tight black jeans, with a bulge that is either wool socks or proof that God plays favorites." Neville could feel the week's listlessness falling away. Of course, the gorgeous man would open his mouth and ruin everything by being inane. But Neville would savor impossible hope until then.

"Who is he talking to?"

"Nobody. He looks like he's waiting. Right now, he's the only person not laughing at whatever Jane just said."

Lise craned her neck.

"I can't see anything delicious in Jane's circle. Why don't you engage this lollipop, so I can see him up close?"

Neville threaded through the crowd while Lise went in search of more champagne. Neville appreciated her patience. She didn't have to snatch at a piece of candy the instant she saw it.

The good-looking stranger was still on the fringes of Jane's conversational circle. She was laughing over a cutting remark at the expense of a former lover, her court echoing her. All except the stranger.

"Good evening," Neville said with all the charm he could muster.

"Good evening," the dark man echoed. Was there a hint of surprise in those lustrous mahogany features? His voice was rich, with a hint of gravel. His eyes were so dark that Neville couldn't tell where the pupil began and iris ended. He stopped searching before it became staring.

"Neville Bicknell Winthrop, at your service."

"I would introduce myself, but our host is eager to do so later this evening. I see that you are a great reader, Neville."

"Well, yes. I own more than twenty thousand volumes, many of them rare. I couldn't live without books."

"You've read Ludovicus Prinneaus' *De Vermis Mysteriis*." The stranger showed pearly white teeth. Neville tried not to quaver. The gorgeous man knew incunabula.

"I own a copy. The hideously dull 1490 Blackletter edition, printed in Düsseldorf. Very rare and expensive. Blasphemy did not make for a lasting legacy until the twentieth century." The pride of Neville's collection was locked safe and untouchable by all but himself in a temperature and humidity-controlled vault, away from unappreciative eyes and unwashed hands.

Neville saw Lise approaching. He clenched, afraid that she would ruin the fragile intimacy he and the dark man had built. When she was close enough to be included in their conversation, she stopped. The feared torrent of words and attention-whoring never came. The stranger didn't say anything either. He spared Lise a momentary glance, then turned those dark, bewitching eyes back to Neville.

"I have leads on a few related volumes, if rare and esoteric books interest you." Neville would tell any silly, stupid lie to get this man into bed. He ached with need. "A collector in Beirut is selling a copy of Antoine-Marie Augustin de Montmorency-les-Roches, le Comte d'Erlette's infamous *Les Cultes des Goules*. And I've heard that a copy of Friedrich-Wilhelm von Junzt's *Die Unaussprechlichen Kulten* was recently sold at an invitation-only Hong Kong auction. Rumors say the purchaser was from New York." The last at least was true.

Again a flash of white teeth, this time a predatory snarl. Neville took a step back and glanced over at Lise. She stood, drink in hand, a blank expression on her face.

"She can't see me," the stranger offered. "No one can but you. Because they haven't read what you have."

Neville waved his hand in front of Lise's face, but she didn't react. She was breathing, but she didn't respond. When he turned back to ask what was going on, the dark man was gone. Neville's heart sank. It had been some time since he had been dismissed so abruptly. Had he come on too strong?

He turned to Lise and discovered a sly smile on her face. "When do we find this tasty newcomer of yours? I'm dying for some variety——"

She stopped when she saw Neville's dumbfounded expression.

"And I'm guessing that you can't find him either."

He caught her by the shoulders. "What just happened?"

"Are you having a flashback? You're not your usual intelligible self." She shook his hands off.

"Tell me about the last five minutes."

"You said you saw someone yummy over here. You walked over, I followed discreetly. When I got here, you flaked out and asked me what just happened."

Neville was silent, searching his memory. How could she have missed the handsome stranger? She had stared at him for more than two minutes. He looked in the direction the man had gone, but couldn't find him in the shifting mass of people.

He had seen the man. Spoken with him. He could not have imagined the vivid impression, the hint of musk that the dark stranger had left in his wake. So what had happened to Lise? She had looked at him, didn't remember him, hadn't heard a conversation not two feet from her. Impossible.

"Would you happen to know what the big to-do will be this evening?" Lise intruded on his thoughts.

He should leave, go home. Something inexplicable had just happened, and Neville's skin prickled. But leaving would mean losing his chance to find the dark man. Could he go home, retreat to his books, give up on ever seeing the luscious man again? He couldn't bear the possibility.

"Simon is playing this one close to the vest." Lise continued in the face of his silence. She glanced in the direction of the locked and chained door off the library.

Nouveau religion bored Neville. Sixties-holdover hallucinogens and shabby rockstar showmanship were no substitute for authentic ceremony. The centerpiece of Simon's occult parties were old and forgotten rituals from the dark corners of the earth. And though Neville did not believe in any god or divine power, he longed to find something beyond mere humanity, some evidence of existence after death.

"Do you think tonight will compare to the Mithraic baptisms?" Lise asked.

Despite his turmoil, Neville smiled. How many people could say they'd been showered with gallons of hot bull's blood? While the experience had been primal and powerful, he couldn't say that he'd touched the divine through it.

"Simon mentioned that he'd brought a Yale anthropologist this evening. I may feel the need for an stimulating conversation about erotic Moche ceramics." Lise was determined to keep the conversation going.

Neville sighed, and gazed down at the century-old cherry floor. Perhaps some absinthe would make the night more comprehensible.

Simon walked into the center of the library striking a small chime to produce a clear, piercing note. After three peals, conversation subsided.

"Your attention, please. Everyone's attention." Simon wore an embroidered smoking jacket, which was odd. He was a fashion victim, and this look was ancient. When Neville spotted the stem of a briarwood pipe peeking out of Simon's pocket, he realized the smoking jacket was an attempt to look collegiate. He was trying to get into the Yale anthropologist's pants. Neville smirked, turmoil fading from his mind.

"Ladies and gentlemen," Simon continued. "I intend for this evening's entertainment to climax at the Witching Hour, and it will take a bit of preparation. Those of you wishing to partake, please make your way to the locked room off the library. The rest of you, well, go back to whatever you were doing."

Not that anyone would miss this. Partygoers flowed in Simon's wake, into the library and the mysterious locked room beyond. With all eyes on him, Simon took a dramatic second to search for his keys. This was the moment he lived for, more than the occasional tumble with an anthropologist. He drew out the slow, sexual insertion of the key. With a turn, the lock jumped, and Simon pulled the overly-theatrical chains off the door handles. With a push, antique doors stolen from an Italian abbey groaned open.

The crowd pushed into the newly-revealed ceremonial room. The walls were murals of an Alpine sunset, rose and gold with dark mountains looming in the distance. On a skeletal lectern of curling wrought iron sat an enormous black folio.

"Tonight, we perform some special tantra." Simon caressed the tome on its lectern; eighteenth century European was Neville's assessment from this distance. "We shall take a page from Friedrich-Wilhelm von Junzt, who travelled far and wide, a seeker after mysteries, like us. *Die Unaussprechlichen Kulten* holds rituals described nowhere else. Tonight, from a lost lamasery at the roof of the world, we will indulge in a ritual to summon . . . " he paused and glanced down at a small card in his hand. "Alasya Paramatattva, the Crocodile of Ultimate Truth."

A hot prickle crept up Neville's neck. They were going to perform something from the *Kulten*? Strange Roman and Zoroastrian ceremonies were one thing, but this might be going too far. And hadn't the gorgeous stranger mentioned its sister grimoire *De Vermis Mysteriis*? The convergence disquieted him.

And yet, what if it worked? To be present for evidence that something existed beyond the mundane and prosaic world, even if it were the terrors von Junzt and d'Erlette wrote of. To call a god down, regardless of what god it was, would be a spectacular triumph.

"None of my tantric studies involved sheet music," Lise said, scanning the page that was handed to her. "But that was to satisfy my inner demons, not summon them."

The entities described by Prinneaus and Le Comte resembled demons in the same way that ostriches resembled sparrows. But Neville reminded himself that he didn't believe in them. So what would be the harm?

The ritual consisted of a strange rondel of four different choruses that chanted unpronounceable words in different time signatures. Simon accompanied the cacophony with a weird, monotonous tune on a *kangling*, a Tibetan trumpet made from a human femur. Neville could not laugh off the bizarre chant and grotesque music as the usual ritual garbage. Something insidious and perniciously inescapable lurked in the sound, as if it had been orchestrated by someone who had never experienced music.

The noise continued for some time, the auditory chaos magnified with each repetition of the chant. On top of the din was a jarring, off-key layer, as if from a flawed or broken flute. No one was playing such an instrument, it must have been an auditory hallucination brought on by the atonality.

In the midst of the ear-torturing noise, Neville spied the gorgeous dark-skinned man in black and white standing on the edge of the crowd. As far as occult entertainments went, this was a bust. If Neville had wanted to sing nonsensical music he would have joined a church choir. At least he knew the dark man wasn't a figment of his imagination.

Even as the thought crossed his mind, the crowd drew back from the stranger. The chanting died away, and the audience stared.

"You have called, and I am now here, without noise or inconvenience." Neville remembered that voice from their all-too-brief conversation, but now it flowed with naked power. The assembly gasped, and Neville recognized the quote from the *Grimoirium Verum*, a book of prosaic conjurations. What was this man playing at?

"I see that congratulations are in order. Despite your ignorance and fear, and you have pierced the Outer Darkness and finally arrived at a truth." The haughty words stabbed like shards of ice. Had the summoning truly worked? The thought was enormous and terrifying.

The man swept the room with his chill gaze, and no one was able to meet it. Men knelt before their gods because no one wanted to look them in the eye.

"I see. A collection of charlatans looking for the truth behind their own lies."

The crowd reeked of confusion and fear. Although the words were full of contempt, Neville was awed.

"This audience is brief, but you shall have the truth you seek." Then, like a magician, he vanished.

*   *   *

For the next week, Neville retreated to his vault, with only his beloved books for company. He tried to concentrate on the familiar pleasures, but memories of the exquisite dark man would not leave him be. What was he? Magician, trickster, demon, God? Neville was drawn to his treasured copy of *De Vermis Mysteriis*. What about the book had allowed him to see the Alasya Paramatattva? He pored over the fragile pages, wondering which of the shuddersome horrors described might wear the guise of the Crocodile of Ultimate Truth.

After days of wading through Prunneaus' dense Latin, Neville was exhausted and wrung out. In a moment of weakness, he paged through a newspaper, hoping the mundane prose would rest his tired mind. Instead, he discovered that a Yale professor of anthropology had killed himself by leaping out his New York publisher's window.

The story was lurid enough to quote several witnesses. The anthropologist, normally reserved and polite, had emerged from an elevator and charged straight for a tall window. After bloodying his nose and then fists in a frenzied attack on the unyielding glass, he had grabbed a chair and shattered the window. Without a second's pause, he threw himself out the new aperture, killing himself and a pedestrian ten stories below.

Disturbed, Neville called Lise to ask the name of the Yale professor at Simon's party. When she didn't pick up, he left a message. Lise, normally eager to trade gossip, had not gotten back to him by the time Neville went to sleep.

Nor did she call the next day. Was she out of the country? Neville tried her number several times, and each time her cold, remote voice mail recorded his worried tones.

He was finally distracted by a call to his cell phone. He picked it up, and someone was breathlessly telling him that Jane Waite had strangled herself.

Neville could say nothing. He hadn't liked Jane, but it was a blow to realize she was dead. Lise was still not responding to his calls, and he worried that something had happened to her, also.

Jane's funeral was a solemn, closed-casket affair. The whispered undercurrent that flowed through the pews said that her husband had found her and loosened the ligature, only to watch in helpless horror as she screamed "Alasya Paramatattva" and tore at her face. Only death had stopped her convulsions.

Neville scanned the mourners for the dark, sardonic god, but did not find him.

He spent two anxious days alternately worrying over Lise and studying Prinneaus' recondite Latin. His diligence was rewarded with a name. "Nyarlathotep," called the Crawling Chaos, and the soul of the Outer Gods. This mordant, mocking figure who sometimes appeared as a dark pharaoh sounded like the Crocodile of Ultimate Truth. But this identification did not bring any comfort or protection. He brooded on this for hours, scouring the book for any hint as to the entity's weaknesses. He found none.

Helpless, Neville tried calling Lise once again. To his surprise, the line was picked up.

"Hello?" The voice was not Lise's, but older and matronly.

"Um, hello. Is this Lise Endicott's phone?"

"This is her phone, and I am Sister Mary-Lucia."

"*Sister?* Lise ran away to a cloister? Don't you have to believe in God to become a nun?"

"She asked if I would assure you that she was alive if you called. She did not want you to worry."

"Can I talk with her?"

"I am sorry. She is in seclusion at the moment, contemplating the new life before her."

"You have to be fucking kidding me."

"I assure you we are not. This order has been the salvation of many troubled young women..."

Neville hung up, his mind spinning. The god. It was hunting them down one by one and... doing what? Jane Waite had long played dangerous sex games. He didn't know anything about the anthropologist. But Lise was as cynical and world-weary as anyone he had ever known. She hadn't prayed to anything but her own appetites in the eight years he had known her. How was a retreat to a convent some sort of truth that the Crocodile shown her?

He needed access to the *Kulten*. He had to have some sort of defence, some way to understand this thing before it came for him. He called Simon, and as expected, got his personal assistant Zelney.

"You haven't heard?" The fear and shock in Zelney's voice let Neville know he was too late.

"No." Neville felt hollow. The pursuing doom was consuming his friends. "Tell me he's alive."

Zelney choked a little, and gave him a hospital room number. Then hung up.

Two hours later, Neville was pacing outside the designated door, an abyss yawning in his stomach. It couldn't be as bad as he imagined, could it? Anticipation had to be the worst part. Had to be.

With a bracing and surreptitious sip of brandy, he opened the door. Simon lay on a bed, hooked up to a couple of leads. A large bandage obscured the left side of his head, including his eye. Simon's expression was not the familiar, knowing smile Neville had come to know, but open and empty.

"Simon?"

The patient's one good eye blinked rapidly.

"Hello?" His voice had changed into something lonely and forlorn.

"Simon, it's Neville. Can you see me?"

The person, and Neville couldn't decide if he truly was Simon anymore, squirmed as he tried to get a better look. His usually fine motor skills were gone. Considering the head trauma, that wasn't surprising. Simon, if he was in there still, faced a long period of recovery.

Neville approached, and Simon's good eye followed him. With a sinking feeling, Neville realized that Simon's eye was empty, all personality lost.

Oh God.

What happened? Who did this to you?"

"I did." The simple statement was flat, final, and chilling. Simon mimed snipping something with his trembling right hand, then jammed the fingers into the dressing over his ruined left eye.

Neville wrestled Simon's hand away from the bandage. Simon resisted for a moment, straining to reach his eye, whipping the threatening fingers back and forth. Then the frenzy was over, and Simon relaxed back into the bed.

"Why? What happened?" Neville was nauseous with fear. What could make a man stab himself in the eye with scissors? Had he really destroyed his own forebrain, lobotomized himself?

Simon's blank eye regarded him, and the monotone voice came from somewhere unimaginably distant.

"I didn't want to think about Him anymore."

Him. Of course Him.

"Nyarlathotep?" Neville whispered the name.

Simon exploded in a screaming fury, hands clawing at Neville, fingernails digging bloody furrows into his face. Neville tried to fight him off, but Simon had a madman's strength, leaping off the bed. The monitors screamed, mingling with Simon's animalistic yowl. He slammed Neville into the wall. A hand came up under Neville's jaw and his skull cracked against the plaster wall once, twice, and the third time something gave way.

Then they were surrounded by a horde of white-clad figures. Simon's fingers were pried off Neville, and Simon was dragged, screaming and thrashing, into the bed. Neville reeled out of the room, his last glimpse of Simon being held down and pumped full of chemicals.

A card waited for him when he got home. It sat, perfectly centered, a cream square on his dark blue table cloth. The door was not broken in, and the locks hadn't been picked, as if the messenger had appeared out of thin air, dropped the envelope, and vanished.

He stared at it, not sure what to do. The entity destroying his friends had no need to warn him or command his appearance. And yet, something told him the envelope was poison; if he didn't touch it, Nyarlathotep could not touch him.

What if he just wanted to talk? What if he wanted more than talk? The possibility of gazing into those dark eyes, of touching that perfect skin... he tore the envelope open.

Flawless copperplate writing invited him to lunch at an outdoor café at eleven A.M. the following day. Neville sat considering the card. Avoiding the encounter was absurd. The Crocodile of Ultimate Truth did not need to wait for him in a café. He considered running, hiding himself in Bangladesh. But what good would it possible do? How could anyone run from a god, or the truth?

He spent a sleepless night among his books. What would happen to him? What could Nyarlathotep reveal to him? What would happen to his books if he went mad and destroyed himself?

He tried to imagine what it would be like to be dead, to not exist. The only image he could conjure was a terrifying eternity of hopeless, disembodied drifting. But proof of god, no matter what god, was evidence of immortality of the soul. Wasn't it?

The café was empty when Neville arrived. Grey clouds loured above him. Across the street, a broken-winged pigeon flapped at the foot of Saint Francis' statue. Neville tried not to glance at his watch too often. He buried his nose in the menu, hoping that it held no special significance.

He had not yet made up his mind when the chair opposite him shifted. He lowered the menu and the Alasya Paramatattva sat down. His spotless white suit was exquisitely tailored. Neville was consumed with longing.

"Try the curried chicken salad. You'll like it." His voice was even more masculine and commanding than Neville remembered. What should one do when the Crocodile of Ultimate Truth suggested a lunch item? *E. coli* was not a truth, was it? Neville put his hands on the glass-topped table to keep them from shaking.

A pert waitress smiled at them both, and took Neville's order. He could not persuade his guest to order, even though he volunteered to pay. Then she was gone, and they were alone. Neville dared to look into the empty black eyes, and found himself in the uncomfortable position of staring into a bottomless abyss. He tore his eyes away, realizing how wrong Nietzsche had been. The abyss does not stare back. The abyss merely is; cold, uncaring, eternal.

The silence grew, until Neville had to say something or scream to fill the emptiness.

"Would it be impolite of me to ask questions?"

"You are free to do as you please, Neville, just as I am." The flash of teeth was as friendly as a tiger's snarl.

"Who are you?" Neville asked in a whisper.

"I have a thousand names, am perceived a thousand ways. I have been called the Black Pharaoh of Khem, and the Blind Ape of Truth." With each claimed title, Neville was granted a vision. He saw the dark man with a blue and gold Egyptian *nemes* on his head, two columns of perfumed smoke rising before him. This shifted to a wildly-flailing yellow baboon with a golden collar and empty pits for eyes. "Men have worshipped me as the Howler in Darkness, and the Bloated Woman." Neville saw an unutterable monstrosity with cancerously tortured skin and a bloody tentacle emerging from its grotesque head. The vision faded to an inhumanly obese woman with an elephant-like trunk and two side-facing mouths screaming in triumph over a field of bloody, eviscerated corpses. "I am older than this planet, more ancient than the eons before the stars were kindled. I have seen civilizations, races, and aberrations of reality that would drive you mad. I am not some anthropomorphic projection, I am entirely different from everything you could ever conceive of."

Neville reeled at the visions and the words. What slumbering horror had they awakened? What hubris to attract its attention.

"Your little group of friends summoned me in order to alleviate their boredom." If there was emotion in the voice, it was alien to human experience. "I considered many ways of sharing my irritation. A nearby supernova to irradiate this planet to lifeless rock, or perhaps inspiring some terrorists to a nuclear detonation in this city. But, interesting as fusion is, I decided that your assemblage of seekers deserved something for their accomplishment. They sought truth. Their reactions have been entertaining."

Neville looked up, and was trapped in the all-encompassing void that was the Alasya Paramatattva's gaze. For an instant, Neville glimpsed a black protoplasmic horror with bloody fangs and razor-edged tentacles that howled from an limitless ocean of carnage, of unstoppable fury like an endlessly-erupting volcano, and hate so cold it could snuff out stars. He gasped, the vision so clear and present that he cringed.

Oblivious, the waitress set his salad down. Neville caught his breath. He thought about looking for a reaction from the mahogany god, but would not risk being swallowed by that terrible, empty gaze again.

He pushed a trembling fork of salad into his mouth and chewed. He could not taste it. He had to escape, to get away from the horror in barely-human form that sat so frighteningly close. With a trembling hand, he put his credit card on the table between them.

"I am here to give you the gift of truth, Neville."

He clutched the table and choked back a moan.

"You have always wondered how you would face death. It is such a contradiction to this culture, so divorced from your daily existence, and yet such an obsession. There is an excellent chance that in six months, you will put the barrel of a cheap revolver in your mouth and pull the trigger."

Neville tried to shut out the words. He would shoot himself? What could drive him to that? He opened his mouth to protest, to ask, to curse, but Nyarlathotep silenced him with a raised finger. Neville rocked for a moment, his inner turmoil a physical churning in his stomach.

The little waitress returned, and handed Neville's credit card back to him.

"I'm sorry. You've been declined."

Neville started. The dark man reached out and tapped the bill with a finger. The waitress nodded, smiled at him, and left.

"Your trust fund is gone, and your credit account is over its limit, your stock holdings have evaporated. All the money you have left is in your wallet."

Neville's mind reeled. Death was too great an unknown to contemplate, but poverty was all too real.

"Of course, you could live comfortably if you sold your books," the dark man said.

Sell his books? He would sooner kill himself.

The Crocodile's mocking laughter rang in his ears. Far too late, he understood something of the otherworldly horror they had stupidly attracted the attention of. He had his truth, for all the good it did him.

Dear God, Neville prayed, let there not be an afterlife.

For Wilum Pugmire

DANIEL POWELL teaches a variety of writing courses at a small college in Northeast Florida. He is an avid outdoorsman and long distance runner, and he enjoys fishing the tidal creeks of Duval County from atop his kayak. He shares a small home near the Intracoasta Waterway with his wife, Jeanne, and his daughter, Lyla. Daniel's fiction has appeared or is forthcoming in *Cthulhu 2012*, *Redstone Science Fiction*, *Brain Harvest*, *Well Told Tales* and *Leading Edge Magazine*. He maintains a web journal on speculative storytelling at www.danielwpowell.blogspot.com.

The Timucuan Portal

by Daniel Powell

We'd been in the house on Arkham Lane for a little over three months when it happened. Ours was the two-story colonial in the left corner of the cul-de-sac—number 619. We were in the process of unpacking, with many of our things still in boxes.

I don't imagine the government will be returning any of it anytime soon, but that's ok. It's all pretty much spoiled now.

I was hanging a set of drapes in the bedroom I shared with Marilyn when my boy burst into the room, anguish in his voice. "It was there, Daddy! In the bushes!" he cried. They were words that cut me to the marrow at the time and ones that will haunt me—hell, maybe *all* of us—to the end of my days.

I stood there staring at my little David, him dressed in dirt-streaked red shorts and an old teal Jaguars t-shirt. He was wearing flip-flops and there were bits of leaves and brush in his shaggy hair. He held his right arm out to me with his palm open and his fingers splayed wide. His arm was covered in a thin coat of blackish sediment—like he'd dipped it clear to the elbow in a barrel of crude oil.

"Davey!" I said, dismayed by his tears. He was a tough little guy and usually made it a point not to cry when he hurt himself. "What happened, Bub?" I went to him and knelt and put my hands in his hair to comfort him.

"There was something rustling in the bushes behind the shed, Daddy! I was playing there with Sam and he's gone! Sam went into the bushes and…and he's gone!"

I wiped the tears from the corners of his eyes and his arm fell to his side. Some of the gunk smeared on his shirt.

"What happened to your arm, Davey?"

"I reached *into* it. I was trying to pull Sam back. But it got him, Daddy! And it was wet. I had a hold of Sam's leg and he was barking and when it touched me, it was wet!" He started to cry again and I hugged him to my chest and then hurried him down the hallway to the bathroom.

"I'm sure Sam's okay, Davey," I said as I worked the soap into a lather. "He's a big dog. He can take care of himself."

Whatever Davey had been into, it was just as sticky as maple syrup. It took

133

fifteen minutes of scrubbing to get his arm clean. By the time I was finished, my boy looked exhausted. His flesh was a bright pink from the scrubbing and I herded him down to his bedroom and helped him change into clean clothes.

"I think I need to sleep now," he said. Such simple words. He walked over to his bed and crawled on top of the covers and was out like a light.

I headed into the kitchen, where Marilyn was putting contact paper down in the cupboards. I grabbed a beer and told her about what happened to Davey.

"What do you suppose it is? You don't think he made it all the way to the creek?"

"Must have," I replied, but I didn't believe it myself. Our home backed up against the Timucuan Preserve, a tract of thick Florida jungle bisected by a series of tidal creeks and cypress swamps. The saw palmetto and mangroves grew so densely behind our house that I didn't think a boy, even one as slight as Dave, could penetrate them. "He said Sam ran off. I'll go see if I can find him."

"Need a hand?"

"I'll manage," I said, and headed out to the back yard. There were thunderheads grouping in the east and the sky just above the preserve was a sickly yellow color. There would be a gully-washer in an hour or so—one of those Florida storms that blew an inch of sideways rain for twenty minutes before tuckering out and evaporating into sunshine.

I crossed the lawn and headed down the gentle slope to the rickety old utility shed. It was a clapboard affair and looked like it might tumble over at any minute. I had a mind to knock it down myself just to keep Dave out of it.

"Sam!" I called. "Here boy! Come on out of there!" I squatted at the side of the shed and stared into the jungle. It looked like a bone garden, all those knobby stalks of cypress and mangrove jumbled together like that. I whistled. "C'mon Sam!"

And then something moved in the brush. Something big. I heard it crashing around out there. "Sam?" I said. I called out for the dog, but I thought it might be something else making all that noise. I knew there were bobcats and bears in this part of the woods. A neighbor said that the park rangers had once counted sixty-seven alligators sunning themselves in the cypress swamp not a quarter mile from my back door the summer before we'd moved in.

It could be anything.

I took a step closer, squinting into that thick tangle while that thing fidgeted in the underbrush. I kept calling for the dog but I stopped when I heard the voice. It sounded like an old man. I couldn't make out any words, but the tone was plain as day. Something was angry. I strained to hear it, to put reason to it and rationally identify it, and then the rains came.

The yellow clouds spilled raindrops thick as cherry tomatoes and they chased me inside, my shirt soaked through in less than twenty seconds.

Marilyn and I checked on Davey. He slept like the dead while our new home was battered by the warm rain. True to form, the squall played itself out within thirty minutes and when I went out front, a few of my neighbors were out in the street, watching the flash flood slide down the storm drains.

I crossed the street to where Tom Riggins, an older man who lived alone after doing thirty years in the Navy, was using a rake to push a clog of leaves out of the opening to the drain in front of his house.

"Hello Tom," I called; we shook hands. "You haven't seen Sam, have you? Davey said he ran off."

The old man had clear blue eyes and he narrowed them when I posed my question. "Dog's missing, is he?" He bit his lip.

I laughed. "I wouldn't go that far. I imagine he chased a squirrel into the jungle. I just wondered if maybe you'd seen him. Dave's kind of worried about him."

Riggins ran a hand over the grey bristles of his buzz-cut. He leaned against his rake and fixed me with a stare. "I think you'd be wise to fence that back yard, Dennis."

I nodded in reply. "We plan to, eventually. You thinking the deer will get at Marilyn's tomatoes?"

"It's not the deer I'm worried about. There's something else in that stretch of woods. Something hungry. It's taken a number of the neighborhood animals in my time here. Cats and dogs. I don't believe it's a bear or a gator though..."

We shared an uncomfortable pause and I watched the storm clouds trundle out to the west. The sun was back with a vengeance and my damp shirt was sticky in the heat. "I'll keep that in mind, Tom. If you see the dog, would you bring him by?"

"I will," he replied, returning to the leaves. "You keep Davey away from those woods, Dennis. The Timucuan is a beautiful place, but I don't like that stretch behind your house there. It doesn't *feel* like the rest of it."

I suppressed a smirk and waved my goodbye and when I went back inside, Marilyn was anxious. "He's got some kind of rash. Come take a look."

Calling it a rash was generous. There were maybe a dozen quarter-sized welts on Davey's forearm. They were bright red and rose up on the skin like chicken pocks. "Should we wake him up? Take him to the emergency room?" She was two degrees from full-blown panic, and I was headed in that direction myself.

I shook my head. "Let him sleep. I'll put some calamine lotion on it and we'll just watch it. I think we might have poison oak out behind the shed there."

Her brow wrinkled at the words. "The shed? He knows the woods there are off limits."

"I know, but he said Sam ran off. He said he tried to pull him back, whatever that means. I think he just tired himself out, but if it gets any worse we'll take him to the emergency room."

I put the lotion on the welts and they did go down some, but Davey was still out of sorts that night at dinner. He sat and picked at the chicken and cole slaw on his plate.

"Not hungry?" I asked him.

He weakly shook his head.

"What's the matter sweetheart?" Marilyn asked. "Is it about Sam? He'll be back soon."

"No he won't," Davey replied. He spoke in a monotone before fixing his eyes on me. "It's *forever* in there, Daddy. Eternity. He won't be back."

I shared a look with my wife. Our four-year-old son didn't speak like that. I mean, he just *didn't*.

"Sure he will," I said quickly. "Sometimes dogs just need an adventure. But they always come home."

I said it, but I was having a hard time believing it. I'd heard something out there. Something big. And Tom Riggins had said lots of animals had gone missing over the years.

Davey just looked at me with those blank eyes. "It's forever in there, *Dennis*. Don't ever forget it. Glorp!"

"Davey!" Marilyn said. She sprang up from her chair and went to our boy and stroked his face near his temple. "What is it honey? Are you feeling ok?"

He stared at her for a moment and then he nodded. "I'm tired, Mommy. Can I go to sleep?"

It was only 7:30, but we put him down to bed. I checked on him every twenty minutes or so until just after midnight, when I finally turned in. Marilyn was snoring lightly when I woke up two hours later, but it wasn't her snores that stirred me.

It was the muttering coming from down the hallway.

I crept down to Davey's room, trying to make sense of the sounds that were coming from inside.

"*R'lyeh. Nyarlathotep. Shub-Niggurath.*"

It was the same tone—that same dark pitch—of the harsh muttering I'd heard earlier in the preserve.

"*Yog-Sothoth. Tsathoggua. Azathoth.*"

I went inside. Davey was sleeping on his back. He was chanting in that foreign tongue, in that strange voice, repeating the same words over and over again. I shook him, trying to wake him. The welts on his arm were back. They looked like they had grown.

"Davey," I said, then tried it a little louder. "Davey! Son! Wake up."

His eyes flashed open and it took him a moment to recognize me. "I was dreaming of them, Daddy. I saw *all* of them."

"What did you see, Dave? What did you see?" I knelt at his bedside and patted down his sweat-soaked hair.

"All of the old ones, Daddy. All of the *ancient* ones."

"Davey, do you feel ok? Do you want to go to the doctor?"

He shook his head . "I just want to sleep. Wake me up if Sam comes home. I have something I need to ask him."

And just like that he was snoring again. I pulled the blanket up to his chin and kissed him lightly on the temple and went back down the hallway to my bedroom.

I never saw my son again.

It was Marilyn that found him missing. We'd slept later than usual so it was just after 7:30 when her shriek startled me from a dreamless slumber. I sprang out of bed and ran to Davey's room.

His bed was empty, the sheets crumpled in a ball. The bay windows were open wide, the thin cotton drapes waving lazily in the faint breeze.

"He's gone," she said, her voice a choked squawk. "Our boy's gone."

I went to my wife and gave her a hug to try to reassure her. "I'll take a look in the back yard. He might just be in the woods, Mary. He might have just gone looking for Sam. It's going to be ok. Call the police. Tell them to come right away."

I slipped into a pair of shoes and ran out into the dew-streaked grass in my pajama bottoms and an old t-shirt. "Davey!" I shouted at the top of my lungs. "Davey!"

That's when I saw them. His pajamas sat in a pile near the shed. It was as though they'd been sucked right off of him. Or, he'd been sucked right *out* of them. I ran to the edge of the forest, fighting to erase the horrible image of my little boy running nude through all of that shadowed foliage. "Davey!"

I pushed my foot into the trees there. I had to go in. I had to try. But when the doorway opened, I jumped back into my yard. I only saw inside for a moment, but I knew in that instant I couldn't go any further into those woods.

You see, there was a tunnel there in the jungle. I know it sounds crazy, but it's true. It's been written up in all of those journals. I can't bring myself to read them. I don't need a scientist's description. I've seen the things at the other end of that portal.

Marilyn once read a snippet to me, but I had to beg her to stop when she got to the part about the eyes. *The creature has many eyes...perhaps thousands of them...and tentacles that sprout from beneath its face like the petals of some horrible flower...*

What more can I say? The government compensated us for our home. A team of scientists lives there around the clock. They are researching the portal. They are trying to make sense of something that can't be explained.

But if you ask me, and believe me, just about everyone with a stake in this thing has tried, my son Davey said it best.

It's forever in there, Daddy. Eternity.

JOSEPH S. PULVER, SR., is the author of the Lovecraftian novel *Nightmare's Disciple*, and he has written many short stories that have appeared in magazines and anthologies, including Ellen Datlow's *Year's Best Horror* and S. T. Joshi's *Black Wings* and *Spawn of the Green Abyss*. His highly-acclaimed short story collections, *Blood Will Have Its Season* and *SIN & ashes* were published by Hippocampus Press in 2009 and 2010 respectively and as E-Books by Speaking Volumes in 2011. You can find his blog at: http://thisyellowmadness.blogspot.com/

No Healing Prayers

by Joseph S. Pulver, Sr.

Midnight.
Moonlight.
Cold.
The howling sun, far from this place with no hope for tomorrow, running with things that fear what the cold moon brings.
Captain Jack sits on his front porch. Shotgun on his lap.
Coffee gone cold.
Waiting.
Waiting for The Thing That Sails On Tears.
The Black Goat.
Sat there every night this summer. Staring at the blackness. Listening to the sound of the empty road.
A yard without children's toys.
Without flowers.
The withered dreams gone, over some rainbow.
Captain Jack didn't follow.
His wife followed the lullaby into a dream. Something soft and quiet he hoped. Tried to tell himself.
Tried.
Tried to penetrate it, like it was a year or a river.
Over and over.
Three years of nights. Centuries of days. No sleep. No solitude. Rain and winter and dust were his bread.
Tried to get under the skin of that stone.
The look in his eye said he wasn't convincing.
His leather hand and the Mossberg shotgun said he was convinced of something else. Said they'd decided on a hard truth—It was coming. And they were ready for the dance.
Wouldn't be lightning.
Wouldn't be roaring wind.
Wouldn't win the gamble.
Knew it.

Knew might-have-been would see no bright morning sunrise.

Take what you get.

Knew it.

Always had.

Didn't know another way.

Not then.

Sure not now.

Captain Jack looked at the stars. They weren't falling.

Didn't figure they would.

Back in the first War, when he was a boy, and they sent him a million miles from yonder, he came to understand it.

Back then, when he came home to her and her cello and the stairs that lead to their bedroom, he understood.

Cold is cold. Hard fact.

Nothing is nothing.

Didn't change.

You fight for your life. Hope the thread don't snap, or get cut.

Second War they didn't have God on their side to change The Truth. Came out the same way.

Saw a lot of blood. Layered on the earth. Soaked in. Saw it as lesson. Heard it scream. Saw it spread. Smelled it. Got the taste of it slammed in his mouth.

Saw cold. And hard.

And young men, ragged, overrun with panic, just wanted to get home and become old men that had had a taste of potential, that didn't come back.

He moved the Mossberg *590 Persuader*.

Remembered the feel of her breast . . . When her eyes were sails that didn't read the verses of winter.

Looked at the moon.

Cold.

Hard times.

No land of plenty.

Remembered her sun hands.

Touching them . . .

The 5 o'clock whistle . . . running home . . . dinner . . . her smile . . . the world melting away . . .

Every morning, up at 5 o'clock . . . The job. Hard work, dog day sweat . . . The Railroad . . . the tracks roaming from here to more . . . the 5 o'clock whistle . . . Her smile. Her sheltering arms. The world melting away. The world being fine . . .

Two sweet years.

Put his money down on this little house. Bet on Eternity. Worked to make it so.

Worked hard. Put his shoulder into turning water into wine.

Never stroked fleeting.

Didn't curse.

Didn't let his fingertips get bound up in vain.

Cold hard moonlight.

Silent.

Couldn't breathe it.

Didn't embrace flowers.

Two sweet years. Didn't need Paris or extra. Didn't care about a Gulf Coast vacation, or the language of empty prayers.

Had her heart, a rose, and no secrets between them. Wasn't missing a thing.

Tombstone.

Handkerchief.

Preacher Man, talkin'.

Cold black sod.

Midnight.

Moonlight.

Waiting.

*   *   *

Ask.

The Coloreds, the Whites, the this-and-that buzzing of the town drunk puffed up on the kicking heat spun from a bottle.

Sift rumor, or the swells—filled with "Happened." and "Look."—under eyelashes.

They say The Piper Man came down the road that night. His trouble-eyes chugging.

Brought his hateful drought music. Stretched it over her. Silenced her cello.

Say the whippoorwills and the loons closed their throats. Took to tight corners.

The Piper Man came.

Danced, they say.

Dragged his claw-foot around the house. Marked it. Carved it out of the world.

Lifted his hand.

Then he played.

Called.

Called The Black Goat.

No censor to fasten it to confinement, barricade came down.

And it came.

Came and took all her dances away.

Then, they say, The Piper Man laughed.

*　　*　　*

Creek out back dried up.

Brambles thick as tar. Braided like rage-hard fingers white-knuckle tight.

Fence gate broken.

Empty house at his back.

Shotgun's loaded. Hard stuff. Bite and shred the guts out of most anything.

War and no hope for tomorrow.

Black thoughts.

Blood and rain and mud.

Frost.

The end of the world. Nights he talked to the wind over her grave and thought of putting the gun in his mouth.

Shotgun's loaded.

Coffee's cold.

Bitter.

Enough to keep Captain Jack awake.

Not that the stone cold hate would step aside for Morpheus.

Not tonight.

Captain Jack looks at his wedding ring.

Same moon the night her married her. Night they came to this house to live. Night they stepped into a dream . . . Night at her grave he lost all human customs in a furrow of Forever.

Cold hard moon.

Looks the same.

Cold as black sod.

Fireflies gone.

But the stars don't fall. Don't shiver.

A shift in the blackness.

Just there.

Not a silent death.

Footfalls on the black road. Thick cackling—infernal, muted, dripping with burn-it-all-down hunger. Hell-bent flute notes, long, brittle claws scraping and etching metal. Scattered. A flame of Other Spaces. Crypt-brewed wolfspell expanding, mounting . . . Wants. Flows . . .

Captain Jack hears the evil. The dark sounds of a rough beast coming. Hears the crack of its claw-foot when it hits the hard road.

Cold midnight moonlight.

Just enough to see The Piper Man.

Business end of the shotgun comes up. Won't turn back.

Or turn tail.

Or be overrun.

Won't blink in the face of unattainable.

Bad thoughts.

Tombstone.

Handkerchief.

Preacher Man, talkin'.

Cold black sod.

Midnight.

Moonlight.

Waiting.

A flash of white light. A little inferno inside it.

Hell.

Coming for bones. Coming for flesh.

Coming to drink tears and tenderness affirmed and every contour between.

The corpse-coffin sound of Hell shouting in the trees. Something black in the road.

"Whatever will be . . . Will be."

The Piper Man laughs.

Shotgun leveled . . .

(Grand Funk Railroad "The Railroad")

for Gary Myers & Robert Bloch

ADRIAN TCHAIKOVSKY, born in Lincolnshire, England, is the author of the "Shadows of the Apt" fantasy series that started in 2008 with *Empire in Black and Gold*, which follows a world with equal parts steampunk and insects. Trained in zoology, psychology, stage fighting and law, Adrian is currently living in Leeds and trying to balance the demands of a day job, a writing career, a family and far too many hobbies. He is a keen gamer, tabletop, online and live-action, and first encountered Lovecraft decades ago by way of a role-playing game, since when the author has exercised an unhealthy fascination over him. His latest book, *The Sea Watch*, sixth in the series, was published in February in the UK, and has its own share of tentacles.

The Dissipation Club

by Adrian Tchaikovsky

This is a story about my friend Walther Cohen. He and I work a business together, or rather it's his business, and I pitch in. People call on Walther Cohen when there's no other agency that fits, and where the rules don't apply. Someone once described him as a ghost-hunter. Actually what they said was "shabby little ghostbuster" but that's what they meant.

We do ghosts. Walther does. We do what comes, and what gets his interest. Most of the time it's timewasters, nutters, people who think they're being haunted. People who would give their right arm to have something interesting happen to them. Most of the time it's bunkum. And most of the rest of the time Walther just gets on with it. He sits people round a table, or he potters about with ouija boards and geiger counters and a whole host of kit he's inherited or bought up or invented. Sometimes he calls me, when he has a feeling. Walther's all kinds of intuition, and when he gets a certain shiver about a case, he gives me a shout, and I take the week off from minding doors to come help out. That's me.

This is a special case. You should know that from the start. We're no pushovers, Walther and me. A month before this case there was a thing in the Southampton sewers that was taking tramps from the street and eating them, and we went into those same sewers with chalk and compasses and holy water and sorted it out. I've seen a lot, and what I've seen's nothing to what Walther's seen.

This is the case. This is the one that meant more than all the others, and pushed us too far. This is the one I said I'd never write down.

Walther Cohen wears white suits and a white trilby and looks like Son of Man from Del Monte. I, in my best monkey suit, look like an ape. There are few places we look right together, and the office of James Vanderfell wasn't one of them by a long shot.

You might have heard of Mr Vanderfell, if you're into shares and money-stuff. If you haven't, he's an American, a businessman, owns shares in everything up to and including the Pope, the way he told it. Not the sort of person Walther and I normally deal with. I didn't know where to put myself. Vanderfell's office wasn't really his office, but he owned most of the company whose office it was, or that's what I reckoned. He was one of those artificial-looking people. He was tanned, his hair was grey, his face was stern and lined, and all of it had been precisely done to him to make him look right as the successful businessman. His appearance was probably worth more than Walther, me and the office together.

He didn't like the look of us much either, even though I'd come in my suit. Walther was in his whites, of course, and had put his white trilby on Vanderfell's desk without asking. He took a seat without asking, too, and I stood behind it like a butler. Walther doesn't make friends easily and, unless he likes you, you work out pretty quick that he doesn't really care what you think of him. It's got the spit beaten out of him three or four times since I've known him, including once inside. He leaned back in the chair, and was obviously considering putting his feet on the desk, when the Big Man finally spoke.

"You must be Cohen," said Vanderfell. "You're awful forward for a man who hasn't been hired yet."

Walther shrugged as if to say that the patronising of Mr Vanderfell was of no interest to him. "I don't imagine I was high on your list, Mr Vanderfell," he said easily. "So if we're here talking you must be feeling quite needy. What can I do for you?"

Vanderfell narrowed his eyes but I could tell that Walther was having none of it. After a moment when I thought we would get thrown out, the American sighed.

"I need you to find someone," he said.

"Not quite my line of work," said Walther lightly. Vanderfell scowled at him.

"Like you said, I'm out of options. I've tried the police and I've tried P.I.s and I've worked my way down the ladder until it was you or The Amazing Boffo. You come marginally more highly recommended. I want you to find my son."

Walther took a moment before replying, and he was more serious when he did. "How long has he been missing?"

"Four months," said Vanderfell. "That's how long it took for your police to write it off, and for every other guy I put on the case to decide they didn't want it. My son, James Vanderfell Junior, has vanished, Mr Cohen, and everyone's telling me that he's just run off around Europe or eloped with a girl, but it isn't so, Mr Cohen. Something has happened to my son, and I'm not being told what." Whatever his faults as a moneyman you could tell he really cared about his boy.

"Still not my line of work," Walther said, sounding slightly irritated.

"I've had a file made up for you," Vanderfell said, as if Walther hadn't said it. "Everything I've found out. Everything the investigators sent me before they decided to go quiet." He pushed a thick buff folder across the desk. It was unlabelled.

Walther looked at his hat for a bit, as though he expected it to do something. His hands had opened the file, were leafing through the papers inside. "I don't do missing persons, not without more. I'm sorry, Mr Vanderfell."

"You've seen how much I'm offering, for any proof," the American said hoarsely. I think before his son disappeared he would have shouted at us and thrown us out, but he had been discovering that even his money and power had limits.

Walther shook his head and opened his mouth to turn down all that money we could have used, and then his hands stopped.

"I'll do it," said Walther quietly. A shiver went through him as he said it and I knew he'd hit on something. When he stood up he looked pale, even wearing white.

We're not private investigators. Walther's business is the abnormal and mine is keeping his skin whole while he's looking into it. We don't do missing persons, messy divorces, all that. Not without more, as the man said. Walther wouldn't say, though, what had changed his mind about the case. We went over the old, cold leads from the file pretty quickly. Whoever had been ahead of us had been thorough, but drawn a blank real quick. "Which is odd," I said. "For Vanderfell's money, people pad things out. This case is three years' easy living to any private eye." Walther wasn't telling me what had hooked him, and because of that I wasn't asking. I'm stubborn like that. We were at my place, the room I had this week, near where my work was. It was about what you imagine, for a rented room in London. I hadn't really unpacked and the landlord hadn't really had it cleaned.

Walther nodded, leafing through newspaper reports. The missing son had made the papers once or twice, then sunk without a trace like everything else. If it wasn't a millionnaire businessman being thwarted you'd think it was a cover up, but Vanderfell's type are usually on the other end of the business when cover ups are handed out.

There was a lot of background information on file. Most of it was just groundwork, irrelevant stuff, put in to make it look like work was being done. Foreign trips in the last year (many), schools (prestigious), work (high paying, low skilled and obviously got through family connections). Eventually even stubborn wears thin. "What am I supposed to be looking at?"

"The PI talked to some of Junior's old chums," Walther said. I found the relevant pages, saw the school.

"Isn't that your posh place?"

"That's not it, but yes," Walther agreed. "Harrow, dontcherknow." Walther never has much money, but his family used to, is how I reckoned. Certainly he came down through the right schools to be a social someone. As for me, I always said my best school was prison. Before that I didn't have much grasp on education.

"But that's not why you're interested?" The stuff from the old chums was thin, odd recollections, nothing the PI had found useful.

"Because we share an old school? Certainly not." Walther poured himself a glass of wine and visibly considered not pouring me one. "You know me better than that, Michael."

I didn't, to be honest. I liked Walther but he was private. He'd never really let me in on his past. I just shrugged and read every damn line of those reports until I drew all the blanks there were. "So what?" I asked.

"Interview with Robin McCalfrey, second page, fourth paragraph." He didn't even pause to remember it, which told me he'd memorised it before to show off.

I read:

"Recalled plenty of women dated JV, no serious, no longer than three months, no pregnancies/scandal. I asked members of societies/clubs? Went through list of usual (as per KP interview). Something else. Prompted mentioned 2yrs ago JV accepted into "Dissipation Club" must check. No other mention. JV drunk when saying and celebrating. Never said when sober."

"So what?" I asked again. I realised as I looked up that Walther had been watching me like a madman.

"I was wondering," he said carefully, "Whether you might recognise it? Not familiar? Not at all?"

I shrugged. "Not to me. But it is to you?"

He nodded. Walther usually looks bright, on edge, kind of like a drug addict in an odd way. Now he looked tired. "Look it up on the Woo-wa," he instructed. Meaning the internet, which Walther doesn't have any truck with. Computers is one of the things I learned inside. I fired up my laptop and Googled it right in there, with apostrophes.

"Not much," was the charitable way of it. No news articles. A few red flags on the conspiracists' websites, which is less than most multinationals get. There was some place in inner London, the posh end, called the Dissipation Club, was about the limit of it.

"What do the conspiracists say?" Walther wanted to know. There was an odd tone to his voice. He knew it all, already, but he wanted to see what other people knew, or thought they knew.

"There's one site saying that it's all to do with companies that want to ruin the environment - mind you, not just ones that happen to ruin it, but actively want to ruin it. There's another here- says they're a branch of the Freemasons, or it's a Mason club, or something. But then it reckons that the Freemasons are running the world for the benefit of the Jews," I explained. "They list a whole load of places."

"For the Jews, is it?" Walther mused. "Well nobody told me. I wonder how I claim my share."

"There's planning permission," I said, scrolling. "Someone wanting to build... objection from the Dissipation Club... permission denied. Well, posh London, hardly surprising."

I carried on ogling Google, paging down links that were less and less to do with anything. "Well, they've been where they've been for a long time." I found notes to do with repairs to the building during the Blitz, and then some note regarding the order of repairs after the fire of London, where the Dissipation Club also seemed to jump the queue. "There's a photo of some MP here." I showed him. It was ten years ago, some secretarial scandal, the harassed-looking man snapped on the steps of a smart but discrete-looking place. The words "The Dispation Society" were cut in deep, neat capitals above him. I saw Walther shiver when he saw the photo.

"Dispation... Does that mean anything to you, Michael?"

"Still no."

He nodded, and then, without precursor: "Can they know what you're searching for, on the Woo-wa? That you're looking for them?"

I didn't know, to be honest. "If they were someone like Vanderfell, with his money, maybe they could," I said. "You think we might get visited? I can move out of here, no problems." I live near where my day work takes me, around London. I don't own much. I slapped in a search on "Dispation Society" too, just for kicks. "Hey, Jack Dee's a member."

"Who's Jack Dee?"

"The comedian," I told him. "The miserable one. Oh wait, this is John Dee. Never mind."

Walther had that face on that suggested I was being stupid, and so I pulled up the article, which turned out to be some student thesis on Elizabethan history. Some crank called John Dee was being accused of witchcraft. Some of the people who stood up for him were his fellow members of the Dispation Society, or so the writer had got from some letter of the time. Their evidence had seemed to clinch the deal for Dee, anyway.

"Fifteen Ninety-nine," Walther said. "That's a long time for a gentleman's club to be going. Long ago enough that nobody had heard of mass media, and so people didn't worry about... leaving references lying about."

"Walther, are you going to tell me what's going on, or what?"

"What," he said.

"Walther-" I stood up, nearly knocking the laptop over. "Tell me-"

He stopped me with a single gesture. He was looking far more serious than usual. The quirkiness, the easy humour he puts up against the world most of the time had slipped a cog.

"Michael, this is serious," he said. "Really serious. It's an old case, to me. It's not something you're involved in yet. Depending on how the Woo-wa works you may never be, if you walk away now. Vanderfell's put me on an old scent again. It's a sign, to me, not to leave things unfinished. But you don't have to come with me."

I left a decent-sized gap before answering. You have you, when people say that sort of thing to you. The answer was no surprise to him, surely. "Go for it. I'm in," I said. "So spill it."

"Not yet. I want you to hear another angle first, before you make your mind up," Walther told me. "Call the authorities."

"Meaning Hawker?"

"Meaning Hawker."

Detective Sergeant Hawker goes back a long way with Walther. I got to know her just after Walther and I got out. It was GBH for me, breaking and entering for him. Hawker passes us jobs, sometimes, when something nasty turns up on her patch. She helps us out, when we need a little digging in the police files. She's been on the force about twelve years and she's pissed off at being passed over, basically, and she doesn't care much about the rest. I put in a call to her from a call box, which is how it works, and we arranged to meet in a week's time.

What happened in between was we had an unaccountable run of bad luck. It was not what you might expect from the films or the novels. Nobody cut my brakes or poisoned my coffee. Walther didn't get run over by a mysterious vanishing car. All the things that conspiracy theorists love to spout nonsense about, none of that happened. My current employers told me not to turn up the next day because they didn't like my attitude, but then I had been a bit surly, to be honest. Walther got picked up by the police and held for about three hours, and then put in a line-up with four large men who looked nothing like him, and then let go without charge, even with an apology. I had some court proceedings come through for some rent I hadn't paid a year before, and I got stop-searched by some policemen. Someone threw a brick through Walther's window and spray-painted "poff" on his door, but it wouldn't be the first time. Little things.

Nobody mentioned the Dissipation Club to us at all. There were no threats, no warnings to leave well alone. The librarians at the British Museum wouldn't release some special old books for Walther to see, but then his record was hardly spotless there. Just little things. Things that made our lives complicated, that tied up our time in various ways. For anyone other than Walther it might have gone unnoticed. Walther has intuition, though, like I said. He knows when someone's messing with him.

We were meeting Hawker at a pub we all knew, and Walther and I turned up first. After exchanging stories I asked right out, "If we start prying, is this going to get serious?" I asked.

"I'd move out," Walther confirmed. "Don't leave a forwarding address."

"And you?"

He gave a grin that was humourless. "They know where I live already."

"Walther, is this... supernatural? Have we been jinxed or cursed or something?"

He shook his head. "This is just someone being very, very subtle in telling us to bugger orff."

Hawker arrived then. She's a solid-looking Irishwoman who looks like she wouldn't hesitate to break your arm, given any excuse. When Walther mentioned the Club she scowled.

"This again."

"This again," Walther confirmed. "But I'm bringing Michael into it now. So I want you to tell him your take on it."

"My take?" she snorted. "My take's that they're a pack of cheating bastards who keep people like me down. It's a rich man's thing, this club of theirs."

"Freemasons," I said.

"Freemasons be damned," she said, and added some fairly serious language about freemasonry. "Freemasons aren't the half of it," she said. "This lot at the Dissipation Club are like freemasons *for* the freemasons. It's all posh lads like your man here, and rich lads, and family lads with places in the country, like Burke's f'ing peerage under one roof. And if you're not in with them, or if one of them doesn't like you, then you're buggered back and sideways, because you'll never get anywhere in life. Look at me. Am I where I should be, for my capabilities? For my experience? No, 'cos I'm Irish and I'm a woman and I'm not a member of the f'ing Club."

She went on like that in the same vein for about an hour, and we bought her drinks. She knew that a lot of her superiors, and more of their superiors, were either in this club or in the pocket of someone who was. It was just more freemasons to me. I was born at the bottom of the barrel. It didn't seem to make much difference to me whether it was a top club or a real tip-top club, if even middle-ranker clubs wouldn't take me in, save to stand at their doors and keep people out.

"Sod them," I said. "I'm still in."

After Hawker had left we went to a ratty little room Walther had rented, with cash and without questions. I sat like a lump until Walther smiled and said, "All right. I've been investigating the Dissipation Club for some time. I made one serious sortie, years before you met me. I was quite young. I got burned."

"So where did you hear about them?"

"This was when I was at school, last year there. Someone I knew, his father died. All very stiff upper lip stuff, you know. Except that a week later the two of us got out and got blind drunk on White Lightning, and he said all sorts of stuff about his old dad. He went on about how his dad had reckoned everything was on the up, on the brink of some great success. What a terrible shame it had happened just after getting into the club. What club? said I. He said he wasn't supposed to talk about it. That his dad hadn't been supposed to tell him. It was a secret club, you see."

"The Dissipation Club."

"I got it out of him," Walther agreed. "Quite possibly he didn't even remember telling me. However, a week later he was gone from the old Alma Mater and I never saw or heard from him again. But I remembered. I wanted to find out."

"What happened?"

"I asked a lot of questions. I splashed a lot of money around. I visited their clubhouse in London. I stood right where that MP had been standing. I talked to the staff, pretending I wanted to join. I found stuff out. It was one of the first investigations I did. I was as thorough as I could be, with what little they'd left me."

"And?"

"Historically? The Dissipation Club, previously known as the Dispation Society, has around for a long old time, Michael. There are references in documents from the reign of Elizabeth One, as you found, but they don't say it was *new* then. In fact some of them, some of the records I pirated from the British Museum way back, say that it was reckoned extremely old."

"So?"

"More recently... If you dig, really dig, in old newpapers, in the paper records, you find things. Not the Woo-waa, I'm sure. That's changing all the time, and I know damn well that the people we're dealing with can make all the changes they want. But if you dig and you dig, you come across missing people, Michael."

"There are always missing people."

"Oh yes, but missing poor people aren't news. These are rich people. People with titles. People of family. People with money by the bucket. People like my friend. Like Vanderfell Junior. There's a stir, just a little, when they vanish without a trace." Seeing my face he was quick to stop me interrupting. "And yes, that happens too. They commit suicide or run off to Brazil, but I did my research and I talked to a lot of people. I was the regular sleuth on a trail of clues. I found three names who were definitely linked to the Dissipation Club, and who had vanished, years apart, going back to the twenties. In fact since then I've found five more."

"And?"

"And what do you think I did, so full of youthful enthusiasm?"

"I think you went to the club and wanted answers."

"Full marks," Walther admitted. His face creased, showing old pain. "They were very polite, and very uninformative and, although I saw a few odd things, I didn't get the chance to explore. They put me back on the pavement, and that's when things went wrong."

"Things?"

Walther smiled. "Why, everything, Michael. Absolutely everything. The family home repossessed, old debts surfacing, shares falling through the floor, friends not wanting to know me, getting thrown out of university. *Everything*, Michael. You must have wondered what happened that I went from Harrow to that place I live in."

"I thought your dad put it on the horses," I said without thinking.

"My father joined the statistics I was researching," Walther said tightly. "Only in his case they found the body. He'd jumped into the Isis when he found out he was bankrupt. He'd written a note, they think, but he forgot to take it out of his pocket. He couldn't even get that right."

"They killed him?" I said, agog.

"No," Walther told me gently. "They didn't need to. He couldn't live without it. Perhaps they thought I couldn't either, but I did."

"So it's personal."

"Oh yes." Walther smiled again, as hard edged as I'd seen him. "And I've been keeping their file at the bottom of the stack, all this time. I'd never forgotten. I knew that the case would be handed back to me by someone, someone like Mr Vanderfell. It's time."

"What do you want to do?"

"I want to go pay the Club another visit. After all, we know where they live too. Coming?"

I am not at home in posh London, which is that bit around the west leg of the circle line with names like Kensington Something, and a whole load of other pieces of London Green Park way, or near where the lawyers hang out. London's a strange one though. You get real ratholes right next to the high society. I worked out that I'd done a few jobs within an easy walk of the Dissipation Club.

"We're just going to walk in?" I asked him. "Just walk right in? What if they shoot us or something?"

"They didn't shoot me last time," was Walther's only logic. "Just about everything else, but not that."

I didn't put into words my thought that they might save the shooting thing for people who called twice. Walther would just have told me that if I didn't want to come I could wait outside. I'd already left a message behind, to be sent to a few friends if I didn't call later to stop it, so they'd know where I'd gone. With a mob like this I wasn't sure it would matter.

The building was just like in the photo with the MP. The outside didn't look so old, but it had been redone a lot, and I knew I'd see those big old beams and low ceilings inside, whatever the outside looked like. The grey stone arch read "THE DISPATION SOCIETY" just as I'd seen. I made some comment to Walther that they couldn't spell worth a damn in those days and he gave me a funny look.

The doorman met us. He was ex-army in neutral dress. He wasn't got up in fringy epaulettes or in uniform, just a solid man in a long coat. I didn't think he had a gun underneath it, but that was probably because it would have spoiled the tailoring.

He wasn't going to let us in, and that would have been that. I didn't reckon I could throw him around, and anyway, it was hardly the time or place for it. Then he said, "Messrs Cohen and Liupowiktz?" and he got my name right first time, which is rare. In Prison I was Loopy first off, and that went to Nutter after I knocked a few of them about. I tell my employers I'm Mr. Lupo. To Walther I'm Michael. I don't hear my real name on a frequent basis.

"Got it in one," said Walther, and the doorman just stepped aside and let us up the steps. That scared me a lot. It's just like the supernatural, that. It's the world working in ways it shouldn't.

We went in to their hall. It was a big old place all right, with a panelled wooden ceiling and walls, and coats of arms on some of the walls, painted a long time ago in little, lots of them. The carpet was so thick you almost had to wade through it. There were huge leather armchairs and little tables. Two or three plumy old boys were sitting around smoking cigars. There was a waiter in a red jacket with a silver tray. He was also ex-army, my guess. Walther's whites and my monkey suit got a good few disapproving looks, which was almost worth the price of admission.

A waiter, a second ex-army waiter, came over and asked us if we'd like anything to drink, and that some Mister Hamley would be with us presently. Walther ordered a brandy and I said I'd have the same because I didn't fancy ordering a pint somewhere as upper crust as that place. Walther took an armchair and actually looked quite at home. He got a Times from a third waiter and began to read the business pages. I went over to look at a wall that had something as commonplace as photos on it. There were a few cricket teams, looking like they hadn't seen this side of the first world war, and there was a group of soldiers obviously about to be sent off into the middle of it. There were also some photographs of famous people. I saw some prime ministers there, and a few others I recognised. When Walther appeared at my elbow I said, "Look, Elvis!"

"The popular singer?" he asked, as if he only vaguely knew who I meant.

"No, Walther, the astronaut." I seldom got short with Walther, but Elvis was worth it. "Was Elvis a member of the Dissipation Club?"

"He was not, although he did perform here once," said a new voice, and we both turned to see one of the old boys, or a new old boy. He was turned out in blazer and cravat, and what hair he had left was white, but he wasn't so narrow in the shoulder at that. He had a moustache, and he could have sat for Agatha Christie as a retired Indian Army Colonel or whatever they are, who sometimes turn out to be the murderers. I looked into his eyes and decided that he could be the murderer quite easily.

"Mr Harmondersly," Walther said, only what he actually said was "Mr Hamley." He showed me how it was written down later. I don't think I'd have been able to treat the man as seriously if I knew he had a trick name. Walther said it in a weird way so you knew the other letters were in there somewhere.

"Mr Cohen." Mr Harmondersly was all polite, and he took us from the lounge into an office that was bigger than almost any room I've lived in. There was a great big desk and some brown old legal documents on the wall behind glass, and big bookshelves floor to ceiling behind Hardmondsly's chair that were all full of books in the same binding, like you get in professors' rooms. Harmondersly sat behind the desk, and we got seats before the desk, and even our seats were leather-upholstered and carved and everything. I had to remind myself that these were the bad guys.

With defiance, Walther put his hat down on the big man's desk.

"It has been quite a while since you last visited us, Mr Cohen," Mr Harmondersly said, with a pleasant smile. I knew he was the man Walther had spoken to before, who had ruined Walther's life. "In a way I'm surprised we've not met sooner. To what do we owe the visit?"

"I've been biding my time," Walther said. "Doing my research."

"Admirable." Mr Harmondsley nodded, and another butler that I hadn't even seen gave us refills of our brandy before stepping out. "You'll excuse me if I can't give you long. I have a guest speaker due shortly."

"Speaking on what, might that be?" asked Walther, not to be outdone in the politeness.

"Club business." Harmondersly brushed him off. "When you sat before me eight years ago, Mr Cohen, in fact I may say when you *confronted* me before, you had some remarkable allegations. I could not but help admire your imagination. Are you here on some kindred business?"

Walther reached into a pocket and pulled out a crumpled piece of paper, passing it wordlessly across the desk. Harmondersly unfolded it and read, without reaction.

"What should I remark upon?" he asked.

"The words are names, nine of them now," Walther said. "The numbers are dates upon which these people disappeared. All these people are linked to the Dissipation Club. I can prove it. The documents that prove it are in a safe place, and people have instructions to pick them up unless I tell them not to." Because this was pretty much what I'd done on this case, except for not having any documents or any idea what was going on, I felt proud of myself. Mr Harmondersly looked delighted, like Walther was a kid who'd been very clever at school.

"And this evidence you have, you've brought copies of course." He was not remotely bothered, and Walther was not bothered about that. The two of them were like old friends playing some kind of weird game, or like spies from opposite sides. They understood the rules and I didn't.

Walther produced his copies obediently: news cuttings, photocopies, scribbled notes on torn sheets of paper. Harmondersly looked over them patiently, despite his having appointments. At the end he smiled at Walther.

"Well I am surprised, Mr Cohen. I'm surprised that you took the time to find so much circumstance before darkening our door again. The Dissipation Club has a great many members who are newsworthy, and some of them have met unhappy ends. So have a great many people. It is a dangerous world."

"Not unhappy, unexplained," Walther said. "These people have disappeared without trace. All of them. What would you say to that?"

"That it is also a mysterious world, wherein our ability to uncover answers is oft-times unequal to nature's ability to obscure them, Mr Cohen. I understand that you have built a cottage industry on the uncovering of problematic answers, and so I understand why this revelation may be difficult for you, but it is true nonetheless. We live in imperfect times. We always have." I cannot believe how polite he was, saying this. Posh people have a special politeness they use to insult people.

"What do you think the press would make of this, Mr Harmondersly?" Walther demanded.

"Do you really think this is the sort of story that any newspaper would be interested in running?" Harmondersly enquired. The implication was unsaid, but I could hear it hanging there. Of the three of us in that room, it wasn't Walther or me who had the phone numbers of Fleet Street in our address books.

"Ah, well," said Walther, sounding deflated.

"Did you have anything else to accuse us of, while you are here, Mr Cohen?" asked Mr Harmondersly.

Walther looked at his accumulated evidence, made a couple of halfhearted gestures to it. It had been so thoroughly and briefly dismissed that I was amazed to see it still physically there. He looked utterly thrown, having prompted no reaction at all from his enemy. Hardmondersly smiled, just the kindly old man. I would have thought Walther was completely off his mark, if he hadn't just then tipped me the wink.

"Come on Michael," he said, "Let's go." He stood, and I went ahead of him, looking angry and disruptive. Harmondersly went with me, and I turned suddenly in the doorway and ran my brandy into him. It went all over his shirt and blazer and probably caused more property damage than I would if I set fire to my room, and to top it all I dropped the glass so that it broke against the wall, rather than hitting the morass carpet. Harmondersly looked aghast, and I looked mortified, and Walther did what he needed.

I have no idea what he set up but when we were three steps out of the office a fire alarm went off. There were no sprinklers, and suddenly old men were jumping out of armchairs, looking for buckets of sand. Harmondersly put us into the hands of one of the bouncer-waiters and made himself scarce into his office and we were almost out onto the street when Walther declared "My hat!"

He ducked under the waiter's arm and I got in the way enough that he was gone back after Harmondersly. The waiter hared off after him, but he was coming back out with his hat even before the man had reached the doorway, and without Harmondersly feeling his collar.

When we were out on the street he kept his hangdog look, but gave me a wink out of the corner of his eye.

We found a pub a good ten streets away and it was all I could do, on that walk, not to shake it out of him. As it was he waited until we had two pints on the table before he told me.

"Simple things. They can lean on the press and they can ruin families and they can make even rich people disappear, but the simple things work, like a match when the power's gone. When I got the fire alarms going Harmondersly was back into his office, why?"

"Because there's valuable stuff in there he wanted to save."

"Close enough," Walther allowed. "And when I went in there, what did I find?"

There was no answer to that, so I waited it out. He was brimming over with it and I didn't have to wait long.

"Not Mr Harmondersly, for starters," he told me. "But better than that. Rich people and their plush carpets, Michael. You don't have to be a Red Indian to read the tracks. Mr Harmondersly was indeed going to check on something precious but, whatever it was, it wasn't in his office. The shelves behind his desk open out. You could see where the pile had been smoothed over, a neat little quarter circle."

"Leading to what?"

"I don't know," Walther told me, "But I'm going to find out. We're going back."

"Now?"

He shook his head. "I think we've exhausted the subtle approach. Next time we're back with a vengeance, and we'll find our own way without the guided tour. A frontal assault, Michael."

"We're going to break in?"

"In one."

I thought about this. It was nothing that we hadn't done before, individually or together and for reasons investigative and criminal. It was just that a top London gents' club was a bit out of my league.

"Security systems," I said. "And probably they have staff on site at night, if there really is something there worth protecting."

"If?" Walther asked. He was genuinely hurt. "Michael, if you don't believe that there's something there, you have no business coming with me." And, right after, "If you don't think there's something funny going on, what do you think is? Vanderfell and the others just walked into the river on a bender?"

"Something's going on," I admitted. "Something that gets rich people killed, that they don't want people to know about."

"And you'd guess?"

I thought about that as well, and I gave it enough time that Walther got a second round in. "Two things," I said. "One, it's some rich man's whorehouse, kids or something, and every so often it goes so far that one of them gets squeamish. So they rub him out and cover it up."

Walther nodded.

"Two," I went on, "It's some rich man's sports thing, fighting or hunting or something, maybe even hunting people, extreme bloodsports. Only it's dangerous and sometimes the hunters get killed."

Another nod.

"I don't think it's our usual," I said, which was stupid, as our usual was everyone else's unusual. "Spooks and stuff, I mean. It's the rich, and they're doing something so bad that they actually have to cover it up, but it's just the rich."

Another nod. "And?" Walther said.

"And I'm in," I told him. "I'm with you."

"Good," he said. "Call Hawker. I have a plan."

What happened was this: At about two in the morning one Thursday, when even London is mostly off the streets outside the commercial district, someone lobbed a brick through one of the windows of the Dissipation Club. In fact what they did was lob a brick into the windows, with force. As the windows were a bit better than windows normally are, the brick ended up stuck there.

The Club's minder was at the door straight away, with a murderous look in his eye. He came out as soon as he'd finished unlocking the door, which took a while. He heard shouting as he did it, a woman's voice. When he got out he was met by an off-duty policewoman who'd just seen the culprits. She showed him her ID and everything. It turns out that these two blokes, a big one and a little one in a white hat, had just run away when she challenged them. When she mentioned the white hat the minder wanted to know as much as she could tell him. She obliged, going into considerable detail.

Meanwhile, Walther and I just walked in behind him, quiet as you like, into the silent lounge of the Dissipation Club. Hawker can be very distracting.

She wouldn't hold the man for long, so we made hotfoot to Harmondersly's office where Walther reckoned this secret door was. The carpet made sneaking about a piece of cake, frankly. The lounge and the office were still lit. I got the impression they didn't care much about the electric bill.

We could hear Hawker finishing up even as Walther started to search for the catch. I couldn't see anything, just a big bookshelf. Walther's hands passed over the bindings as though he was just looking for a good read.

"I think he's coming back," I whispered. I couldn't hear Hawker talking any more.

Walther grinned at me, and I knew he'd found it already and was just mucking me around. He tugged a book at doorhandle height, that looked a bit wooden now I saw it. A moment later the middle shelves swung out towards us, revealing darkness, and some stairs that went right down and around, and steep. We stepped in, as quiet as we could, and pulled it gently closed after us.

If the minder had thought to check, then we'd have had to throw him down those stairs or something. The plan was vague on that point. I'm guessing they didn't pick their nightwatch for imagination. No doubt he poked about in the office and just ducked out. Perhaps he didn't even know that part of the bookshelf was an exit.

We clicked our torches on. There were no lights at all down here, no switches and no fittings. The stairway spiralled down, stone-lined, looking old, the ceiling black from soot. The air from below was just like cold breath. We looked at each other. Walther was still grinning.

"I'll bet the Blitz didn't touch this," he said. "I'll bet the Great Fire didn't touch this." He went down the stairs faster than recommended, skidding a few times, torch beam waving wildly but always catching himself.

We went down four turns before it came out in a vaulted chamber, low-ceilinged and made up of a net of arches, rows and rows of pillars that made the stone above us a complicated lattice of crosses and squares. The stone here was mostly red, said my torch, but the arches were picked out in pale. My torch found a neat stack of boxes and crates at one end, and the biggest wine rack I ever saw.

"What now?" I asked. "What are you expecting?"

"I'm not expecting anything," Walther told me. Even whispering, the space did odd things with the echoes.

"Even if we find some kind of proof or something, what will we do with it?" I pressed. It was a bit late for this kind of reasoning, but I went on. "Harmondersly was right, the papers won't buy it. No-one will."

Walther turned sharply, staring down my torch. "Michael, two things: secondmost is that if I can spanner their works in some way then, as God is my witness, I will. But firstly, when we find out, then I'll *know*. I'll know what it was for. I'll know why. And *that*, that's the point."

"Walther," I said. "It's a cellar. They keep their cheese and wine down here."

He smiled and directed his torch behind me. I looked and saw the door. It fit one of the archways that led beyond the cellar, dark old wood with a big ring handle. Tilting his hat at a cocky angle, Walther led the way to it and tried to open it. His smile slipped slightly when it wouldn't turn. My own torch found the big rough-cut keyhole.

"Would you do the honours?" he asked me. I knelt down and reached in my pocket for my picks. It's a grand old art form that's dying out in a lot of places these days. Kids would rather knock in a window and just grab stuff. There aren't so many people like me who care about the trade. Anyway I almost needn't have bothered here. It was a simple old lock, well oiled, and big enough that I could probably have lined up the tumblers with my finger. As it was my pick was too delicate but I managed it by using an actual key to flip them straight. Walther and I exchanged another glance and I pulled the door open.

The room beyond was pitchy, and we flashed our torches about a weirdly civilised scene, seeing flashes of silver plate, polished wood. Then Walther leant in and flicked the lightswitch.

The chandelier above us glowed into life, and revealed the grandest dining room I ever saw, let alone the poshest one ever put in a cellar. It was the same décor from upstairs, same carpet even. The walls made up in portraits and framed legalese papers what they lacked in windows. There was a massive fireplace, wood stacked neatly beside it. The table, which could have seated fifty people with elbow room, was made from a single slab of some kind of wood, varnished dark red and inlaid with... scenes.

I tried hard to make out what those scenes were showing. It was some sequence of events, but it went round the table's edge and it was impossible to tell where it started. It was done in mediaeval style, everyone with big heads and standing weird, all half-front on to me. Some of them were hunting. Some of them were on boats. There was a knight-looking chap lying dead beside a black lake, who could have been King Arthur for all I know. A comet or a falling star turned up a few times. Two blokes on a horse were doing a Saint George act, and while normally Saint George is killing a dragon about the size of a cat, this one made up most of the table's centre. It was all coils of neck and tail, claws and teeth. Someone had a lot of red and black left over, after finishing the edge, because they'd spent a lot of time and table on that dragon.

I couldn't help but recall that the furnishings upstairs had been lots of reddish and dark shades, just like the colours in here. There was even a red cross as part of the table inlay, a fancy-pointed one. There was a lot going on in that table. The background turned out to be more of the foreground, when you looked closely. Balancing the red cross was the pyramid-eye thing the Americans use on their money, and I've flogged enough trick rings to recognise the set square and stuff that the Freemasons use.

"Walther, you have got to see this table," I told him.

"Look," was all he said.

I'd passed over what he'd found, because I'd thought it was just one of those lists of names. People who died in the war or maybe a list of the club chairmen. It was just like those, names and dates, black with gold lettering. Walther was pointing to the most recent addition.

"James Vanderfell," I read. "Two thousand and six." I shivered, but it was excitement as much as anything. "We were right. You were right."

"I was," Walther agreed. "And they're all there. Everyone I've linked to the club, and a few I couldn't prove, and..." He looked on and on.

"Every seven years," I said. Each name had a single date. Each date was seven years before the next. Before Vanderfell Junior was a Captain Graham Cordwright, nineteen ninety-nine.

It was a big board, taking up half the space from floor to ceiling. It had three columns, in medium small writing, and little Jimmy was halfway down the third. Our eyes were drawn inexorably up and up.

Walther had already got there. I'd heard his hiss of breath. When I joined him, the top of the first column, the style was illegible, for all someone had touched it up in gold leaf recently.

"Sir Geoffrey Martlet," Walther said, his voice shaking a little. "Eleven Forty-five."

The silence crept in after that. Walther stepped back almost reverently from the board. "Photo it," he told me. I did, on my phone.

He was looking at something else, when I'd done that. There was a big glass-fronted drinks cabinet but on top of it, close to eye level, were three things.

Two were cups or bowls, one silver and the other gold, both set with twiny patterns. Between them was a little golden stand, just a block with two fingers sticking up at each end. It was crude as anything but it was almost certainly solid gold. The prongs were holding a knife.

It had a blade of copper, and a hilt wound with cold wire. I touched it, and it cut my finger a touch, almost no pressure. You can get copper sharp enough to shave with, you see, although it blunts in no time. We looked at the cups, which were broad enough and big enough to be bowls, really. When I got them down we saw that the golden one had a certain discolouring, on the inside surface.

"Enough of it," Walther said what I'd bee thinking. "Over and over, enough of it, and even the most diligent staff can't quite get it clean."

"It's a cult," I said, because labels are useful when you're scared.

"Onwards," was all Walther said. There were two doors to this room. One of them, on cursory investigation, proved to be a kitchen.

That gave me a funny turn. I couldn't make myself go to the back where the freezer was. It's one of those things, those unspeakable things that just won't go away. There's a kind of horrible awe to the idea of eating other people. It's all kinds of symbolism and power. The Dissipation Club were rich and greedy. To eat their own species would be in reality what they did every day metaphorically. To eat one of their actual own would be... fitting.

There was a bit of meat in the freezer, or so Walther said. He recognised venison and boar and steak and some kind of small birds. It didn't look well stocked, but he said, "Seven years to the next feast perhaps? And there aren't any leftovers from Vanderfell Junior, if that's what you're thinking. If they ate him, they ate him all up." He said it like he was telling Goldilocks, just to make me shudder.

The kitchen didn't go anywhere else so we were left with the other door. There was a draft from under it, colder than cold.

It was locked, but the lock was the same clunky old thing as the last and I had it open in a moment. It opened onto another set of stairs, spiral again, going down.

"We'll either hit the sewers or the Metropolitan line in a minute, won't we?" I asked.

"I'm willing to bet they made a special detour for both, to avoid this place," Walther said bleakly. "Come on."

I didn't want to. The feeling about the freezer hadn't left me. I'm not imaginative but my mind was full of ghouls and Morlocks and things just then. Walther, in the doorway, looked back at me, giving me a smile. It would have been pointless to ask whether he had any idea what was down there. He didn't, and that was why he had to go look.

"Walther, you're all kinds of psychic," I said. "Aren't you... feeling anything?" I was. I really was.

"No," he said, with a little frown. "Not a thing." He turned and went into the dark.

It was a count of seven before I could follow him. I was sweating despite the cold, my teeth jumping. I've seen some stuff, in my time, but I was scared here. It wasn't what had been done, or was being done, whatever that was. It was that rich people were doing it. Monsters you can sometimes reason with. I was scum off the streets, and a monster would have had more time for me than Mr Harmondersly.

But I followed Walther in there, God help me. I followed him down those stairs. They were grey stone now, and the stones were quite big, all different sizes. To take my mind off it I asked, "How old?" to Walther, two turns below me.

"Early medieval," he said and then, "Older." The echo told me he was at the bottom.

I joined him. The ceiling here was even lower, making me stoop. Walther had taken his hat off. Our torches were all the light there was. When you've only got the beams of two torches, it's very difficult to completely get the feel of a place, seeing it only in small slices. The room was big. There was what I thought was a big stone coffin in the centre, like a knight's tomb. It was just a slab, though. The cupboard-things at the sides were stone basins. There was a certain amount of staining there, as well.

There were big stone-stoppered jars, two feet high. I counted eighteen of them. When Walther lifted a fist-sized stopper the smell was weird and vinegary, and very strong. He closed it hurriedly.

There were designs on the walls. They were made of lots of little pieces of stone, and a lot of the pieces had gone missing. Walther's torch beam searched them out, trying to find them, seeing hands, feet, trees. Too much was gone to tell, but the odd piece just reminded me of that table. I saw the same falling star or whatever it was, almost intact.

"There's more stairs," I said. Walther nodded. Not a spiral flight, but a straight descent, and one that nearly killed us more dead than any monster because the stone was worn into bows, and it was so steep I reckoned they could have put a lift in without taking the stairs out.

I had lost track of how deep we were, now, but when we got to the bottom I couldn't but notice that the walls were just faced with big slabs of stone. A bit of torchwork told me that it was rock behind them. We were in a cave that had been cut out to be bigger than the dining room, with pillars keeping the cramped ceiling in place, and there was nothing in there, no decoration, nothing: just another doorway beyond. Our breath plumed white in the little lights we had brought with us, and we took turns to change batteries, because the light was failing. The air smelt of something musty.

The opening on the far corner was cut roughly rectangular, and it led into an identical room. Our torches picked out the same pillars, the slabs that made the walls, before they settled on something pale at the far end, next to a further dark hole.

We advanced cautiously and I stopped when I saw what it was, although it was clear enough they wouldn't be making trouble for us.

Something had been done to them. Their skin was gone like leather, dried over their bones. Someone had given them a real beef jerky treatment, and I thought of the room back there, with the slab and the sink and the jars, and what they might do there, after the business with the knife and the bowls was finished with. The man furthest from the opening was recognisable though. We'd both seen his face in the file enough times.

"I think we've found Junior," I said.

There were three of them, sitting with their backs to the wall as though guarding the opening, or as though waiting in line. They had their legs crossed, their arms folded across their chest. I didn't touch them, but when Walther did it looked like their skin was hard as wood. Each had a long line across their throats, the edges peeled back a little, that told just how they'd ended up. They wore white robes, and they had gold necklaces, a disc on a woven gold chain. The disk had marks on it, but they just looked like lines. Walther lifted one up, peering closely, not caring how close he brought his face to a mummified dead American.

"I've seen this before," he said, hushed. "Nowhere near here. There are stone tombs, the Scottish islands... old writing, Michael. Old."

"What does it say?"

"Alas, I don't know. Nobody does. Or that's what I thought before coming down here. Perhaps it's a curse on those who disturb this place." He grinned, half desperation, half desperate cheer at having found out so thoroughly much more than he'd thought. "Perhaps Junior and his friends are symbolic guardians, to stop us going further."

"And will they?" I asked.

"Only one way to find out," he said, and walked straight past into the low opening. I was frozen to the spot for a second, and there was utter silence. "Walther?" I said, and then "Walther!" and damn the echo, but there was nothing.

I made myself follow him. The dead trio didn't move. Walther was there, just beyond the doorway, but he was frozen and I froze too. For a very long time neither of us had words for it. At last it was me who found something to say.

"Disneyland," I said in a raw, horrified voice.

Walther blinked and snapped out of it, turning his torch on me. "I'm sorry what?"

"Disneyland," I said again, because that was all it reminded me of, in the whole world. If you haven't been to Disneyland then any big fun park will do. It's the same with all of them, the way they make use of their space. You spend most of your time there queuing, and they make you line up, up and down, up and down, the interlocking barriers compressing a half-mile queue into a neat little box. It was Disneyland. It was Disneyland for the dead. The barriers here were almost the same, and everyone was waiting in line, except that they were sitting down, white robes in graded stages of decay, legs folded, arms crossed, and each with their lucky medallion.

Walther was counting, depth by width, and I really didn't want to know the answer. I couldn't stop looking though. My torch just went from rank to rank of dried-kipper faces, a study in gradual dessication in seven-year intervals.

"Gaps," I said. It was true. Every so often there was a space, five or ten or so bodies wide, just left empty. It was as though the whole thing would make a picture or spell something out when viewed impossibly from above.

"That's awkward," Walther said. "If we had all hands present and accounted for there would be space for two hundred, but if they're going to leave gaps I won't bother." A moment of calculation and he said, slightly shakily, "But even if one out of spaces is just punctuation we're already beyond Sir Geoffrey Martlet. We're before the Norman invasion, at one every seven years."

My torch was shaking and I brought it down to the floor at my feet. I tried several times before I could say it. "In- in the far corner, Walther. There's-another hole."

I didn't think I could bear it, to go queue-jumping in that place: to sidle along the waiting ranks, brushing against the paper-dry dead, but when Walther went, I followed. I'm stupid like that. Sometimes I just cannot believe how stupid I am.

Neither of us suggesting vaulting the barriers. The ceiling was low and the barriers were wood that might not have borne us, and besides, it would have been disrespectful. So Walther and I wound our way in and out of the patient corpses, speeding when we found a gap, slowing again at the next of the deceased.

Walther actually chuckled, halfway there. "I'll say one thing," he said. "This is certainly very British." And we pushed our way to the front of the queue.

It was not the front of the queue. The hole lead into another carved out cave, and that one was full as well with the snaking lines of the ancient dead. I saw Walther's lips move a couple of times, seeing the same pattern: economy of space with a shotgunning of random gaps, some of which must have been twenty dead men long. There was little deterioration of the bodies, even compared to Junior two rooms back, but it was there, and I said, "How long?"

Walther shook his head. "They can't be every seven years. I won't believe it. If they were all here we'd be... before the Romans came here. Before the birth of Christ." He swallowed. "Before the Roman Empire even started maybe."

"Walther," I said slowly. "There's another-"

"I know. I don't care. I won't believe it." He said that, but he was already moving down the zig-zags of the dead. I had no trouble following him now. That was because I had realised that the room of ancient dead people in front of me was matched by a room of ancient dead people *behind* me, and I wasn't going to get left with it.

We were halfway through the room when the light went on. It was another torch but it was a big, bright white one. Suddenly everything around us was better lit up than either of us wanted. We turned automatically, trapped in a maze of corpses. Of course we just saw the light but someone said, "I really must commend you." He said it quietly but the only other sound was us and so we heard it very clearly.

The voice was familiar, and when the light was turned a little we could make out Mr Harmondersly standing in the entrance we had come through, all smart in his blazer as though we were not standing waist deep in a dead-man's theme park. He had a gun, and although it was pointed at us it was almost a relief to see something I could understand.

"Mr. Cohen," Harmondersly said. "You have done remarkably well."

"Not quite well enough," Walther noted, actually leaning on one of the barriers, as though he and Harmondersly were just chatting, without gun.

Harmondersly began to make his careful way towards us. I could see he was used to it. He didn't jog a single body and the gun never wavered. "You might as well continue," he said. "You might as well see all of it."

"How many more rooms?" Walther asked.

"The next is the first. Go on ahead of me, if you would."

"What if I'd rather just push you into shooting me now?" Walther asked him, not going anywhere.

"Oh but you wouldn't, Mr Cohen," Harmondersly said. "You'd rather find out, and then be shot. Tell me it isn't true."

Walther's face showed that it was, and with a shrug he went on, weaving down the lanes of the dead. Their skin was taut over skull and bones, this far in. There was not even a rag left of any robes they might have worn. The air was cool and dry, though, and there was not a hole or mark on them, save for the cut throats. Seeing so many, I was an expert on the subject right there. Each man had his throat slashed cleanly, without ragged edges. The angles were all so very similar, like whoever did it was copying from a book.

We got to the next opening. Walther stepped inside, torch moving. I looked to see if Harmondersly was close enough to rush, but he was two lines back. The time to jump him would be at the entrance, I knew, but it would be tight. His hair might be white but he held himself well, moved easily. I reckoned he was another old army bird. A stray shot would go badly for me or for Walther.

I followed Walther in, very tense, looking back. I bumped into him, because he was stopping to stare. I looked where his torch went.

It was another room of dead men, although the gaps were larger, an entire row and a half in one case. I knew Walther would be trying to count back the years, but just then I didn't want to know.

This room was more of a cave. At our end it had been shaped a bit, propped up. At the other end it was just the natural rock, and the natural rock was doing something unpleasant. It disappeared. The far end of the cave just fell away, a twenty-foot chasm that was utterly, completely dark.

There was a click next to my head. It was Harmondersly cocking his revolver. It was easily close enough to make a grab for it, but what the films don't teach you is that, reactions aside, it's quicker to pull a trigger than move for a gun. I'd missed my chance. The old boy had come up behind us quicker than I'd thought. He nodded, and Walther and I moved along a bit.

"So what's the story?" Walther asked? "You owe me that much."

"Because of what we did to you? We owe you nothing," Harmondersly said. "For finding your way here, however... Perhaps you should tell me your conclusions to date. It would save time."

"The Dissipation Club is continuing a tradition of murder that goes back… a very long time," Walther said. I was making sure to stay between him and the gun, so he had to speak almost under my armpit.

"And our victims are…?"

"Members of the club, it would seem. I'd guess new members, who are promised some social advantage when they join, and then done away with."

"And why would we do such a thing?" Harmondersly asked.

"Cheap thrills?" Walther suggested. "Or maybe you are a cult. Maybe you think you're bringing the second coming."

"Does it matter?" I said.

Harmondersly's smile was just visible in the light of his lowered torch. "Mr Cohen knows that it matters. 'Why?' is always the most important question. How long, Mr Cohen?"

Walther gave a kind of hopeless laugh. "Well all things being equal, Mr Harmondersly, there's space for enough bodies to take us back to around fifteen-hundred BC, but I don't believe it."

"Your logic is impeccable," Harmondersly congratulated him. "However, all things are not equal, and the interval between formal meetings of the Club was only standardised around the time of the Crusades." At Walther's brief nod he added, "Before then the interval was frequently longer than seven years. Our tradition cannot be dated with accuracy, but it came to these isles before metalworking did. My earliest counterparts watched Stonehenge being built. You are looking at the honoured dead of over five thousand years."

Walther said nothing, and so Harmondersly added. "Kindly make your way to the edge, Mr Cohen."

"Well of course. The best view from the good seats," Walther almost mumbled. He was doing it, too, making his subdued way towards that chasm. Of all things I didn't want to go any nearer, but at the same time I wouldn't leave Walther unprotected, for what little good I could do.

"He's going to push us in!" I hissed.

"Is that what you think?" Harmondersly asked, not confirming or denying. He followed us at a leisurely pace. I tried to work out whether we could wait until he was at the far end from the entrance and then just hurdle our way to freedom, but he would get far too much of a chance to shoot us, and it was a good bet that he was a good shot. I had to hope he'd come close again.

Walther was at the end by this point, with me three corpses behind him. Close to, the pit was huge. The cold draft was coming from it, too, and it smelled funny. It smelled bad, but not any smell I could put a name to, not anything I'd ever smelled before.

"What, then?" Walther asked, on the edge of the abyss. Harmondersly's torch lit him up like a firework in his white suit. He looked back at the old man. "What then? I'm here. You've got a gun. It's the end. But tell me. What have you got down there?"

"The reason for all of this, Mr. Cohen," Harmondersly said. "What its name is I cannot say, but the Romans called it Dispater."

Walther choked on that and I had to ask twice before he'd tell me.

"The Father of Wealth," he said. "God of the underworld, to the Romans." He managed a little grin. "You're thinking it was Mickey Mouse's dog, aren't you?" because we'd had that conversation before. "They got Pluto from the Greeks, but from north and west Europe... they got Dispater. The Dispation Society. The Dissipation Club. Oh very clever."

"I'm glad you approve," Mr Harmondersly said.

"And he's down there is he?"

"Yes."

"You seem very certain. What does he look like?"

"No mortal eye has seen Dispater for two thousand years," Harmondersly said. "The earliest and only description says it is a thing of all shapes and no shape, a horror of shadows. I paraphrase, of course."

"Of course. So how do you know he hasn't died or moved on, old Dizzy?" Walther's irreverence was wasted. Harmondersly was unflapped.

"Because of the evidence you have passed by. Why do you think there are gaps in the ranks of the dead, Mr Cohen? Because when Dispater wakes, he is hungry."

With the pit at our backs, with that constant, sour breath coming out of it, I let out a bit of a whimper at that point. Walther's hand found mine and squeezed.

"It came from the skies, the writings say, like a mountain of fire, and it is hungry. It sleeps for many generations. Sometimes it wakes." Harmondersly was saying it like it was a church reading. "When it wakes, it is drawn to its sigil, stamped in gold, and it feeds, consuming always the freshest first and working its way back, through the years of our sacrifices, until it is sated. Sometimes its hunger is swiftly assuaged, and sometimes it feeds long and long. The space I am now standing in represents at least two centuries of offerings, at one sitting."

"Why leave the gaps empty? Poor economy of space." Walther was trying to be calm, but his voice was ragged.

"Where Dispater has fed," Harmondersly said, "No corpse will rest easily."

I let out another sound.

"And so you run your little murder club to feed it," Walther said. "And what gives you the right? Because you're rich? Because you can?"

171

"Yes!" Harmondersly was fierce with it. "Because nobody else can. For five thousand years those who govern and rule have appeased this hunger, whether they be Britons or Romans, Saxons or Normans, Englishmen or Great Britons once again. The secret is kept because it is too awful for the world to know that this devouring thing lies here beneath the earth, and must have human flesh when it wakes. The practices of the Britons that so appalled the Roman invaders had their origins here, but when the Romans understood then, their governors and generals kept them, and kept them underground. These men around you are kings, Mr Cohen. They are senators and chieftains and noblemen of the British Isles, and they are not unwitting victims. Each one knew the risk he ran, to protect Britain from the devouring hunger of Dispater. Through the centuries we have kept faith. We have put ourselves forward for this service, the rulers and the wealthy, the Dissipation Club. The men whose names you passed to me, Mr Cohen, are not victims, they are heroes, who made the ultimate sacrifice for this country and this world. Dispater is called the father of wealth, but like so many gods he devours his children."

"I'd have thought you'd just take tramps from the streets," Walther said, and at last Harmondersly looked insulted.

"Our trust is a sacred one. We are not murderers. We are those with the wealth and power to keep this greatest of secrets, and for that wealth and power, we pay the price, every seven years."

"And others pay the price, for your secrecy," Walther almost whispered.

"Do you not think the secret justifies such payment?" Harmondersly asked him.

Walther was quiet a long time before I heard him sigh. "God help me," he said. "Maybe it does. How many people know about this?"

"The members of the Club only, and they are chosen carefully. The most responsible, the most entrenched, the most honourable, the most reliable. They are sounded out well before they are approached. Almost always they are drawn from the highest echelons of society, so that they have power with which to defend their sleeping charge from inquisitive men, such as you."

"Ah yes, me. And what now? You want Michael and I to pop down there and see if Dizzy's sleeping peacefully?"

"Occasionally however," Mr Harmondersly said, as if Walther hadn't spoken, "There are those who, despite all our efforts, uncover the truth of the Dissipation Club. I am not a villain in some American film, Mr Cohen. If I had wanted to kill you then I would not have bothered with all this explanation."

Another heavy pause before, "Are you offering..."

"I am offering you membership in the Club," Mr Harmondersly said carefully. "With your persistence, I feel that you have earned it."

"It's a trick," I said immediately. "You can bet who'll be sitting next to Jim Junior come the time."

"It would be an overly complex plot if I intended to let your friend go only to arrange his death in seven years' time," said Mr Harmondersly with the contempt of a rich man for his inferiors. "Mr Cohen, you are an educated man. You are a man whose mind is strong. You come recommended by your clients. You are of good family, though fallen on hard times."

Walther grinned at that, without humour, and he must have been thinking of his father. Harmondersly meant him to, to show Walther he was being open at last. "Our duty is sacred, as I hope I have imposed upon you," he went on. "You would have no greater chance than I, to be the chosen one. Mr Cohen?"

Walther paused a long time, on the brink of that. "What," he asked at last, "about Michael?"

"Mr Liupowiktz does not meet with the entry requirements of the Dissipation Club," Harmondersly said, and I felt Walther bunch up beside me, ready to spit in the eye of Dispater if he had to, but the old man was going on. "Mr Liupowiktz can however take a place on the staff. He would seem to have the qualities of capability and loyalty that we require. Perhaps he would even serve at the next club meeting, if he still suspects foul play."

"You want me to be your waiter?" I spat at him. He regarded me coldly.

"Is it so demeaning?" he asked. "Your name, Mr Liupowiktz, would at least not go into the silver cup, as mine has done many times. Mr Cohen, have you an answer for me? If you are considering your family fortunes, these can of course be repaired."

Walther let out a brief, hard laugh. "Oh I'll not take charity, Mr Harmondersly. I'll take from you exactly what Vanderfell offered us, because he won't pay up when I draw a blank on his son. I'll take a promotion for a friend of mine, who's been short of one for a long time. Other than that, I won't take a penny from you." He looked at me, and I'm not sure whether he was apologising or not. "But I'll take your offer. How could I not?"

I was waiting to find out if it was a trick, but Harmondersly put his gun away right then. He and Walther were from the same world. They had an understanding I couldn't break into.

"Tell me though," Walther said. "I've always been sensitive, to all manner of things. I'm standing here next to a pit that's full of stargod, and... nothing."

"You were born in this country, Mr Cohen," Harmondersly said. "You have lived in the psychic footprint of Dispater all your life. In order to escape it, to feel the lack of it, you would have to journey to Eastern Europe or Africa or cross the Atlantic. And there you would feel the touch of other beings of the same nature and magnitude. The thing that sleeps beneath the Pyramids is called Apep, by the ancient priesthood that has always guarded it. The others we cannot name. Their guardians are secret enough to evade even our searches, but they are tended, for if they were ever unleashed upon the world then believe me, everybody would know it."

He was walking back now, making his practised way up and down, and Walther was following him. Being stupid, though, I turned and looked down into the pit with my torch.

I was expecting just rock and a drop, but at the very edge of the light, where it was thinned down to almost nothing, I saw something shiny and slick, and it moved.

I followed right after the others, after that.

We blew Vanderfell off, and he didn't seem surprised. He obviously didn't think much of us. Not a satisfied customer. We went back to our lives, and all the little irritants stopped, of course. DS Hawker got her promotion.

And in a few years time, Walther has a dinner appointment, and they'll have to find a way to fit me into one of those red waiter's jackets, because there's no damn way I trust any of those rich bastards.

DAVID ANNANDALE is the author of *Crown Fire*, *Kornukopia* and *The Valedictorians*, thrillers featuring rogue warrior Jen Blaylock. His short stories have appeared in numerous anthologies of horror fiction, including *Dead But Dreaming*, *The Asylum, Volume 2: The Violent Ward*, and *Wild Things Live There: The Best of Northern Frights*. He teaches literature and film at the University of Manitoba, writes film reviews for *Videoscope* and UpcomingDiscs.com, and is working on a book about video games, along with many other stories and novels of horror and mayhem, because that is what the world needs. He lives in Winnipeg with his very patient wife and family.

Lure

by David Annandale

Don Hubbard realized he needed a drift net. He stood beside the Circulation desk of Dunfax University's Edgerton Library, just past the security turnstile, in a straight line from the entrance. Not hard to spot, and still he kept having to call out to his students as they wandered by, oblivious, eyes nothing but big orbs of disorientation. One of too many signs of the times. It was late February, he'd just handed out the final essay assignments in his freshman English course, and the library was obviously terra incognita for his class. He wasn't surprised. It was the same story every year. But it depressed him every year. Too many of the faces showed no curiosity, only puzzled, resentful confusion at the absence of spoon-fed information. He would try to break through that barrier, but he was already feeling drained by the knowledge of his inevitable failure.

When he was sure there were no more trailing minnows to gather, he led the way past Circulation to the library's computer lab. The students spread out in the room, sat two to a monitor, instantly started to surf. Hubbard's mental image shifted from fishing to herding cats. He walked down the rows, shutting down Facebook pages and webmail. "Your attention to the front, if you don't mind," he said, in his best Incipiently Angry Dad voice.

And at the front was Mike Glick, the reference librarian, who should already have had his Power Point presentation up on main screen, but didn't. Surprise, surprise. "Well," Glick swallowed. "Welcome." He stabbed at his computer as if he could make it boot faster. Leaning against the rear wall, Hubbard saw fingers play with keyboards, monitors flicker with ADD. He stifled a groan, let the apathy creep in. So they weren't going to pay attention. Their loss when it came to the grades. They were adults. There were limits to how much hand-holding and discipline-enforcing he could bring to the table, especially on his sessional salary. He was carrying a full course-load, three-in-the-morning marking sessions were regular events, and his reward was to graze the poverty line. Sometimes he was just above, other times just below, especially those summers when the competition for the off-season courses was fierce. He had a mantra. He'd learned it as a graduate student when he'd joined the other toilers in the trenches of the English Department's utility teaching. The mantra was *They Don't Pay Me Enough*. He'd been paid barely enough to eat, so certainly not enough to care. What was true then was even more true now, the "PhD" at the end of his name growing stale, his best-before date long-since expired. He'd put in over ten years of one-term-at-a-time teaching gigs. He'd spent eight of those years applying for full-time positions, what few there were in an academic world cinching its belt tighter every day. No luck, and now there never would be. Whatever new jobs appeared were earmarked for the newly minted Doctors of Philosophy. His thesis, never reworked into a book, was old news. He could read the writing on the wall. His destiny lay in the academic service sector. He accepted that. He did his job. He did it well. But it had been a long time since he'd gone any extra miles.

Glick finally opened up his presentation and began to speak. Hubbard tried to stay focused on what he was saying; there might be the odd keener with a question later. The effort was killing. Hubbard liked Glick, had done lunch with him a couple of times, but his delivery was a drone punctuated by long pauses, hesitations and self-corrections. Then there were the digressions, as he abruptly remembered information he should have conveyed five minutes earlier. These tutorials on using the library resources spared Hubbard some prep, but the effort to stay awake was the harder strain.

Thirty minutes in, Hubbard had long-since lost the train of Glick's explanations, and was reminding himself again not to bother with this exercise next year. At last, Glick reached the only really coherent and useful part of the hour. The students were each assigned a random book title. They had to search the on-line catalog, find the call number, and fetch the actual physical specimen. Then the drone was over. Even standing, Hubbard had been wrestling sleep. He took the class out of the lab, thanking Glick as he walked past.

Up now, to the second floor, to turn them loose in the book stacks. The students hesitated before the aisles, the herd bunching together in reaction to a threat. Hubbard didn't know if it was the sheer number of books that was making them skittish, or the simply the presence of books. He feared it was the latter. He hoped it was the former. If it was, he found it hard to blame a clutch of eighteen- and nineteen-year-olds from quailing at their first sight of the main collection. The library was something in Dunfax that had been done right.

Dunfax wasn't a big town, and was smaller than it had been in its early-70s prime, back before the industrial sector had shut down, one plant at a time. The community would have been lost in its south-western corner of Manitoba if not for the University. In a good year, close to fifteen thousand students poured in, most from the giant catchment of rural communities dotting the Manitoba, Saskatchewan and North Dakota prairie. The big draw on campus was the Agricultural Sciences, but the Arts had a library out of all proportion to the size of its departments. It was the legacy of Jonathan Edgerton, a grain baron and lover of literature who had had the financial acumen to die of a stroke in 1928, thus ensuring his fortune went intact into a gigantic library endowment he had set up for the fledgling institution. The endowment was still the library's lifeblood. New acquisitions didn't pour in the way they once had, but they still arrived. In the rare moments he had for his own research, Hubbard could do a lot of digging right here, without the recourse to inter-library loans.

To a first visitor, though, the library was an intimidating collision of too much and too little. The book stacks were legion, marching off in rows that disappeared into the distance and concealed the far walls, along which carrels huddled close to the inadequate windows. There were too many rows, and there was not enough space. There was barely room to walk down a given aisle. It was impossible to crouch face-on to a stack. The lighting was low, enough to read by, but only just, and the far ends of the aisles dropped off into dimness. There was wealth here, but it didn't believe in making itself easy of access.

"Check the call number range," Hubbard told his group. "There's an indicator at the end of each aisle." On yellowing cardboard, written in fading marker, true, but visible all the same. "Okay?" he said. They all stared at him. "Off you go." He pushed out with the palm of his hands, sending them in on their way. "Go."

They went, none too happy about things, but they went. He felt a twinge of envy. There were some bright lights in the class, and this exercise would click for them, make them shine a little bit brighter, and they would experience the fresh joy of the rush the library could offer. It would blossom for them, unfolding labyrinthine layers of knowledge petals. They would start to see the books as something other than an obsolete medium whose analog page flipping was an inconvenient substitute for the digital. Every worn binding would offer the promise, or at least the potential, of another little epiphany. There were also the little pleasures, the serendipitous trivialities that led nowhere but were a kick to find. He remembered, as an undergrad, researching a paper on Chaucer and stumbling over a bowdlerized version of *The Canterbury Tales* cleaned up for children. The book's author was dead and forgotten, its project was dead and ridiculous, but it clung to its little shelf space all the same, a hard, dusty little package of hope that it might yet prove useful, or, if nothing else, grant one more reader an amused snort.

Hubbard checked his watch. They had ten minutes. More than enough, even for the most numerically obtuse. One by one, they trickled back, assigned books in hand. A few had to be sent out again when they came back with nothing and wanted to give up. But then the job was done, and it was time to wrap things up. "English 1200!" he called out, breaking the silence of the stacks, but not by much. The massed walls of books muffled and swallowed his echoes.

"Time!" He waited one more minute for stragglers. There was one. Then, with his minnows gathered once more, he translated a couple of Glick's more gnomic utterances back into English. When he was finished, he said, "Clear? Good. Go check your books in with Mr. Glick, and I'll see you Friday."

And that was the last class of the day. So then it was off home to his one-bedroom apartment, and the routine day wound down in its routine way until the call came and the darkness descended.

It was past ten, and he was deep in marking hell, plowing his way through the fourth C-minus in a row, when the phone rang. "Don, it's Ellen Jacobson." The Chair of the English Department did not sound happy. Hubbard tensed. He got along with Jacobson, but they didn't socialize, rarely spoke on the phone, and never after hours. "You have a student named Bryce Browning in your 1200 section?"

Normally, Hubbard would have to check his class list. His memory for names was atrocious, and even now, six months into the regular session, he could connect the faces and names of fewer than half of his students. But Bryce Browning owed his parents some serious payback for the terrible alliteration, and his was the first name Hubbard had learned this year. "Yes," Hubbard said. "Why?"

"Was he in class today?"

Hubbard thought for a minute, trying to visualize the afternoon's group. There were forty students in the class, and most of them had shown up. He remembered Browning was one of those who hadn't been able to find his book right away, and had been sent back into the stacks. "Yes, he was. What's going on?"

"He's missing. I've just had his parents and the police on the phone, and we're trying to figure out when he was last seen."

"What?" Hubbard frowned in disbelief. "He's an adult. It's draft night. Has it occurred to anyone that he might be at a bar with some friends?"

"It has, and that's being looked into. But I was just speaking with Mike Glick, and Bryce is your only student who didn't turn a book in this afternoon."

"Really?" Hubbard flipped through his memories, trying to spot Browning's face as the class wrapped up.

"Did you check that everyone was back?"

"I took them to the library, not Kandahar," he snapped. "And no, I'm not in the habit of taking attendance at the *end* of class. Are you?" For Christ's sake, what was being implied here? That he should never let anyone set foot in the library unchaperoned? What the hell kind of bullshit was this? He wasn't taking the blame for anything. (But now, a sudden, sick worry: why did he think anything had happened that required blame?)

Jacobson didn't answer his question. Instead, she said, "Would you mind meeting me at the library?"

"When?"

"Now."

Ridiculous, he thought, as he shrugged into his winter clothes. Ridiculous, he thought, as he waited for his ten-year-old Echo to warm up. "Ridiculous," he kept muttering as he drove to campus. The word was an incantation, meant to become reality through repetition. But he didn't repeat it enough, because there were two police cars in the street and a dozen people on the sidewalk when he pulled up in front of the library. A local constable was controlling access to the entrance. Through the doors, Hubbard saw Jacobson, another officer, and an anxious-looking couple. Jacobson spotted him and spoke to the officer, who waved him in.

As Hubbard joined the group, Browning's mother turned blood-shot eyes on him. "You were the last to see him," she said. "Where is he?"

Hubbard opened his mouth, had nothing to say. The officer stepped in. "Was there anything about Bryce's behavior today that was unusual?" he asked.

"No. Nothing."

"Did you speak to him this afternoon?"

"He had a couple of questions about the assignment, and he was having some trouble figuring out the way call numbers worked. That was it."

The officer's nod was full of significance, as if Hubbard had just confirmed all sorts of terrible guesses. "We should get started," he said, and waved at the constable outside. The other man waved back and opened the doors, letting the search party in.

The volunteers spread out through the library. The police took most of them to the second floor for a systematic sweep through the stacks. Hubbard was in this group. He walked down his assigned set of aisles, calling the boy's name, hearing nothing back but the calls of the other searchers. And even those noises were faint. For the first time, the sound-dampening qualities of the place struck him as being just a bit too impressive. The shouts fell into air that was suddenly thick, congealed. It stopped the sound waves in their tracks, enforcing an inviolable law of silence. It wrapped itself around Hubbard. It was constrictor, and it was lead curtain. Hubbard opened his mouth to call again, desperate now to pierce the air and kill its spell. Instead, it forced his way into his mouth and smothered his call. "Bryce," he said, and the word was stillborn.

He sought his mantra. He needed to chant the chorus of "ridiculous" and have the word mean something. Of course it meant something. Of course he'd been right earlier. It was ridiculous to expect to find Browning in the library. It was ridiculous for anyone to think Hubbard bore the slightest responsibility for the student's disappearance. It was ridiculous to cast him as some sort of daycare worker. Ridiculous, ridiculous, ridiculous. See? There was the mantra.

It didn't work. At this moment, in this place, in the stacks at night, there was very little that could be dismissed as ridiculous. Darkness seeped in through the windows and took the lighting down still further. As Hubbard turned a corner and started down a new book aisle, the far end was the shadowed blur of near-sightedness, fuzzy and grainy, buzzing with potential revelation. The books were no longer the material embodiments of knowledge. Now they were the bricks and mortar of secrets, the dark walls of a labyrinth that led not to enlightenment, but only to more shadow.

The gloom deepened as he worked his way farther into the library. The calls of the other searchers faded. His throat was raw, and that, he told himself, was why he wasn't shouting Browning's name anymore, and not because the air was now so thick that he was scared he wouldn't be able to hear himself at all. What was the point in calling anyway? If Browning could hear and could answer, he would have done so. The only useful thing was to look down every aisle and confirm that he wasn't in the library, that there was no body lying in a corner. Then the spreading shadow would lift, and the building would be just be a large repository of books once again. Hubbard held his eyes straight, rigorously scanning every inch of the floor of every aisle he walked. In his peripheral vision, the books leaned in, amused. He tried to blot them out, and the more he did, the more their presence became insistent. His vision tunneled, dim and long. He fell into a trance, taken by the plodding rhythm of his steps, numbed and dulled by the browning, fluorescent twilight and the treacle of the air. The tunnel he was moving through darkened, narrowed, irised his vision down to nothing.

He stopped. Jesus, H. and Christ, what the *hell* was wrong with him. He gave his head a sharp shake, scattering cobwebs. His vision cleared, though the light was still lower than it should have been. "Okay," he muttered, and his voice was perfectly audible. Of course it was. Only he couldn't hear any other members of the search party. The library's silence was massive but expectant, like a stone holding its breath. He looked around, seeking bearings from the call numbers. There were none. The book spines were leather, old, cracked, and unmarked by labels or titles. Hubbard stared at the stacks, curious. He'd never been in this area of the library before. What was it? Storage of yet-to-be-cataloged books? That didn't seem likely. It was an open invitation to chaos to have these out where anyone could take them down and leave them lying around. Were the labels on the covers? He picked a book at random on the nearest shelf and reached for it. The ball of his thumb touched the spine. The texture was odd. It felt like scales. He pulled the book down. It was heavy in his hand, its cover a featureless, matte black. And yes, it *did* feel like scales. It was cold, too. Then he frowned. No, he was wrong. The book wasn't cold at all. It was warm like a cat. He began to open the cover. As he did, he felt something at his back. He didn't look. He didn't have to. His mind reacted with sure and terrible knowledge to the gaping of a maw. A gorgon call tugged at him. He gasped with the effort to resist. His fist tightened on the book, clamping it shut. The pull lessened. He leaned against the ether riptide and forced himself to take a step. That gave him the strength for a second step, which gave him a third, and then he was running down the row between the dark and leaning shelves, fleeing the absolute-zero cold that fingered his neck and dared him to look, look, look.

He did look, as he turned the corner to race down the main aisle. It was just a glance, a mere flicker, surely not enough to turn him into a pillar of salt. He was very nearly wrong. His heart froze solid, became a stone that forgot, for an eternal second, to beat. In the shadows at the far end of the stacks, there was a rip in the air. It was a coil of fog and darkness. It pulsed with muscle. It showed teeth. Hubbard saw all of that in a fraction of a second. It gave his flight wings. He whined through clenched teeth as he tore down the length of the library, racing for the promise of light and sanity.

Contemptuous, the library released him to the fragile sanctuary of the recognizable. He descended to the main floor. The lights were on. There was no one around. He checked his watch. It was after two. Jacobson had called four hours ago. The search for Browning must have been over and done for ages. That was why he'd stopped hearing the calls. He'd lost track of time. He'd worked himself into a panic attack. He'd hallucinated. These things happened.

The book was still in his hand, heavily real. But it wasn't warm anymore. It was just a book. As he walked to the exit, he paused by the Circulation desk. His impulse was to leave the book here. He made the deliberate decision to ignore the instinct. If he gave in, he would be validating the irrationality of his nerves. He would be granting the impossible a solidity it did not deserve. He didn't open the book, though. There was enough residual terror still buzzing through his system to prevent that. He looked over the cover, confirmed that there was no bar code, and walked through the library's turnstile. No alarm registered the unauthorized removal of university property.

Outside, he stood for a moment beside his car, breathing in the sharp air of the Manitoba winter. This was a different cold from the one he had felt (no – thought he'd felt, *thought*) in the library. It had a brute, tensile strength that cut through bullshit and cleared his head. There was a purity to this cold. It was as brutal as it was mundane. It left no room for cosmic terrors or metaphysical panic. Even so, as he looked around, the parking lot, the library and the other university buildings all had a brittleness to them. A thinness. He suddenly found himself thinking of Potemkin villages, and didn't know why. Nor did he want to. He shut that train of thought down and got into his car.

Home once more, and his answering machine's light was blinking. He ignored it. Nothing that could be dealt with at this time of night. Nothing that couldn't wait until morning. He looked at the book he held. It could wait, too. It wasn't cowardice that made him decide against opening it now. Not at all. He was exhausted, that was all. Time for bed. Pure common sense. He tossed the book onto the kitchen table, where it could damn well wait until the rational light of morning.

But in the morning, there was too much of a rush. He wasn't delaying; he was running late. There was barely enough time to wade through the phone messages, all from Jacobson, wondering where the hell he'd wandered off to. He grabbed the book and shoved it into his briefcase as he headed out the door. Time enough for mysteries later. First the ordinary bullshit of the day, bullshit that had never felt so welcome.

He was able to keep up the pretense of hurry until he reached his office. The English Department occupied the tenth floor of the Humanities Tower. Most of the other sessionals shared broom-closet offices that lined the center of the floor. Their only view was the main corridor as seen through glass doors. Hubbard was lucky. He'd been in the Department long enough to become a fixture, and five years ago had been granted a full office with an honest-to-God window. The Tower was the tallest building on campus, and the view was a panorama of snowy-roofed, ersatz neo-classical architecture sprouting from the winter prairie. The sky was cloudless. The sun dazzled. The day was all sharp edges and clear definitions that brooked no presence of shadow. Hubbard took in the view's curative, then sat down at his desk.

And now he couldn't hurry anymore. It was barely past nine. He didn't have class until one-thirty, and it was another section of English 1200. There was no prep to do. He could teach "The Love Song of J. Alfred Prufrock" in his sleep. He had marking to do, but he would normally have done that at home, then rolled in after lunch. There was no reason for him to be here this early unless he was trying to avoid being alone. He couldn't allow himself to grant that possibility. If he did, he would be giving the events of the night a dangerous level of credibility. He opened up an essay. Focus, he told himself. Read yet another piece on "A Rose for Emily" that was little more than a mangled regurgitation of his class lecture. No luck. He couldn't even make himself go through the motion of staring at the page. Instead, he stared at the book on his desk. He still hadn't opened it. Temptation fought with anxiety. Together, they created paralysis.

He overcame it. "This is ridiculous," he said, finding that mantra again. He grabbed the book and opened it. There was no title. The pages were a creamy white, silken to the touch, paper that was decadent in its luxury. Symbols writhed over them. He flipped through. Page after page of arcane diagrams. Sometimes there were dense blocks of runic writing. He was outside his field here, didn't know a thing about ancient forms of writing, but he sensed he wouldn't find these runes in any reference work. Their shape bothered him. It had a complexity beyond any ideogram he'd ever seen. Worse, though, was that complexity's *morality*. The contortions were somehow obscene, vicious, insane. Clusters of runes seemed to vibrate in his peripheral vision. Twice, he thought for a moment that a diagram was about to slip off the page.

He closed the book. He stood up and backed away from his desk without realizing he was doing so. He caught himself, took a breath. Steady, he told himself. Nothing happening here. There was nothing to understand in the book, nothing to fear. The day was still as it was. The brittleness he felt was his own nerves, rubbed raw by his imagination. Nothing more. Nothing worse.

He thought about Bryce Browning. He hadn't asked anyone whether the student had been found. He analyzed his lack of curiosity, understood it as fatalism. He was assuming Browning was gone for good. He was assuming he had been swallowed by what he had seen in the library last night. There were so many things wrong with that assumption, so many deeply frightening implications, that he cast it aside and marched down the corridor from his office to find Ellen Jacobson. As he walked, a headache bloomed. It felt like a fishhook in his frontal lobe. His left eyelid fluttered.

Hubbard reached the end of the hall and poked his head into the Department's general office. He saw Jacobson's adjoining door open. The secretary was on the phone, so Hubbard gave her a vague wave and walked past her desk. He rapped on Jacobson's doorway. She looked up and gestured him in. "Close the door," she said. When he had, she asked, "What the hell happened to you last night? Did you get lost?"

"Actually, I did."

"I don't think this is the time to be funny, do you?"

"I'm not trying to be. Did you find Bryce?"

"No. Not a trace. Obviously, he must have left the library. At least that—"

Hubbard didn't hear the rest of her sentence. The hook in his head was given a sharp tug. The pain was silver bright. It receded, dropping back to a throb. In its wake, it left the unwelcome residue of epiphany. The vision was partial, a mix of toxic fragments and nightmare intuitions, but suddenly what he had seen in the book was no longer purely incomprehensible. He didn't know the language of the runes, but he had a sense of the meaning behind them. Beyond the fragility of the rational and the real, hostile immensities watched and hungered. If they were shut out, it was just provisionally. Hubbard broke out in a sweat. He leaned against the door to keep from falling. "Sorry, I missed that," he said to Jacobson. The mere act of speaking to another human being was suddenly a supreme act of faith.

"I said, at least that should let us off the hook, legally. His parents are still raising hell, though. Not that I blame them. I'd be frantic, too." Jacobson gave him a hard look. "Are you okay?"

"Touch of the flu, I think." The tug came again. Silver. Bright.

Jacobson spoke. Her words were nonsense, a hiccuping buzz of insects. She lost definition, as if she were an image on a grainy film. Hubbard tried to blink her back into focus. Color bled from her. She moved towards the gray and blurred. He gasped, fumbled for the doorknob. He tried to say, "Excuse me." His mouth opened and he made sounds. They were as meaningless and unformed as Jacobson's. The doorknob felt soft as he turned it. He fumbled the door open and stumbled from the office. The floor now had give beneath his feet. Behind her desk, the secretary was becoming brown and cloudy.

He ran as best he could down the hallway, back to his office. There was nowhere to go, but the momentum gave him the brief illusion of flight, and the action of his body slowed his thoughts down, delayed the inevitable arrival of wisdom. But only by so much. The book and its venom of symbols continued to resolve itself in his mind. By the time he reached his office, he knew that those terrible gods were not shut out from the world at all. They were its creators. Reality was their toy, to be torn down at will. On his desk, the book was now the only sure and clear object in the room. He fell against his window with his arms spread in appeal and embrace. He needed the day and its sun as surely as he was going to lose them. And his loss was coming, because the knowledge fragments were knitting themselves into coherent wholes with each yank on the hook in his brain. He knew what that book was now. It was a lure, dangling in this fragile reality, waiting for such unwary fish as himself. He was caught, and he was being pulled out into a realm of lethal truth.

Hubbard sobbed as, before him, the curtain was drawn back. University, prairie and sky came unstuck. On the left hand side, the peeling began, and Hubbard saw the world begin to roll up, a backdrop that was no longer needed. Behind was the pulse of black and muscle, teeth and eyes. As the light failed, the last of the book's wisdom unfolded (silver and bright), and there was no comfort in knowing that, as alone as he was, what came for him would be coming for all.

RICK HAUTALA was born and raised in Rockport, Mass. After graduating from the University of Maine in Orono (a classmate of Stephen King's), he has published more than thirty books, including *Untcigahunk: The Complete Little Brothers*, *Occasional Demons*, and *Reunion*, and more than fifty short stories. His novella *Indian Summer* will be published by Cemetery Dance Publications this spring. With Mark Steensland, he has had several short films produced and has recently an adaptation of Robert E, Howard's *Pigeons From Hell* to Paradox Entertainment. He lives with author Holly Newstein in Maine. You are invited to check out his website www.rickhautalacom.

The Call

by **Rick Hautala**

I've been working on this journal for almost thirty years. Ever since I was twelve years old. You'd think I would have finished it by now and gone on to write something else, but I have to keep writing and re-writing it if only to make sure the memories and the fear stay fresh and alive in my mind.

I *want* to remember.

I *have* to remember because I don't want to have what happened to my father happen to me. So at least four or five times a year—sometimes a lot more often—I take down the old journal and read it straight through, and then I write ... and I revise ... and I remember.

I have no idea when it started for my father. It had to have been long before I was born, back when he was a kid, growing up in Hilton, Maine. I do remember that, at some point, the dreams got so bad for him he told me one morning at breakfast that there were times when he actually couldn't distinguish between waking and sleeping.

That idea really bothered me.

I was just a kid at the time, remember. Couldn't have been more than five or six years old, but I'll never forget that particular morning. My dad and I were sitting across from each other in the breakfast nook, in our usual places, eating what we always had for breakfast--cereal, usually Cheerios, and orange juice for me; scrambled eggs, wheat toast, juice and coffee for my dad.

My mom died when I was three years old, so I don't have any memories of her that aren't colored by the old photographs I've seen of her and how my father described her. But memories of my dad—and that morning and what happened afterwards—are still sharp and clear.

I work at keeping them that way.

My father was a good man ... a good father. I don't remember him as anything other than patient and understanding, even when I screwed up royally. Now that I'm older, and married, and have a son of my own—he's named Matt, after my father—I think I understand a little better why my father was the way he was. At the time, though, especially that morning, all I knew was that I was worried sick that he was going to die, that I was going to lose him like I'd lost my mom.

That morning ...

It was spring, maybe March or early April. I remember how the sun was shining warmly in through the kitchen window, but the view of our back yard out the kitchen bay window was of a brown, dead world. The only snow left on the ground was in the shadows under the pine trees that bordered our property, and I remember a swarm of brown sparrows fluttering around the feeder my dad and I had built together the summer before. I could hear them chirping even through the closed window.

I also remember being confused and frightened by what my father had said, and then he told me a story that confused and frightened me even more. He said it was something called a Zen *koan*. I don't remember exactly how it went, but it was something about a man who was upset because the night before he'd dreamed he was a butterfly. His friend or teacher or something asked him if he could be sure that, right then, he wasn't a butterfly, dreaming he was a man.

I'm still not sure I get it.

But then my dad proceeded to tell me how for the last several nights, when he was dreaming—when he was *in* his dreams, they were so vivid that he felt as though he had been awake all night. When he awoke up in the morning, he said he felt so tired he might just as well not have slept at all.

He didn't look so good, either.

I remember thinking that. His eyes had puffy, dark bags under them, and his face was pale and drawn, really pasty-white. To my little kid's eyes, he sure looked like someone who might be living two complete lives instead of one with no time left over for any real sleep.

My dad worked at Martindale's Rope and Twine Factory, in Biddeford, Maine. It wasn't a glamorous job, by any stretch of the imagination, but he worked hard, and we got by. I don't remember ever going without food or clothes, although—like any kid, I suppose—there were toys and stuff I wanted that I didn't get, even for Christmas.

It wasn't until a little later, once I was in junior high school, that my father died, and that's what this is an account of, as best as I can write it. Of course, there are lots of things—especially what my father was thinking and feeling at the time—that I can only guess at.

But I was there when it happened, and I saw what I saw, no matter how unbelievable it might seem even to me.

Even now, thinking about it, I get a chill deep in my gut. No matter how much over the years it seems more and more as though it had to have been a dream or a nightmare, I know it really happened. I know because it killed my father.

But even if it didn't happen the way I remember it ... even if it *was* just a dream, I know dreams and nightmares, no matter how intense, fade over time … like memories, and I have to remember this one. I have to keep it fresh in my mind so I don't end up convincing myself that it didn't really happen, and then fall into the same trap my father fell into.

The whole time I was growing up, I remember thinking how my father didn't look very healthy. He was always on the thin side, even in his wedding photos, but by the time I was in seventh grade, I remember lying awake many nights worried sick that my dad had cancer like what had killed my mother, and that he was going to die, too, and leave me all alone in the world.

And that's exactly what happened.

He died, and from the seventh grade on, my aunt and uncle, Pauline and Mike, raised me, but my father didn't die of cancer … not unless it was cancer of the universe.

Now there's a concept!

Cancer of the Universe.

Every now and then, especially in the months before he died, my dad talked to me about his dreams. I remember many mornings when he looked haggard and tired, and he would ask me over breakfast what I had dreamed the night before. He taught me early on to pay attention to my dreams, but I'm sure now that it wasn't just out of interest or curiosity. He was checking on me … making sure I was okay … not being threatened. No matter how casual he tried to be about it, I always felt like there was an undercurrent of danger when he asked me about my dreams, as if he didn't quite trust his own dreams and was afraid that mine would get to be as bad as his.

He never told me any of the details of his dreams, at least not that I recall, but he seemed to move through life with a dark cloud hanging over his head, shading his face even on the sunniest days. That's the only way I can describe it.

Anyway, it was a bright, sunny morning in spring when I was in seventh grade that my father looked particularly worn when we sat down at the table for our usual breakfasts. By then I was convinced he was wasting away from some dread disease he didn't know about or he did know about and didn't yet have the heart to discuss with me. So I got really nervous when he told me he wasn't going to work that day, and that he was going to call school and tell them I wasn't coming today and we were going for a drive.

I protested.

Not that I wanted to go to school or anything, but there was something about the way he said it that I could tell something was *really* wrong. All I could think was, he's going to take me to the doctor's office or he's going to check into the hospital where the doctor would break the news to me that he had only a few weeks—or days—to live.

"Hey. What's the matter, Sport?" he asked, scruffing my hair.

He called me "Sport" a lot.

"You got something against missing school and spending the day with your old man?"

"It's not that," I said, and I remember that I was burning inside, dying to ask him if he was okay, or if he was going to die. Instead, all I could manage was a feeble, "So what are we gonna do?"

"I was thinking about taking a little drive up north," he said with a thin smile. The circles under his eyes looked like smears of black shoe polish.

"You mean up to Hilton?" I asked, and he nodded.

I remember thinking how his smile looked forced ... not at all natural or normal. And I remember that all I did was nod in agreement and focus as hard as I could on the cereal floating in the milk in my bowl, all the while thinking, *He's going to die! ... He's sick, and he's going back home to die!*

Crazy thought for a little kid, don't you think?

Anyway, we finished breakfast, cleaned up the dishes, and got into the car. As we backed out of the driveway, I wanted desperately to ask him why he wanted to drive to Hilton, especially today, but I couldn't because I was still tingling with the dreadful anticipation that he was going to admit something horrible once we were on the road ... something I didn't want to hear.

The drive north went okay. I've never been much for long car trips, even now. After two or three hours in a car, I start getting a little twitchy. But this particular day, I remember, was mild and sunny. The grass was green, and leaves were bursting out all over the place. As we drove, my dad told me he wanted to take the long way and see some of the scenery while we were at it.

My father was born and raised in Hilton. It's not much of a town, but I always had fun whenever we'd visit. I remember thinking how it must have been kind of a cool place to be a kid. Although I haven't been back in ages, probably only once or twice since he died, I can imagine that, even now, in spite of cell phones, the Internet, and MTV, it's probably retained some of that quaint "small town" charm it had back them. There are places where the Twenty-first Century still hasn't arrived.

We stopped along the way and ate lunch at Moody's Diner on Route One before heading west along Route 201. My father didn't seem to be in any particular hurry, and as far as I could tell, he wasn't in a bad mood or depressed or anything. I do remember thinking how he seemed ... distant, maybe, is the word. It was like he was preoccupied, thinking about something other than the drive. I'm sure now that it was his dreams he was mulling over. He was living half of his life, and right up to his dying day, I'll bet he was trying to figure out how those two lives he led—the one awake, the other dreaming—might coincide.

We got to Hilton a little past three o'clock in the afternoon. We drove through downtown but didn't stop even though my father recognized a couple of people and waved to them as we passed. At the edge of town, I could see Watcher's Mountain through the trees, off to the west. We turned onto a narrow dirt road that wound through a dense stand of pine trees. I didn't recognize the road, and I was suddenly afraid.

"Where we going?" I asked.

This wasn't the road to the old family homestead—I knew that much. My father's parents were both dead, and my dad had only one brother, my Uncle Mike, who lived with his family in Saco. I'd been thinking all along that we had come out here so he could drive past the old house, and my dad could reminisce.

"I just wanna check something out," my father said.

At least now, I remember hearing a certain tension in his voice, but at the time, I think I just shrugged and settled back in the seat, waiting to see where we ended up.

The road was a typical dirt road, the kind you find all over Maine. It wound through a long corridor of dense pine forest that shut out the sun except at high noon. I had my window open, and I remember the strong smell of pine resin wafting around me. I've always loved that smell, but for some reason, on this particular day, the smell made me sick to my stomach. I could hear birds singing, deep in the forest, but their songs didn't seem very cheerful.

"So--uh, where are we going?" I asked again.

I wasn't afraid of my father. I'd never been afraid of him even the few times I'd made him angry by doing some bonehead kid thing. I trusted him like I've never trusted another person, before or since. But I realize now it was fear I was feeling.

It was fear for my father as much as fear for myself.

The tall pine trees blocked out the sunlight, and my father's face was all but lost in shadow. I kept trying to think of this excursion as fun, but I remember thinking this was how it must feel when you're driving to a funeral.

"There's a small lake out here that I want you to see before I--"

He stopped himself before he finished the sentence, but I mentally finished it for him--*before I die!*

He was going to die ... at least he *thought* he was going to die, and he wanted to share something with me ... a family secret or something.

"Look over to the south there. See?" My father leaned forward and squinted as he pointed off to the right.

Through the trees, I caught a glimpse of sunlight, sparkling on water. It looked like quicksilver flashing between the dense stand of trees.

"That's Watcher's Lake," my dad said. "And you see all these woods around here? We own it all."

"Who does?"

"Us ... Me and Uncle Mike ..." He paused and took a deep breath. "And you."

"All of it?" I asked, amazed as I scanned the area.

I think now that I should have been more excited than I was. I certainly was impressed, but the deep, cold gloom of the forest had seeped into the car and into my mind. Whatever else you could say about the land, it certainly didn't seem cheerful, even on a warm May afternoon. I could just imagine what it was like out here on a dreary winter day.

"The old homestead is on the other side of the mountain."

I knew Watcher's Mountain well enough. It was a bit of a hike from my grandparent's house, but there were a couple of times back when we visited in the summer, when my grandparents were still alive, that my dad and I climbed it. I almost remember seeing a lake or pond from the mountaintop, but no one ever said anything about it to me ... not until right then.

"So how come we never come swimming out here?" I asked, and my father gave me a funny look. It makes sense to me now, but at the time, I remember being confused.

"We just don't," he said, and there was a certain finality in his tone of voice that made me know that was the end of it, so I let it drop.

My father took a turn onto an even narrower dirt road, not much more than a path, really. I could see we were getting closer to the lake. Something—probably the suspension—was making a real loud bumping sound underneath the car. I was jostled up and down in my seat so much that, when I spoke to my father, my voice sounded all chattery.

"Why we coming down here today, then?"

My voice trembled with fear, but if I had known then what I know now—especially after what happened an hour or so later—I would have been a lot more frightened.

"I want to check on something," was all my dad said.

He frowned as he hunched over the steering wheel and looked up at what little patch of sky he could see above the pine trees.

"We probably should have waited, though," he said, talking more to himself than to me.

I knew he was he worried about it getting dark soon. Plus, the forest had this ... this *feeling* to it. Maybe it still does. It was like night came here a lot sooner than it does any place else on Earth. I suspect memory and imagination have played tricks on me, and I've exaggerated this feeling more than I should. But I swear I have a clear memory of feeling like the trees were closing in around us, and the sky was pressing down like it was made of something heavier than air. All around the car, the shadows under the trees were dense, so dense it looked to me like they were opening up in front of us and then closing back behind us once we were past, keeping us in this kind of bubble that separated us from the real world.

"Maybe we could come back tomorrow," I offered.

"It may be too late tomorrow," my father said, and I could tell—and I'm positive this isn't something I made up later—that he said the words before he thought it through. He caught himself, and the expression on his face made it clear he wished he hadn't said anything.

"Too late for what?" I asked, unable to choke back my question even though I was afraid of the answer.

My dad forced a laugh and scruffed my hair.

"Hey, Sport. Don't you worry about it, all right?"

I could tell he was forcing it. The look in his eyes made me feel plenty worried.

The car crested a long, slow hill that curved around to the right. At the top, it dropped off, much steeper. The lake was close by on the right as we started down the hill slowly, the car bouncing all over the place like the shocks were gone. The shadows deepened around us like black water, swallowing us even though I could see sunlight reflecting off the water. The narrow dirt road ended at the bottom of the hill, and through a stand of pine trees, I saw a small wooden shack.

"Is that—" I started to say but then cut myself off, knowing that my father would eventually tell me what was going on ... if he wanted to.

As we pulled to a stop, I could see that the building wasn't big enough to be a summer camp or anything. It was just a tiny shed that looked like it was used either as an outhouse or for storage. Its shingles were rotted, and some of them had fallen off, giving the shed a funny, gap-toothed look. Dark, black moss was growing up its sides like a fringe of uneven beard.

"Want to take a look around?" my dad asked.

The car was as close as he could get it to the small shed. I remember thinking I should be excited about being at the lake. It was an adventure. Even though it was too early in the year to go swimming, I could have waded along the edge of the lake and explored.

I looked at my dad, wanting really bad to ask him again what we were doing out here, but I couldn't get any words out. I could hardly breathe.

"I don't really like this place," I managed to say, and I know my dad heard the tremor in my voice.

The sun was tipping the edge of the western horizon, making the forest on the opposite shore look like it was on fire. After a moment or two, though, I noticed something curious about the lake. The sky was streaked with bright red and orange clouds, but the water was dull and gray. It looked like how I imagined it would on a winter day, just before a blizzard. It was like the lake absorbed rather than reflected the sunset. I wanted to say something to my dad, but I wasn't sure how to phrase it.

"I just want to have a look around, is all," my dad said as he snapped open the car door and stepped outside.

I sat where I was for only a second before deciding that I would rather be with him in the woods than left alone in the car, no matter how weird and creepy this place was.

The pine needles made a funny crunching sound under our feet as we walked slowly down toward the water. A soft, hissing sound of wind whistled high in the trees overhead, but I couldn't feel even the faintest stirring of a breeze against my face. Even with the sun going down the air was heavy and warm. Even so, a shiver ran up my back, and a cold tightening twisted deep in my gut.

"Dad ... Why'd we come out here?" I asked.

I was trying hard to keep my voice steady, but it was shaking and weak.

"I have to see something," he replied, and I could tell by the dreamy edge in his voice that, once again, he was talking as much to himself as to me.

"It's about the ... dreams."

I wanted to ask him *What dreams?* but I already knew. He meant the dreams where he feels like he's not asleep, where he feels like what's happening while he's asleep is really happening.

"It was a long time ago," he said, his voice distant and so low I could barely hear him above the sighing of the wind overhead and the crunching of the pine needles beneath our feet. "And it happened out here."

I wanted to ask: *What happened?* but couldn't.

We were close to the lake, now, and I felt a faint stirring of wind coming in off the water. It carried a damp, fishy smell that made me gag. Even with the wind rushing across the water, though, the surface of the lake was as flat and smooth as a polished mirror ... just like a mirror except for one thing: a mirror reflects objects. I couldn't see even the faintest trace of reflections in the water. My eyes were having difficulty adjusting to the odd lighting, like I was looking at something that had a different dimension to it or something. I know how weird this sounds, but something made me really afraid of the water.

"There used to be a camp here. Long ago. We came out here ... my friend, Glenn Chadbourne and I." My dad's voice got distant and dreamy. "We weren't supposed to be out here. We knew that, but—you know how kids are. We did it, anyway."

I couldn't shake the feeling that he wasn't talking to me, that he had forgotten that I was there with him. He stared out over the water, and I remember thinking that the lake must have been looking weird to him, too, because his eyes didn't seem to be focused right. They had a milky, glazed cast that scared me. They reminded me of the eyes of this blind kid in school, Billy Randall.

The wind picked up, and as it did, I heard a low, hollow whistling sound. At first I thought the sound was coming from behind me, maybe from the old shed, but when I turned to look in that direction, the sound shifted and seemed to come from behind me again. I turned quickly, trying to get a fix on it, but no matter where I looked, the sound thrummed softly, like someone was standing behind me, blowing gently into my ears. At times, I imagined it was the faint sound of distant music. And with the sound, the smell I'd gotten a whiff of earlier got much stronger, like something was rotting.

"It was in the summertime," my dad continued, still acting like he was unaware I was there with him. "Just around sunset ... like this ... only in the summer. We'd been playing baseball, down at Pingree Field. We'd ridden our bikes to the game and were heading home, but for some reason ... for some goddamned reason—I don't even know whose idea it was—we decided to come out here instead."

"Were you gonna go swimming?" I asked.

The sound of my voice seemed barely to intrude on his awareness. He shook his head slowly as through he was in a dream and was struggling hard to wake up. I was gagging from the decayed smell that was getting much stronger. It reminded me of rotting fish or sour vomit and ... something else ... something so horrible and noxious that it's still indescribable, no matter how hard I've tried over the years to find words for it.

"Yeah, but then ... Glenn disappeared," my father said, "and ... Oh, *Jesus!* It's happening again!"

I looked up at my dad, wondering what he was talking about. In the gathering gloom, his eyes widened, and he pointed with a trembling hand out over the water. The flat, dimension-less surface of the lake was still, perfectly smooth and unruffled, but now that the sun had dropped behind the trees on the far shore and stars were twinkling in the sky, the color of the water rapidly deepened as well.

Too rapidly," I thought, and then my father whispered hoarsely, "See ... Out there ... There it is again."

As much as I didn't want to look, I tracked my eyes out over the water. After a moment or two, I saw what he meant. The center of the lake was ... *thickening* is the only word that comes to mind. The water was turning a deep black—as black ... no, *blacker* than the oncoming night. And in the very center of the lake, a round patch of darkness was spreading out slowly like an ink stain seeping into cloth. But this stain didn't fade on the edges as it spread out. It deepened, if that's possible, as thick, winding strands of pitch black radiated from its center.

I stared at what was happening to the lake, almost overcome by a feeling of intense vertigo. I couldn't resist the nauseating feeling of falling forward, spiraling headfirst into that thickening darkness. No matter how desperately I wanted to look away, I couldn't. Twisting, waving, black arms reached out to me, and I watched in stunned, silent horror as a hideous shape gathered and took on a three-dimensional quality as it rose up out of the water. Coiling strands of darkness clawed at the night, spraying fetid water in all directions. I knew if that darkness reached me and touched me, I would be destroyed by a cold vacuum as deep and lifeless as space.

"... *run* ..."

I heard the word distantly; it barely registered in my brain. I couldn't move ... I couldn't breathe or swallow or blink my eyes. Frozen with fear, I didn't move as the darkness deeper than the night quivered and reared up above the water's surface. Black tendrils twisted and writhed, taking on hideous shapes that I was and still am powerless to describe. The horrible stench of rot and death filled my throat and chest, gagging me.

"*Bobby! ... Run! ... Get the hell out of here! ... Now!*"

My father's voice came to me as if from an impossible distance, but no matter how hard I tried, I couldn't make sense of what he was saying. Vaguely, I knew I had to save myself, but I was frozen with fear, riveted where I stood.

The black, amorphous shape shifted and grew into impossible dimensions as it covered the night sky, blocking out the stars and casting a thick shadow across the land. Thick, rounded shadows streamed across the ground, swallowing, embracing everything in their path as they moved closer and closer to where my father and I stood.

Still unable to move, I suddenly felt something grab me roughly by the shoulders and spin me around. As soon as I wasn't looking at the monstrosity on the lake, its hypnotic grip was broken. My body was rigid as I lurched forward and then, just to keep my balance, I started to run.

Even after all these years, I find it impossible to describe the fear that gripped me as I ran. It wasn't just my imagination. The cold and horrible emptiness of that darkness gathering behind me filled me with terror. I realize now, all these years later, that I wasn't just imagining it. There was a cruel, unfathomable intelligence inside that darkness that didn't so much want to destroy me as it had no awareness or regard for pitifully small human fears and emotions. It was the cold, uncaring destructive power of the eternal void that swept away whole worlds as easily and unthinkingly as it destroyed human life.

I have no idea how, but somehow I made it back to the car. I have a single, clear mental image of my hands fumbling to open the car door open, and then, more vaguely, I remember hurling myself onto the front seat and slamming the door shut behind me before rolling onto the car floor.

Even then I knew that I wasn't safe as I cowered on the floor, whimpering and curled up in a fetal position with my head ducked down and my hands covering my head. The darkness outside was still rising, still swelling and gathering power, sucking it from the night. I heard a soft, strangled cry, but it took a while before I realized I was making the sound. By the time I did, I knew ... I could feel that the darkness had retreated. My face was streaked with tears and snot as I cautiously raised my head and looked down toward the lake.

The night was too dark to see clearly, but stars were shining through the trees. Behind me, a half-moon had risen. It cast a silvery glow over the shore. Long dark bars of the shadows of trees scored the shoreline like pinstripes. I remember being surprised that the lake now seemed to be "normal," whatever that meant. Its water reflected shimmering starlight, and far out in the center, I could see that a gentle breeze was ruffling its surface, giving it a beaten metal look.

"*Dad?*" I called out in a strangled voice. I raised my head and slowly unfolded my body, looking all around.

I already knew the terrible truth of what had happened.

My father was dead ... *gone* ... destroyed by that indescribable darkness that had risen up out of the lake.

He was gone, and I—somehow—had been left alive. "I alone am escaped to tell thee."

I haven't got any clear memories of what happened next. I know from what my Uncle Mike told me afterwards that I managed to drive the car out of the woods. Just after I got onto the main road, I ran off the shoulder of the road, smack into a tree. A passing patrol car found me unconscious behind the wheel some time later. I told the policeman that my father was missing, and he went back to look for him, but—of course—never found him. The authorities concluded that he'd gone for a late night swim and had drowned, but his body was never recovered.

I never told anyone—not even the police—what I had seen. I knew no one would ever believe me. I was positive they'd think I was crazy, maybe even take me away from my aunt and uncle, and lock me up in a nut house. For years, I was consumed with grief over losing my father, but more than that—infinitely more—I was filled with the deep, indescribable terror that has consumed me ever since that night.

There's still so much to tell ... about how my aunt and uncle raised me, and how I tried to deal with what had happened that night. I've never stopped feeling as though my entire life is a dream, that I am a walking, talking phantom that has absolutely no business being here on the earth. I've kept this journal and, over the years, have worked and re-worked my description of that night because I think it will help.

But it hasn't.

Not really.

Ever since that night, I've been lost in a surreal feeling that absolutely nothing is real in this life ... nothing except the nameless horror that I saw and felt that night when I watched a dimensionless darkness rise up from the waters of Watcher's Lake and consume my father. Even now, one small, rational corner of my mind insists it had to have been a dream, that it couldn't *really* have happened the way I remember it, but I know what I saw.

And I wonder sometimes ... all the time, in fact, if it's still out there ... if that nameless darkness still lurks in the depths of Watcher's Lake ... or if Watcher's Lake is, somehow, a lens that focuses it from whatever dimension it originates.

For the last several months, I've been having some disturbing dreams about what happened back then, and I've been toying with the idea of driving up to Hilton just to take a look around. I still own the property and the lake, so I know no houses have been built along the shore. Everything should be exactly as it was that night more than thirty years ago when my father disappeared.

If I do go out there, I probably won't go down to the lake. Or if I do, I'm going to make damned sure I don't get too close to the water's edge ... especially if it's late in the afternoon. I know how fast it gets dark out there in those woods.

Still, I wonder what might be out there in Watcher's Lake, and I wonder what I might find if I were to drive down that narrow dirt road and take a look around. It's a beautiful autumn afternoon. Maybe when Matt gets home from school, he and I will hop into the car and take a little drive up north. I'll bet we can get to Hilton long before dark.

DONALD R. BURLESON's fiction has appeared in *Twilight Zone*, *The Magazine of Fantasy and Science Fiction*, *Cemetery Dance*, *Inhuman*, and many other magazines. He is the author of twenty-two books, including several novels and short story collections. His most recent short story collection is *Wait for the Thunder*, from Hippocampus Press. His nonfiction books include *UFOs and the Murder of Marilyn Monroe*, *UFO Secrecy and the Fall of J. Robert Oppenheimer*, and *A Capitalist Christmas Carol*. He is a professional mathematician and semi-retired college professor, and lives in Roswell, New Mexico with his writer wife Mollie.

Christmas Carrion

by Donald R. Burleson

Mate Ellis was dead, to begin with. The trouble was, he wouldn't *stay* dead.

Nor would any of the others--Jack, Scar-Face, Long Tom, Spanish Joe, Peters. All of them were dreadfully disinclined to lie quiet in death. But Mate Ellis was the most unquiet of the lot.

It was the Yuletide, and light grey-white flakes of snow were silting down beyond the windowpanes to settle in pale mounds among the gnarled winter-blasted trees and the curiously painted stones in the front yard. All the world, out there, was ghastly and cold and dead. Inside the ancient little house in Water Street, there was at least a modicum of warmth from the fireplace, and sitting in his wan cone of lamplight with his antique bottles ranged in front of him along the edge of the tabletop, the Terrible Old Man--for so the foolish denizens of Kingsport, Massachusetts called him--the Terrible Old Man reflected, once again, on how ironic that epithet truly was.

What was terrible, on many such nights as this, was the idea--and the reality--of sitting up late into the night with the undead.

Yes, the folk legends that circulated about him--he knew of them, he overheard the furtive references to him when he went to the market, paying for his goods with two-hundred-year-old Spanish coins of gold and silver--the whispered folk legends were misguided, though founded in part upon truth.

Inside the neck of one of the old bottles, the tiny leaden pendulum suspended there from the hoary cork began to swing, at first in a barely perceptible motion, then more vigorously.

"Yes," the old man intoned, "yes, Mate Ellis, I know ye be there."

After all these incalculable years, he ought to know; Mate Ellis and the others were there, in essence, and had always been there, since the time (long before the earliest memories of anyone else in Kingsport-by-the-Sea) when the East India clipper ship *Bellerophon* had gone down off the coast of Borneo taking the old captain and all the crew down to the nighted depths with her, and only the captain had come up alive, or alive in any ordinary sense of the term. Now the spirits of the departed others haunted these bleary glass bottles, and haunted the Terrible Old Man--kept him alive, alive well beyond his years, with their spells, yes, but haunted him still.

How many of these imbecile townsfolk had crept up to the old man's windows of an evening, over the years, to see him in converse with the pendulums in the bottles--to see him talking to them and then to scutter away in terror and tell breathless tales the next day, around the coal stove in the village store, tales about the evil old man and his bottled daemons? Puling lackwits, all of them, to think what they thought!

Did they really suppose that he was master here? Could they really think that he delighted in these nocturnal exchanges? Perhaps, through the grimy diamond shaped panes, they couldn't see his hands tremble.

Well, tonight, at least, there were no watchers at the window, for it was the Yuletide, the immemorial winter solstice time, and people in the village of Kingsport made the Yuletide an occasion of much gravity and ceremony, pouring out of their doorways, as they did, to form silent lantern-lit processions in the narrow and winding streets, processions that converged at the crumbling old church on the central hill--for what purposes the old man could scarcely have said to this day, for he had never taken part in their observances, though in his time he had seen more winter solstices than any man alive of them. Tonight was the Yuletide, and the processions had already gone their way to the church, and the streets were empty, and the old man was alone.

Well, not really alone.

Again the same pendulum swung in the same bottle, describing an angry little arc, and this time it moved with such force that the bottle itself wobbled and rattled on the tabletop and nearly fell over. On an impulse, the old man reached for it and drew out the brittle stopper, pulling the pendulum out with it.

There arose at once an acrid cloud of smoke that smelled of death and decay and things from the sea. Choking, the old man pushed his chair back and stood up, swinging his arms to clear the foul mist that filled the room, only to see, then, standing before him, the lean figure of old Mate Ellis, his tarnished cutlass sheathed by his side, his seaman's clothing hanging on him in clotted rags like so many scabs upon the skin, or upon places where there should have been skin. Even in life, Mate Ellis had been a remarkably ugly man, but he was more so now, his face pulled into a revolting leer, his mottled flesh grey and diseased-looking where it did not fall away altogether, his lich-eyes rheumy and pustulent, his mouth hanging open to reveal rows of blackened teeth surrounding a beefy tongue that lolled wide to release, from beneath it, one long, fat seaworm that dropped with a puffy sound to the wooden floor and lay there writhing. Licking what remained of the lips, the tongue withdrew into the abhorrent mouth, which smiled and began to speak in a gurgling voice that recalled fathomless sea waters and less namable things.

"How be ye, Captain?"

"I--" the old man gasped, his throat suddenly dry and aching. "What do ye want with me, spirit?"

"Much," Mate Ellis said.

"Can ye sit down?" the old man asked.

"Aye, I can," Mate Ellis said, belching a cascade of rancid salt water onto the floor.

"Do it, then," the old man said, shuddering.

The spectre shifted his cutlass and sat heavily at the opposite end of the table, deposited the protruding bones of his elbows upon the tabletop, and said, "Ye no longer be one of us, ye pitiable landlubber."

"What do ye mean?" the old man asked, easing himself back into his own chair to face the visitor.

Mate Ellis glared at him with those mucoid eyes and spat. "Ye make me sick. And it ain't just me. Here, ask the others."

Reaching across the tabletop, he pulled the cork stoppers from the bottles one by one, and a medley of foul gasses filled the air, gradually clearing to reveal the assembled figures, the crew, on whom the old man had not looked for countless years, though their restlessness in their respective bottles had never let him suppose them irretrievably dead any more than Mate Ellis was. There, across in the corner, was Scar-Face, his old scar a livid slash across his half-decayed face. Near him was Spanish Joe, his rotting mouth open to emit a torrent of vile yellow drool. Standing just behind Mate Ellis, who remained seated at the table, were Peters, Jack, and Long Tom, their dead eyes floating in their sockets like oysters, dead but alive, peering at the old man with an intensity that turned his blood cold to see it. At length Mate Ellis spoke again.

"Is it as I say, lads?"

Long Tom cleared his throat with a sound that made the old man's stomach lurch. "Aye, and more. It isn't just pitiable he is, but unfittin' to live."

"Aye." This time it was Scar-Face, whose gaping scar now seemed to open and close along with the speaking mouth. "Ye revolt me, captain. To think how we once saw ye standin' at the helm with the good salt air a-blowin' yer hair wild and free and with full sails drivin' the clipper proud and mighty before the wind. Ye were a man then."

"*Sí*," Spanish Joe spoke up, turning his head more into the lamplight to face the old man. As the head turned, the eyes in their sockets came around more slowly than the rest of the face. "*Un hombre*. A man fit to breathe the air."

"Aye," Peters said. "I've seen the time ye stood by the foremast, cutlass in one hand and knife in the other, captain of yer ship, by God, and a gale turnin' her nearly over in the water, and a boardin' party swarmin' over the deck and four of 'em comin' at ye from every side, and ye took 'em down like dogs, every scurvy one of 'em."

"Aye, Captain," said Jack, one of his eyes rotted away beneath the tatters of his patch, the other eye glaring at the old man with a cold phosphorescence. "If 'Captain' I ought ter still call ye. I remember the time when the old first mate, what was there before Ellis, stood up to ye and questioned yer judgment, and said as how ye ought to give up yer authority, and ye drew on him without a word and cut him in half where he stood."

"Those were fine days," Mate Ellis said, picking up one of the glass bottles and looking at it for a moment and setting it down. "But look what ye are now. Where is that fire that burned within ye, old man? Ye sit by yer window like a feeble little granny knittin' her a shawl. Ye talk to yer old crew what's been kept in them bottles, and we talk back, but ye don't listen, ye don't catch our drift. When them town people say they fear ye, old man, ye ought to make sure ye *deserve* their fear, but ye don't. If they really knew ye, they'd split their hulls laughin' at ye."

"Aye," Peters said, looking about and addressing himself to the others. "Look at him, now. There's ships lyin' at the bottom of the sea with their keels rotted clean away that has more backbone than him."

The old man was appalled to hear all this, but swallowed hard and forced himself to speak. "I have sunk that low, then, ye say? Is this what ye have come to tell me? Why tell me at all, then? What good is there in it?"

Mate Ellis sat forward and fixed him with a deadly gaze. "We've come to offer ye hope."

"Hope?" the old man said. "Hope for what?"

"Yer salvation."

"My salvation?"

"Yer reclamation, then," Mate Ellis said.

The old man looked around at the eaten-away faces. "I don't understand."

"Ye'll have three visitors," Mate Ellis said.

"Spirits, like these?" the old man said, waving his hand at the group.

"Nay," Mate Ellis said. "Thieves. They would presume to take liberty with a weak old greybeard, and make ye tell the whereabouts of the treasure ye keep, and haul it away, these three."

"When will they come?" the old man asked.

"This very night. The first will come to see if ye are asleep. Expect him when the bell tolls midnight. Then--"

The old man motioned for him to stop. "Can't I take 'em all at once, and be done with it?"

Mate Ellis seemed to be considering this, and turned to look at his companions, who one by one nodded their assent. "Aye," he said, "that might even be the better way."

"What am I to do?" the old man asked.

Mate Ellis drew his cutlass and slammed it broadside on the table with such force that the oaken beams overhead creaked and dropped a sifting of dust. "What ye do depends on what ye *be*," he said. "And ye'll get no help from us." The light in the room grew grainy and clouded with a medley of foul mists, and the bottles on the table seemed to suck the clouds into them; abruptly, the old man was alone again. He replaced the corks, noting, as he did so, that Mate Ellis had left his cutlass on the table. The old man sat and leaned his head upon his elbows, and felt like weeping.

But the clocktowers in the town were tolling. Great cold iron waves of sound reverberated in the air out there, one after another, ten, eleven--twelve.

And then there was another sound, a fumbling at the latch out back, at the gate in the great wall that stood between the back yard and Ship Street.

The old man's stomach felt cold. He closed his eyes.

In a moment, the fumbling was at the latch of the back door to the house itself, and the old man heard the door swing open on its rusted hinges. He opened his eyes to find two young men standing in the room looking at him.

"Are ye the ones whose coming was foretold?" he asked. "And if so, why be there only two of ye?"

They looked at each other in evident bewilderment, and one of them spoke. "I don't know what you're talking about, old man. Anyway, we've got business with you."

"What business do ye have with me?"

Snorting with derision, the other man spoke this time. "It's Christmas time, old sailor. Now, at Christmas time, you know, a man is supposed to be generous."

"What do ye mean?"

"They all say you've got money hidden here someplace. A lot of it."

"I have no money," the old man said. "Only what I need to live. I'm old, and I do not work. Why do ye torment an old man?" His voice came out tremulous, and he hated himself for it.

"Because," the first man said, snapping open a switchblade knife, his face impudent, belligerent, self-assured, "we want what you got. All of it. We mean to take it, so let's stop wasting time."

Somehow, the presumption in the young man's face and voice suddenly so enraged the old man that something hot and wild and unbridled came alive within him, and he snatched the cutlass up off the table and stood up.

"Aye," he said. "Time is given, only so much to any man, and it be a deadly sin to waste it."

Lunging across the room, he brought the heavy blade to bear upon his problem, and kept slashing and slashing and slashing even when the gory tangles of flesh and shredded clothing had long since ceased moving. Kicking the two mangled bodies with a savage fury that felt wonderful because it brought the blood rushing warm and honest and good to his ancient cheeks, he stepped over the carnage that lay at his feet, took his coat from the rack beside the back door, went out into the snow, and made his way to the back gate, having a feeling that the prophecy was to be taken as given, and that his task was not yet quite done.

He was not mistaken, for in the little lane onto which the gate opened, an automobile waited. A lone figure, another young man, emerged from it and came to meet him at the gate, and it was a timeless sensation brought to glorious life again to see the terror in the man's muddled little eyes as the blade began its work.

When all was done and the old man was back inside, he stood the cutlass in a corner and dropped upon his knees, clasping his hands together.

"Thankee," he said, his voice tremulous, but tremulous this time with emotions with which he could be pleased. "Thankee, Mate Ellis, and Peters and Spanish Joe. I say it on my knees, Scar-Face, aye, on my knees, Jack and Long Tom. Ye spirits and the Yule time be praised, for I be now the man that I would not have been but for this."

It was an exceedingly long, snow-ridden, bitterly cold New England winter, and it wasn't until the first real thaw in April that three chopped, twisted, and decomposed bodies were found in a little-visited recess near the harbour. According to the newspapers, the police had no clues, no concrete evidence with which to approach any particular suspects. The viciousness of the slayings would be the talk of the town for a long time to come.

For one citizen of the town, perhaps more than any other, it had been a Yuletide to remember.

Ever afterward, when the pendulums chanced to move in their bottles of an evening, in the mellow lamplight in the little room in the old house in Water Street, they moved with a certain quiet deference.

And ever afterward, in the ancient little village of Kingsport beside the sea, when the loungers at the village store whispered dark things about the Terrible Old Man, it was for good reason. As one of them said, reflecting upon the old man's presence in their midst: "God help us, every one."

For H.P. Lovecraft and Charles Dickens

ERIK T. JOHNSON's writing has appeared in or is forthcoming in such places as Hugo award-winning *Electric Velocipede, Shimmer, Space & Time Magazine, Underworlds, Sein und Werden, Structo, Morpheus Tales,* The British Fantasy Society's *New Horizons, Pellucid Lunacy,* and *Best New Zombie Tales Volume 3.* His website is www.eriktjohnson.net .

The Depopulation Syndrome

by Erik T. Johnson

I.

There are signals all around us, transmitted by strange entities with no interest in humanity's survival. Light itself travels through the emptiness of the vacuum without a care for the eye or plant. There are signals that carry dark information along unseen channels, which since slime began have sought a receiver. These signals do not care what effect they have on the receivers, and flesh is as good as anything else if only it will carry the inhumanly cold message.

II.

Allergic reactions are a peculiar example of signal-processing, in which the body interprets information from the world as problematic and destructive. Throughout my life, I have experienced such reactions to a variety of things: circus peanuts, moldy leaves, the tracks of a cockroach, beloved pets. Exposure resulted in my lungs tightening and atopic dermatitis, rashes blooming in random spots on my arms and legs. My flesh was my enemy.

The highly-allergic person is not at home in the world. When I was young I imagined I belonged on some other, isolated planet, where nebular formations, solar winds and dead atmosphere would not contaminate me like the pollen-filled sunshine—a world without sun, flame, sea or earth. There is something alien about being an allergic individual, and perhaps such people are more sensitive to other forms of the unworldly. But across the country, allergies are increasing in quantity and intensity and today I know this far-off planet of my dreams is not far off. It is a nightmare orbiting your doorstep.

I had always wanted to belong to this world and when I was in my twenties, I undertook an extensive series of immunotherapy injections to reduce my reactions to food allergies and environmental pathogens. The treatments were highly successful and I soon found myself enjoying autumn leaves and peanut butter and jelly sandwiches, mundane pleasures that had long been beyond reach.

All that changed again about ten years later, when I undertook an expedition to the Rhymeshead area of upstate New York in the autumn of 2009. I had heard bees were disappearing from their colonies in exceptionally large numbers in this desolate location. Having recently published a well-received article in *American Apiculture* on Israel Acute Paralysis Virus and worker bees, I thought myself up to the task of solving the mystery, not knowing I would become a part of it.

III.

One of the few things I had not been allergic to were bees, and early in life I took to studying them. Although I earned my living as a professor of Information Science, as an amateur entomologist and sometimes apiculturist I naturally took great interest when Honey Bee Depopulation Syndrome (HBDS) was first described in North America in 2006. Many today are familiar with the term, as more and more bees go missing from hives with devastating effects for agriculture. Although the scientific and popular journals are full of theories, such as *Varroa* mites and the effects of electromagnetic radiation from cell phone towers, in the apocalyptic days to come everyone will know the true meaning of this phenomenon. It will be called nothing, then. There will be no words to describe it because all the mouths will be eaten.

IV.

Set in the lonely hills of Rhymeshead, New York, Ghostmoth was a small, once-thriving university town sequestered between a row of abandoned rubber factories to the east and the Rhymeshead River to the west. Besides its quaint Victorian architecture, the town was distinguished by inexplicably having the highest rate of allergy sufferers per square mile in the United States. But years of immunotherapy meant this no longer concerned me.

I drove past the ramshackle town and into the wilder, northern reaches of the area, where the houses grew more and more dilapidated as I went deeper, until the few scattered homes I saw were completely abandoned and tattered like people lying near the epicenter of an explosion.

I stopped my car by a field near the edge of a dense wood and got out to stretch my legs. Almost immediately I felt an itching sensation on both my arms and discovered vaguely star-shaped welts rising there, suddenly removing me from the world the way the first drops of rain take you from a clear day. At the same time, I heard a low droning, as of bees congregating, somewhere through the tightly-grown birch trees.

I got back into the car, rolled the windows up and turned on the air conditioning, but the itching continued. I took an allergy pill and waited twenty minutes. The bumps on my arms increased in size, bulging outward like sacks of pennies. Seeing there was no escape from this unknown allergen, I once again left the car and decided to find the source of the sound.

Although I moved through closely-packed trees, I could tell others had preceded me from cigarette stubs and the occasional boot-print. Soon I came upon piles of pants, jeans, shirts and underclothes. The marks on my arms shook like jelly though they were hard as teeth to touch. I felt them being pulled outward by an unseen force. At length I came upon a yellow-grassed clearing that sloped down toward a bog.

At least a hundred naked people danced by the bog's edge with weird aquatic motions, twisting themselves about like pieces of meat tossed by a wave. They stumbled and swirled around and past each other in ecstasy or the limits of pain, kicking up peat with their feet and hands, clawing and flipping about. Their bodies were covered in fleshy stalks about four or five inches in length, which protruded from star-shaped red patches ending in purplish bulbs. One man I cannot forget was rolling on the floor wildly, seemingly trying to snap the growths off of the eyelids where they had taken root.

The buzzing that had drawn me there came from thousands of swollen bees hovering and sitting on the plant-like protrusions on the dancers' bodies. These were the same type of worker bees, with their modified ovipositors, that had gone missing in the area; only their bodies were bloated to the size of small mice. The bees appeared to be gathering something from the fleshy stalks, as though harvesting pollen from pistils. Their purplish-black stripes rippled weirdly like the flashing of squids and I realized the bog itself was rippling to an invisible tide in the same rhythm.

The bumps on my arms began to redden and rise. I scratched and they grew at the scraping of my fingernails as though nourished by bruising. The itching increased in intensity and I felt compelled to run toward the bog and douse myself in the fetid water. Sweaty dancers squirmed around me like chunks of slimy food digested in a gut, filling the poisonous air with broken laughter. I heard their words borne in snatches on the dry wind, as though passing under a spinning fan whose blades each had its own voice, some distorted beyond recognition:

"We called it fifth . . . The transmitter transmits . . . b'thnakl-thog . . . world spurts . . . bone ask and perceive . . . h'laqtra-kratom . . . "

Then the contorted people began chanting, all at once and from wherever they stood, lay or crawled, the obscene stalks vibrating like reindeer-bells along their quivering bodies:

The sun must fade, flesh must dawn.
The flame must fade, flesh must burn.
It calls, it calls!
The sea must fade, flesh must storm.

The earth must fade, flesh must turn.
It calls, it calls!
To nothing ever never falls.

The song was in no key, ranging across the twelve-tone scale randomly as drops in a blood spatter. But part of me wanted to join in with them, too and the cognitive dissonance was splitting my skull. I forced my mouth shut and was about to hurl myself into the bog, praying for the itching to stop, when I saw the holes in the rippling watery ground, each a terrible abyss that spiked my eyes with sharp emptiness, the nothing at the rotten centerlessness of the universe. The distended bees flew in and out of the holes as from a hive. Some purplish light belched deep below the reedy surface. I looked in horror at the sacciform stalks swaying on my arms and now depending from my chin and neck.

The repulsive bees came to me, perching on the dark, bulbous tips of my flesh where it grew in little towers from my arms, my face and neck. I felt their mandibles and legs scratching, the stalks expanding, the shrill cachinnations sifting through my pounding head.

With the strength of an outraged lunatic I tore the growths from my arms and face and tossed them aside. I ran until my asthma collapsed me on a brown, rocky knoll. I lay there sweating, gasping, bleeding amidst buzzing and howling laughter merged together like the voice of a mad perpetual motion machine. The bees did not follow.

V.

Now I know why the dancers laughed. I removed the starry growths from my body. But I could not remove what was already *growing in me*, what the missing bees brought and injected into the allergic protrusions, those monstrous channels for incomprehensible information. I am full of holes, like the surface of the Rhymeshead bog. I am bloated with the abyss.

VI.

Across North America, bees continue to leave their colonies bereft of workers. Allergies are on the rise. Recent reports indicate food allergies alone have increased by 65% over the last year. Theories abound, from global warming to an obsession with cleanliness rendering the immune system rabid and delinquent.

But I have received the signal directly from the transmitter. It calls. I learn new songs. It is preparing bodies to receive the final packet of information. You may be merely sneezing now, just a little itchy. But soon the whole world will be another, much colder planet. Soon the world will hear the buzzing, laughing of the Human Being Depopulation Syndrome, scratch stars rising on their bodies, feel stalks bursting from hands clasped in prayer, meet prodigal bees urging them to dance, filling them with blackest signal, returning to the transmitter at the place where nothing goes, where I go now.

CODY GOODFELLOW has written three solo novels—*Radiant Dawn, Ravenous Dusk* and *Perfect Union*—and three more with John Skipp—*Jake's Wake, The Day Before* and *Spore*. His short fiction and comics work have recently appeared in *Dark Discoveries, Crimewave, Creepy, Cthulhu's Dark Cults* and *The Bizarro Starter Kit (Purple)*. His first short fiction collection, *Silent Weapons For Quiet Wars*, won the Wonderland Book Award in 2010. As co-founder and editor of Perilous Press, he has worked on quality hardcover editions of modern cosmic horror by Michael Shea, Brian Stableford and Richard Lupoff. He lives in Los Angeles.

"Uncle Sid's Collection" is 85% true. Only the names have been changed.

Uncle Sid's Collection

by Cody Goodfellow

Uncle Sid likes to gamble, but there is no question of his hopping a bus to Vegas or even the local Indian casinos, and money holds no real fascination for him, anyway. So Dana accompanies him to the private storage places when they have auctions on abandoned lots.

If she helps load the junk into Sid's van, she can have her pick. Last month, she found a mint run of the syndication LPs for the *Dr. Demento* show, from '74 to '79. But mostly, she just likes to see Uncle Sid excited. Sometimes, he gets so worked up, he almost talks in front of strangers.

Sid puts in a couple blind bids on spaces that afternoon, under a saggy canopy in the parking lot. Gray rain falls on the hot tarmac and turns to steam. The pavement glistens like spoiled whale blubber as they roll up the door on the lot that Uncle Sid won.

"Three hundred bucks, and for what?"

Sid picks up a rake and wades into waist-high drifts of loose trash, fast food wrappers shredded to fine confetti, headed for a stack of stained cardboard cartons in the far corner. His big sneakered feet shuffle across the floor as if to ward off stingrays. A looming, alarmingly fat man, Sid looks like a giant, balding toddler when there's nothing to lend perspective.

Dana follows him into the storage space. Dark inside. Darker than shadows. Botanica candles, pillars of melted glass and ash, everywhere. Sheet-metal walls black with scribbles, scrawls and overlapping, insane doodles and diagrams. Used-up Sharpies among the garbage like spent shell casings. Somebody spent a long time in here, hammering out their manifesto or masterpiece in pitch blackness. Not a word of it is legible.

The fetid air resists the stirring of the summer breeze. It reeks of ammonia and chemicals, and the sour, musky tang of an animal burrow. Dana thinks, *Crank kitchen.* Tweakers lost their apartment and tried to live in their storage space.

A few gawkers yawn and walk away, relieved they didn't fall for it. "Nothing in here but trash, Uncle Sid."

Lifting one of the cartons tears it open like a carelessly stuffed mummy. Books black with mold spill out. "Found a cherry '72 Husqvarna 250WR in a

217

place over in Arcadia, once. There's bound to be something."

Dana trips over something and stumbles into the trash. Her inhaled scream sucks plastic snowflakes down her throat.

Still talking about motorcycles, Uncle Sid stoops in the far corner. "Told you," he mutters.

Coughing up plastic, Dana feels for whatever she tripped on. Her hand gets mired in something slimy with broken sticks in it.

"Fuck a duck," Dana calls out, wiping black foulness on her jeans. "I think something died in here."

Uncle Sid doesn't turn around. He's found a bicycle, or what used to be a bicycle. Schwinn Stratocruiser 77, maybe 79. It's not rideable, though

Dana kicks away the trash around her until she can see what she was sitting in. A black puddle of ooze surrounds a partial skeleton like a long, coiled snake in a viscous black pool the size and rough shape of a dog or coyote. The head is missing. "Jesus, there's a dead dog in here."

Uncle Sid ignores her, and presently, she comes over to see it. "Fucking tweakers wreck everything."

Every inch of the bicycle has been wrapped in layers of coathanger wire, and a bewildering array of odd metallic implements are jammed into the spokes, while a bunch of knives are wired onto the fork and the rear axle. Uncle Sid turns the pedals, and the wheels spin. The knives play the junk in the spokes like a music box. A jingling, liquid jumble of chimes like crickets and gamelan bells make the hairs on Dana's forearms stand on end.

"Weird," Dana says, "but it's all junk."

"It's still good," he says, like he says about everything. "It just needs to be fixed."

She kicks the ribcage of the dead dog, and finds its head, nestled in the shriveled pouch of decayed bowel in the shallow basket of its pelvis. No sign of the legs or the tail "C'mon, let's get the fuck out of here."

"Go get the dolly from the van."

"No way! This shit is worthless it's just shit!"

"It's *my* shit. Go get the dolly."

She goes down the corridor inside to stay out of the rain. All the way to the van and back, Dana wonders if the freak who holed up in the storage space is still out there. Who could do something like that to a dog, even after it's dead?

Uncle Sid is still playing with the musical bike when she got back. "I'm so hungry," he says, "I could eat my own head."

*   *   *

Dana has been living with Uncle Sid for three months, since she split up with Tony. Mom offered to put her up in the game room, but Dana knew she didn't mean it. Besides, she counted getting away from her stepfather as one of her greatest life accomplishments, and wasn't about to go back. Uncle Sid has a four bedroom mid-century ranch house in the middle of a nice quiet neighborhood close to SDSU. And he lives alone.

Uncle Sid fits nine of the fifteen traits of a serial killer. A big, shy loner who drives an ancient primer-gray Ford Econoline van, never been on a date, but a wizard with anything mechanical. Dana knows he would never hurt anyone. If he didn't kill Dana and her friend Julie Hess when he babysat them the night they egged the entire neighborhood from the roof of her house, he simply doesn't have violence in him.

Dana's Mom would never let her have boy toys, least of all guns. Uncle Sid once found her an old Mattel toy portable radio that transformed into an assault rifle at the flick of a switch. Boys were terrorized, Mom was none the wiser, and Uncle Sid became the keeper of all mysteries, in Dana's world.

Mom says it's hereditary, the hoarding. Mom never kicked it, she just turned it inside out. Throwing everything away that's not nailed down is how she gets her buzz, since she stopped drinking. Everything Dana owned before high school, Mom threw or gave away.

Sid cleaned all of his shit out of a bedroom close to the front door. For a while, Dana relished the tacky mid-century bamboo bachelor pad furniture with bowling trophies and weird Shriners' relics everywhere. In the yawning voids between sleep and looking for work, she could prowl the other rooms and excavate the lively strata of Uncle Sids hoard.

The house is cool, cavernous mid-century modern, and would have fetched a million if Uncle Sid hadn't turned it into a junkyard. He inherited it from Grandma Ellen when she died, last year. Her last tenant lived there for three years and somehow managed never to pay a dollar of rent. She'd always be out of town when Ellen sent Sid to collect. Mother said it was because Grandma Ellen had begun to lose her marbles, but Uncle Sid flatly insists the tenant was a witch. Bills still crowd the mailbox for her: DOLORES ZURBARAN. Uncle Sid keeps them in a box by the front door, but when he's not looking, Dana burns them.

At least four TVs in every room, only half in color, still wired to a massive Skymaster antenna like a pterosaur skeleton on the roof. Living the dream.

The big backyard was landscaped to dramatically emphasize a sunken patch of dull gray dirt where the lawn died and none of the watermelon seeds Dana planted ever sprouted. Uncle Sid said there used to be a swimming pool, but the witch filled it in. Dana lay down on the earth and pressed her ear to it once, imagining she heard the muted, mournful cry of a car horn.

To the casual observer, Uncle Sid might not seem to have any emotions at all. Dana's mother told her Sid stopped maturing inside at age seven, when his parents got divorced. Grandma Ellen married a sadistic merchant marine who terrorized Sid until he wet the bed, then made him wear his pajamas to school. Understandably, his emotional center packed up and moved off across a thousand miles of internal tundra from the nearest sensory input.

He might not seem to react to anything, but then a response will come like a feeble telegraph message, so long after the fact or so beneath notice as to seem an unrelated tic. He is pathologically shy until he felt you were safe, and then he never stops talking about the weather, about things on TV forty years ago, about some unlikely tangent of impossible local trivia banking off of some casual thing you unwittingly said. Dana's earliest memories play to the monotonous narration of Uncle Sid explaining how Dr. Seuss and Raymond Chandler belonged to a secret society that sacrificed animals to keep something from dragging California into the Pacific.

Uncle Sid leaves her alone, fixing broken appliances and old motorcycles in the garage, or collating his treasures in one room or another, the crackly AM radio blaring Rush Limbaugh, Paul Harvey or *The Shadow* and *Inner Sanctum* reruns out of the intercom speakers throughout the house until dawn.

It's the world in purified microcosm. What could be more perfect? Who needs the thrift store, when you can look under your bed and find mounds of exotic jetsam? Who needs the museum, when there are closets filled with Beardsley and Nagel prints and police mugshot albums? Who needs the library, when she can find *The Hollow Earth Codex*, *The Secret Teachings Of All Ages* or *Phyllis Diller's Guide To Marriage* in the stack on the toilet tank? Whenever shes stoned and bored, she rummages in a random pile and turns up some awe-inspiring relic to cherish for a while, then sell on eBay. It's fun while it lasts, but after the dead-dog auction, Uncle Sid's collecting gets way out of hand. He starts collecting people.

She wakes up to find a cross-eyed Vietnamese man standing in her room with his hat in his hand. His misaligned eyes, glassy with lust for her and/or the chintzy ceiling chandelier, flick away only when she covers herself. "So sorry looking for bathroom."

"Don't use mine!" she screams, too late.

Dana rolls out of bed and pats down the sheets for her smokes. Her baggy boxer shorts and holey Link Wray T-shirt smell musty, but she can't get to the washer in the garage, anymore.

Sid was always an avid collector of everything, could only let something go if he knew it was wanted by someone, if it was useful. He goes out early in the morning and often isn't back until dark, and Dana can only guess what he's up to. Buying up failed garage sales or haggling at the swap meet. Sid can't bring himself to look a stranger in the eye, unless he's buying something. The tide of incoming junk has reached the ceiling in the living room, spilling over the breakfast bar and into the kitchen, where she found a wee gray mouse furiously treading water in the dishpan, last night.

She doesn't mind the junk. But Sid's taken it too far, gone to war with open space with the mute stubbornness of a larva building its cocoon. And almost every time he goes out, he comes back with somebody.

Dana goes in the kitchen to make some waffles. Uncle Sid's on a barstool in a foxhole trenched out of his junk, reading an old book called *How To Read A Book* and eating ice cream. He squints owlishly at the book through a pair of granny bifocals for a minute, then tosses them in a bucket and tries another. He sits under one of Dana's favorite things, a gigantic black velvet portrait of a Mexican bandito with a gruesome scar deforming his face into a sleepy snarl.

Across from Sid is her least favorite thing, even though he could have been the model for the portrait. Sid's new friend Ricardo looks like a bandito gone to seed, with his graying Che mustache and blue bulldog jowls, and his scars. A Chilean Allende Socialist, he was set on fire by Pinochet's Caravan of Death for breaking a curfew. He sensibly emigrated to America and became the laziest Communist handyman in the free world. Except for his personal neatness fetish and his endless leftist lectures, he is perfect company for sedentary Sid.

"Mice in the kitchen again." She feeds some Eggo waffles into the toaster.

"You leave a mess, Miss. You think you are aristocracy, but you must see someday, that you are but another of the proletariat."

"You're wearing one of my shirts again. Did you get it out of the dryer?"

"From each according to his means, to each according to his needs!" He huffs and peels off the Amoeba Records shirt and flings it on the floor like a broken peace treaty.

Dana doesn't rise to the bait, so he retreats to cribbing notes in a legal pad. Against her will, Dana looks on, intrigued when he flips the pad over. The book on his lap is one of the moldy things from the storage space lot. It's very old, three columns of dense serif-crazy text per onionskin page, and in Spanish. Some of the words are spiky symbols, like spiders crushed into the ink. The header reads LAS CANTATAS DEL DHOLES. *The sad songs?*

"Is that from the storage shitbox? Sure smells like it."

Peeking over Ricardo's shoulder at the yellow notepad, a glimpse of his odd block script translation: THE SUN BENEATH THE SEA, THE GRAVE OF THE UNBORN ESCHATON, THE FROZEN FIRE OF CELESTIAL LARVAE.

"Cool, let me see."

Ricardo closes the book on the pad and tucks it into a pile of obsolete phone books under the table.

The thought of something Ricardo doesn't want to talk about *ad nauseum* piques her interest, but her wits are still dull. Her coffeemaker is filled with swamp-stinking herbal tea. "What the fuck, Ricardo?"

"Have some mat instead. It's good for all humanity."

Ricardo moved in two weeks ago. Uncle Sid cleared out the other three bedrooms for guests, but he doesn't sleep in any of them, himself. He sleeps-- if and when he sleeps -- in a Barcalounger in a trench in the family room, parked in front of three TVs, all tuned to the same channel. A huge Magnavox with the tube burned out provides the sound. A 20" Sony with a broken vertical hold flashes the color in a dizzying endless barrel roll, while a puny 10" black & white with a busted speaker shows a fizzy keyhole view of the program. Somehow, Sid prefers this to one functioning TV. Buying a new set is out of the question.

"Is that Asian guy moving in, too?"

"No, he just wants me to fix some stuff." Vague wave at an AKM assault rifle and a cheap gun show conversion kit on the counter in the phone nook.

"What about the bicycle? Did you fix it yet?"

"Not broken." Sid switches reading glasses again.

"It was too fucked up to strip for parts."

"It's not a bicycle."

"Well, what is it, then?"

Ricardo shows her an old *National Geographic* cover. An ugly lump of rust and coral from the bottom of the Aegean Sea. Weird gears embedded in the gnarled surface of some kind of elaborate, ancient machine. "I postulate that it's an Antikythera device. A great mystery of the ancient world."

"What's it for? Was it a clock?"

"More than likely, yes, but it could predict the alignments of the planets, eclipses and tide changes and perhaps much more."

"It couldn't be that great, if some tweakers in a storage space could make one."

"A mystery of the modern world."

After breakfast, she goes poking into the linen closets. One shelf is filled with slide projectors and carousels stuffed with strangers decaying snapshots. In another, a trove of tape recorders, and in the back a massive Ampex reel-to-reel. The tape on it is a hypnotherapy session from 1978. A heavily drugged young woman with Baroque mental problems starts talking about what causes earthquakes. She thinks the cause is her dead father, eating the earth. Not very interesting, but five minutes into it, the shrink begins fellating the patient. A hatbox filled with tapes in the same stabby writing, spanning decades. All with the same ending.

*   *   *

Digging in the backyard, a week later. Rosy dawn sunlight coaxes the lizards out of the mounds of broken ornamental brickwork to do their morning pushups. She counts at least five different varieties: skinks, swifts, alligator lizards, a pygmy iguana and some kind of monitor fixedly watch her work.

The other two bedrooms are filled, but she doesn't know how many people live here, now. Uncle Sid apparently has a girlfriend. She's not sure, but she thinks the White Man is living in the backyard. A filthy sleeping bag rolled up among the pile of incomplete bicycles in the corner. When she comes out to make coffee in the morning, she sees him kneeling in prayer, hands outstretched to hug the fallow ground. He looks like a castaway: emaciated, with wild white hair and a Karl Marx beard. Has the hollow thousand yard stare and leathery, freckled skin of the terminal homeless, but his white shirt and painter's pants are always spotless. He almost never comes in the house, but a lot of weird vitamins and nutritional supplements and unidentifiable fruits and vegetables turn up in the kitchen fridge. Plenty of room, since someone ate every crumb of her food. The White Man cooks all their meals. Dana claims a microwave and a mini-fridge from the living room. She eats alone in her room with the door locked.

White Man creeps her out, but she's afraid to ask Uncle Sid about him.

Afraid of Uncle Sid.

The junkpile has spilled out into the yard in robust ziggurats and dunes of debris. A key copier, a rusty Ditch Witch and a spaghetti-mound of cracked PVC pipes cover Ricardo's aborted vegetable garden. She's digging in the dead dirt over the old swimming pool, a plot for a mix of wildflower seeds she found when the junk tide turned in the study, revealing antique, perhaps indigenous strata. The seeds are older than she is, but seeds are viable for centuries, Uncle Sid told her.

Ricardo patrols the yard, restless without his garden, picking up stones and stacking them in neat, knee-high columns around the perimeter.

Dana's shovel breaks through the rocky topsoil and stabs into damp, unyielding rust-red clay. She offers to let Ricardo plant his cabbages here, but he pointedly ignores her. Since Rhoda and the White Man moved in, Ricardo has acted like he's sinking into senile dementia.

Her shovel skids off something hard in the ground. Plastic. Buried treasure. In a house stuffed to bursting with forgotten valuables, what would anybody see fit to bury?

Plunging her hands into the hole, she scoops out noisome clods of clay until shes uncovered the top of an old sun tea jar. *Lame*, she thinks, but keeps digging.

Caked with filth, the jar resists coming out of the soil. She scrapes away the clinging red clay from the clear plastic jar as she starts to try to unscrew the lid.

The jar shifts in her hands. The weight inside is solid, and it moves. She's sure of that, even after she drops it and lets out a little screaming giggle. Afraid to pick it up, she peers closely into its filthy contents.

Fur, feathers, scales and chitinous exoskeletons press against the sides. As near as she can tell, its a rat or cat, a fish, a dove and a scorpion. Some kind of loony ritual burial that the witch left behind, or an exotic White Man delicacy: hobo roadkill kimchi.

"Put it back," Ricardo says. His shadow spills over her to leak into the hole in the ground.

"What is it?"

"Just put it back." Out of breath, or choking, holding a rock in his shaking hand like he's about to throw it or dash her brains out.

"Is it yours?"

"*Put it back.*"

"Okay, Jeez." Dropping the jar into the hole, she hastily buries it and drops the shovel.

"I'm scared, Ricardo." She waters the grave with her fat, helpless tears. "He's sick, and he doesn't know who his real friends are."

"The world is too large, lady." Taking out a handkerchief to wipe his wire-rimmed spectacles, he looks around as if all this shit just dropped out of the clear blue sky. "He tries to make a smaller world, tries to become bigger, tries not to change. We all must become what the world makes of us. This place is a place of healing. What is broken, will be mended. What was diseased, will be devoured, and made new."

"You're all talking like the White Man," she says. "Talking cult bullshit and tripping out on that stupid bicycle"

A crow swoops down into the yard and tries to scoop up the iguana, but the lizard squirms in its talons and pins the bird to the ground.

Ricardo grabs her arm and lifts her up, too weak to hurt her. "Stay away from the device, he says. It does not measure eclipses. It causes them. And *stop fucking with my fucking rocks!*"

She watches him over her shoulder as she retreats into the house, stamping on the filled grave and chanting under his breath as he begins to build another cairn of rocks.

It isn't until she gets back to her room and slams the door and looks out the window that she realizes that the iguana isn't trying to escape the crow, but raping it.

Of all Uncle Sid's recent acquisitions, Rhoda is the worst.

Sid talks about her like he never talks about anything. On and on about how she used to be a mud wrestler and an actress, but he can't name any of her films.

Dana wants to support Sid's fumbling attempt at normal manhood, but she just can't. Rhoda looks like something he could have built in the garage. Emaciated, wiry yellow limbs carelessly swathed in flaking crepe-paper skin, concave except for her absurd artificial breasts and collagen-injected lips. Odd ridges and veins of leaking silicone fan out from her bogus bosom like some kind of cybernetic leprosy. Bleach-blonde fiberglass for hair and eyes like runny, infected blue sores open so wide, you can see the holes in her brain. Nervous system and liver shot to hell, yet she drinks more than she eats. Her Chihuahua barks incessantly and spite-pisses on anything Dana leaves outside her room. When Sid's not in the garage or in his recliner, bathed in the compound eye glow of his broken TVs, he sits in her room, basking in her wetbrain babble and turning the pedals of the musical bicycle.

Dana's in her room on the bed after midnight, watching cartoons and burning a bongload of anxiety medication. Headphones on and blasting African Head Charge, muddy tribal thunder that perfectly blots out the noise from the garage. She sets the bong on the nightstand and crushes a bug shaped like a silverfish, but it's purple and bigger than her ring finger. Gangly, multi-jointed legs twitch in perfect spasmodic counterpoint to her headphone music.

Her eyes won't focus, but when she closes them, she feels like she's falling into a bottomless pit lined with giant, grasping hands. Her TV shows a snowy closed-circuit vision of the garage.

Junk fills the room to the rafters, but a cluster of junk people -- Sid's people -- sit in a bowl-shaped trench, maybe ten of them packed in around the bicycle. Stark naked, sweaty and soft, like botched stuffed animals

White Man turns the pedals and they howl and gibber and hit themselves in time with the hypnotic gamelan polyrhythm. Like a sleepwalker, Ricardo scoops up trash with a shovel and feeds it to Uncle Sid.

Her uncle sits on a washing machine like a brazen idol, with his legs tucked out of sight under his elephantine bulk. He is a baby again, huge wobbling head pressed against the rafters, mouth sagging ear to ear to accept the shovel, toothlessly gumming VHS cassettes, laundry detergent samples, broken computer keyboards and a Chihuahua with its bulbous head twisted off. Glowing with a sullen, molten orange light that burns brighter with each bite through folds of fat to reveal something inside like a fossil trapped in amber, or the ripening fetus in an egg held up to a candle.

Dana turns away and falls out of bed and reaches out to catch herself against a rack of antlers wrapped in cellophane. Rhoda's hips falter under her weight even as Dana recoils and trips on her bed.

"WHY ARE YOU SCREAMING MY NAME?" Rhoda shrieks in her face. Naked and shaking, she bursts into ammoniac tears and reaches out with curled, cracked nails. "Have you seen my dog?"

"Fuck off!" Dana shoves Rhoda away and her hand glancingly touches her ridiculous fake tits. Hard as milk jugs filled with sand, they wriggle under her hand. A patch of jaundiced skin sloughs off under her fingernails.

Dr. Blythe comes in and takes Rhoda by the hand and leads her out like a half-empty helium balloon. Then he comes back into the bedroom and yanks Dana's headphones off.

Blythe looks uncannily like Richard Widmark, if he had a coke problem and a stroke. A once-respected psychiatrist, he used to treat all the socialite wives in La Jolla, but a motorcycle accident left him in a coma for a year. Ricardo says he still has metal in his head, so be gentle. Rhoda was one of his secretaries, and he took care of her in her own studio with a steady flow of pill prescriptions and a vodka IV drip, until she got too wasted to use for sex. Then he gave her to Sid.

He smiles at her, and its like he's trying to use those old novelty chattering teeth for dentures. "I guess you think you're too c-c-cuh-cool to have any manners, but if you weren't om-nom-nom-nominally a girl, I'd chuck your ass out in the s-s-s-stuh-reet and stomp some man-nuh-ners..."

Long before he's finished the sentence, she's got her phone and an air rifle out. The Wrist Rocket slingshot with its leather pouch of steel ball bearings would be more effective, but nothing says *Get the fuck out* like a gun.

Blythe backs out, still smiling like his teeth are trying to escape. "This is *His* house," he hisses, "and in His house nothing is wasted. Will you serve, or be swallowed?"

"I'm calling the cops," she snarls, backing him down the hallway to the garage. "What are you freeloading fuckers doing to my uncle?"

"Healing him," Blythe whispers, hands out to embrace her, pupils dilating to hold her in what he probably thinks is a hypnotic gaze. The hallway is lined with bookshelves and mildewed crates of comics, making the path too narrow to wriggle past him.

"I want to see him," she says. The White Man slips into the hall, blocking the garage doorway with his glistening nakedness.

"Soon," Blythe says, and behind her, Ricardo pounces.

Dana screams. The air rifle is ripped away, the phone smashed to the floor. Thrashing under the moaning men, she claws at the bookshelves and they tumble to bury her like bricks closing over a sinkhole.

"The world is too big," says the White Man, "so he has remade it here, smaller and simpler. We are making ourselves pure, and anointing him to become what he will be, in the bosom of his family."

"I'm his family!"

"We are his *true* family. Closer than you."

"Uncle Sid! Help me!"

"He will see you now," says the White Man, "but you will not see him." He raises a canvas Windmill Farms shopping bag and tries to slip it over her head.

Dana throws her head back to smash Ricardo's nose. He flails backwards and she turns and knocks him down and tramples him, racing for the door.

Blythe and the White Man run after her. She throws a hat rack and a bookshelf into her wake. They trip and fall, screaming her name.

In her room, she slams and locks the door, throws some clothes into a duffel bag, sobbing so hard she whistles.

She notices the neat cairn of rocks in the far corner of her room just before it crumbles and falls apart.

Something heavy thuds into her door. The upper hinges groan and pop out of the frame.

Dana jumps backward, looking around, grabbing things in a panic: her alarm clock, her Bob's Big Boy coin bank, a fistful of CDs. She can go out the window, climb the pomegranate tree and hop the wall, but she can hear them outside, lying in wait.

"Dana, come out, honey." Uncle Sid's voice, soft and ashamed of itself, comes through the door. She goes over and almost opens it, but she slips in something viscous and cold in a puddle on the floor. It's seeping under the door. "It's okay, nobody's going to hurt you."

She wants to tell her uncle that she loves him and she's scared out of her mind, things are way too weird, but she just grabs her bag and jumps out the window.

"I don't want it to happen like this," he calls out. "I don't want to go alone!"

She flies over the wall and across the neighbors yard, then out into the street. Nobody's waiting for her, nobody pops up in the back seat of her car.

She starts the car and peels out and is on the freeway before she starts crying, and realizes she has nowhere to go.

*   *   *

227

Tony was ecstatic to see her for about two days. Mom had already filled the game room with a pool table. When she realizes her unemployment check has been sent to Uncle Sid's house, she breaks down and resolves to confront it with both eyes open.

She hasn't slept right all week. Dreams that only get worse when she tries to stay up. Buried alive in Uncle Sid's house. When she finally lets go, she realizes she's not going crazy. The nightmares came from him, trying to reach out to her. Begging her to come back.

The house is so white it glows in the starlight, as if it were sculpted out of ice cream, as if the moon shines on it alone, though tonight, she heard on the news, the moon's light is doused by a penumbral lunar eclipse.

The pomegranate tree in the side yard is dead and slumped against the roof, like something ate its roots. Six cars and a camper are parked in the horseshoe driveway. The little plot of ground where she planted zinnias and dahlias is covered by an overturned Jacuzzi.

She never should have left.

She feels a tug of shame that its her money, her possessions-- her own infertile cocoon -- that dragged her back. If Uncle Sid wants to run a halfway house or a cult, that's his business.

They're taking advantage of him, she knows it. Poisoning him, maybe. But nobody lets anything happen to them, that they don't really want to happen.

She picks her way through the debris in the front yard, wondering why the neighbors haven't sicced the city on them. The porch light is off, but the faint witch-glow of many televisions play on the few unblocked windows. The chocolate brown front door hangs open just a crack. She hesitates, thinking one more time about coming back with the cops.

It wasn't an accident, no, none of it. The storage space he bought was registered to a *D. Zurbaran*. The White Man, Rhoda, Blythe and Ricardo all came in hopes of being changed, or just helping Uncle Sid to become something to punish the world

Sure, that makes sense. She kicks the door open and flips the light switch, but nothing happens. The darkness rustles and chitters, and she knows it isn't Rhoda's Chihuahua. How many more obsolete people has he taken in? How many are hiding in here, amid the junk?

Her bedroom door won't open. Stuff piled to the ceiling against it spills around the door like an avalanche. The wall is soft and cold, like a dead man's love handles.

"No room, no room," the White Man says from behind her. She whirls around and brings up the gun-- a real one, lifted from Stepdad's collection in the basement.

228

He laughs at the gun, scratching his long white beard. His eyes are black, all pupil from lid to lid. Steam or smoke leaks out of his tear ducts. "You don't belong here but He wants you."

She smashes the gun into his face and screams for Uncle Sid. The White Man stumbles back into a pile of photo albums and football body armor that closes over him like a wave. He burrows into it and disappears.

Dana climbs over shifting hills and treacherous chasms to get to the living room and Uncle Sid's recliner.

All around her, the living junkpile rocks like the ocean, chewing its contents into a homogenous soup of dust and dead memory. A rogue wave breaks and spits the White Man out right in front of her. His spotless white painter's pants and T-shirt are dirty. His beard is black with slime.

"Never too late," he crows, and hurls a flickering TV. Hit on the head, the tube bursts like ball lightning in her face, she can't even find the floor, crushed, she can't move, can't even breathe.

"Take my hand, young lady," Ricardo rasps, and she can't find him, but he pulls her out of the rubble.

"You're using him, you're making him crazy."

"We're making him into a god," brays the White Man. "Come and see!"

"Where is he?"

Something drips on her -- Ricardo's tears. "We buried him in the backyard."

This last brings her up short like a fist to the ear. "You killed him!"

Ricardo says, "He's not dead just buried."

"This house is an egg," says White Man, "a seed filled with all the nutrition he'll need to effect his final transformation. He's gone as far as he can, in his present state."

"What did you do to him?"

"The Dholes that eateth the Earth like the worm gnaws the tooth! This world is sick, but He shall eat its disease!"

The light from the flickering TVs reveals what she's holding hands with. A huge, reticulated worm with the blind head and knurled, stunted limbs of a naked mole rat. Outsized teeth grate at each other in a nervous frenzy, as if they will grow together the moment it stops gnawing. The slavering jaws and dull, vestigial eye-spots twitch in some desperate imitation of a smile.

His voice like knives on whetstones, Ricardo pleads, "He needs you, Dana -- needs us all... the world is wounded... its sickness must be devoured..."

Whatever he's become, she is sorry she has to shoot Ricardo. The junkpile heaves and screeching cyclones of teeth burst out of the lard-soft walls.

Dana leaps and crawls for the door, but she's swimming upstream, as the whole foundation gives way with a weary seismic moan. Cracks shoot up the walls. The ceiling sighs and comes crashing down in a drywall monsoon.

Dana leaps for the doorway, claws and teeth ripping out hair and raking her back, and everything is circling a vast yawning drain beneath the house, everything is going down into a mouth, and they want to take her with them. She crashes through the frosted glass of the atrium window and hits the overturned hot tub on all fours, but she never stops running until the ground beneath her feet ceases to rumble like an unquiet stomach mumbling her name.

Nobody calls her, nobody comes looking. A sinkhole under a hoarders house makes the end of the local news: water main draining into improperly filled-in swimming pool leads to tragedy, local man Sidney Swensen missing... neighbors called him a quiet man who kept to himself...

Dana tries not to sleep for three days, but when she does, she sees the Earth from space. When it passes in front of the sun, she sees it is hollow and rife with colossal worms -- no, one worm, coiled upon itself over and over, gorging itself on the molten mantle of the unbearably fragile Earth.

She can live with it, even if she has the dream for the rest of her life. She will not let her possessions add up to more than will fit in a single suitcase. And if ever the stack of rocks in the corner of her room should happen to fall over, she will pack her suitcase and run, until there is nowhere left to hide.

BRIAN M. SAMMONS has been critiquing all things horror, science fiction, dark, or just plain icky for over a decade. His reviews and columns can currently be found in the pages of *Cemetery Dance* magazine, on the web at Hellnotes. com, and in seven other magazines and websites. Not being satisfied at being a humble and handsome critic, Brian has penned a few tales himself. They have appeared in such magazines as *Bare Bone*, *Cthulhu Sex* and *Dark Animus*, and in such anthologies as *Arkham Tales*, *Horrors Beyond* and *Twisted Legends* among others. He has also written extensively for the *Call of Cthulhu* role playing game in an attempt to corrupt as many new, young minds as possible. Despite all this, Brian is often described by his neighbors as "such a nice, quiet man", and he loves animals. His webpage is: brianmsammons.blogspot.com

Father's Day

by Brian M. Sammons

By now the school must have told mother that I am gone. That I had slipped away and snuck into the city by myself. This was not allowed. It was forbidden for anyone as young as me to go to the city alone. But in my case I would be in more trouble than most because of who I am. Or what I am.

I am a freak.

Mother does not mention it, but I know. I can see things about myself that are different than others. My fingers that are partially webbed. My skin that is equal parts pink and smooth and green and scaly. Even the way that I blink my eyes is wrong. I am like no one else that I know, not even mother. That is why I had to leave and come to this city. I need to find out who my father is because I know he is the reason for all my differences. He is the reason I am a freak. I must know who he is. *What* he is.

That is why I came to the city of Innsmouth.

Right now I walk between large structures. It is dark out but there are no lights inside them. This is not where people live, this is where they do things. I've never been here before but I know this. I may be a freak but I'm not stupid. In fact, I can understand some things better than others my age. That may be the only gift I got from my father. Like now, I'm staring at three words. I don't know what one of the words means but the other two are *family* and *clinic*. I know these words because mother told me about them when she told me stories about this place.

This is where mother came to become pregnant with me.

While mother doesn't tell me everything she has never told me an untruth. So I believe her even when I don't understand. I know that she also has the old beliefs. I know that one of those beliefs has to do with the mating of our kind with the *others*. I know that there are some in this city that also share our faith in Mighty Dagon but that these people are now few and keep their beliefs secret. This is because a long time ago there was a great tragedy at Innsmouth and many worshipers, both our kind and the *others*, were ended. But I also know that our beliefs are strong and enduring and go on no matter what. I know this because I am here, I am alive. I am a testament to these beliefs, or so mother has told me.

She also told me about this *clinic* place. I don't understand but I know that father left his seed here and that those in this place that share our faith made sure that mother got that seed. With that seed mother had me. That seed is the reason I am different and that is why I am at this *clinic* now. The people inside will know who my father is and they will tell me.

I will make them tell me.

I move close to the *clinic* and look through an opening. I see someone inside, a female. I can tell this by her long hair. She is sitting and doing something and there is a little bit of light around her from overhead. There is no other light in the structure. I know this means that she is alone. I bang on the barrier between us and she looks up. She is startled. She gets up and moves closer to me, to see me. Then she does see me and she starts screaming like I knew she would. She starts to quickly move away so I come smashing into the *clinic* with her. There is some pain in doing that, but not much. I easily catch the female and grab her perfectly smooth neck. I hate her neck. I squeeze it and draw blood when my claws cut her. I must calm myself, there is so much anger inside me.

"Father...who is father?" I croak out to her. My throat is very dry.

The female shakes, her eyes leak and she makes strange small sounds but she doesn't answer. I squeeze her neck more.

"Father left...seed here for mother. Who is father?"

"I don't know," she says to me. Her trembling is doing something to me, making me feel funny. Something deep inside me is stirring, making waves in my stomach. I want to hurt her and I don't know why. Is this something I got from mother or father? I must know.

I think back to stories mother told me about how I came to be. I remember the strange name she called herself when dealing with the *clinic*. It was a name to keep things secret but maybe this female needs that name to find my father.

"Mother name was...Mar...Mary. Mary M...Mash? No, Mary Marsh. Mary Marsh was mother name. You find the seed giver for Mary Marsh."

"Yes, yes, just please don't hurt me," the female says.

I say nothing.

"I need to go...go over there," she points to where she was sitting before I came. I let go of her. She slowly moves back to where she was and does something I don't understand. There is a square with different colored lights that she looks at as her fingers tap on a small flat thing before her. I have never seen anything like this before but I don't care, all I want is to find father. Soon another box is making noise and spitting something out. I recognize that it is paper. The female rips off the paper and holds it to me with a trembling hand. There are some dark lines on the pale paper. They are words! I take paper and read words. I am smart and I read them but I don't understand.

"What this?" I say.

"That's his, I mean your father's, address." She says.

I say nothing.

"Don't…don't you know your address?"

"No, what address?" I say.

"Oh, I can show you if we can go to the door," she says. I don't understand but I let her go. I can catch her if I want to.

She moves to where I had smashed through and points outside to a long, thin black pole with two green things sticking out of it at its top. On those green things are words.

"That's a street name," she says, not trembling so much anymore. She then points to my paper with her short, red claws. "You need to find a sign like that with this street name: Bay Side."

"Bay Side," I say after her.

"Yes, it is over there," she then points away from the city towards the ocean.

"Once there you will have to find these numbers," she points again to my paper then to the outside of the clinic where there are numbers. "See, like this. Those numbers will be on his house. Do you understand now?"

I look at her for a long time then I look at the paper and then at the numbers on the *clinic*.

I think.

I blink.

"Yes, I understand."

"Good, then will you let me go, please? I have done everything you wanted, can I please just go now?" the female says.

I think some more. My anger is sleeping inside me and she helped me. No need to hurt her. No need to end her.

"Go," I say.

She moves away from me fast and I start to move to where she had pointed. Towards the ocean, towards father.

*   *   *

It is darker now and raining, I am happy for that. I like being wet, hate being dry. The rain helps this. I wonder if mother is looking for me. Did she come back to the city of Innsmouth to find me? Was I allowed to? How will I be punished when I return to her? I think about that and much more as I move through the dark city, looking for the words *Bay Side*. I am tired. I have traveled a long way today, longer than I ever traveled before. But I go on, I must find my father. I must know him.

After much hard walking I find the words *Bay Side*. Next I find the numbers that match the numbers on my paper. This is it, this is where my father lives. He lives where the land meets the ocean and the smell of salt and brine is heavy. Where he lives there is light inside and as I move closer I hear sounds. Speaking, inside there are people speaking. Is one of them my father?

I move to the front of the structure, to the thing the clinic woman called a *door*. I bang on *door* and I hear speaking inside stop. Then noise coming closer. Then *door* swings away from me and before me is my father.

He is so strange, so different from me. My dry throat has no voice.

He is taller than me, but shorter than mother. His eyes are brown and quick blinking. They are behind two crystal pools he keeps on his face. He has hairs around his mouth and hairs on top of his head. They are sand colored. His skin is almost completely covered in hides of different colors, just like the woman in the *clinic*, but still I can tell that he is smooth and pink all over beneath them.

He looks long, hard and blinking at me. He doesn't say anything.

"Father..." I say at last and reach out my green, scaly hand to touch his smooth pink one. But my claws are too sharp and his skin too thin and my touch makes him bleed.

"Daddy who is-" an unseen someone says then moves slowly out from behind my father so that I can see it. It is young. I smell that it is female. I feel funny in my stomach again and anger.

Lots of anger.

I know that the young female is the offspring of my father, that she is almost part of my brood. But she is not like me. She is ugly and strange but she is all like father. She is not a half-blood. She is not a freak like me and I hate her for that.

And I hate my father for seeding me.

After long silence my father finds his voice. He starts to speak something but I don't hear it. All I hear is my roar. It is as loud as the thundering waves and deep as the depths with rage. My claws flash. I rip through his blue hide and through his warm pink skin beneath it. He gasps like a newling taken to the surface for the first time. I would laugh at that if I didn't hate laughing so much. Laughing is another dirty thing I got from my father, like my thin pink skin and my blinking eyes the color of wet sand.

Mother never laughs.

Father falls to the ground and I am on him quick. My claws go up then flash down, go up then flash down. I am like the great eaters when they smell blood in the water. I am out of control but for the first time in a long time I feel good. At last I feel like I know who I am.

Father is no longer fighting. He only twitches and blows red bubbles. My ears come back to me from the roaring in my head and I hear something. It is a loud, angry noise. It is also a fear noise. It is coming from the young, pink, female. My near-broodmate. And I know what she is doing. It is called *screaming* and I like the way it sounds. It makes the waves in my stomach roar. It makes my tainted blood rush in my body. It makes me feel like Mighty Dagon.

I smile at this. I know that I shouldn't but I can't help myself. I have too much of my father in me. I hope mother would forgive me just this once. Then I leap at the screaming, eye leaking female. My nearly webbed fingers spread, my claws wet and ready.

*　　*　　*

I have been here for a long time. I hear that the rain has stopped and I feel a change in the air. I know the sun will be up soon. I do not care. All around me is red and wet. The smell of it makes my head dizzy. It still makes my stomach feel strange and below that, between my legs, there is a tingling. All over I am tired. My claws hurt from tearing, but it is a good pain.

Then I hear something from outside this structure. Something is moving closer. Perhaps it is another of the *others* that dwell here, like the older female that had come here after I had gone back to father. I quickly caught her and ended her so I know I can end whatever is coming now.

I am ready.

I am fearless.

Fear is one thing that I did not get from my father.

I get down low, ready to leap, ready to claw and bite…then I stop. I can smell who is coming.

Mother has found me.

She moves closer, opens the *door*, and first I don't know her. She has the colored hides that the others use covering her, but then she lets the hides fall and I can see her beautiful scaly skin. He large, unblinking eyes pin me to the ground like a needlefish. In her eyes I am not scary, I am not Mighty Dagon, and I am not a freak. I am just her youngling and she loves me. I know that because I love her too.

I get love from my mother's blood.

She holds out webbed hands and scoops me up to bring me close to her heart. She softly claws at my scales, avoiding the thin pink spots, and I nuzzle into her neck and lightly bite. I know everything is now fine. I know that she is not angry at me for leaving the school and coming here. Just as I know that we will stay the day here with what's left of my father and his brood before returning to the sea. I know that while we wait she will tell me more of the old ways. Of the mixing of blood between us and the *others*. Of how one day I will loose all the marks of the surface dwellers and become fully a child of the deep. And in the long aeons to come, none of this will matter. I know all this because she has told me this before. But now for the first time I believe her.

DARRELL SCHWEITZER won the World Fantasy Award in 1992 for co-editing *Weird Tales* (which he did between 1988 and 2007). His fiction has also been nominated for the World Fantasy Award and the Shirley Jackson Award. His novels include *The White Isle*, *The Shattered Goddess*, and *The Mask of the Sorcerer*. His short fiction has appeared in *Twilight Zone*, *Amazing Stories*, *Night Cry*, *Cemetery Dance*, *The Horror Show*, *Whispers*, *Interzone*, and in numerous anthologies. His story collections include *Sekenre: The Book of the Sorcerer*, *Tom O'Bedlam's Night Out*, *Transients*, *Necromancies and Netherworlds* (with Jason Van Hollander), *The Great World and the Small*, and *We Are All Legends*. Also look for his story-cycle/novella *Living with the Dead*. He is also an essayist, reviewer, poet, interviewer, the author of books about H.P. Lovecraft and Lord Dunsany, and editor of *Discovering H.P. Lovecraft*, *The Thomas Ligotti Reader*, *The Robert E. Howard Reader*, etc. He is also famous for rhyming Cthulhu in a limerick.

Innsmouth Idyll

by **Darrell Schweitzer**

Much, much later, he realized that this afternoon had contained the happiest moment of his life; but he didn't know that at the time, of course. When you're fourteen and it's summer, days tend to blend together. This particular day was a Sunday, and after a typical service at the Hall which didn't mean a whole lot to him, Timothy hurried home and changed out of meeting clothes into plain cut-offs and a t-shirt and ran down to the beach barefoot, to where Hezzie had whispered that she would meet him. Her name was Hezekiah, actually – they had such strange names here – something he'd have to get used to growing up in this incredibly run-down, wreck of a town in what he liked to call – in what he thought was an oh-so-clever display of attitude – "the ass-end of nowhere." It was the ass-end, too, which is to say they didn't have internet here and they *hardly* even had phone service, and when TV went from analog to digital that was the *end* of that, no more channels from Boston and no sense even *asking* about cable; it was like living in the *Stone Age*. But here he was because his Uncle Abner and Aunt Emily had brought him here, "to be close to your kind of folks." Which made no sense because he didn't know anybody here. But he had to go where they took him, because he was an orphan and lived with them, his parents having come to a bad end in a "fishing boat accident" nobody wanted to talk about.

But on this particular summer day, not one bit of that mattered, because the sun was warm and the hot sand felt good beneath his feet, and the prettiest girl in town, who was actually older than him by slightly over a year, had asked *him* to meet her in secret on this beach. It *had* to be a secret. He did not want the other kids in the neighborhood mocking him about having a girlfriend, when he wasn't sure he had one, wasn't sure of anything.

But she had asked him, and that was pretty amazing.

She said she'd meet him between the second and third of the "fingers," which is what the local people called a peculiar rock formation which thrust out into sea like an outstretched hand, webbed with beach in between each point. Once when he and Hezzie had looked down on it from the cliff-road above, just after he'd first met her, right after he'd just moved into town, and she'd pointed it out to him, he'd said, yes, it looked like the paw of the Creature from the Black

Lagoon – which he thought was funny, but he stopped laughing very suddenly when she apparently didn't.

The sandy beach ended up against the first "finger," and he considered for a minute wading out and around the stone point, where waves broke and sprayed, but it looked like it was three or four feet deep out there and he wasn't ready to get totally soaked yet, so he climbed, gingerly slipping his fingers and toes into cracks in the rocks.

From the top, he could see the next stretch of beach, which was deserted. He jumped down, a good ten feet or more, and didn't land as nimbly as he thought he would, but instead went sprawling in the sand. He got up, unhurt, brushed himself off a little, and hurried on his way, not even pausing to look at what might have washed up by the tideline and lie half buried in the sand. He knew this was where some of the people from the Hall came down at night, to do whatever it was they did, and people said they sometimes found gold on this beach, but he didn't see any, and he wasn't looking anyway.

He climbed the next outcropping and descended a little more carefully this time, backwards, like going down a ladder. When he got to the bottom, someone yelled, "Hey Timmy!" and he turned around suddenly.

She was there, and she was, to his eyes, the loveliest thing he had ever seen, dressed in faded cut-offs like his own, only they came down a little below the knees, and a very loose tank-top which had a logo on it with a fish – something about a reef and a school swimming team – and her hair was tied in place with a bandana, and she was wearing flip-fops on her feet, and before he could take in any more details the Frisbee she had thrown hit him in the face and knocked his glasses off.

"Ow!" he said.

She kicked off her flip-flops and ran to him, picked up his glasses and put them back on his face.

He felt where the metal bridge of the glasses had banged into the top of his nose.

"I think I have a cut," he said. "Do I have a cut?"

She took his glasses off again and brushed his hair aside and looked.

"If you do, it's a little one and you'll live. Here. Let me make it better."

She kissed him, not on the cut, but tenderly, on his forehead.

That was pretty amazing too, as much so as the mere fact of this meeting, because no girl had ever kissed him before, anywhere, or even gotten this close to him, besides which he could tell that she wasn't wearing a bra under that very loose tanktop. He started to wonder what she'd look like wet.

She handed him his glasses, and when he'd put them on, she ran away from him backwards until she was twenty or thirty feet away and launched the Frisbee once more.

"Now catch it this time!"

He caught it and threw it back to her, and for a time they ran back and forth across the beach, playing with the Frisbee, his mind pleasantly blank, until at last she caught it one last time and didn't throw it, and the two of them sat down side by side near the water's edge, just close enough for the lapping tide to wash over their feet. There were shells half-buried in the sand there, but no gold.

She asked him how he liked living in the town, and he told her, frankly, that it was okay, he guessed, but there were parts he didn't like, like no cable TV.

"There is the library. You do, read, don't you?"

He did read. He was a big Harry Potter fan. He also liked science.

"There are more books in the Hall. They keep them locked up, but when we're older, we get to read those too. Everybody does. They're kind of like science."

"Kind of?"

"Only kind of."

She reached out and took his hand in hers, and he tensed, because no girl had ever done that to him before. He didn't know how to respond except to let her do it.

The conversation drifted. Later, they had lunch. She'd brought an actual, old-fashioned, wicker picnic basket, the likes of which he'd only seen in a Yogi Bear cartoon before.

Later still, they lay side by side in the warm sand. She edged against him. She reached over and took his hand again. He let her do it. That was it, the moment of absolute contentment, a haze of gentle hope and wonder. He had to admit that he wouldn't mind lying beside her forever, just letting this go on and on. To have a friend like her, to be here, that was all he wanted.

Lazily, they talked about what they both would be someday. He said he might like to be a writer, and write books, or maybe an astronaut, or maybe both. He admitted he hadn't made up his mind yet.

"We'll have to move away from this place," he said. "Not much opportunity here."

"Maybe not," she said. "It could surprise you."

That was when she sat up suddenly and said, "Let's go swimming!"

Before he could say more than "Huh?" she had tossed away her bandana and shaken her long, dark hair loose, and pulled off her tank top, under which she had indeed not been wearing a bra.

He stared, but he was looking at her back, and he noticed that she had a thin stripe of fine scales down her spine, like tiny fish scales, a little darker than her skin, but somehow on her it didn't look ugly or freakish at all.

Then she got up and stepped out of her cut-offs. She hadn't been wearing any underwear either, and now she crouched down by him, entirely naked, only a little covered by her hair which draped down below her shoulders, and all he could do was stare wide-eyed and say, "But – but – but –"

"It's all right," she said, as she undressed him, all the way.

"But – but –"

"It's called skinny-dipping. We do it a lot."

"We?"

She grabbed him by the arm and ran into the water, dragging him along. If he had any stirrings of lustful interest, that came to a sudden halt as soon as the waves broke over his crotch.

"Holy crap! That's cold!"

"Mind your language!" she said, laughing, pretending to scold him. She let go and swam on her back out into the water, her amazing breasts floating in full view, like water wings.

He remembered a line intoned by one of those weird, wrinkled, smelly Elders at service back at the Hall, "When we were so very, very young and still mammalian."

He knew enough science to know what "mammalian" meant.

Still?

He stood there, shivering.

"Come on!" Hezekiah shouted. "Swim! You do know how to swim, don't you?"

In fact he knew how to swim very well. Back in his old school he had won junior medals on the swim team. One of the coaches had said that for a skinny little kid he was the most phenomenal swimmer he'd ever seen.

He swam out toward Hezekiah, and after a moment or two he didn't feel the cold. He forgot his embarrassment as they raced, and played tag in the water. Once, laughing, she broke to the surface beside him and said, "Isn't this great?"

"Yeah," he said. He looked back toward the beach and was more than a little surprised at how far they had come. He could see the beach and the cliffs overhead, but he couldn't see their discarded clothing on the sand. They were too far out for that.

But she didn't seem at all worried, and he decided he wasn't either. He *was* after all a very good swimmer, like the coach had said.

Then she took him by the hand again, and led him, swimming down, deeper and deeper until the water began to get dark. She seemed to be able to hold her breath forever, and he was amazed at how long he was lasting, but finally, more because he thought he should be feeling a lack of air than because he actually was, he broke free and swam a very long way to daylight and the surface.

She popped up beside him.

"It's okay," she said. "You won't drown. You *can't*."

"*Can't?*"

"You'll see."

She grabbed him from behind and hugged him. Under any other circumstances having those remarkable breasts of hers pressed against his bare back would have been wonderful almost beyond his ability to describe, but now he wasn't so sure. He struggled.

"Wait-wait-I-don't—"

"Yes, you *do*," she said, and before he could react she hauled him underwater in her arms as if he were a sack. Her grip and the movements of her legs were incredibly strong. She drove the two of them down, down, until the depths. They came to the edge of an underwater shelf and plunged over it, deeper, deeper. He was beginning to panic. He knew he should be drowning, he would *inevitably* be drowning, but somehow while she touched him and held him he wasn't.

He kicked feebly. They plunged downward.

Then he saw something moving down below, something *huge*, and he did panic, and he did fight her with all his strength, and he screamed underwater, which only made a gurgling sound, as it seemed the whole black bottom of the sea moved as *one piece* – too large to be a shark certainly, too large even to be a whale – impossible! Impossible! He knew enough science to know that nothing was that big. But it *was* that big, and it opened an immense, pale colored mouth, baring teeth like spikes, no, like broken pillars, thick as snapped-off trunks of trees—

It's going to eat us! he tried to scream, but only gurgled.

And then her heard her voice, Hezekiah's voice, inside his mind, as if she were talking to him in everyday, soothing tones. "No, it won't hurt us. Calm down. *It is our father. The father to us all.*"

All he could do was surrender, and go limp, drifting with the current as she swam, holding him.

The thing's eyes opened, like twin moons coming out from behind dark clouds.

And it spoke, at first growlings and rumblings and crackling, but then, to his utter amazement, he *understood*, as if something had switched on inside his head, and he could pick up signals on this new frequency.

The thing spoke, and it welcomed him, and Hezekiah, and its speech was not quite in words, more in concepts, images, like something from a half-remembered dream. It was like watching a landscape rush by from a train window, he thought. You get the broad sense, but miss the individual details.

He saw great vistas in the ocean's depths, and he saw with something other than human eyes, in other wavelengths, so that nothing was entirely dark to him. He saw massive stone columns, draped with seaweed, rising from the ocean floor. He and Hezzie were swimming among them. She'd let go of him now. He swam by her side. He reached out and took her hand. All around him, the water seemed suffused with strange light, in a color he could not quite define. He heard something, in his mind, which filled him with awe, something like a vast hymn, which went on forever, which sounded from the beginning of time until the end, like a current carrying him along, something to which he would add his own voice, he understood, in time, when he was ready.

There were others around him, who could speak to him in fragments of words, in actual languages, for all they seemed to have nearly forgotten how and much of what they said didn't make any sense.

So much didn't make any sense. He tried to sort it out in memory after the visions stopped, and the double-moon eyes closed and dissolved into the darkness, and he and Hezzie were drifting – forever it seemed – up, up toward the impossibly distant surface.

When they broke the surface, gasping, it was *dark*. He looked around, alarmed, and he could only see the stars above, filling the sky with their brilliance, and the lights of the town, along the coastline, so far away that they almost seemed to be more stars.

Something strange had happened to them. Time had been suspended somehow. They had been underwater for hours.

But Hezzie was with him and then he was not afraid, and they held on to one another as they half-swam, half drifted toward the shore.

The tide was coming in and it was very strong. It would take them where they needed to go. He was sure of that. As long as his face was in the water, he could still hear the singing.

It *was* cold though. He was trembling almost uncontrollably and coughing as they crawled up onto the beach and groped around for their clothes.

*   *   *

Much, much later, he realized that for all his future might be filled with incredible visions, with adventures, with possibilities he could not even imagine, the last perfectly happy moment in his life had come to him that afternoon, while he was still innocent, while he could still lie beside Hezzie on the sand, with no wish or expectation that anything would ever change.

Because he heard the music now, and he felt the tide that carried him farther and farther away from that perfect moment, and he knew that he had undergone a kind of baptism, and the music and the tide would never cease.

The author of over 50 mostly pseudonymous novels and a lifelong Lovecraftian, WILL MURRAY has been writing about HPL since the 1980s, chiefly in now-legendary journals such as *Crypt of Cthulhu, Lovecraft Studies, Studies in Weird Fiction, Dagon, Nyctalops, Books at Brown, Lovecraft Annual,* and *Fangoria.* He was one of the three founders of Friends of H. P. Lovecraft, which was organized to place the memorial plaque on the grounds of the John Hay Library on the centennial of Lovecraft's birth in 1990. A contributor to numerous anthologies, Murray's Mythos stories have appeared in *The Cthulhu Cycle, Disciples of Cthulhu II, The Yig Cycle, The Shub-Niggurath Cycle, Miskatonic University, Weird Trails, Reign of Cthulhu,* and the forthcoming *Cthulhu 2012.* Many involve the semi-fictional Cryptic Events Evaluation Section of the National Reconnaissance Office. He periodically threatens to write more. Murray lives in Massachusetts, has explored Arkham Country extensively, and is a professional medium and a trained remote viewer, among other arcane accomplishments. He has never encountered H. P. Lovecraft, living or dead, but cannot rule it out in the future. If there is one.

The Hour of Our Triumph

by Will Murray

In the weeks immediately after the sun was quenched like a candle and the moon ceased to be visible in the unending, eternal night, mankind eked out a precarious existence, living off the thinning resources of a steadily-cooling Earth.

Travel was still possible. But the means were scant. Money had stopped circulating. Only the basics mattered—the perishable foods were long before consumed. Foodstuff were the new coinage, although other considerations were bartered. There was a brisk business of assisted suicide, for those who had no compunctions about killing the willing. The willing being those unwilling to suffer along with the rest of doomed humanity.

For the entire frigid month of November, humanity realigned itself. Ominous clouds gathered in the sky unlike any seen before, their cobalt bellies hanging lower than natural clouds ever did. Unhuman visages could be glimpsed in the roiling chaos of their formations. They radiated a dull hunger. A new reality was taking hold. The Old Ones were in the ascendancy. But few knew it. The public struggled through a darkness of misinformation within the eternal night that had enveloped suddenly mortal Mother Earth.

Word came of out Egypt that Nyarlathotep had raised the old city of Cynopolis—the accursed City of Dogs—from the desert sands and was again accepting the worship of men. When Nyarlathotep walked the Earth, the Old Ones could not be far behind....

A new moon arose to take the place of the old. A pale self-luminous apparition resembling a blind bony eye, it careened madly across an unchartable sky. After a week, it went into eclipse, and mankind realized it possessed a dark bituminous companion. No discernable transits were ever discovered. Men went mad under the influence of their dyssynchronous gaze. Colloquially, they were dubbed Alpha and Omega, but those who were versed in Earth's dark prehistory called them Nug and Yeb. And perhaps they were the hellish twins spawned of Shub-Niggurath.

For a brief period, a comet was sighted. But it was a vaporous yellow, like a sickly candle guttering in anti-stellar space. It possessed no detectible tail. Over the course of three days, it grew in apparent size, as if headed toward Earth. But when the planet completed its next revolution, no nation beheld it. For it was no longer there. Another cosmic anomaly quickly forgotten in the downward spiral some called Ragnadammerung.

Then a fragment of something massive all but obliterated a vast portion of Texas, shaking the western hemisphere with the force of its impact. Early reports speculated on an asteroid impact—as if the weakened Earth had not endured indignity enough.

There were still working scientists, of course. One journeyed from surviving Houston to look over the scene of devastation. He witnessed a still-boiling sea of black vitreous material bubbling mightily, and pronounced it the work of a 20 million ton extinctor asteroid. It should have spelled massive global climate change, but that shoe had already fallen. Now it was just a local problem.

After that scarred portion of Texas had cooled, others examined the remaining matter, took samples, conducted analysis. A NASA geologist determined conclusively that what had fallen, while similar in composition to an asteroidal body, was in fact a fragment of Earth's lunar companion, unseen in the eternal night for over a month.

The news was suppressed, of course. What the American public did not know could not hurt them. Yet.

There was no point in searching the heavens to determine how much, if any, remained of Earth's original moon. The sun and the stars had been extinguished by a fast-spreading star-plague. No earthly light could illuminate the night sky. It was as black and impenetrable as the obsidian heart of Texas.

Duty is a funny thing. Long after men abandoned their churches and families, a few clung to their sense of obligation to their fellow men. In the aftermath of the unthinkable, some police, National Guardsmen and doctors attempted to fulfill their normal functions.

Count me as one of them.

While mankind reeled under the bewildering assault of astronomical anomalies, wondering if the Universe had gone mad or almighty God become wrathful, the unofficial unit of the National Reconnaissance Office known as the Cryptic Events Evaluation Section toiled onward, alert to signs that the Old Ones were beginning their final incursion into Earthly reality.

We had no battleplan. We were just doing our jobs. CEES had been holding back the night for so long that when it finally clamped down, we simply continued operations as if events were somehow reversible. We knew better. But we had to try. There was nothing else left to do.

My name is Van Arrowsmith. I'm a CEES-NRO Task Force Leader. My specialties are Artifact Identification and psychometry. At Princeton, I majored in archeology, minoring in geology. That's why I was assigned to fly to Mount

Redoubt in Alaska when it grew a cap.

The remnants of the National Geologic Service continued to monitor all active volcanoes in the U.S. Transmissions from their static cameras could still be viewed via their website. Without ambient light, there was normally not much to see. The first images that got CEES' attention showed that Mount Redoubt had become active. A smoldering red glow danced along the crater rim. It uplit something that looked like a gigantic piece of candy corn horn jammed into the cone, virtually filling the crater to the cracking point.

That got the Director's attention. I was tasked to look into the phenomenon. Lucky me.

As the noisy Bell Ranger helicopter orbited the crater, I felt my mouth go dry. I thought I was prepared. I was not.

The horn—or whatever it was—extended so far up into the thrice-damned blackness of night that no upper root could be discerned. The narrow portion thrust into the crater mouth had a greenish, glassy quality. Cracks were showing in the volcano's sides, as if it were about to burst.

"Try to fly to the top of that thing," I ordered my pilot, Cartomancer First Class Nubia Rezendez. She doubled as a crypto-mythographer. She gave it her best. The turbines soon began laboring.

"We're at our ceiling," Nubia shot back over the rotor whine.

Above us, the monster continued indefinitely upward, defying all calculations of size, nature or origin.

I painted the side of the thing with a cabin-mounted halogen light. Fifteen hundred candlepower illumination painted the target. Pale green, it was. While glassy, its surface was rough and striated. It reminded me of old chalcedony. Or something that had been removed from an ancient tomb. I had studied prehuman artifacts which possessed that identical color and texture. No scientific analysis had ever cracked the secret of their composition. We couldn't be sure if they were organic or mineral. Or otherwise.

"Okay, give it up," I said finally.

We descended, setting down at the base of the volcano on the Cook Inlet side. Alaska was no colder than any other spot on Earth. Still, the desolate terrain abounding with plutonic rock formations of cooled magma made it feel positively polar. Once in a while, a faraway cracking sound told of an indigenous evergreen tree splitting in agony from the sheer cold. I heard three such reports inside of a dozen minutes. But it was like this everywhere. In another month, from palms to pines, the last living trees would lie shattered.

Surveying the impossible vista before me, I was reminded of Devil's Tower in Wyoming. But this thing was taller, vaster, more forbidding. The backglow from the vomiting lava gave its lower shank a hellish, foreboding luster. You couldn't see anything of it beyond that hazy red illumination. But knowing that it reached far into the sky made a coldness settle into my stomach.

"It's thicker at the top," Nubia pointed out. "Like someone had stuffed an upside down mountain into the caldera to cap it."

"Or to ignite it," I returned.

"You think so?"

"No volcano could extrude a plug like that. It's not hardened magma, or any form of vitreous rock. I'm certain of it."

Nubia eyed me skeptically. "In these hellish times, how can you be sure?"

"Point taken. But the sheer volume, the way it spreads up and out for miles, simply insults the laws of physics. I can't accept the theory."

We stood in silence, watching fingers of lava crawl down from the crater, hissing and spitting as they encountered rapidly-vaporizing snow.

I mused, "If I could get up there, I could…."

"Psychometrize the material?"

"Exactly. But the lava owns the crater rim. I'd be scalded like a parboiled hotdog."

"From a safe distance we could chip off a piece," she suggested.

"With what? Cold chisels don't come in sizes fit for Paul Bunyan."

Nubia grinned gamely. "My Heckler & Koch MP5 might blow off a good hunk. If we fly high enough, it should fall free of the cone. Just have to find it in the rocks."

I frowned. "I'll have to get authority to try. This reads like a Class A incursion—not something to mess with."

I got on the horn to Washington. The news was bad.

"There's another one just like it impacting Gibraltar," the Director told me. "And we have reports of a third in the North Pacific."

"Permission to shoot off a sample," I requested.

"Permission granted. Make a report of your findings ASAP."

"If I live."

We got back into the air. I used the MP5's underbarrel flashlight to scope out a section where a dislodged piece would land clear of the volcanic cone. There was no guarantee that if I knocked off a fragment, we could find it again. But it was all I had by way of a line of attack.

"Hold her right here," I told Nubia.

"Copy." She settled the chopper into a steady hover mode.

Training the halogen light on the center of mass of the target, I sighted carefully and fired a continuous burst, emptying the entire magazine.

I couldn't miss.

And I didn't. I heard a definite cracking sound. The cockpit filled with burnt gunpowder stink. My eyes teared up. I wiped them clean, then searched the greenish mass for damage.

Suddenly, the thing was not there. I pulled my flashlight off its underbarrel mounting, swung it around wildly. The cone of light faded off into a starless void, illuminating nothing.

Nubia blurted out, "It's gone, sir!"

"But where the hell did it go?"

"I didn't see. I had my eyes on my instruments."

"Damn it!"

We orbited the zone over the crater. But the impossible thing was nowhere to be seen. I had only taken my eyes off it for a fragment of a second....

I gazed upward. All was unrelieved night. I cursed the utter absence of moonlight. Then I remembered what had happened to the moon, and mouthed a silent prayer for it instead.

I looked down at Mount Redoubt. The volcano's maw was a red open wound. Lava bubbled incandescently, the lurid vomit of hell on Earth.

"Definitely gone," I said. "Land!"

We searched for over an hour, but found nothing. In the days before Sundark, I would have called off the search until daybreak. But day was destined never to break again.

I was forced to report failure.

The Director of CEES said, "Valiant try. Return to base. We'll see if we can't throw you against the one on Gibraltar."

Back at headquarters, I was debriefed by Director Cranston—his first name was classified superblack—and his deputy by candlelight.

"Did it retract into the volcano?" asked Cranston.

"Impossible, sir. Its volume precluded that."

"Not if it was an ultratelluric substance," Deputy Director Christo suggested.

"Point taken," I admitted. "I still doubt it."

"Could it have retreated into the sky?" wondered the Director.

"That assumes that it came down from the sky," I pointed out.

The Deputy Director frowned like an old Bulldog. "It didn't just pop out of existence like a soap bubble, now did it?"

"For all I know," I said in exasperation, "it dissolved into another dimension."

Director Cranston steepled his fingers together. "We can't rule that out, now can we?"

"We can't rule anything out," I agreed.

"Especially since our man in Gibraltar reports that the artifact that he observed there is no longer there," he noted.

Two days later I was standing on the shattered spine of the Rock of Gibraltar. In the old days, it had been one of the Pillars of Hercules, reputedly the outer limits of the known world. More recently, it has stood as a symbol of Earth's unyielding endurance. Now it lay split like a diamond under a jeweler's chisel.

I picked through the shale and limestone rubble, looking for fragments of the spiky thing that had bisected it. I found nothing other than marine fossils left over from the Jurassic commingled amid the indigenous greenish-gray marls and gray cherts. Whatever had done this, it was formidable. Yet 9mm rounds could fracture it. That meant it was composed of matter common to local space—and therefore vulnerable.

I conferred with our agent on the island. Our breaths made dueling plumes.

"Was there any indication of its coming, Carlos?"

"None. But on the day before it appeared while the city below slept, an object was seen in the sky. It was an intense yellow, and internally luminous. We thought it was that phantom comet. For it seemed to grow larger, as if it were approaching. But after an hour, it simply winked out of existence."

"First I've heard of this. Did it look like a comet to you?"

"No. It reminded me of the eye of a wolf. But no wolf could be so large, and besides wolves possess two eyes, not one great orb."

"Anything else?"

"Meteors. Many meteors."

I nodded. Increased meteor activity had been reported worldwide. Could mean anything. Or nothing. "Carlos, exactly when did the horn go away?"

He gave the day and hour in local time. I ran it on my handheld device, converting it to Greenwich Mean Time.

"Tallies with the event in Alaska," I noted. "Tallies precisely."

I got on the horn and reported my findings.

"So they both vanished at the same time?" the Director said.

"To the minute."

"Maybe they're connected in some way. Shooting one transmitted a pain signal or telepathic distress call to the other. Both went into panic mode and took off."

"Took off for where?" was a question I dared not raise.

Instead, I asked, "Any late word on the North Pacific sighting?"

"Yes. It's gone too. No witnesses. Unconfirmed reports of a fourth horn in the interior of Mongolia, but no updates since. Come home, Arrowsmith."

On the flight back to the USA, I plotted the locations of all known horn impacts on a global map. They formed a curve or arc. That told me nothing. With so much water between the known contact points, there could be many others. And as big as they were, we had no way to connect those dots.

Hurtling over the inky Atlantic Ocean, I received intel that in the Gobi desert, there was now a sandpit the size of Nevada where the fourth horn had impacted. It too had vanished inexplicably.

I got on the radio. "So there were four in all?"

The Director came back. "Four verified. There could be six or eight of the damned things for all we know. Global communications are spotty. We don't know if Australia or New Zealand are still on the map, or not. All communication with them has been out for days."

"What's our next move?" I wondered.

"We wait. And hope we've seen the last of these things."

"Why don't I revector to Alaska to resume search for that horn fragment?"

"We have people on the scene now, doing just that."

"Good luck to them," I grunted, remembering that inhospitable place of plutons.

By the time I had returned to CEES HQ in Chantilly, Virginia, Lake Michigan was returning to Earth in the form of a hot rain mixed in a superheated mist. This far south, its precipitation was only a welcome warm shower.

Deputy Director Christo met me. His face was stark. All the spleen and bile was out of his voice. I had never seen him so shaken.

"We have high confirmation it's another segment of the moon. It smacked into Lake Michigan, and the impact turned it and portions of the adjoining Great Lakes into steam. Virtually all life in some surrounding states has been boiled alive."

I said nothing. What could I say? My God? The almighty wasn't even listening.

"A secondary piece pulverized upper Vermont," he added.

"That means there's more coming," I breathed, thinking those meteor showers must be lunar.

"We think that's why no one has heard from Australia and New Zealand. It also explains why water levels in the South Pacific have dropped so significantly."

I didn't bother to point out that such a devastating impact would have created global tsunamis. The fate of Australia was not my problem.

"Where is our Alaska search?" I asked instead.

"Active but so far unproductive. But we aren't giving up. The Director wants to see you in his office."

Director Cranston looked up when I knocked my way in and got right down to it. "Our remote viewers are reporting that the falls of moon crust and the horns are connected."

"What are their perceptions of the horns?"

"They get a lot of imaginal and associative junk. Ants. Humans. The relationships thereto. These things are so massive, our viewers are having trouble adjusting their non-physical eyes to the scale of the phenomenon. Even when the monitors send them back in with expanded parameters, they say they feel like fleas trying to survey an ocean. They can't make any head nor tail of it."

"Consensus data?"

Cranston threw up his hands. "No consensus. Absolutely none. After reading the session summaries, I'm reminded of the blind men trying to feel out the shape of the elephant. Everyone has a fragment of the puzzle. We just don't have the numerical viewer strength to obtain sufficient pieces to intelligently assemble a complete picture."

"Anything else?"

"There is. They all came back from the Matrix complaining of tooth problems."

"What kind?"

"Toothaches. Nerve pain. The usual things that send a person running to the dentist. Half of them are out looking for one now."

"Good luck to them," I muttered. Dentists were high among the early post-diurnal suicide waves. "I wonder if the stress of viewing caused them to grind their teeth until something gave out?"

"I'll take that theory," grunted Cranston. "Less for me to worry about. I want you standing by until something breaks."

"What makes you think a psychometrist can do what a crack remote viewing team can't?" I asked bluntly.

"The fact that it's hand-on. Stay handy, Arrowsmith."

I spent the day pouring over our collection of prehuman artifacts. Whenever I was on assignment, I found moving among these relics helped me to warm up. I grabbed a soapstone effigy, cupped it in my cool hands and closed my eyes.

The first images were slow in coming. I was rusty from too much travel. But I cleared my head, and dropped down into a receptive Alpha brainwave state. Soon enough something resolved in my mind's eye.

Visions of tropical forest filled my brain. I had a sense of Viet Nam or Cambodia. Maybe Thailand. My skin relaxed with a sympathetic warmth. I was getting a rare kinesthetic response.

I looked at the catalogue card: "Unknown artifact found near Angkor Watt ruins, Cambodia."

"Good enough for government work," I said to myself.

Moving among the glass cases and shelves, I reached out and then retreated from various displays. My higher senses were kicking in. I let go of the outcome and let my fingers wander. Almost of their own accord, my eyes closed.

I touched something cool.

The object my fingers grasped felt spiny. I recoiled, dropped the thing and captured it with my other hand before it struck the floorboards.

What lay in my left hand was a palm-sized stone ring. The inner rim—the donut hole, if you will—was filled with sharp spines. They are what pricked my fingers.

The ring itself was flat, yet it was carven to suggest some form of life. There was a solitary eye spot at the apex of the upper ring, what might have been gill vents at the edges, and taken all together, the spiny hole must have represented a mouth. If so this creature was almost all mouth.

But most disturbing of all, the material it was carved from resembled in color and surface texture the great horn which had almost split Redoubt Volcano asunder. Chalcedony or adventurine, from the look of it.

Pressing it carefully between flat palms, I psychometrized it. My first impressions were of a flounder or sunfish—or some other form of bottom-feeding fish that lay flat on the ocean floor as a means of protection and defense. A vague idea flittered through my memory of a flat fish that allowed sand to half-cover it as it lay supine on the ocean floor.

I shrugged off the clammy, uncomfortable fish-feeling and tried to go for the origins of the effigy.

They never came. I heard clairaudiently a collection of syllables that I recognized to be prehuman, but could not convert them into sensible speech. But best I could do was capture a very weak "Norn." Or something like that. Maybe it was "horn."

Going to our database, I looked up every variant spelling. Other than the three Norns, or Fates, of Icelandic myth, I found nothing that fit the creature depicted by the carving. Not that they did. The three Norns were supernatural giantesses, each one representing past, present or future. The whole concept of future made me shudder involuntarily. Did any future exist for Man?

I was still searching the World Wide Web when I was summoned to Director Cranston's office. I dropped the fierce-featured carving into my coat pocket for later study.

"Here's your fragment," he said, indicating a cedar box.

"Anyone touch this?"

"No. It was picked up with virgin tongs. No human fingers came into contact with it, so it's vibrationally pure."

Carefully, I opened the box. Bringing a candle to it, I waved its fitful light over the interior. Nestled in cotton wadding was a glassy greenish shell with broken edges. It was pocked and striated.

"That it?" the Director asked.

Nodding, I lifted it out of the box carefully. It was heavier by weight than it should have been, given its mass. I flipped it over. The underside was a dry, brownish substance that reminded me of decayed tree bark.

"Exterior surface suggests a mineral origin," I muttered, "but the anterior portion reminds me of organic matter. What could it possibly be?"

"You tell me," invited Cranston.

Closing my eyes, I laid one palm against the glassy side while the other clamped the dark inner matrix. I waited for the images to appear.

Instead, a red-hot needle of pain stabbed my jaw. Howling, I dropped the hellish thing and grabbed my chin. Contact broken, the pain should have gone away. It didn't. It seared me to my knees.

Cranston ran to the door. "Medic!"

By the time a doctor was on the scene, I had solved the problem. The pain had gotten so fierce, I had yanked out the offending lower incisor by its roots. Bloody, it lay on the floor next to the despicable thing that had created a wave of sympathetic agony.

Novocain had me too numb to speak intelligibly. I wrote it all out for Cranston:

"The RV team had tooth problems due to feeling sympathetic pain. I got a bigger dose of the same contact feedback."

"Get anything else?"

"Are you kidding? I dropped that damnable thing like a red-hot potato."

"So we're at a dead-end?"

I shrugged. I was in no mood to pursue the subject. My lower jaw was throbbing. I had never before felt such searing agony. It was going to be a very long time before I was up to touching that damned horny crust.

A day later I was feeling more human. I walked to work, counting the uncollected corpses which littered street and sidewalk. The number had doubled since the day before.

Deputy Director Christo grabbed me the minute I passed through the last of three security layers.

"We want you to take another pass at the fragment."

I swallowed my original retort. "Is that an order?" I muttered through the cotton packing stuffed into mouth.

"We correlated your experience with our RV unit. Guess what? Everyone experienced excruciating pain in the same tooth—the lower left canine. Yours was worse, so we figure you're on to something …"

They locked me in my private office with the cedar box. I fortified myself with a cup of brandy-laced coffee, then fought off a rising panic response as I lifted the lid.

There it lay, as innocent as a sleeping scorpion.

Gingerly, I touched it.

To my everlasting surprise and relief, nothing happened. My cotton-packed tooth socket throbbed lightly, but it had been doing that steadily since dawn.

Carefully, I gathered up the fragment, looked it over and shifted into a receptive state of mind. My eyes closed.

This time, I heard a different clairaudient word. It sounded like "Haiti."

I let the breathy syllables pass. They repeated. Then came a chaotic cloud of disconnected images. I saw dogs, wolves, jackals. The figure of Anubis, Egyptian god of the dead, strode across my mind's eye, turned his forbidding canine profile to stare at me with emerald eyes that made me feel like a helpless meal. He bared his teeth in a silent snarl. I dismissed this as analytic overlay. Anubis is often identified with Nyarlathotep, and late reports out of Egypt were growing grisly.

I shook over that image and refocused. Conceptual images of predators came and went. I saw hyenas, coyotes, sharks. Vultures, ants, beetles, paraded by in profusion. I recognized that each was a symbol of some type of scavenger.

A round unhuman maw suddenly yawned at me. Its inner jaw was a circle of teeth and I was instantly reminded of the chalcedony effigy I had used to psychically warm up the day before.

The phantasmagoric stream concluded with a sense of being swallowed by an unfathomable blackness. I had a shivery sense of how Jonah had felt before he breathed his last.

That sent me running to my handheld device.

Haiti was a useless topic. Too broad. I searched for the word "scavenger." I might as well have Googled "mother." I got so many hits it was ridiculous. But every species I had seen, and more, was represented by that word.

What did I mean? Was the horn off some kind of cosmic scavenger? There was no other interpretation?

Then I remembered that the author of Earth's misery, the multi-fingered stellar corruption know as the Sothis Radiant, had originated in the star Sirius. Sirius the Dog Star. Known to the ancient Egyptians as Sothis. Dogs are scavengers....But what did it all mean?

I was pondering the imponderable when my cellphone rang.

It was the Director. "In my office, Arrowsmith."

Both Cranston and Christo were waiting for me there.

"We have a fresh sighting," the Director told me. "We're sending you to Peru. There's another horn come down. This one is jammed into Amazon rain forest."

"Take a team with you," Christo interjected. "See if you can't pulverize it, send it back to wherever it came from."

"Understood."

We were in the air in less than an hour. Nubia was flying the high-winged Cessna Skymaster. I had recruited two others to the team. One of them was an ex-Star Gate remote viewer named Velikovski. The other was just muscle—a former Marine. I forgot his name as soon as I heard it. He looked worried. Who could blame him? Marines could tackle any enemy, handle any battlefield situation. But not this.

I killed time by briefing them on the situation to date.

The Marine grunted. "Norse Norns. Haiti. Scavengers. None of it correlates."

"A lot of earthly myth and legend cloaks the reality of the Old Ones," Velikovski mused. "Maybe we need to sift through the data and see if anything matches up."

With nothing better to do, we pulled out our handhelds and began keying. I took Haiti.

I got a lot of Voodoo junk, some Zombie legendry, and old reports of minor incursions. The first Black republic in the Western hemisphere had been a beachhead for those from Outside since it was originally founded.

I gave it up after an hour. "Anything?" I asked Velikovski.

"The three Norns don't appear to correlate with anything in the Necronomicon," he said. "They are practically identical to the Greek Fates."

"Which might mean they're anthropomorphized symbols of so-far unknown prehuman entities."

"Or not. Nothing quite like them was recorded by the Egyptians. They were a legacy culture, you know. A lot of older lore filters through Egypt. Anubis equates with Nyatlathotep. Nut and Geb may be a transmission or corruption of Nug and Yeb, who remain unfathomable unknowns—"

Abruptly, the aircraft went a sharp screaming bank. The distinctive sound of the centerline engines grew wilder. We grabbed for our seat armrests, buckled up where we weren't.

Once she got the plane righted again, Nubia called back, "Take a look to starboard. Try not to panic."

All eyes veered to the starboard windows. I saw a great smoldering blur down on the ground. It backlit looming mountains. I didn't recognize them.

"What am I looking at?" I demanded.

"Popocatapetl. A volcano near Mexico City. It grew a horn."

Once she described it, my eyes were able to make sense of the tableau. It was just like Redoubt, but bigger. The lower horn burned like a weird coal. The rest of it disappeared into the immensity of uncaring space.

"Guess we can cut our Peru trip short," the Marine grunted.

"Circle," I ordered.

Nubia sent the aircraft in a wide sweep around the phenomenon. I could hear her talking to Chantilly base. She broke radio contact and shouted, "There's a string of them,
spaced hundreds of miles apart, all the way down to Patagonia."

"All jammed into volcanoes?" I asked.

"No. This is the only one."

"Still, it can't be a coincidence that this group includes a volcano among its impact sites."

"No, it can't," Nubia agreed. "Didn't you wonder if the other one was trying to ignite Redoubt?"

"Just a theory."

"But a good one," Velikovski chimed in. "Let's work this problem."

As Nubia kept us in a holding pattern, we worked our handhelds. I switched with Velikovski and took the word Norn. I must have been really rattled because I accidentally typed "Horn." Since it was going to be my next search, I read what came up. Skimming swiftly, I learned that horns were often composed of skin-covered bone, or sometimes keratin, such as a rhinoceros horn. I also discovered that a deformed horn was known as a scur. Sounded like a perfect name for a minor deity or star-spawn.

"I don't think this thing is a horn," I said slowly. "Horns don't have hard-shell outer coverings."

"What is it then?"

One of the side effects of doing supersensory work is that it requires one to flatten the brainwaves in order to become receptive. The flatter the waves, the easier it is to pick up non-local signals. But the slower the cycles, the fuzzier the normal thought processes. I had been doing research for so many hours straight that my brainwaves were resuming normal dynamics. I was back in Beta—Beta where brain functioning was sharper and critical thought became more clear.

"I've been in a damn alpha fog!" I exclaimed.

Everyone looked at me.

"That isn't a horn. It's a tooth!"

"Tooth?"

"Or fang or tusk," I added.

Blank looks scrutinized me.

"Think it through. That's why everyone who made psychic contact with it got hit with sympathetic pain in their right lower canines," I explained. "That thing up in Alaska was the equivalent of a right lower canine tooth. We broke off a piece of its enamel and exposed the pulp with its sensitive nerves endings."

A cold silence settled into the cabin. Nobody wanted to follow my thought to its logical conclusion. If we were now looking at a canine, or analogous tooth, how big was this damned thing?

A cold chill rippled along my skin. Big enough to take a preliminary bite out of the planet the size of Australia.... I suddenly understood why water levels in the Pacific had fallen so drastically. Something had to fill the continent-sized cavity.

Suddenly sweating, I went back to my handheld. This time I typed the word correctly. I rummaged through everything I could find on the three Norns who governed men's fates.

Synchronicity plays a big role in my work. You do enough psychic operations, and you become a kind of synchronicity generator. Events cluster. Coincidences abound. In other words, shit happens. There's no good explanation for it. It just does.

I was starting to read about the hounds of Norn when Velikovski suddenly started swearing.

"What is it?" I asked. Bathed in the instrument backglow, he sat heavily in his seat. His mouth hung open like his jaw muscles had lost all tension. The whites of his eyes looked unhealthy, like yellowing ivory.

"I mistyped the word," he said thickly.

"What word?"

"Haiti. I left out the first i."

I mentally spelled it. Rang no bells with me. "So?"

"You do it." His words had that dry-mouthed texture.

I did. "Hati." Up came a hit. "Says it's one of Saturn's moons," I reported.

"Go deeper."

I did. The second hit was more detailed. I began reading aloud, unaware of what my words really meant.

"'In Norse mythology, Hati Hroovitnisson is the wolf who chases the moon, brother to Skoll, the wolf who pursues the sun. And both of whom will inevitably consume their eternal prey at the time of Ragnarok.'"

My words died in my throat. I swallowed, and swallowed again. All the saliva had dried in my mouth tissues. My tongue felt heavy and alien in my sticky mouth.

I had just been reading about the hounds of the Norn—a traditional Icelandic term for wolves.

"Hati is also called Managarm, the Moon Hound," Velikovski said quietly.

My racing thoughts went back to Gibraltar, and the yellow comet that had loomed closer and closer, only to wink out. Wink. Like a canine eye.

Up ahead at the controls, Nubia began to shed tears like rain bouncing off stone.

"Sir, the old Norse believed that at Ragnarok, after the sun and moon and stars disappear from the sky, the Fenris wolf will break his bonds and sink his fangs into the Earth, shaking it and causing all trees and the mountains to fall." Her voice broke. "It's all happening."

I joined her and got Chantilly on the horn.

Director Cranston answered.

"It's the end, sir," I reported.

"End? End of what?"

"Ragnarok, sir."

"Talk sense."

"We now have a better idea of what quenched the sun," I continued. "And what happened to the moon after it went dark. It was bitten into pieces. Now whatever fell scavenger is tasked to approach in advance of the Old Ones, it's trying to do the same to Mother Earth."

"Scavenger?"

I pulled from my pocket the one-eyed artifact that was all teeth, and tried to imagine the immensity of the stupendous maw that was now trying to swallow the world of Man. I could not.

"Imagine a shark the size of a gas giant," I croaked. "A one-eyed jackal capable of consuming comets. An inconceivable thing that is almost all mouth and no stomach. A ravenous devourer. If you plot every contact point from Patagonia north, you will be able to measure its jawline. And you will probably discover that the monster's teeth have punctured a circle around the entire globe. For God help us, this beast is structurally built like the rings of Saturn."

The silence from CEES HQ was prolonged. The sound of the Skymaster's combined tractor and pusher engines moaned interminably.

I went on. "Sir, I think the reason that some of these tusks are making contact with volcanoes is to trigger catastrophic pyroclastic eruptions. It's part of a process of destructive consumption calculated to—"

Now I was crying. It was in my voice, clogging it.

The Director would have none of it. "Get a grip, Arrowsmith. We can still fight these things! Can you take a shot at the one you have in view?"

Something in me shook off the smothering horror of the shadow that loomed over us all.

"We can try, sir." I flung back to the others. "We're going to open up on that thing. Right now!"

Everyone grabbed a machine pistol. The Marine yanked a window open. Nubia chandelled us into position.

Crowding the open port, our eyes squeezed tight against the biting slipstream, we fired in unison. All three of us.

The effect was almost instantaneous. I should have seen it coming. Velikovski and I doubled over, our teeth on fire.

Pain had me writhing on the floor. Velikovski literally bit his tongue in two, spitting out the bloody tip. Stoically, the Marine kept firing. As psychic as a bag of hammers, he was naturally unaffected. He was Earth's last hope. If only—

But it was no go.

Unable to stand the pain, Velikovski leaped onto the Marine, grabbed his MP5, shot him dead. Then he trained the smoking weapon on his own anguished head.

I heard it more than I saw it. Tears of agony were streaming down my cheeks. But from the procession of ugly sounds, I assembled it all in my mind.

The thud of two bodies hitting the cabin carpet told me that it was all over.

I crawled back to the cockpit and sank into the copilot's chair. I don't know how I got that angry tooth out, but I did. I used a pen knife.

I looked over at Nubia's stony profile and spat through bloody teeth, "Land if you can."

I'll never forget her thin, bitter words. Her last words: "Why bother?"

She banked the plane. Down below, I could see the tapering tusk of the Norn Hound Managarm—or maybe it was Skoll or Fenriswolf—inexorably forcing itself down into Mount Popocatapetl's fiery gullet, causing its massive cone to burst and crumble, as fire fountains and superheated magma spurted in all directions.

Even over the airplane's prop scream I could hear the Earth cry out in her last convulsion as gargantuan jaws steadily, remorselessly began to bisect her cold crust like it would crack a coconut shell.

As the dying Earth screamed, we screamed too, knowing that the fiery fissures erupting below meant there was no longer any place to land....

The Hour of Our Triumph

PETE RAWLIK's literary criticism has appeared in the *New York Review of Science Fiction* and *The Neil Gaiman Reader*. His fiction has appeared in *Talebones*, *IBID*, *Crypt of Cthulhu*, and *Tales of the Shadowmen Volume 7: Femmes Fatales*. Born in North Dakota he currently resides in the State of Florida. His lifelong fascination with horror began at age four when his father read him "The Rats in the Walls" as a bedtime story. His collecting of Lovecraftian material borders on the pathological and has on occasion been deemed socially unacceptable. As of 2010 he has yet to be charged with any crimes. His doctor hopes that through therapy and a proper regiment of anti-psychotics he will soon be fit to stand trial.

Here Be Monsters

by Pete Rawlik

The doctor tells me that I was found unconscious, floating amongst wreckage in the South Pacific near 47° 9 S and 126° 43 W. He says the wreckage has been positively identified as belonging to the *Dionysus*, and that all others, the nineteen other men that made up the rest of the crew are lost, that I alone have survived and I must tell the tale. I have no reason to doubt him. I saw them die, all of them, but they did not die when the ship went down, they were dead before that, killed as much by their misplaced faith as by the thing that rose up out of the sea to shatter the *Dionysus* and scatter her across the sea.

May the Blessed Mother have mercy on them.

For the record, you may call me Dorian Morgan, not my real name but the one that is on all of my identification. Ostensibly, I am twenty-six years old, a graduate of Arkham College where I majored in Oceanography. For my Masters degree at Miskatonic, I studied the influence of various sampling techniques on water quality nutrient analysis. I am an employee of the Rowley Oceanographic Center and assigned to the Research Vessel *Dionysus* where I worked analyzing deep-sea water samples. Officially, the *Dionysus* was studying the after effects of the submarine nuclear testing that had been conducted in the early Nineteen Sixties, for which we have a permit from the Department of Defense.

Unofficially, secretly, we had come to pay homage to one of our Gods and witness His rebirth.

The People, the race men call Deep Ones has dwelt on the Earth for millions of years, and in that time we have come to worship many Gods. The oldest of us still pay homage to our progenitors, who have long since passed from the world, they still live, dreaming what cool inhuman dreams their cool inhuman intelligences allow; that which is not dead can lie eternal, and in strange eons they may return to us. Others are content to worship the first of us: Father Dagon, Mother Hydra who still dwell deep in the abyssal oceans, where time is cold and slow and the sounds of the world are little more than whispers in the dark grey light. If one is inclined, the descent can be made and an audience sought. But you do so at your own risk. The deep abyss is a barren wasteland and while our ancestors are content to take sustenance from the dead things that drift down from the surface, they are not opposed to adding a little convenient fresh meat to their diet. The hybrids of the People, those whose ancestry is mixed with either human or other sources, have come to know another God. The Sleeping God dreams and some of us can hear echoes of those dreams. And from these dreams all of us know our place in the world, and our part in His great work. The Pure People cannot hear the call, they are too pure, too close to the progenitors, and are unable to violate their genetics. We hybrids, whether land-born or sea-born have heard the call for hundreds of years, and though we are weaker than the Pure, we can do things they cannot. We can break the seals, we can wake the Sleeping God, and we can make him free.

He is not an easy God to follow. He is indifferent, he cares nothing for sacrifices or worship, and he answers few prayers. Men have called him anti-anthropomorphic, for he cares nothing for the works of man. Their cities and roads, their art and their monuments to their dead, mean nothing to our Lord of the Green Abyss. And for this we embrace him as our savior, for it is he who would wipe out our pestilent land dwelling cousins and leave us as rulers of the world. This he would do for his faithful servants; all we had to do was be patient. God was in his tomb waiting to be reborn, when the time was right.

IÄ Cthulhu!

Others had tried, and once in 1925, they had come close. The city of R'lyeh had risen, and a band of the faithful aboard the *Alert* had made their way to that remote island. They had done what was necessary and the seal had been broken, the Dreaming Lord had been released. But then another ship, the *Emma* had arrived, and after a fierce battle the interlopers slaughtered the faithful. The *Emma* was scuttled, and as it sunk beneath the waves the humans took command of the *Alert*, and later used it to attack our Lord himself as He climbed back into the world. By all accounts Cthulhu retreated back into His tomb, to await another chance to be reborn.

That time came sooner than expected. The ages-old prophecy had for centuries been misinterpreted. Scholars who had read the prophecy and interpreted the word "great" as meaning "many", and thus when the stars were right our lord would be free, but "great" should have been interpreted as "large" not "many". The prophecy wasn't talking about a shift in stellar alignment, but rather a change in the sun itself, such as the increased solar activity that leads to more ultraviolet radiation, energy our Lord needs to be reborn. In the last couple of centuries the sun enters into that phase every thirty-five years or so.

And so it was in 1962 the United States military conducted Operation Fishbowl, a series of underwater nuclear tests that were designated Bluegill, Starfish, Starfish Prime, Bluegill Prime, Bluegill Double Prime, Checkmate, Bluegill Triple Prime, Miskatonic, and Kingfish. They hid the truth, saying such tests allowed them to refine the yield of these horrific weapons, while all the time we knew they were bombarding our Lord with radiation in a vain attempt to destroy Him, all they did was prevent His rising. And their warships kept us from coming to His aid, for another thirty-five years.

We used the time wisely, we were patient, and our memories are long. It took us years to create the Rowley Oceanographic Center, to hide behind double- and triple-blind corporate partners, to fool the Government into thinking that we were a legitimate, innocent organization. It took even more work to slowly build up our reputation as a serious and respected organization, rivaling the Cousteau Society and Greenpeace. We worked hard to avoid controversy, always supplying data and facts, but leaving the interpretation up to others. We focused on environmental disasters, and gained a reputation as an impartial and level-headed group capable of serious scientific work. Most of our early work was in the New England area, Boston Harbor, Cape Cod, and Kingsport Head. We worked with the Army Corps of Engineers in Guantanamo Bay, and with the South Florida Water Management District in the Gulf of Mexico. We funded research projects, created scholarships, hired the best and the brightest. But all the time our goal was to gain access to the area where we knew our Lord lay dreaming. And in time the memories of men faded and their warships withdrew. It took time but with relatively little effort we gained access to the area under the pretense of scientific research.

We came to this place in the South Pacific where the mate Gustaf Johansen said the *Emma* went down, and the *Alert* had been commandeered to interrupt the rebirth of our God, sending Him back to fitful slumber. There was no doubt in our minds that our Lord and his city were hidden somewhere below this vast desolate portion of the ocean. All we had to do was find Him. So we came.

What fools we were.

We came, the twenty of us, the central cabal of the conspiracy that was the Rowley Oceanographic Center, as pilgrims summoned by our God to release Him from His slumber. So we came to this remote and forgotten part of the world in an attempt to do that which so many others had failed to do. Too many times had His followers been thwarted, and the Sleeping God had failed to awaken. Too many times had His servants been slaughtered by lone but learned men, by teams bent on destroying our people, by the governments of men who rightly feared His coming. It had been seventy-five years since the *Alert* had briefly raised the Tomb-City, only to have it sink down again, but we would succeed where they and all others after had failed. There was nothing that could be done to stop us.

We were so naive.

Had we only looked at the history, at the dozens of attempts that had been made to raise our Lord, we might have guessed at why they had all failed, why Great Cthulhu had not come up out of the ocean and laid waste to the cities of men. In retrospect it was so obvious, but all my friends had to die for me to see the truth.

In the cold waters of the South Pacific I clung to the side of the *Dionysus*, all around me were my brothers, the faithful, the chosen ones, the high priests of Cthulhu. The *Dionysus* was abandoned, adrift; we would have no need of her anymore. With my free hand I clutched a twenty-pound weight. As one, we let go of the ship and let the weight drag us down beneath the surface into the cool, bright ocean. Down we went, plummeting faster than we could swim, schools of baitfish and predatory sharks fled as we rocketed past. I looked up and saw their graceful silhouettes as they swam across the face of the sun.

Deeper, and the light faded to a murky green dusk. A reef appeared, a submerged atoll of coral atop a seamount peak. Crabs and echinoderms, mollusks and exotic fish came out to stare at us and then were lost as we sank deeper and deeper. A hundred feet down and the sunlight vanished, but still we were aware of our surroundings. As I plummeted past a fleet of infant giant squid being pursued by a pair of gulper eels, I could see the first dim lights of the upper terraces of what I knew had to be the remnants of R'lyeh.

We have dreamed of R'lyeh, molded images of it in clay and stone. Such visions are mere shadows; the truth is beyond anything we could dream. Seen from above, the city is built in vast spiraling terraces that jut out from the base like mutant fungi. Channels and tunnels honeycomb the metropolis. Shoals of wondrous, unfamiliar creatures banked effortlessly in the current, their scales and eyes glittering back the pale light of the ubiquitous bioluminescent fish that crawled and swam around the towers. Squids with wings, fish with tentacles, and monstrous crabs with two sets of claws roamed through these waters, and I instinctively gave such things a wide berth.

The current suddenly quickened, and we found ourselves inexorably drawn down past the upper tiers and deeper into the subaqueous abyss below. Further and further down we went, following the faint trace glow that leaks from the lower tiers. Age and depth had taken its toll on the once magnificent towers, for they were covered with the parasitic and antiquated growths of a million years of algae and coral and mollusks. Blind crabs monstrous with thorny points and thick spiny hairs scuttled across grey colonies of unknown corals. Ancient anthropomorphic things floated past, with remoras and other parasites writhing hideously in their wakes. Once the pinnacle of the food chain, they had long ago ceased being predatory, their once sharp and gored stained teeth had elongated into brittle hair-like sieves, each breath, each movement of gill, each vast mouthful of water was a passive act of feeding.

Then, as quickly as the creatures had come into view they were gone. The strange current that carried us had suddenly accelerated and we plunged down. We were drawn deep, for how long I cannot say. The grey lights of the upper city rapidly grew dim and faded, and my sense of time warped and then failed me. I had a sense that my companions were still with me, but I could neither see nor feel them. Blind and deaf I retreated into the dark recesses of my own mind, for this descent was so much like my earliest fragmented memories of my life in the ocean.

I am sea-born, and my mother spawned me into the wild currents of the open sea. The first thing I remember is the ocean, and the ocean was everything. It surrounded me, supported me, carried me, it brought me food, it sang to me, it showed me the world, taught me how to survive, and how to live. How long I dwelt within the sea I cannot know. I know that once I was small, and then later I was larger, and then much larger. Once I feared the fish that swam swiftly through the shoals of the warm currents, and then the fear was gone, and then later those same fish feared me. I was beautiful then, graceful, and I swam in the seas without a care in the world. There were others like me, the graceful swimmers, some were alone, and others were grouped together in schools of a dozen or more. If one of us was beautiful, a dozen of us swimming together were simply magnificent. I have these memories, but they are not continuous. It may be that in my youth, in the youth of my species, of the sea-born, we exist not as wholly sentient creatures, but rather as animals with occasional flashes of consciousness. It may be better this way. Should the butterfly remember her life as an earthbound caterpillar? Should a crab dwell on the fears it had when it was nothing but helpless plankton?

Without warning my memories retreated and I became less blind, able to once more sense those about me. I knew instantly we were in danger, the great towers had widened, grown fat as we neared their bases, and the space between them had grown thin. We clustered together, a school of minnows in the dark open abyssal ocean, and I knew the others, like me, longed for a return to that state of unconsciousness that had shielded our minds when we were juveniles.

The thing that came out of the darkness was titanic in size, larger than the elder deep ones who dwelt in the old cities, though it shared their general shape and characteristics. It emitted light from a series of tentacles set about its mouth. It was a cousin of ours, an ancient hybrid Deep One, though in this case it wasn't humans that had contributed to its genetic code, but rather as the tentacles revealed, this creature's ancestry drew in part from the spawn of Cthulhu himself. As we dropped down, we watched a demigod rise up out of the darkness to greet us. So intent were we on studying the magnificent creature that we failed to comprehend that the thing was angling toward us. It focused on us with a single glassy black eye, and then in an instant a great transparent membrane rolled over that eye and its mouth opened wide revealing rows of razor sharp teeth. It tore through us like a shark through a school of bluefish. Blood filled the water, and three of our companions were gone.

Panicked, our tight school broke up and we dashed apart, seeking shelter in the crags and angles of the tower walls. Still we were adamant in our task, and those of us who could dove deeper into the city, searching for the door to the tomb of our God. We consoled ourselves in the knowledge that soon we would be masters of the world sitting at the right hand of God. I crept along the walls fascinated by both the diversity and amount of life found at such depths. Ancient currents carried fragments of bone and cartilage into drifts that piled up against the curved and bulbous walls. Vast colonies of barnacles covered the edifices and creaked open to extended vast feathery tentacles to harvest great quantities of the slowly falling debris and curled back into their calciferous pentagonal shells. Choked with debris and colonized by the strange invertebrate forces of abyssal decay, the byways of the city had become impassable, and I floated across vast deposits of detrital snow, searching for my elusive goal.

A mile above the bottom we gathered back together, and from our vantage point those of us who were left stared in horrified wonder at the great temple that occupied the center of the vast plaza that lay before us. There was no doubt, we had reached our goal, and this was the tomb of Cthulhu, in its entire hideous alien splendor. It was a vast lozenge shaped trapezohedron that jutted up out of the plaza. The resting place of our God was a great black crystal monolith, a thousand feet tall and half as wide. Unlike the city surrounding it, the surfaces of thing were clean, smooth, uncolonized by the myriad forms of sea life that had come to inhabit the city. There were no markings upon the titanic sarcophagus either, no writing, nor runes, nor any pictographs, or drawings. It needed nothing to declare what it was; we all knew what lay before us. And as we swam nearer to the cyclopean construct, the sight of it and its condition filled me with a growing sense of dread.

About the base of the construct were the accumulated remnants of thousands of years. Skulls and other bones littered the floor, as did bone daggers, stone axes, flint knives, the rusted remnants of guns and helmets. Nearby, a plane and a submarine hosted a nascent reef, and all about there were the scattered pieces of shell casings, and bomb components. The tomb had become a midden documenting the last two thousand years of history. Unable to stop ourselves we grew closer, and in doing so the truth of things began to unveil itself. The Great Seal that had kept the tomb closed was gone, and though it boggles the mind even now, the alien sarcophagus was open, only slightly, but open nonetheless. We peered into that vast darkened hold, reverent in our faith up to the last, but what we saw in there shattered the last of our resolve, and we fled from the sight of what lurked inside in blind and unbridled terror.

We flew up out of the ancient alien city, without caution or care and in doing so we drew the attention of the great monstrosity that had already devoured three of our number. It roared as we passed it and fell in behind us, pursuing our ragged and demoralized band with a vengeance. I gave it no heed. I was blinded by emotion, driven insane by the contents of the crypt of Cthulhu. So when the beast caught up and swallowed two more of us, I barely even noticed.

When we reached the lower tiers I watched through fear clouded eyes as the great monsters that lurked there scuttled away, fleeing from the creature that struck at us time and time again filling the sea with our blood and the stench of death. The descent, our sense of time dilated by wonder, had seemed to take only minutes, but the ascent, driven before a devouring predator, seemed to take hours. And as we reached the upper ocean our pursuit intensified. Blood and panic had scented the waters, and more mundane but equally deadly predators joined the titan that had chased us from below. Sharks with cold dead eyes came at us from above, and those monstrous crabs swam up off the coral atoll to pick off any stragglers or scraps. In minutes we were surrounded, and though we ourselves were well armed, and killed more than a dozen sharks, the combination of exhaustion and despair left us vulnerable to attack. The sharks took six of us and I watched one of my friends succumb to a swarm of vampire octopi. Five of us broke the surface just yards from the *Dionysus*. We swam, we swam for our lives and when I reached the ship I turned and found myself alone.

I clambered up the ladder. The sea was quiet. My heart was like a drum pounding in my brain. Things moved so slowly. There was a great eruption of water, the air filled with the stench of death and blood. Two monstrous tentacles each as thick as telephone poles, smashed across the ship, and I felt the beams beneath the deck snap into pieces. The sky reeled, and something in my brain exploded. I saw the face of the creature bearing down on me, before I slipped into the cold sea and blessed, welcome unconsciousness. I dreamed of monsters marching across the sea floor on roiling tentacles spiked with chitinous claws.

I will escape this prison that masquerades as a hospital ward. I will return to my people. I will tell them the truth and they will reject the false God. We will return to the old ways, to the old Gods. Those that refuse will be slaughtered by the righteous, led by the one who has been to R'lyeh, seen the tomb of Cthulhu, and seen the truth.

Yes, I have seen the truth. Seen the great black crystalline tomb, and what lies inside. The tomb of our God was open, had been open, and Great Cthulhu was free to stalk the Earth and lay waste to the civilization of men. He had lied to us, for ages He had sent forth His dreams, promised us the world, but it was all lies, and in the end, just echoes of lies. He was free, had been free for decades! The thing, that terrible thing, that we saw in the tomb proved it. I understood so much in that instant. Understood what it meant to truly be anti-anthropocentric, why so many cultists had failed to free our Lord, why so many plans had been foiled by so few. I understood, and in that moment my mind, my wondrous mind, snapped.

When he rose seventy-five years ago, when Johansen piloted the *Alert* in a desperate attack, we assumed that great Cthulhu had retreated, climbed back inside His tomb, to wait for another more propitious time. We were wrong. The city of R'lyeh, the tomb of Cthulhu sunk back down into the ocean, but the thing that floated back inside wasn't the injured Cthulhu, but rather that terrible thing that had lain there for seventy-five years.

It took time for us to understand what we were seeing. It was a ship, a human ship, a schooner with two masts. It was old, covered with a thick layer of detritus that made identification nearly but not entirely impossible. But there, on the bow, the letters were clear. Four letters and the world as we knew it was destroyed.

After untold epochs, dead but dreaming beneath the ocean, He had risen, He had come up into the world of men, that fateful year of 1925, and He had done nothing. He left us, abandoned us, He cared nothing for the works of man, and therefore did nothing. Like an animal too long in a cage, He was finally free, and He left without a backward glance. He left to stalk between the stars, left the Earth behind, and the men who crawled upon its surface. He left us, His faithful servants, abandoned us with nothing to mark his passage save a derelict ship that had drifted into his former tomb. A ship that had gone down just hours before R'lyeh sunk back beneath the waves. A ship that lay there still, that marked the date of Cthulhu's release better than any monument ever could, a ship that after all these years still bore the name of *Emma*.

May Father Dagon forgive me.

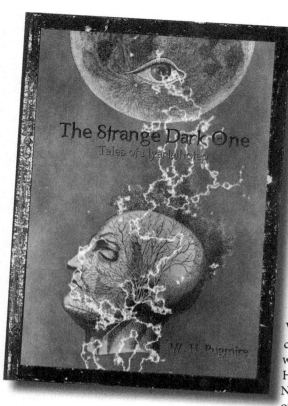

With

The Strange Dark One,

W. H. Pugmire collects all of his best weird fiction concerning H. P. Lovecraft's dark god, Nyarlathotep. This avatar of the Great Old Ones is Lovecraft's most enigmatic creation, a being of many masks and multitudinous personae. Often called The Crawling Chaos, Nyarlathotep heralds the end of mortal time, and serves as avatar of Azathoth, the Idiot Chaos who will blew earth's dust away. Many writers have been enchanted by this dark being, in particular Robert Bloch, the man who, through correspondence, inspired Wilum Pugmire to try his hand at Lovecraftian fiction. This new book is a testimonial of Nyarlathotep's hold on Pugmire's withered brain, and these tales serve as aspects of a haunted mind. Along with stories that have not been reprinted since their initial magazine appearances, The Strange Dark One includes "To See Beyond," a sequel-of-sorts to Robert Bloch's groovy tale, "The Cheaters"; and the book's title story is a 14,000 word novelette set in Pugmire's Sesqua Valley. Each tale is beautifully illustrated by the remarkable Jeffrey Thomas, who is himself one of today's finest horror authors.

Coming soon from

Miskatonic River Press

See how it all began...

15 Tales of fine Lovecraftian fiction, edited by Kevin Ross and the late Keith Herber.

First published in 2002 by DarkTales Publications, this highly regarded anthology soon went out of print. In following years collector's copies have fetched as much as $300 on Ebay.

Now back in print, with corrected copy, authors' biographies, and a new Afterword from editor Kevin Ross, the book has found a whole new legion of fans.

Dead But Dreaming includes tales by Ramsey Campbell, Stephen Mark Rainey, Loren MacLeod, Patrick Lestewka, Darrell Schweitzer, David Barr Kirtley, Mike Minnis, Walt Jarvis, Brian Scott Hiebert, Adam Niswander, Lisa Morton, David Bain, Robin Morris, Mehitobel Wilson, and David Annandale.

Dead But Dreaming is available direct from the publisher at www.miskatonicriverpress.com, as well from Amazon.com and other fine booksellers worldwide.

Miskatonic River Press

THE H.P. LOVECRAFT HISTORICAL SOCIETY

LUDO FORE PUTAVIMUS

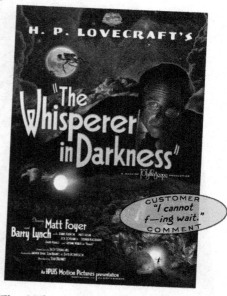

The Call of Cthulhu

Widely acclaimed by critics and audiences throughout the world, this black and white, silent film version of HPL's classic tale has been called the most faithful and effective Lovecraft adaptation to date. Features an incredible original symphonic score, available as a soundtrack CD. The region-free DVD features titlecards in 24 different languages and a behind-the-scenes featurette that some enjoy as much as the movie itself!

The Whisperer In Darkness

HPL's iconic tale bursts onto the screen in the style of the classic horror films of the 1930s. Skeptical folklore professor Albert Wilmarth discovers a century-old manuscript describing weird creatures and demonic rituals in the remote Vermont hills — setting off a chain of events that will lead him deep into the mountains and to the very edge of madness as he confronts the true purpose of these shadowy visitors from the dark edges of the universe.

A GENUINE Plythoscope PRODUCTION

Dark Adventure Radio Theatre

Experience some of Lovecraft's best stories in the form of 1930s-style radio drama, with great acting and all-original music. Our lavishly produced 75-minute CDs are accompanied by elaborate prop documents, photos, and maps, bringing the stories to life in your hands! Collect the whole set packaged in a nifty custom-made collector box shaped like an old time radio!

WWW.CTHULHULIVES.ORG

Thomas Ligotti is beyond doubt one of the Grandmasters of Weird Fiction. In *The Grimiscribe's Puppets*, Joseph S. Pulver, Sr., has commissioned both new and established talents in the world of weird fiction and horror to contribute all new tales that pay homage to Ligotti and celebrate his eerie and essential nightmares. Poppy Z. Brite once asked, "Are you out there, Thomas Ligotti?" This anthology proves not only is he alive and well, but his extraordinary illuminations have proven to be a visionary and fertile source of inspiration for some of today's most accomplished authors.

Coming from

Miskatonic
River
Press

The New Classics of Lovecraft Country!

Miskatonic River Press is very proud to offer two well-received collections of Classic Era gaming matierial for Chaosium, Inc's Call of Cthulhu® roleplaying game. Journey to the locales created by Lovecraft himself. Drive back the darkness in Arkham, Kingsport, Dunwich, and Innsmouth.

New Tales of the Miskatonic Valley and *More Adventures in Arkham Country* contain the triumphant return of such veteran authors for the game as the late Keith Herber, enigmatic Kevin Ross, and ever-secretive Scott David Anioloski. Join the madness!

The Triumvirate of Modern Horror Gaming!

Kevin Ross, editor of *Dead But Dreaming* and *Dead But Dreaming 2*, and author of such gaming classics as *Escape from Innsmouth* and *Kingsport, City in the Mists* has produced one of the most disturbing horror campaigns to date. *Our Ladies of Sorrow* pits the investigators against The Sorrows -- ancient goddesses of grief, madness, and death who, in their multitude of forms, have preyed on Man since he first began to dream. These lengthy scenarios mix elements of ghost stories and mythology and emphasize subtle atmospheric horror and terror on a very personal level. For as the investigators strip away their foes' many masks, they themselves become the prey of The Sorrows, culminating in a terrible choice that could save their lives -- but leave them forever haunted by their grim sacrifice...

THESE AND MORE AVAILABLE AT MISKATONICRIVERPRESS.COM AND AT FINE GAMING STORES THE WORLD OVER!

Horror for the Holidays

Edited by Scott David Aniolowski

"When the footpads quail at the night-bird's wail,
And black dogs bay at the moon,
Then is the specters' holiday – then is the ghosts' high noon!"
-- Sir William Schwenck Gilbert, *Raddigore*, Act 1

Holidays. Special days of commemoration and celebration. Feasts and festivities. Remembrance and revelry. But what dark things lurk just out of sight, in the shadows of those celebrated days? Forces beyond our comprehension, yearning to burst into our warm and comforting world and tear asunder those things we hold most dear. As the wheel of the year turns and we embrace our favorite occasions, let us not forget that beyond the light is a darkness, and in that darkness something stirs. Some nameless thing that brings us *Horror for the Holidays!*

Coming Soon from

Miskatonic River Press

Dissecting Cthulhu
Essays on the Cthulhu Mythos

Edited by S. T. Joshi

Forthcoming Non-Fiction from Miskatonic River Press:

The Cthulhu Mythos is H. P. Lovecraft's most dynamic invention. His bold vision of a cosmos filled with baleful "gods," forbidden books of occult lore, and a constellation of richly imagined New England cities was the perfect vehicle to express his "cosmic indifferentism." The Mythos has become one of the most imitated tropes in horror literature, and hundreds of writers have made their own extrapolations on it.

But many misconceptions remain about the Cthulhu Mythos. Its very name was not invented by Lovecraft, but by his disciple August Derleth. Derleth altered the Mythos in significant ways, and it is only recently that scholars and writers have returned to the purity of Lovecraft's own vision.

This collection of essays, gathered by pre-eminent Lovecraft scholar S. T. Joshi (*Black Wings, The Rise and Fall of the Cthulhu Mythos, I Am Providence: The Life and Times of H. P. Lovecraft*) prints many of the seminal essays on the Cthulhu Mythos, ranging from pioneering articles by Richard L. Tierney and Dirk W. Mosig that strip away Derleth's misconceptions about Lovecraft's pseudomythology, to penetrating studies by Robert M. Price, Will Murray, Steven J. Mariconda, and others probing key elements of the Mythos— its use of gods, books, and topography; the influences that Lovecraft absorbed in fashioning it; and its wide dissemination by generations of later writers. All told, this book provides an invaluable guide to Lovecraft's most intriguing but most misunderstood creation.

Coming from

Miskatonic River Press